Dedication

To Milly and Milo, my cuddlesome twosome!

Acknowledgements

As always, my very grateful thanks to everyone who has helped me with, or who has read (and especially left a nice review of) my Artesans of Albia series. I could not have done it without you.

To Dave; to my parents, Barbara and Dennis; to my brother, David: I love you all!

To Milly and Milo: thanks for all the cuddles and walks.

To my editor Diane Dalton: special thanks for your expertise, enthusiasm, and encouragement.

To Mikey Brooks: for yet another brilliant and atmospheric cover. I adore it.

To NTN (David Snell, David Shepherd) and to Susan Mallett: many grateful thanks for the music and the fun.

To Bob Watson: for website advice and maintenance.

To Janet Morris: special thanks for that wonderful endorsement.

To anyone who has reTweeted, posted to Facebook, or otherwise helped spread the word through social media, and to anyone who has taken the trouble to write and post a review.

I hope you enjoy this book!

Praise for the Artesans of Albia series:

"Cas Peace's *Artesans of Albia* trilogy immediately sweeps you away. The series propels you into a world so deftly written that you see, feel, touch, and even smell each twist and turn. These nesting novels are evocative, hauntingly real. Smart. Powerful. Compelling. The trilogy teems with finely drawn characters, heroes and villains and societies worth knowing; with stories so organic and yet iconic you know you've found another home—in Albia. So start reading now. I, for one, can't wait to find out what will happen next.

~Janet E. Morris, author of *The Sacred Band of Stepsons* series; the *Dream Dancer* series; *I, the Sun*.

✦ ✦ ✦ ✦ ✦

"*King's Envoy* surprised me in the most delightful way. Cas Peace has a most beguiling method of pulling you into this well thought out world she has created. You simply fall in love with her characters, and then you cannot put the book down. The characters are authentic. The story is captivating, and overall, this is one of the best reads I've come across in awhile. So—if you have the notion to escape for a moment, I know a portway to where the metaforce is calling. Come into the Fourth Realm and . . . enjoy."

~ American Girl! *Amazon reviewer*

✦ ✦ ✦ ✦ ✦

"As a fan of the late great David Gemmel I think I have finally found an author who is similarly inspiring. It's how fantasy should be written. Less about the world building and more about the characters. I didn't want to stop reading."

~ML. H, *Amazon reviewer*.

✦ ✦ ✦ ✦ ✦

"A superb read. Non-stop intrigue and action. I literally could not put it down. Anyone needing a good series to read should take up Book 1 and get started. Cas Peace has created an unforgettable hero(ine) in Sullyan, and a world that ranks alongside Middle Earth and Westeros."

~David C Snell, *Amazon reviewer*.

Published by Albia Publishing 2016

First American Paperback Edition

Copyright ©2016 by Caroline Peace
Editing by Diane Dalton
Cover art by Mikey Brooks, www.insidemikeysworld.com
Author photo by Dave Peace

Visit Cas Peace at her author website: www.caspeace.com

ISBN-10: 1-939993-69-5
ISBN-13: 978-1-939993-69-4

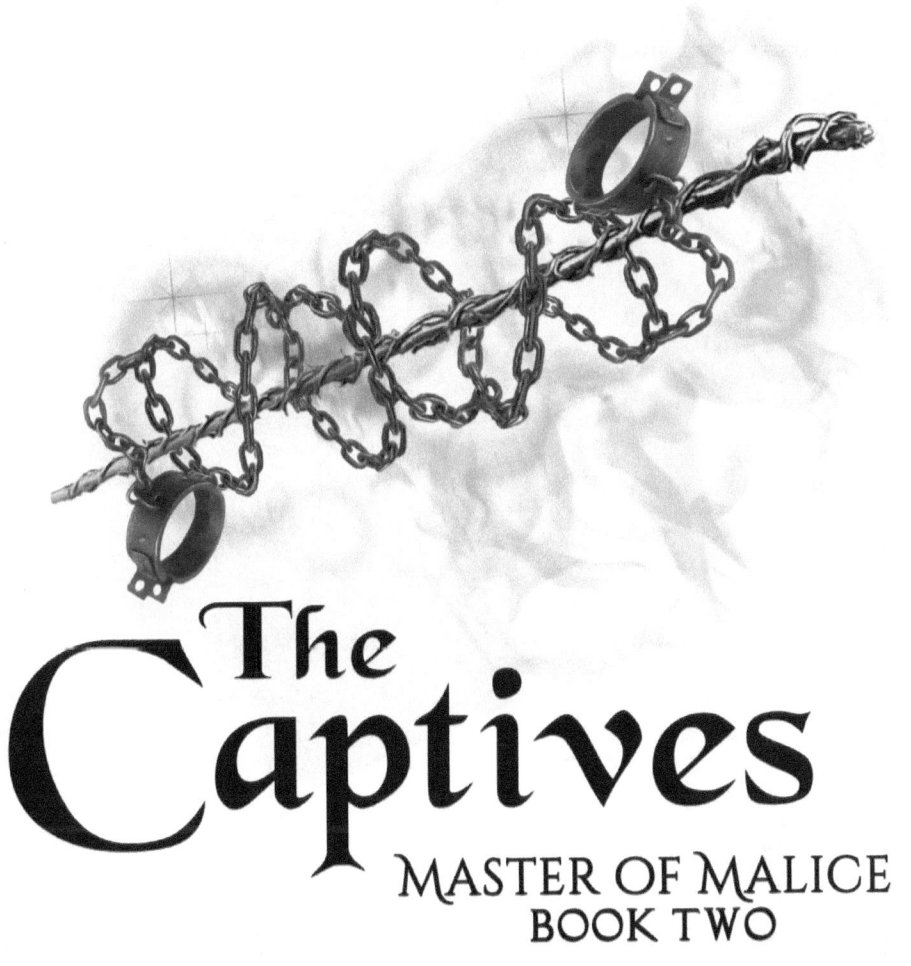

The Captives

MASTER OF MALICE
BOOK TWO

Cas Peace

Albia Publishing

The Kingdom of Albia in the Realm of Albia, (not to scale)

Realm of Andaryon. (not to scale.)

Chapter One

Princess Seline woke to the sound of the servant delivering the overloaded breakfast tray. Bessie did not stir, so she got out of bed and went to collect her own plate, wrinkling her nose at her nursemaid's mountain of food. Seline liked to take a walk in the castle park after breakfast, the earlier the better. Bessie knew this very well, yet always lingered over her extravagant meal and interminable morning ablutions. Sometimes Seline suspected Bessie of deliberately dallying, especially after Seline had given her a difficult time.

Seline had had enough. She was not a child anymore, unable to dress herself or find her way about. She did not need a chaperone, certainly not within the bounds of her own house. She finished her fruit and bread, drank the milk, washed quickly in water heated over the nursery fire, and dressed in simple, warm clothing. It might be gray and dismal outside, but she still wanted her walk. She did not see why she should wait for the sloth-like Bessie, who had only just fetched the breakfast tray to her own room to eat. With the noise of her exit concealed by Bessie's clinking cutlery, Seline emerged into the hallway and made her way toward the stairs.

She passed the east wing door and wondered what the vagrant was doing. She was still annoyed he had refused her help. Surely he would need food and drink? What she had taken him the previous evening would not last more than a day. He would find no sustenance in the deserted east wing.

She had half decided to ignore his refusal and smuggle him more food when she remembered she had given him the only key to the east wing. One of her favorite curse words nearly escaped her lips, but she bit it back just in time. She would have to be careful of that. Bessie would inform the King if she ever heard her charge uttering obscenities.

Seline stamped past the doorway, irritation growing as she realized she had lost her only refuge. Until the vagrant returned the key, she had no bolt-hole. She sighed. That would teach her to offer her help so quickly. The prospect of helping her mother had excited her, and she had not thought things through. She ought to have kept the key or ordered the vagrant to have a copy made.

Feeling petulant, she decided to stay outside as long as she could. Let Bessie come and search for her, although the lazy maid would likely send some lesser servant instead. Well, the Princess was under no obligation to obey servants.

Holding her head at an arrogant angle, Seline stalked past the guards, ignoring their greetings, and emerged into the morning chill.

✤ ✤ ✤ ✤ ✤

"What the Void's going on, Brynne? What can have happened to Jinny?"

Taran had gone through elation, fear, anger, puzzlement, terror, and confusion after Sullyan's startling statement that the burned skeleton in the ruins was not Jinella. At first Taran's soul had swelled with hope and gladness. But then his memory of her frantic mental contact intruded, and the terror or pain that must have engendered it plunged him back into fearing what had become of her. Knowing he had lain insensate for twenty-four hours, useless to both to her and his King, ate away at him, and he completely missed the thing that most troubled Sullyan.

Sullyan could hardly blame him. He was looking at the personal danger and terror, thinking only of his love and what had become of her. Sullyan, worried though she was for Jinella's safety, was much more concerned by the murder and elaborate subterfuge perpetrated here: the killing of a woman who superficially resembled the Baroness and the planting of her body, dressed in Jinny's jewels and clothing, in order to … what? Throw them off the scent long enough to spirit her away? But the fire alone did that. By the time the conflagration had burned itself out, whoever had taken Jinny was long gone.

No. This elaborate charade had an entirely different purpose. There was a pattern here, a clue, she was certain. She just was not sure yet what it was.

She turned to regard Taran, her heart lurching with pity. He burned to do something to help Jinny, yet he was helpless, bound by his commitment to Elias and without any clue as to who might have taken her or where she might be. Sullyan could only imagine how she would feel if it were Robin. She would be climbing the walls to find him.

"I cannot say, Taran. I am as confused and fearful as you. But I will pledge you this: once I have attended the duties that await me, we will sit together and reach for Jinella's mind. If she was able to overcome her lack of talent once, she might do so again. You and I together might be able to sense her. I will stand for you; you can use my strength and skill, along with your intimate knowledge of her, to seek her out. More than that, I cannot offer you."

Taran squeezed her shoulder, too full of fear and hope to express what he felt.

✢ ✢ ✢ ✢ ✢

They arrived back at the castle just before mid-morning and rode into a garrison courtyard strangely devoid of people save for a lone swordsman on patrol. Sullyan shot Taran a look as she slid from Drum's back, leaving him to dismount as best he could with his injured leg. She yelled for a groom to take Drum's reins as the patrolman caught sight of them. He raced to meet them, panting as he threw Sullyan a hurried salute, but she gave him no time to catch his breath. "Where is everyone? Why is no one else patrolling the garrison?"

"They're all inside the castle, Colonel. Something's happened..."

Sullyan sprinted for the side door leaving Taran to hobble after her. Fear knotted her stomach—not more bad news! She pounded up the stairs, calling urgently for information.

On the upper floor, Sullyan accosted a servant who appeared flustered and confused. He gabbled an incoherent message in which the only clear words were "dying" and "Levant." Sullyan took off at a trot and Taran followed more slowly as she made for Levant's suite.

She ignored the quick, soft footsteps on the carpet behind her, her attention riveted on the tight knot of people gathered outside Levant's door. She wheeled to face Taran as he reached her, but then stared angrily past his shoulder at someone behind him.

"Princess. What are you doing here? Why are you alone? Where is your maid?"

Her tone was sharp. Seline drew herself up to deliver a proud retort, but Sullyan was in no mood for the young girl's pertness. Whatever had happened was one strange occurrence too many, and her duty to her King overrode the sensibilities of anyone who got in the way of her execution of that duty.

She swung round on the nearest guard. "You. Take the Princess back to the nursery and give her to her maid. Do not leave her alone. See that they both remain there, do you hear?"

Seline drew an outraged breath, gray eyes snapping with haughty pride. "I don't have to do what you say. You're not my father; you can't order me about like that!"

Sullyan stared at her coldly. "Colonel Vassa and I are responsible for your safety while your father is away, and you will follow any order we give you. Protest to the King when he returns, if you wish. Until then, Madam, you will obey me. Now go to your rooms."

She waved her hand and the guard led the spluttering Princess away, her angry protestations loud in the hushed hallway. Sullyan ignored her, reserving her pity for the hapless guard, who had to endure Seline's spleen all the way to the nursery.

Sullyan entered Levant's suite, nearly gagging as a dreadful smell hit her like a sledgehammer. She covered her mouth, trying to hold on to the contents of her stomach.

This was more than Rendan Levant had managed, judging by the carpet by his bed. And it was not the only indignity his body had suffered.

He lay on his left side, breathing harshly through a slack mouth, his skin a ghastly shade of green. His eyes were open but unseeing, glazed over by a strange milky film. His nightgown was drenched in sweat and bunched around his legs, tangled with the bedclothes when his body convulsed. Urine and excrement soaked and covered everything. The remains of a half-eaten meal lay on the floor, scattered by the suffering man's uncontrollable spasms.

Sullyan crossed to his side, laying her hand on the clammy brow. She struggled to draw breath through the fug of sickness and stench of vomit. "Who found him?"

"I did."

Colonel Vassa entered the room, followed by two healers. He stood back, a hand to his mouth, as they approached the sick man to examine him. "When I did not find him in his office, I looked first in the garrison and then in the dining hall. One of the servants told me he had brought a tray in at dawn, so I came back to see if he was still here. I found him like this."

A yell sounded in the hallway and the guard who had escorted Seline pelted into the room. "She's dead! The nursemaid is dead! There's blood and vomit and—"

Sullyan let out a curse. "Where is the Princess, man?"

"I left one of the other guards with her, Colonel."

Sullyan nodded. "Get back there and make sure there are two guards with her at all times. Touch nothing in the room—nothing, do you understand? Your lives may depend on it."

The guard ran off and Sullyan turned back to the healers. "Has he been poisoned, Endor?"

The older of the two men nodded, his broken-nosed face nearly as green as Levant's, whose breathing was growing shallower by the moment. "Someone fetch water, lots of water. And salt. *Hurry!*"

One of the hovering servants dashed to carry out his orders as Sullyan turned to Vassa. "Jerrim, these are not random cases of poisoning due to bad food, these are deliberate acts. The person responsible will be long gone, but I recommend we close down the castle. I also suggest we turn out the garrison and check every one of the castle's inhabitants, in case anyone else is affected. Do you agree?"

Though Vassa was technically the senior officer as he was Blaine's second-in-command, and it was his tour of duty at the castle, he did not begrudge Sullyan taking command in this crisis. He simply nodded his assent and left to give the orders.

Sullyan knelt by Levant's side, addressing Healer Endor. "We need a purgative, and quickly."

The master healer was already reaching for his medical bag.

"We do not know which poison was used, Colonel. Bringing it back up may do more harm than good." He produced a packet of purging herbs. "And he's not a young man."

She held his gaze. "He will most certainly die if we do nothing."

Endor opened the packet, shaking his head. "Someone fetch me that jug on the table. And the cup."

Taran did so, and the healer mixed the strong smelling herbs into the water. There was only about a cupful in the jug. Levant must have drunk some before the fever came upon him. The purgative brew would be very strong.

"Turn him on his back and then stand away," Endor instructed. "You should all stand away."

He placed a hand under Levant's head, tilting it back, causing him to open his mouth. Trusting his reflexes to seal off his airway, Endor poured the liquid down Levant's throat, the heavy aroma of purging herbs masked by the vile smell issuing from the sick man's gullet.

When the liquid hit Levant's stomach, he convulsed violently, lurching over the side of the bed, bringing it all up again. Most in the room avoided the splatters, but not all. Those who had not slipped away for a hasty wash and change of clothes.

A servant arrived with water, another with salt. The second healer mixed the two in the water jug and then passed it to Endor. He poured the biting fluid down Levant's helpless throat, heedless of the consequences.

With every infusion, the sick man convulsed, vomiting wretchedly. What came up smelled vile and turned the water murky brown. The convulsions and the effort required to expel the fluids exhausted the stricken man. After the third time, Sullyan stepped in to support Levant's failing strength with her own.

The First Minister was no Artesan, but he knew Sullyan well

and offered no resistance to her probing psyche. With the way thus left open for her, she managed to bolster his energy before it gave out completely. Her face was as pale and clammy as his by the time his response to their treatment eased.

She glanced up at Endor, who was looking to her for guidance. Artesan healing was still new to him and he was unsure how to proceed. "Keep giving him the salt water until what comes back up runs clear. I think he is over the worst. He did not eat all of his meal, if that is where the poison was, so perhaps he did not receive a lethal dose. But the drain on his body has been severe, and as you so kindly pointed out, Endor, he is not a young man." She glanced at Taran. "If you can find a way to support him, Taran, do so."

Endor flushed. "I have never known so old a man recover from such virulent poison."

Sullyan smiled grimly. "Ah, but then you have never seen one attended by Artesans before, have you?"

She swept from the room, leaving the healers to their work and Taran to concentrate on trying to reach the stricken man's inner resources.

Chapter Two

Sullyan ran to the nursery, pushing through the press of Guardsmen checking the castle. She could hear the Princess's voice long before she entered; the girl's haughty whine grated on her overstretched nerves.

"Madam, be silent!"

Seline shut her mouth with a snap, face paling dangerously. Sullyan ignored her anger. "I have no time to deal with your tantrums just now, but if you wish, we will discuss your grievances once I have dealt with these attacks. Or would you prefer me to leave you vulnerable to the perpetrator?"

Seline bit back a retort, recognizing the necessity of Sullyan's actions. She knew whom her father would side with once he returned. She threw herself into a chair, ignoring Sullyan.

Sullyan gave the hint of a grim smile, but it disappeared when she entered Bessie's room. If she had thought the smell surrounding Levant's suffering was bad, it was nothing compared to this. The First Minister, if he survived the next few hours, would have had a very narrow escape indeed. He must have ingested a much smaller amount of the poison than poor Bessie had. Hardened as she was to gore and the dreadful sights of the battlefield, Sullyan had to turn away.

Bessie was dead indeed. The virulent poison had worked its will upon her, starting, by the looks of things, much as it had with Levant. But with more of the substance in her body and no one to hear her or help her, it had run its full, terrible course through her system.

Blood lay everywhere. The violence of her convulsions and the effects of the poison in her tissues seemed to have burst every blood vessel she possessed. Every last drop of fluid in her body had been expelled—one way or another. She must have died in excruciating pain, and Sullyan felt a dreadful, boiling anger at whoever had done such a terrible thing.

Unable to do anything for the good-natured, long-suffering nursemaid, Sullyan left her room and locked the door. No one but the mortuary attendants would see the undignified mess death had inflicted on Bessie.

Something of what she was feeling must have shown in Sullyan's eyes, because both Seline and the guards flinched when she confronted them. She fixed Seline with a heavy look.

"Did you not speak to your maid this morning, your Highness?"

Despite the harshness of her tone, she had observed the proper forms. Seline was constrained to reply, unable to protest ill-treatment.

"No, Colonel. I left before she was dressed."

Sullyan remained unfazed by Seline's hostility. "And is that usual? Are you not supposed to wait for her before you leave the nursery? In view of last night's events—which you must have heard about being abroad so late—was it not foolhardy?"

The Princess flushed at Sullyan's implied rebuke over her late-night foray. Drawing herself up to full height, she retorted, "I'm not a baby. I am quite capable of dressing myself and finding my own way about. This is my home, you know! What harm can I come to here?"

As soon as she said it, Seline realized her error. She saw the recognition of it in Sullyan's eyes and fought against the reddening of her face. She lost.

"All right, I admit it's not always safe. But *I* wasn't killed, was I? No one poisoned *my* food. And if Bessie had not been such a glutton, she might still be alive. That's hardly my fault—oh!"

She recoiled with a squeal as Sullyan slapped her face. The Princess gaped in astonishment. Sullyan had actually hit her. Not very hard, just enough to bring a red mark to her white face. Seline's hands flew to her mouth and tears of fury started in her eyes. She had never been slapped in the whole of her life. Shock made her crumple.

Sullyan regarded Seline in disgust. How could the child be so callous about the death of her maid? Even if she had not particularly liked her, Bessie had never deserved anything like the treatment she had received from the petulant Princess. Elias paid her well, aware how difficult his daughter could be, but Bessie never complained until she had no other choice. Anyone else might have refused to deal with Seline, unable to resist her torments. Bessie had been the best of nursemaids—firm when necessary, pliant when possible. She did not deserve such a death, nor such wounding accusations.

Sullyan fought to suppress her anger, aware that if Seline had not decided, in a childish attempt at independence, to defy the normal strictures of her routine that day, Bessie might still be alive. She chose not to point this out, as it might tip Seline's temper out of her control.

"You will go with Kier and Fergus, your Highness, and will stay where they take you. From now on, you go nowhere without a bodyguard, not even to visit the privy. I will assign you two lady's maids, and they will stay with you night and day. You will obey me in this or I will have you locked in your rooms with a guard posted on the door. Do you understand?"

Still shocked by the slap, Seline remained silent. She glanced at Sullyan through a veil of tears and nodded curt acceptance. Sullyan spoke tersely to the guardsmen, Kier and Fergus, then turned on her heel and left.

She returned to Levant's room, where the dreadful smell had

abated. The healers had cleaned the First Minister and were swabbing his room with disinfectant herbs. She crossed to the sick man's bed and laid her hand on Taran's shoulder.

The Adept was sitting at Levant's side, pouring strength into him as best he could. His unfocused eyes sharpened at her touch and he glanced up at her. She nodded at the prone form. "How is he doing?"

Taran ran a hand through his hair. "I think he might wake up soon. I can feel him trying."

She cast her own senses into the First Minister, feeling the beginnings of resistance to her touch. While unconscious, his natural defenses were weak, but with the reassertion of his psyche, his mind's inborn barriers came back into play. She withdrew and nodded to Taran.

"You are right. You have done well. He seems a little stronger. I think we can leave him to recover on his own now. The healers will see to his comforts. He should be able to take some plain water. His body must be starved of moisture."

Taran straightened from the bed. "What of poor Bessie?"

Sullyan shook her head, the look in her eyes dissuading him from further enquiry.

Vassa appeared just as they were leaving. "There are no more cases of sickness or death. Everyone is accounted for. The men are still searching, but we have found no clues as to who might be responsible. I have cordoned off the castle—no one will enter or leave without our permission. There's a city council meeting in session in the court chambers. We'll need to inform the ministers." He glanced at the figure on the bed. "How is Rendan?"

She led him out by the elbow. "He will survive. He has been extremely fortunate. The poison must have been in the food. Bessie ate all of her meal and she died in terrible agony."

Vassa's tone was bleak. "We'd better question the servants."

Sullyan nodded. "I will inform the General and the King. This is serious, Jerrim. I fear I made a grave error believing the focus of our enemy's attention was on Bordenn. If it is the Baron behind these dreadful crimes, he must be in Loxton province, if not already within the city. I am tempted to ask Elias to return so we can protect him, and yet I fear for his safety if he does.

"And there is a further twist to the tale. The fire at Jinella's mansion did not claim her life, as we thought. The body that burned in the blaze was placed there deliberately to make us think she was dead, but it was not Jinella at all."

"Not Jinella?" Vassa glanced at Taran's pale face. "So she's alive? That's one piece of good news, surely?"

Sullyan grimaced and Taran looked away. "We do not know if she is alive or dead. We only know she did not perish in the fire. I must contact the General, and then I have to arrange for the transfer of the new company from the Manor. If you will inform the city council of our arrangements, I will assist you with questioning the servants. I hope the ministers will react with care. The last thing we need is to upset the populace any more than they already are."

✣ ✣ ✣ ✣ ✣

Elias's second day in Lerric's company was no better than the first. The General passed on Sullyan's recommendation he stay, and although the King agreed with her reasoning, he was not looking forward to more interminable whining from Lerric and bitter accusations from his disgraced former Queen.

He had a brief respite from Sofira's venom, as she was not in evidence when his party reached the dining hall for breakfast. Lerric must have been there some time judging by the food remains on his plate. Despite an obvious awkwardness in his manner—due, no doubt, to the behavior of his daughter the evening before—Lerric remained seated as servants brought fellan and hot bread to Elias, Blaine, and Robin. It was not long before he resumed his catalog of complaints, and the General exchanged a long-suffering look with Elias as they fended Lerric's many veiled requests for reduced levies on his province.

Robin took a brief meal and returned to the barracks, still anxious over the condition of his men, and not just the two sick ones. Morale remained low despite his assurances, and in any case he would rather spend time with them than listen to Elias and Lerric's verbal fencing. He was pleased to find both Col and Pengar looking better. They had finally been able to take a little fluid without bringing it back up.

He sat with Dexter, watching the men go about their duties. He was impressed as always by the comradeship shown by the company. Each man who passed the sickbeds stopped to exchange a word or joke with the bedridden men, though they were only capable of weakly appreciating the gestures.

"Have they remembered anything else about last night?" Robin asked.

Dexter glanced at the two men. "Not that they've said, sir. They seem more embarrassed than anything else, and don't want to talk about it. I have told the lads not to pester them. They know they have to report anything they remember."

"And how are relations with Lerric's men?"

Dexter shrugged. "Not bad, all things considered. They all know about the incident and found it highly amusing, judging by the looks they give us. One or two remarked about it, mainly jokes about insubordination. Our lads know better than to rise to that kind of thing, and they've been told to respond in kind."

Robin was pleased. "What about the two who were with Col and Pen? What have they had to say for themselves?"

Dexter frowned. "No one's seen either of them since last

night. I expect they have been told to lie low, but I think they were both due on night watch anyway, so they are probably sleeping. Do you want me to keep an eye out for them?"

"Do that, Dex, but don't go asking for them. I do not want any more attention than is necessary. I might seek out Bassan in a bit to see what he knows, but if the two men responsible are on night duty, we won't see them again before we leave. It's a bit odd, though, don't you think, for Bassan to allow them an evening's drinking if they were due on watch?"

Dexter shrugged again. "Nothing here surprises me, not after what Wil told us and what we've seen for ourselves. Lerric does not run his men on the same lines as the Manor. It's all very haphazard. No wonder his forces were defeated in the civil war. The idea of the realm being run by the likes of Lerric and this lot is laughable."

Robin was about to respond when he felt Sullyan's questing touch. Dexter, recognizing the signs, gave him privacy as he accepted her contact. His heart sank at her news. She told him her suspicions concerning Denny's death, and about Taran's return to consciousness. She mentioned the unknown body in the fire, holding out little hope Jinella was still alive. The news of Levant's poisoning and the terrible death of the nursemaid went through Robin like a cold shock.

What the Void is going on, Sullyan? This is getting more peculiar by the minute. We came here to clear up the uncertainty surrounding the Baron's apparent suicide, and instead we are encountering more and more mystery. Elias is getting nowhere with Lerric—Sofira hasn't even put in an appearance so far today—and I don't know how much more he's going to take. I am expecting orders to move out any minute. But if there is someone with a grudge against him in the city, someone clever enough to get away with the murder of Neremiah as well as infiltrating the castle to poison the First Minister, shouldn't we recommend he stay away?

Robin sensed his life mate's turmoil. *I agree, my love. I would be far happier if Elias consented to base himself at the Manor, at least until we have investigated this properly. Suggest it to him, after you run it past Mathias, of course. Use Eadan to sweeten the pill. Seline will have to accompany her father, as it is entirely possible the poison poor Bessie took was intended for the Princess. Vassa has shut the castle down and we will question the staff and servants as soon as we can. He has gone to inform the city council they will be unable to leave the castle for the time being. Tell Elias he may have to issue an edict to reinforce our orders—I doubt the ministers will be happy at losing their freedom.*

I am about to contact Bulldog; he will have readied the company that is to replace Denny's murdered men. Inform the General I intend to send another through later today. In the light of recent events, we need a strong presence in the city until we can clear this up.

Robin indicated his agreement, but she was not quite done.

Robin, you must also tell Elias I may have made a grave error in thinking Bordenn is the focus of Reen's attention. If he is behind all this, he has moved faster than I anticipated. It comes as no surprise you have found no trace of him there. But I am still suspicious of Sofira. If Elias has not already done so, ask him to question her on the subject of letters sent to or received from Reen on the island. Be there when he does, if you can. I would be very interested in her reaction, and you and Mathias might just see more than Elias will.

Sullyan broke the link, leaving Robin confused and alarmed. Was she saying she thought these terrible yet diverse occurrences were connected? But why would the Baron set up such a risky ambush in order to murder a whole company of King's Guard?

Why would he want to murder the King's daughter?

Robin experienced a cold shudder as a possible answer came to him. The Baron could systematically undermine Elias's morale and confidence with these savage acts. Striking so intimately into the heart of his home and removing with such ease those who guarded his safety would so distress and infuriate Elias that he might react rashly, as with his disastrous invasion of Andaryon. Any move of that sort would leave him open, vulnerable to further attack. Put in that light, these events made more sense, even down to the poisoning of Levant, one of the High King's staunchest supporters. Yet where did this business with Jinella fit in? Why plant a body to make them think she had died in the fire? Why not just murder her? Robin had to admit, that part did not make much sense.

He rose, tossed Dexter an enigmatic look, and left the barracks. Elias's safety was his prime concern; he would let wiser heads untangle the threads of intrigue.

He found Elias and the General where he had left them. Servants cleared away the morning meal as Lerric suggested he send for his daughter. He felt, as he told the High King in patronizing tones, Elias ought to try talking to her once more. He knew how much she missed her children and was sure they could come to a suitable arrangement. Lerric's manner seemed overanxious, as if he was uneasy having to deal with the King alone. Although why he should be, Robin did not know.

"Your Majesty, General, might I have a word in private?"

Elias's head snapped around and the General eyed Robin with wary suspicion. The young man tried to reassure his senior officer with a steady look. What could have been an awkward moment was saved, yet again, by Lerric himself, who smiled and moved to leave the room.

He chuckled as he reached Robin. "Don't mind me. I heard

about that little incident in the tavern last night. If you want advice on how to deal with drunken men, talk to Bassan. He has the same problem almost every month. He's devised some rather inventive punishments for those who can't hold their ale!"

Robin inclined his head as Lerric continued, still chuckling, down the hallway. General Blaine beckoned to him and he entered the room, closing the door. The servants had all left with their lord, leaving the three men alone. Nevertheless, Robin kept his voice pitched low as he related what Sullyan had told him.

Elias was white and trembling with fury by the time he was done. "How dare they!" he hissed, his voice sharp and dangerous. "If they think they can do what they like in my city then they're very much mistaken! Mathias, why are we wasting time here when whoever is responsible for these terrible crimes is loose in Port Loxton? Even Sullyan thinks it's a mistake us being here. We should leave at once."

Blaine spoke in measured tones. "Be calm, Elias. Let me think."

The King's pale complexion reddened. "Don't tell me to be calm! What is there to think about? There is a poisoner loose in the castle. He killed my daughter's maid and very nearly my First Minister. How can I be calm about that?"

"I'm aware of that, but I also happen to agree with something else the Colonel said. If there is still a poisoner within the castle, it is the last place *you* should be. But I doubt there is. He will be long gone by now. If he has been stupid enough to hide there, Vassa and Brynne will find him. We should not rush blindly back to Loxton, not until we have more information and we know the castle is secure. And certainly not before the extra men from the Manor have been deployed."

Elias drew breath for a protest, but Blaine overrode him, irritation coloring his gruff tone. "Have you considered that goading you into a precipitate return might be exactly why these acts were committed? Can you think of any other rational reason why someone should target Levant, or that poor nursemaid? Levant is your First Minister. His loss would sorely affect your governance of the realm. And Bessie—well, if she was the intended victim, attacking her is tantamount to telling you your daughter is in danger. What two things could more completely guarantee you'd want to rush back to the capital?"

Elias subsided reluctantly. Blaine was right, and Robin wondered whether Sullyan had actively considered the points he had made. They did explain the rather puzzling choice of victims. And the fire at the mansion could have been an accident, although there was still the mystery of the body that was not Jinella's. Unless Sullyan had made a mistake, of course. Robin shook his head. It was still too convoluted for him.

Elias tried again. "What about the attack on Sir Regus, then, and the massacre of Denny's men? Do you think they're connected to the other incidents?"

General Blaine shook his head. "I'm deeply saddened by the loss of a good commander and a trained company of swordsmen. But we all knew brigands had re-infested Loxton Forest. Denny clearly let himself be out-thought. He was expecting an ordinary band of opportunist thieves, but this lot must have found themselves a leader. You know how dangerous that type can be. Might even be some noble's man-at-arms, dismissed from his lord's service for committing some misdeed. Once the city is safe again, I will organize more sweeps. Some of those caves need demolishing or blocking up. That will put a stop to their activities for a while.

"Elias, I'm in agreement with Sullyan. We stay here for the moment, as we planned. She has seen to the safety of your daughter, and I will contact her to authorize an edict in your name to the councilors, if they prove difficult. We could even declare a state of military regnancy until we have cleared this up. Last night's near riot was bad enough. The last thing we need is more civil unrest in the city. If there is an enemy out there—and I am still not convinced—that is exactly what he will be hoping for.

"Now, are you up to facing the Princess again? We may as well fulfill our reason for coming here, and if we're to finally discount any collusion between Sofira and the Baron, I think I'd also like to see how she copes with being questioned about correspondence with a traitor."

✠ ✠ ✠ ✠ ✠

The red-haired man who had once been Othal, swordsman of Lerric's personal guard, looked about him in confusion. He had somehow traveled through a misty, shimmering cloud to this strange place, and he had a task. He had a vague recollection of something dreadful happening to him, something violating, invasive, and agonizing, but had no clear memory of what. Or who had done it. He could not even remember what he had done yesterday. His life before this moment was a blur. All he knew was he hurt and an imperative existed in his mind. If he did not carry out his orders to exacting standards, he would suffer horribly.

Shivering in fear, he scratched at his chest, yelping when his dirty nails caught on a painful spot. He glanced down at his clothing, pulling it away with one hand. The raw, running sore that met his eyes nearly provoked a memory, but it left as quickly as it came. As he readjusted his clothing, Othal forgot both pain and sore.

He hid among winter-bare woodlands, close by a worn path. Evergreen shrubs surrounded black-limbed trees, affording him cover from the wind and the cold, as well as casual eyes. Not that there were any. He had been here since dawn without seeing a soul.

His eyes, prickling from the cold, gazed at the rope. One end was tied to the bole of a tree opposite; the other lay at his feet. He had brushed snow over its length with a branch, also wiping out his own tracks. His subjugated mind did not question what he had done. His actions were automatic. All he needed to do now was wait.

There it was. The thump of hoof beats. His own heart pounded as he readied himself. He took up the free end of the rope, eyeing the pathway to his right, from whence the rider would come. Courage and sure-footedness were prerequisites for runners and their horses. The pair would be moving fast.

Othal had orders not to permanently damage horse or rider. It was vital they be fit to carry out their duties. He must time his attack to perfection. Too early and the horse might see the rope in time to jump it cleanly. Too late and it might tangle its limbs, breaking a leg or its neck. Neither was acceptable. Othal desired the horse to swerve abruptly, throwing its rider, who should land softly on the recent fall of snow.

Well, that was the plan.

The muffling snow was playing tricks on him and the pair was closer than Othal had thought. He was nearly too late with the rope. He jerked it tight at the last moment, but still the horse tripped over it. Squealing in fear and pain, the beast thudded to the ground in a flurry of legs, kicking out and scattering snow. Taken by surprise, the rider yelled, pitching over the horse's shoulder to land heavily at the base of a tree.

Othal leaped from hiding, another shorter length of rope in his hands. He sped to the dazed rider as the horse scrambled upright. He knelt beside the groaning rider and pulled the young man's arms tight behind his back.

The rider yelped again, but Othal took no notice. The youth's eyes flew open, fastening on Othal as the ropes bit. "What the hell do you think you're doing?" he rasped, his pale face spattered with dirty snow. "I'm a King's runner. You risk death by harming me. I carry nothing of interest to you, scum, so you might as well let me go. And my horse is branded, so you won't be able to sell it."

Othal knew this. He knew all about Elias's runner system and how it operated. He had heard Lerric's grudgingly admiring comments many a time, and his sullen laments about not having the funds to set up a similar service himself. Othal ignored the rider and crossed to the shivering horse. He caught its reins, soothing it with a murmured word. He ran a practiced hand down its slender legs, relieved to find no heat in the tendons. He led it forward a few steps. It was sound.

He breathed a sigh of relief. He had fulfilled the first part of his orders. Going back to the young man, who was still trying to convince his captor to let him go, Othal stared down at him. The youth was barely more than a boy, and Othal felt a twinge of doubt. Would the lad be old enough? Would he have the knowledge his master required? What if he wasn't a local? But that was not likely. This place was so remote, so isolated. No one in their right mind would come here looking for employment if they lived far away. Many did not even know of its existence.

Bending to the lad, Othal tapped him below one ear with the butt of his dagger. The youth collapsed, unconscious. Checking that the precious message pouch was still secure on the runner's belt, Othal picked him up and slung him across his horse's saddle. Using the rope he had brought the beast down with, Othal fashioned long reins to the horse's bit. He walked behind the animal, driving it like a plow horse, stepping in the prints of its hooves to mask his tracks as he made for his hiding place. Now all he had to do was wait for his master's call.

Chapter Three

Sullyan's agitation eased when she contacted Bull to arrange the relief company's transfer. The big man took the news of the events in the city with his usual mix of anger, concern, and practical good sense, promising to find more men to send her later. His lack of questions and instant acceptance of her orders was a balm to her burdened heart. She always found his huge presence comforting, the size of his body somehow reflected in the feel of his psyche. His large, generous spirit filled every aspect of his person.

The men were ready. Drawn from the General's command, all were volunteers, as no one knew how long they would have to stay in the city. The loss of a full patrol was devastating; it would take some time to train replacements at the Manor. When he had the leisure, General Blaine would call for replacements from other garrisons, garnering spare men from wherever he could. Until then, the Manor made up the shortfall, as it traditionally did.

Once she ascertained all was prepared, Sullyan quested for contact with Lord-General Anjer. The huge Andaryon answered her almost immediately, picking up the undertone of anxiety she could not quite hide.

Have you been practicing again, my Lord? Her tone carried mock irritation, for she was annoyed with herself at betraying her state of mind. Anjer, a Master, was two full levels below her in metaphysical rank, but she knew he still worked on his control, training with both Aeyron and the Hierarch when he got the chance.

She felt his appreciative chuckle. *You are very kind, Brynne, but I think it was more your lapse than my skill. What is wrong?*

She sighed. *I fear a resurgence of hostilities from an old enemy. I have already made one error and now I question everything. We recently lost an entire patrol to an ambush that should never have happened, and I need to reinforce our presence at the castle. I ask your permission to transfer a body of men.*

Anjer's permission was pure formality and he gave it instantly. They handled the transfer between them, continuing their conversation even as they manipulated the substrate.

Were you planning to come and discuss this with Timar? I can inform him if it will save you time.

As she watched the fresh men emerge onto the frozen grass of the castle park, Sullyan allowed her gratitude to show. *I thank you, my Lord, for your understanding and your suggestion. I may take you up on the offer, although I hesitate to burden Timar with my problems. He will be unable to stop himself worrying over Aeyron, and it may be I am wrong. There is no proof the Baron is behind these attacks, only a lack of proof he is not. That, and the fact I can think of no one else it could be.*

She broke the link and concentrated on collapsing her structure. The men she directed to Valustin, who was waiting to assign them their duties. Then she went to find Vassa, who should have begun questioning the castle servants.

She eventually located him by following the cacophony of angry voices issuing from the council chamber. She grimaced. She had been afraid of this. Elias's ministers were an intractable lot, never pleased when something disturbed their routine. Already agitated by the embryo riot at the castle gates, they distrusted the city's volatile mood. The emergency council session's purpose was to discuss the matter, and the absence of Elias's First Minister did nothing to reassure them. When Vassa told them the reason for Levant's absence, they reacted with predictable panic. And his order that they remain in the castle, where a poisoner might still be loose, triggered their instincts for self-preservation. Vassa had foreseen this problem and had not gone alone. His men blocked the doorway, standing solidly while the furious ministers raged around them, demanding release.

Vassa allowed them to expend some energy before bellowing for silence. The fifteen ministers quieted, but when he attempted to reason with them, they turned on him again. Sullyan exchanged a look with Vassa and raised her own voice. She was habitually softly spoken, her lilting tones ill-suited to anger or volume. When she chose, however, she could augment her voice by channeling metaforce through her psyche. She did so now, shocking the ministers, most of whom were so occupied haranguing Vassa they had not noticed her entrance.

"*Silence!*"

The absence of noise following her command was palpable. Faces turned toward her, fearful, angry. Sullyan made her way to Vassa's side via the top tier of seating, so the gathered ministers had to look upward as they followed her progress.

She regarded them coldly. "Gentlemen, I am disappointed by your conduct. That was a most unseemly display of malcontent for such respected councilors. Is this how you would reassure the people? How can we expect them to remain calm when their trusted leaders cannot?"

"How can you expect *us* to remain calm when we've just been told there's a murderer in our midst? You should be out there hunting him down, not corralling us here like sacrificial lambs!"

Sullyan had no difficulty identifying the speaker, Sir Regus. She heard a vexed sigh from Vassa and recognized its origins. He thought Regus intended to cause trouble.

She thought so too. Known for his aversion to Artesans, Sir Regus often raised his voice in objection to any suggestions concerning their legitimizing or advancement. His lowly position, however, guaranteed his opinions carried weight only with himself, although he did try to influence his fellow ministers whenever he could. Yet his desire for his own advancement meant it was impolitic for him to speak too openly against Artesans in front of Elias, so he usually held his tongue, biting back his objections. Today, he had free rein.

Sullyan answered him curtly. "I think you may safely leave the matter of apprehending the murderer to the King's Guard, Sir Regus. And if you will use your wits for once, you will realize we can best accomplish this and thus ensure your personal safety if we have your willing cooperation."

Regus spluttered. "Personal safety? Let me tell you, Colonel, none of us feels safe cooped up in here. And what good did the King's Guard do the Arch Patrio? For that matter, how safe was First Minister Levant?"

That was too much for Vassa, who took a step forward. "It was only thanks to the swift action of Colonel Sullyan here that Lord Levant is still with us. I doubt she'd be so swift to save *your* miserable hide were you in the same position!"

Regus refused to be intimidated. "That's already been proven, hasn't it? None of you came to our rescue when brigands attacked my wife and me in the forest. Not one of you stopped them robbing us of everything we had. And none of *them* have been apprehended, either!"

This enraged Sullyan, images of Denny's cold corpse before her eyes. "Twenty good men lost their lives trying to apprehend those brigands," she snapped. "Twenty men we could afford to lose less than twenty of *you*, my Lords!"

Her words caused general outrage. The noise in the council chamber rose to unbearable levels, led and fueled by Sir Regus. Soon, Sullyan had had enough. The ringing hiss of steel as she drew her sword silenced the furious ministers. She held the naked blade before them and they glared at her coldly. No one had ever drawn a weapon in the council chamber before.

She stood, staring implacably. A few feet shifted uneasily, but otherwise they were silent. She drew a steadying breath. "That is better, my Lords. Now, I came here this morning for a more pressing reason than to listen to your ill-mannered objections. Colonel Vassa and I have more important tasks than to nursemaid you, and I am commanded to deliver you an edict from the King."

That elicited a few muttered comments, which died beneath her glare.

"My Lords, all this posturing and angry resentment is worthless—so much wasted air. You are constrained to obey whatever commands we see fit to issue, for I have to tell you that from this morning, and until the King himself should rescind it, there exists within Port Loxton and its province a state of military regnancy."

Another profound silence followed her words. Apart from during conflicts such as civil war, it was rare to issue such edicts. In one simple sentence, Sullyan had stripped them of their civic authority, placing them under military rule until the King's pleasure released them. Powerless, faces open-mouthed and angry, they watched the two colonels leave, Sullyan sheathing her sword as she went.

Vassa spoke in low tones as they walked toward the kitchens. "That went about as well as I'd expected. But I didn't expect Elias to issue that edict."

Sullyan glanced at him. "He had no real choice. The near-riot last night and the attacks today took the decision out of his hands.

If the townsfolk hear what happened to Levant and Bessie and react as strongly as they did last night, we will need the structure already in place to deal with them. Bull has readied another company for transfer, just in case."

"When does Elias intend to return?"

"Before nightfall. Come, my friend, let us see if we can find a culprit, or at least a witness, to place before him. These attacks in the heart of his home will trouble him sorely. But I am not confident of success. I have the gravest feeling someone is laughing at us and I do not like it, Jerrim. I do not like it at all."

✢ ✢ ✢ ✢ ✢

Laughter was the last thing on the mind of the person responsible for the acts that had caused such uproar in the castle. Crouching close inside the door to the east wing, the vagrant had heard most of what resulted from the orders he had been given. The poison had reached its intended victims, and they were gravely ill, if not actually dead. Then, he prudently withdrew deeper into the deserted wing, aware of the fearful stench emanating from his ruined, decaying body.

The vagrant was dying. At least, he fervently hoped so. He was weak and sick and the charnel reek, which up to now had not affected him, was nigh on unbearable. As was the pain of his ravaged chest.

He dragged himself into the farthest recesses of the abandoned rooms, hoping to hide for as long as possible. The attacks on Levant and Bessie would elicit a swift and thorough search of the castle, and his discovery would not be advantageous. Not that he did this from any desire to further his vicious master's plans. He accepted Reen had abandoned him; he had reached the end of his usefulness and his master had tossed him aside like the detritus he was. Reen could have instructed the vagrant to leave once he had administered the poison, but he had not. Getting his servant into the castle and into a position to carry out the poisonings had been a stroke of luck, one which would not have happened but for Elias's absence, and the Baron was not about to ruin the effect by trying to retrieve an expendable tool.

No, the dying man was well aware he had been sacrificed, his tasks complete. Therefore, he hid his body—not to buy time for the Baron or confuse his enemies, but so he would remain undisturbed while he completed the process of dying.

What he feared most was the intervention of an Artesan. Having no experience other than what the Baron had shown him, he feared they could keep him alive. He was terrified they might prevent him slipping into oblivion, that they would trap him in the agonizing prison of his ravaged body while they extracted the secrets he held. To die as swiftly as possible was the only thing he wanted now. He craved it like a starving man craves food, like a drowning man craves land. It beckoned him like a promise of fulfillment, and the thought he might lose it terrified him.

His soul was forfeit—he knew that. His spirit had been stolen, his heart no longer his own. The Baron would know he was dying and would come to claim the last dregs, the final, useless drops of this captive life. A life that had done some terrible, unforgivable things.

Before his enslavement, the vagrant had been no blameless paragon of human virtue. He was an ordinary swordsman, not particularly bright, but not brutal or cruel. A simple man with simple desires. He thought nothing of the morals of his actions, had no great regrets or unfulfilled ambitions. His life, when brought for examination under the turning of the Wheel, would yield no cause for commendation or condemnation. At least, not before.

Now, however, he was damned. He was as sure of that as he

had once been sure of his name. The acts forced upon him by his master ensured no hope awaited him, no promise of respite in peaceful limbo before the Wheel turned again, spitting him out into whatever purgatory awaited those with such stains on their souls. What torments lay in store for one whose soul was not his own? He had no idea. Yet if he could die before his master had a chance to suck that final spark, he might just escape the nightmare consequences of what he had become.

And in the end, he was granted his wish, although not in the way he had thought.

He lay surrounded by the stench of his own living death, parched and desolate in the darkness. He was in a cellar beneath the disused kitchens, where he had gone hoping to find water. Food held no interest for him, even though he had long since eaten what the Princess had given him, back when he had thought his tasks might not be over. He had hidden the basket with cunning; it would probably never be found. The Princess's letter still lay within. But his body craved water and he had searched frantically for the merest drop until his strength finally gave out and he realized his master was done with him. Creeping down into the lightless, freezing cellar, the wastrel curled the collapsing wreckage of his body into a corner and waited to die.

Time held no meaning. It could have been hours, days, or months. He lay there, his mind all but shut down, until a familiar presence made itself felt. It woke him with a shudder.

"So, my faithful servant, I see your time has come."

The echoes of that hated voice did not sound through the substrate as a true Artesan's did. The Baron was not speaking as one person to another. The voice issued directly from the vagrant's own mouth, and the words tasted bitter and cruel.

The pain in his ravaged chest blossomed like fire, but he lacked the strength to scream. He felt the scarecrow's amusement

30

through the agony and wondered how it would feel to deal even one retaliatory blow against his tormentor. He would never know. He was completely helpless. He lay under his master's will and stared into the darkness.

"You have done well."

The words were mocking, but they held a ring of truth. The vagrant had never kicked against his bonds, never tried to resist his master's control. By the time he realized what had been done to him, all chances of resistance were gone. And so he had been a model servant, the ideal tool, without which many of the scarecrow's plans might not have come to fruition.

The crawling voice continued. "So I will grant your desire. The life you have left is of no value now. I have others on whom to feed, and soon I will have all I desire. You are fortunate. You die at a time when I can afford to be generous."

The laughter the vagrant thought he would never feel again nearly succeeded in breaking through. That such an evil monster could consider itself generous! Yet he forbore to comment, even to think. Now he could die. It was enough.

⁜ ⁜ ⁜ ⁜ ⁜

The final, pathetic spark of life began to fade, and Reen was pleased. The havoc that must have ensued from the poisoning—and hopefully the death—of two who had wronged him was enormously gratifying. But it was the anticipation of his next move that generated his act of mercy. His current emotional state was far removed from the panic he had felt at Elias's unannounced visit. He was excited—he was elated. He had used his wits to turn the possibility of disaster into potential triumph, and the first real task given his new servant had gone well. The Baron would contact him shortly. And then—then!—he would possess the real tool with which he would pave the way to the total degradation, the utter humiliation, and the eventual destruction of his most feared and hated enemy.

His malicious, indulgent thoughts already far beyond the confines of the lonely, deserted cellar, the Baron did not wait to see the putrid collapse of his servant's ill-used body. The only witnesses were maggots.

✢ ✢ ✢ ✢ ✢

Sofira did not answer Lerric's summons and he was forced to entertain the King and the General alone. Increasingly nervous and fearful, Lerric did his best to convince them Sofira's unhappiness and the welfare of his grandchildren were the reasons for his agitation. And because there was truth in what he said, neither Robin nor Blaine detected any falsehood.

Elias was all for leaving Bordenn immediately when he realized Sofira did not intend to put in an appearance. He saw no reason to pander to her whims, whims designed to anger and upset him. Her vicious remarks the night before rendered him even less inclined to speak with her than usual. But the General, despite his initial resistance, knew they had not fully exploited the possibilities presented by this visit and persuaded the King to remain a little longer. At the very least, they would get a warm meal before having to brave the winter freeze again. If Sofira remained absent, it was one less problem to worry about.

So at midday they gathered once again in Lerric's dining hall, casting appreciative eyes over the array of hot food. Its variety gave the lie to Lerric's constant carping about his province's poverty, although Elias was too shrewd to mention it. He did not want to give Lerric the opportunity to bemoan how little they would have once the King's party left.

Once they were replete and had repaired to the inner chamber with fellan and brandy, Elias and the General traded a private glance. Robin placed himself where he could watch Lerric without being too obvious, and Blaine nodded to his sovereign.

Elias stretched his legs to the fire, captured his vassal's attention, and leaped in with no warning. "So, Lerric, what did you make of the news about the traitor, Reen? I take it you heard what he did?"

Lerric stiffened. His face turned pasty and the goblet trembled in his hand. "What ... what he did?" His gaze fixed on the King's face. "I ... don't understand."

Elias snorted. "Oh, come, man! Did you not hear the news? Surely you heard he escaped imprisonment?"

Lerric's demeanor turned desperate and his gaze flicked between his three guests. "Escaped? I ... hadn't heard that."

Robin, watching Lerric closely, pondered the man's conflicting emanations. Uppermost was a fear that was almost terror. Lerric would naturally feel fear at the news the traitor who so nearly succeeded in killing the High King, and who had come originally from his own court, had escaped. Yet deep within the complex swirl of emotions Robin also sensed a strange surge of hope, almost as if Lerric wanted them to discover something. He frowned and concentrated harder. There was something odd here.

Elias warmed to his deception. "You hadn't heard the traitor escaped justice? Strange. I thought you would have known all about it. We knew Reen corresponded with someone while he was on the island, and the only person who might be ... interested, shall we say? ... in his circumstances was you."

"Me?" Lerric almost yelped the word. "Why would I be interested in him? Why should I correspond with a convicted traitor? I want nothing more to do with the man!"

Robin's frown deepened. Lerric's tone carried a distinct ring of truth, an emphatic assertion that flooded his voice, yet the undercurrent of terror and reluctant hope remained. It was almost as if he was not master of his own emotions, a thought that made Robin distinctly uneasy.

"Ah!" Elias injected a tone of enlightenment into his voice. "Maybe it wasn't you. Maybe it was someone else in your household."

Lerric froze, his eyes haunted. He cast a swift glance at the door, whether in fear or hope, Robin could not say. But the man was desperate to end this conversation, that much was clear.

"What are you saying, Elias?" Lerric's whisper was almost pleading. "What are you accusing me of? Has my House not suffered enough at the hands of that dreadful renegade? Did our family not lose enough? What have we done that you should question us so? Why can't you leave us alone?"

Robin closed his eyes, the better to sense Lerric's emotions. It was clear he hardly knew where to turn or what to say. A great fatigue filled him, as if he had been under tremendous strain, yet there was also a futile sense of bitter anger. His emanations were so complex and convoluted that their import was clouded. Robin gained a strong impression of dark fear, deep unhappiness, and a strange, almost eager hope. The debilitating weakness pervading Lerric's spirit might well lead to collapse. Even as he scanned the man, Robin felt his spirit struggling, almost as if he had decided to voice some kind of revelation. Robin wondered whether he ought to say something to Elias, but the door opened abruptly, saving him from the decision.

Stiff-backed and furious, Sofira stood in the doorway. She glared at Lerric, fear behind her eyes.

"Father!"

Her sharp voice slit the tension like a knife ripping silk. Lerric jumped half out of his skin and his pale face flushed. Elias startled also, but hid his reaction far better than Lerric. Robin could see he was annoyed with himself. Had he not cast aside the feeling that

Sofira still held power over him?

Apparently not.

Sofira strode into the room, her face white and angry. She ignored the other three men and glared at Lerric's sweat-sheened face. "Father, you're not well. Why did you not send for me? Your Majesty, General, I must ask you to excuse my father. He is not strong these days and this terrible winter has further sapped his strength. Had I known your visit would have reduced him so, I would never have left him. Father, you ought to go to your room. You are weary and need to rest. I am sure our distinguished guests will not be offended."

Lerric hesitated, looking surprised. Robin saw him glance up at her, a furtive, guilty look, as if she had caught him betraying secrets. Then his shoulders slumped and a sigh escaped him.

"I beg your indulgence, your Majesty, but I fear my daughter is right. I do feel less than well. Perhaps a short rest will restore me, and I will be fit to speak with you again before you take your leave."

Elias, clearly displeased by Sofira's appearance and intervention, could hardly refuse. "By all means, Lerric. You should have spoken of this before. I had no idea you were not at full fitness. I hope I am not so ill-mannered a guest as to impose on a gracious host."

Lerric gave a small frown, peering at Elias as if suspecting him of irony. But Elias waved a casual hand. "I wish you peaceful rest, Lerric. I will not be offended if you are not well enough to bid us farewell. I am sure your daughter will fulfill your duties admirably."

Sofira took her father by the elbow and guided him toward the door. Robin barely heard their whispered exchange.

"Sofira, I—"

"Be silent! I will speak with you later." Sofira raised her voice. "Go and lie down, Father. I will send a servant to tend you."

Chapter Four

Sofira closed the door and returned to the fire. Elias, the General, and Robin watched her warily. Ignoring Robin, she offered fellan to the others. They accepted. Blaine served Robin himself, a point that was lost on—or ignored by—the Princess.

She sat in Lerric's chair, holding herself stiff and straight-backed, hands resting in her lap. She addressed Elias. "You should not have tired him so. He's no longer strong. The effort of wresting an income from this wretchedly unproductive province has left him a shadow of the man he once was. You could do so much more to help him. The levies you impose are not at all just."

Elias's face darkened. They had all heard the same thing expressed in many different ways over the past few hours. Besides, wasn't she forgetting something?

"If Lerric hadn't rebelled against my father, he would have enjoyed the same benefits granted other loyal subjects of the Crown. As it is, in the light of his rebellion and your betrayal, I consider you both extremely fortunate still to have your lives, let alone the governance of your province. As for the levies, I base them on independent assessments of what you produce and not upon the figures sent out by your father's clerks, as you are well aware. If I believed every message bewailing rain-flattened crops, or flocks wiped out by the murrain, or coastlines damaged by earthquake, my treasury would be paying *you*, rather than the other way around!"

Robin noted Sofira's reaction to the mention of earthquake damage. Elias's acid tone caused her face to pale dangerously, and then flame in anger. She knew he suspected her of fabricating that claim in order to account for the large amounts of gold she had given Reen to fund his scheme with the Staff, though he had never been able to prove it.

"How dare you throw the war back in our faces? We were coerced into supporting the rebellion! My father was caught between Urlow of South Fells and Porras of Garon, both of whom had greater resources and contingents of arms than us. How could he have resisted their demands and survived?"

Elias scoffed. "He could have stood up for himself! Other provinces did so, some less prosperous than this one, I might add. Other lords retained a sense of integrity. Not everyone sold themselves for promises of power. Like the promises held out by your treacherous Baron."

In the privacy of his mind, Robin applauded his King. He had begun to fear Elias had once more lost sight of the purpose of their visit. Maybe he had only been biding his time.

Sofira's face was white and pinched. "What the Void do you mean by that?"

Elias leaned forward. "Admit it, Sofira. You were as deceived by his machinations as I was. He wormed his way into your confidence when he saw my interest in you, and made himself indispensable. He made you depend on him so fully you didn't want to leave him behind when you came to the capital. He used you, Sofira. You were right to denounce him at the trial."

Sofira spat like a cat, gray eyes glittering. "Yes, you'd love that, wouldn't you? You would love me to admit I made a mistake! Well, we are not all as perfect as you, Elias—you and that little Artesan whore! You had to bring her and her demon lover in to save your miserable sham of a trial, didn't you? You did not have enough evidence to convict Hezra without their lies. *They* don't care what falsehood they hide behind, do they? They can do no wrong in your eyes. And in the face of your persecution, I could hardly blame Hezra for pushing some of the blame onto others. I *told* you how he deceived me. I *begged* you to believe me; on my knees I begged you! I admitted, in front of the whole court, how he led me and used me, but would you accept what I said? No! You preferred to believe that ... that *trollop*! You should have listened to Hezra, Elias. You should have listened to Lord Neremiah. They were right when they said she had you under a spell. And it seems she still does!"

Elias's face turned thunderous as Sofira went on. Her use of the word "whore" in connection with Sullyan caused an ugly pulse to jump in his temples, and Robin feared the King would lose control. Yet furious as he was, he was not beyond reason.

"So you defend him even now. Even though you begged me to execute him—even though you demanded the worst form of death my power could inflict. Why? Why is that, Sofira?"

She almost screamed. "Because he was *right*! Because, even though he betrayed me, even though he took my son from me, even though he plotted behind my back—still, he was right. They have you in the palm of their hands, these unnatural favorites of yours. *They* rule in Albia, not you. Hezra was only trying to make you see that. He may have been a traitor. He may have deserved death upon the Wheel. But I still say he was right."

"Is that why you corresponded with him?"

Elias's calm question, at such variance with his former anger, pierced Sofira like a knife to the heart. Her face, white with fury already, turned deathly gray, and Robin saw her tremble. Her eyes widened with fear, fixing desperately on Elias.

"Who ... who told you that?"

He held her gaze. "Ah. I thought so."

Her whole body froze. Robin silently applauded his King for the second time, thinking Sullyan would be proud of his cunning in the face of his former wife's self-righteous anger. For once, he refused to play the game of blame she tried to force on him.

Robin watched Sofira wrestle with her thoughts. Elias had caught her out and she had to think quickly. She drew herself up, staring at the King with frank dislike.

"I don't know what business it is of yours, Elias. I am no longer answerable to you. But since it pleases you to pry into my private affairs, and since you have so underhandedly trapped me, I will tell you that I did indeed write a letter or two to Hezra in his exile. Are you satisfied?"

"What was in those letters, Madam?"

She shook her head. "I am under no constraint to reveal that, my Lord. The letters were private and will remain so."

"Madam, when a convicted traitor and his disgraced former co-conspirator continue to communicate behind my back, I think I have every right to demand an explanation of their actions. Never forget I control access to your children. If you wish to see them and be an influence in their lives, then I recommend you reassure me as to your loyalty. Otherwise, I may conclude you still hold views contrary to my administration of this realm."

Tears of fury and defeat came into Sofira's eyes, but she refused to crumble. Robin wondered where her strength came from. Yet her reactions rang true to what Robin had heard of her. He would compare notes with the General later, but he doubted Blaine had a different opinion. Whatever her faults, Sofira had told the truth. Sullyan's fear she had made an error in believing the Baron had an ally here was borne out. If he was alive, against all odds, then he was hiding somewhere else.

Sofira made no effort to conceal the emotion Elias's threat sent surging through her. She held herself stiffly erect, trembling so badly her voice shook. "Oh yes, that's right, Elias! Hurt me as much as you can. You know how to wound me, don't you? Well, I surrender. I have to, when you hold the weapon of my children's affections over me. How does it feel to be so mighty? I hope you are proud of yourself—I hope you can sleep at night. Since you must know, I wrote to Hezra because I wished him to understand why I said what I did at the trial. I wanted him to know I did it for the sake of my children. Despite his betrayal, I wanted his forgiveness. There, I have told you. Does that content you? Are you pleased you have humbled me into that? Do you enjoy seeing me so helpless?"

Elias had the grace to look shamed. Her courage clearly surprised him, just as it had Robin. She had told him nothing out of character and no obvious falsehoods. Robin sensed the King's discomfort and suspicion that this visit had been a total waste of time. His relationship with Lerric had never been easy; it would be worse now. He had forced the mother of his children to reveal things it pained her to remember, and she would doubtless strive harder to turn the children against him. Elias shuddered.

"Your pardon, Madam. It was not my intention to interrogate you or give you pain. You have my word I will do nothing to turn our children against you. They need their mother, I accept that."

Sofira pounced. "You will let them come to me here, then?"

Mathias Blaine stepped in before the King could reply. Elias should not make hasty promises.

"Your Highness," he said, drawing a furious glare from Sofira, "the hour grows late. There have been harsh words between you, and it is unwise to make decisions in the heat of such dissention. We must soon return to Port Loxton and his Majesty wishes to take his leave of your father if he is well enough. I advise you both to leave the matter for now. Approach it later with cooler heads. Decisions made under such circumstances may fail in the calmer light of day. I wonder, might we trouble your servants for more fellan?"

Robin felt Elias's gratitude for the General's rescue. Blaine had put Sofira under the constraints of guest-right, and she was unable to refuse without contravening those rights. The look she gave him promised retribution should she ever be in a position to exact it, but the General refused to be intimidated.

She rose, waving a hand at the servant by the door. "Fresh fellan for our ... guests." She glared at Elias. "My Lord, I should see to my father. If you have finished your inquisition?"

Her phrasing made Elias flush. He bowed his head. "Madam."

She turned and stalked from the room.

They sat in silence as the servant refreshed the fellan pot, and then Robin dismissed him. He was keen to know whether the General's opinions agreed with his. Once they completed their discussions they would prepare to leave, and Robin knew he would not be the only one to breathe a sigh of relief once Daret disappeared behind their horses' tails.

Elias expelled a breath. He stared at the General, who matched him. "Well, Mathias? Was all that really necessary? Are we any further in resolving Sullyan's mystery, or have I merely antagonized and alienated Lerric and Sofira more thoroughly than they already were? Please tell me you've learned something valuable, because I confess, I'm beginning to rue the day I agreed to this visit."

The General shook his head. "All I can tell you is that I detected no falsehood in Sofira's words. As for Lerric, he is a very worried man, but whether it stems from genuine hardship in the province, as he claims, or some other reason, I cannot say. Sofira is clearly angry with him—very angry—and he fears her, but again, I could not guess the reason. Major, do you agree?"

Robin nodded. "Mainly, sir. I also heard no falsehood in their words. I would go further, though, where Lerric is concerned. I would say he is terrified of something, and I think he came very close today to telling us what it is. If the Princess had not entered when she did, I am sure he would have unburdened himself. It was that very danger, I think, that triggered her anger. I'd give much to hear what she's saying to him right now."

Elias glared at both of them. They had given him little comfort. "Is that all? Sofira is angry and Lerric is frightened? Is that the sum of what you garnered from two days of discomfort and argument? I could have told you that before we came! Sofira is *always* angry. And Lerric has lived in fear of her ever since she was old enough to brush her own hair. That's not news to me."

Robin glanced at the General, unable to offer more. Blaine watched Elias in sympathy. "We now know two things for sure," he said, ignoring Elias's stare. "We know Sofira was indeed Reen's correspondent. And we know neither she nor her father harbor a traitor here. Sofira was very open about her feelings where the Baron is concerned. I doubt she would give him a second glance were he to turn up on her doorstep. And Lerric is unlikely to extend the hand of friendship to a man who brought disgrace on his House. You saw how he reacted to your probing on that score. If the traitor is, by some improbable chance, still alive somewhere, he's getting no help from them."

"I told you that, too, before we came!" Elias stood abruptly. "This whole damned exercise has been a waste of time. While we have been enduring torture, someone has infiltrated my city and my castle, murdered a chief cleric, my daughter's nursemaid, and very nearly my First Minister! Not to mention massacring a valued commander and twenty trained swordsmen. Why are we still here?"

The King strode to the door and the General exchanged a glance with Robin, who nodded. "I'll alert the men at once, your Majesty. We can be ready in thirty minutes."

Blaine raised a brow. "What about the two sick men?"

Robin shrugged. "If they can't ride, we'll make a litter. They will be fine. It's not as if we have far to go."

"Very well, Major. I will leave the preparations to you. I'll inform Colonel Sullyan of our departure time, and I'll see you in the courtyard once his Majesty has taken leave of our hosts." The General dropped his voice so Elias could not hear. "I hope Brynne has some results to show Elias when we return. If not, I would not care to speculate what he might say. He'll want to turn the city upside-down if there's no sign of our murderer."

Robin left for the barracks, heart heavy with wondering what awaited them back at Port Loxton.

✣ ✣ ✣ ✣ ✣

Deep in the bowels of his darkened lair, the scarecrow lay on the truckle bed in a corner. His tortured body was so twisted, so desiccated, comfort meant little to him. He no longer experienced sensations as a normal man would. Right now, his mind was far away from the wreckage of his body, far from the confines of the palace where his intended bride vented her fear and anger on her father, screaming her rage at his cowardice, beating her fists on his chest. Although aware of her distress on a subliminal level, he had more pressing matters to attend.

He had bolstered Sofira's courage while she faced Elias, though she did not know it. He was subtly linked to her now, although not yet in the same way as his servants. He could influence her through her emotions, through her love for him, and it took little of his stolen energy to do so. Yet now he needed every drop of strength to complete this latest, most important, plan. Once accomplished, he would need to feed again, and deeply. Maybe he would even take his pleasure at the same time. Or maybe not. Maybe he would save that for the ultimate slaking, the one he had promised himself from the first. Irritably, he dragged his thoughts away from his lust. He must attend to the matter at hand.

Dismissing everything else from his mind, the scarecrow sought the pathetic scrap of humanity serving as his latest tool. It was ridiculously easy to find, having no defenses left. It was his totally, as if it had never possessed any other life. He had only to think of it to look out of Othal's eyes and see a youth lying bound and gagged in the straw of a ramshackle barn, stray snowflakes swirling through broken wallboards. The youth shivered and he smiled. Was it from cold or from fear? Did the boy see the sullen red light bloom with eerie menace in the eyes of his captor? Reen did not know and did not care. His servant had done well; it only remained to see how well.

✣ ✣ ✣ ✣ ✣

The young runner stared into the face of his captor. He could not understand what was happening. First, the fellow brought down his horse, trussed him, and clubbed him into unconsciousness. Then he brought him to this disused barn out in the wastes of the snowbound countryside. There the boy woke, shivering and fearful, head throbbing from the blow, body aching and cold. Yet his captor did nothing. He simply sat there, unmoving, unresponsive to the noises and movements the youth tried to make.

The boy eventually gave up. The fellow must be simple or something. He must be waiting for his master to come, although what anyone could want with a young runner like him, the boy had no idea. He carried only the usual monthly report from the garrison, for delivery to the Manor. In this snow-locked landscape it would take him at least a week to get there, maybe more if the weather worsened, forcing him into shelter. Runners were expected to carry out their duties whatever the weather, and he had never failed.

The runner stiffened. The red-haired man had not moved, but something caught the youth's eye. He stared at the fellow, a creeping sense of horror growing as he registered the sullen ruby light coming from the silent fellow's eyes. Sweat broke out on the youth's brow as the man shifted abruptly, dropping to his knees in the straw, thrusting his face into his captive's. The youth tried to wriggle away, but the fellow gripped him hard by the shoulder. Unbearable heat surged into him through the rough hand, making its way to his brain.

He fought the creeping fire without knowing how or why. It was not comforting warmth. It was alien, invading and violating, and he wanted to scream. He wanted to run, to fling himself away from it, prevent it from burrowing into his mind like a maggot of corruption. Yet he was helpless. The hand on his shoulder pinned him down, and the pervading heat crept closer to his gibbering mind.

When the needle of fire entered his brain, he screamed. Not even the gag could mask the high, thin sound, but it was muffled enough. There was no one abroad anyway, no one to hear his terrified cry. His limbs stiffened in agony before he slumped, limp and pliant, his consciousness held in thrall, his private thoughts and memories plundered.

✠ ✠ ✠ ✠ ✠

The Baron nearly giggled as he savored the runner's stolen thoughts. The youth was the friend of a relative. He even knew the man! It could hardly be better. He knew the family, their intimate circumstances. Oh, this would be so easy! He would not even have to coerce the lad once he planted the suggestion. The boy would be desperate to deliver the message of his own volition, due to the ties of friendship. They would suspect nothing because there was nothing *to* suspect. The youth would not remember this experience.

He would be totally devoid of falsehood, totally innocent of the scheme he was about to enact.

The Baron liked that. He was attracted by innocence. Serrin had been innocent—innocent and young. Oh yes, this one would serve more than one purpose. This one could be used to satisfy many desires.

Shaking himself from the dark pleasure of his thoughts, he turned once more to the captive mind. He insinuated the knowledge of sickness, distress, of great need. The mission's urgency was paramount. The perceived time wasted in its delivery would add to the sense of crisis, covering any slight discrepancies a thorough questioning might reveal. Gratified beyond measure by the outcome of his planning, the Baron continued his preparations, instructing his servant in his part once the runner was fully primed.

Time was running out.

Chapter Five

Sofira was unaware of the preoccupation of her betrothed. She only had one thought in her mind. Once Elias and his unwanted entourage had left, she could complete the arrangements for her wedding. Clandestine it might have to be, but there was no reason her marriage night should be anything less than the culmination of her desires. Seeing Elias again, the man to whom she once gave her body, made her realize she had lost nothing. Her new lover would restore everything to her—everything and more. Once they wielded, together, the power of his mind and her province, they could begin the work that would restore her to the throne of Albia, and her beloved children. All she had to do was ensure his instructions were carried out to the letter.

Which is why her father's craven soul and spineless whining brought such anger to the surface.

Sofira sat in her chamber, breathing deeply. She had left her father in his own bedchamber, stinging from the whip of her words. She had taught him the error of his ways. He now knew better than to fail her again. She could only pray Elias's witch-lapdogs had not scented Lerric's wavering courage.

Sofira roused herself, checking her image in the gold-framed silver mirror. She rearranged her hair, pulling it tightly behind her head. She had forbidden her father to bid his guests farewell; she would not risk it. She would have to tell Hezra what she had prevented. He would consider it a betrayal of trust if she did not.

And although she was terribly angry with her father, she feared what her betrothed would say when he learned of the narrow escape. She might even have to defend her father against her lover's ire. Yet for now she must appear composed. She must show no trace of her recent fury. She would treat Elias coldly, formally, and speed him on his way. Only then could she afford to relax and turn her attention to gaining her desire.

Straightening her back and smoothing her gown, she wrapped a warm cloak about her shoulders and descended the stairs.

✣ ✣ ✣ ✣ ✣

Never before had Lerric seen his daughter in such a towering rage. Even more now did he fear what the vampirish specter huddled beneath his palace had done to her. Too late, he wished he had given in to his fear and told Elias what they had done. The High King might well have ordered his death, but might that not be preferable to what was coming? Lerric did not know. All he knew was that his last chance, his last hope, even now strode toward the courtyard, hastening to leave this comfortless house, this loveless place of conflict.

Lerric harbored a terrible fear he might never see his overlord again. Sighing deeply, trying to still the tremble of his aging hands, Lerric pulled parchment toward him and took a quill from the rack.

✣ ✣ ✣ ✣ ✣

Robin had gathered the escort and readied the horses. The men waited in the courtyard, the Major holding the King's mount, Dexter holding the General's. Lerric's men stood in attitudes of disinterest, one or two scratching absently at various places on their bodies. Robin grimaced. First winter fever, then illicit narcotics, and now fleas or lice! He heartily wished his party away from this depressing place, even if sadness and chaos awaited them in the city.

Elias and the General emerged from the east tower, and the men came to attention. Sofira, wrapped in a fur cloak against the biting wind, followed them down the stairs and across the courtyard toward the waiting horses. Her bleached face looked hard in the freezing air.

The King turned to her before taking the reins of his mount. He bowed stiffly.

"I thank you for your hospitality, Madam. I am distressed to hear of your father's condition. It was not my intention to cause him discomfort. Please tender him my thanks and my wishes for a speedy recovery. Have you a message for our children?"

Sofira's eyes hardened. "Just send them my love, my Lord, and assure them of my continuing affections. If you are sure it will be no trouble?"

Elias glared at her sarcasm, but did not comment. He nodded, took his horse's reins, and spurned Robin's offer of help to mount. He swung into the saddle without another glance at his former Queen, and kicked his horse forward. The stallion grunted and surged toward the open gates. Robin leaped for his own mount, checking all his men were behind him. The two who had been poisoned rode double with their comrades, still too weak to support themselves.

General Blaine saluted Sofira as he passed, but she ignored him. The escort swept out of the courtyard, Corporal Wil exchanging a wry glance with Captain Bassan as he went. Wil had told Robin that Bassan would be the only one sad to see them go. Indeed, Bassan had told Wil he was seriously considering deserting his lord and following Robin to the city. He was certain his life would improve if he did so, for despite Robin's fault-finding and criticism, he had impressed Bassan with his leadership.

Robin was flattered. He had given Lerric's captain a really

hard time. He glanced back at the man as they continued down the road away from the palace, but Bassan remained where he was. Sofira had already returned to the palace, and Robin swept the lot from his mind.

＊ ＊ ＊ ＊ ＊

The intensive questioning of the castle servants produced precisely what Sullyan feared: nothing. Nothing of any real value, anyway. She and Vassa spoke to the man responsible for serving Levant and Bessie. The fellow was eager to step forward once he learned what had happened. He was fearful and deferential, certain of dismissal at the very least. Yet it took Sullyan only a short while to ascertain the man was innocent of anything other than delivering the tainted food. He was an unwitting tool and had no case to answer. Nevertheless, she detained him in his room, aware Elias would wish to see the man himself. She only vaguely noticed he constantly scratched his arm.

None of the other servants added anything valuable. They saw nothing unusual, and had chased no strangers from the kitchens that morning. None of the tradesmen delivering their produce were strangers, and the food served to Levant and Bessie was not left untended for any length of time. Sullyan was at a loss to explain how the poison had entered the food.

She did, however, prove beyond doubt that Levant and Bessie had been poisoned through the food. The garrison stable lads habitually set traps for the rats that ate the horses' grain, and she obtained a large specimen. It spat and squealed its fury through the bars of its cage when she offered it what remained of Levant's meal, and once it calmed down enough to eat, it quickly succumbed to the poison. She showed its contorted corpse to Vassa, who whistled.

"I'd say Rendan is extremely lucky to be alive." He eyed the stiffening rat with distaste.

Sullyan agreed. "He was only saved by your timely arrival, and by not eating everything on his plate. Maybe he felt unwell before it was finished, or perhaps he was not very hungry. Whichever it was, it saved his life."

"That and your emergency treatment. Have you heard how he is?"

"Healer Endor tells me he is sleeping. He should make a complete recovery once his strength returns. That should please the King, but it will not be enough. We must find out why Rendan and Bessie were targeted. I have to admit, it makes no sense. Are some, or all, of these events linked, or are they coincidental? And we must ensure there are no more. The General informed me Elias will not hear of removing to the Manor where we can best guard his life. Therefore we must protect him here. We must double the guards around the castle and shut it down as tightly as possible."

Vassa nodded. "I've already sent a detail to the kitchens to oversee the preparation of all the food. Another is scrutinizing all visitors to the castle and garrison, whether tradesman or workman, councilor or noble. No one will enter or leave without our knowledge. And the guards on the gates will be doubled, and changed every two hours to keep them fresh."

"And what of the castle itself? Can we be sure our murderer is not still inside? Have we shut the wolf in with the lambs?"

He shook his head. "I've had those extra men you brought through searching the place systematically since they arrived. They've found nothing."

"But have they searched everywhere, my friend?"

Vassa stared at her. "Everywhere. Even the King's own chamber."

"Even the east wing?"

He frowned. "The east wing is securely locked. I checked the door myself."

She held his gaze. "But did you check the key?"

"The key? What—?"

"Is the key still where it should be?"

Vassa paled. "I … I don't know. I assumed because the door was locked …"

She nodded. "But doors can be locked from either side. I think we should subject the east wing to the same scrutiny as the rest of the castle. I have felt drawn to that door twice now, with no good reason. It is time I obeyed my instincts. The King's entourage will arrive soon and it is your duty to greet him. I will take a detail and search the east wing, and I will bring my findings to you in the King's chamber. Mathias will not allow the King to remain at the castle until we have accomplished that."

Reluctant as he was to bear the brunt of Elias's displeasure over the recent incidents, Vassa had to agree. This was his tour of duty; he was responsible. He nodded and she smiled at him, sensing his somber mood.

"We will not desert you, my friend. The General knows you are not to blame. He will not permit Elias to lose his temper. If anyone is to suffer the consequences of temper today, it will likely be me. When Seline hears her father has returned, she will lose no time protesting my shameful behavior. I fear I have lost whatever regard the Princess may have held for me. Not that it would have been much. Ah well. I will be as swift as I can, but I intend to turn the east wing inside-out. Something is pricking at my spine and I will learn what it is if it takes me the rest of the day."

Even with a detail of six swordsmen, it did take her the rest of the day. Discovering that the key to the east wing was missing from the trunk in the King's antechamber, Sullyan wasted no time urging her men to the search. Once they found a locksmith capable of opening the door and she stood in the dark hallway, she feared the worst. A miasma of evil seeped from the musty corridor, and when her torch revealed smudged and unreadable swirls in the disturbed dust on the floor, she cursed and sent the men running in. She stationed guards on the door to prevent the escape of anyone who might be hiding, and subjected every room to the most exacting scrutiny. No conceivable hiding place, no matter how small, remained unexamined.

But the east wing was large, with many rooms. Like the rest of the castle, it had two residential floors, with a service floor below and storage rooms above. Not to mention cellars and drainage channels below ground level. Sullyan was determined not to miss a thing, and so she was still fully occupied when General Blaine opened the substrate to bring the King home.

✣ ✣ ✣ ✣ ✣

Wracked by cold, Jinella huddled beside the remains of the fire in the tiny, dingy hut. She had done her level best to keep it alive throughout the day, even down to feeding it dirty straw from the floor. But now it was dying and there was nothing she could do. The only things left that would burn were the wooden shelf of the bed and her coverings. She wished she had torn the shelf from the wall when she still possessed the strength to do so, but now her hands shook too badly and the bitter cold leached all power from her limbs. She briefly entertained the idea of burning her night robe and comforter. They would flare brightly and quickly die, she knew. Yet she would enjoy a fleeting moment of warmth before the winter freeze claimed her, removing all heat for good. A swift descent into the false warmth of approaching death might be preferable to the struggle she experienced now.

She did not even have the energy to sustain the notion. All the food was gone. She had eaten the last crust of bread hours ago. And she only had half a cupful of gelid water left, a scum of ice on its surface. She stared bleakly at it, tears stinging her eyes. Her hand crept out, fingers trembling so hard she could barely grasp the cup. She brought it to her lips and drank it all, raw throat burning from the icy liquid. The cup dropped to the floor.

Shuffling awkwardly, she crept closer to the grimy wall, huddling against it for its last vestiges of warmth. The stone hut had no windows, but there were small gaps in the stout wooden door, gaps through which she had screamed for help back when she believed help might come. Through these, she knew it was evening and the light was failing. She stared numbly at the door, too cold to think. She would not survive the night with no fire. Once it died, it would only be a matter of hours before her struggles were over. She closed her eyes, willing herself deeper into the moribund state that gnawed at the spark of her soul.

She did not know how much time had passed when the sound of boots crunching on snow reached her ears. The dimly perceived glow of a torch impinged on her sore eyes, but not even the realization that a torch meant rescue roused her from her torpid state. As the wooden bars securing the door were drawn, she stared blankly at the flickering light.

The door swung open and she screwed her eyes shut. The torch was not bright, but the night was dark and her eyes had seen nothing but faintly glowing embers for the past few hours. She heard the low murmur of men's voices, their breath pluming gold in the torchlight, and she realized someone had entered the hut. She shivered violently, half from fear and half from cold.

Rough hands tugged at her, insisting she rise. Helpless, she let them do as they would. Her muscles were cramped and she had no command over them. She heard a muttered curse when the man realized she could not stand unaided.

"Ach, this bloody fire's nearly out."

A sullen response came from outside, but she could not make it out.

"Give me that blanket," said the voice by her ear, and she felt a coarse woolen weight, warm from a horse's back, settle about her shoulders. She could have cried for that small mercy.

He lifted her like a sack and carried her from the hut. She kept her eyes closed. It was easier if they thought her unconscious. Their voices and actions told her they were not her friends. Neither were they shepherds. Even a simple farmer would have treated her better than this. No, they had known she was there, meaning they were the ones who put her there. She had no wish to look at them.

She was hoisted onto a horse and held there by rough hands. The man's breath reeked of pungent tobacco. His cloak was clammy and cold, but she was beginning to feel the benefit of the horse blanket. Her shivers grew worse as blood found its way back into frozen muscles.

"We'd better get her back before she collapses completely. The master will not be pleased if anything happens to her. And you know what that means."

The second man grunted an obscenity, and Jinny's head jerked against the one who held her as his horse surged forward. The beast's exertions brought heat to its muscles, and this permeated slowly through the blanket and comforter, working its way into her body. By the time they had gone a couple of miles, she felt able to open her eyes.

It did her little good. The land was in darkness; no lamp or candlelight betrayed the presence of houses. She seemed to be out in open countryside, which made sense when she thought of how loudly she had screamed from her prison the day before. Having gone to such lengths to hide her, they would not have left her anywhere near human habitation.

She did not try to see the man who held her. Neither of her captors had offered her physical harm so far and she wanted to keep it that way, although she had no doubt harm would come to her when they finally delivered her to their unknown master. Staving it off was her only thought. She kept her muscles loose except for the shivering, which she could do little about. But she did, once or twice, catch glimpses of the second man, who rode his horse alongside hers.

Like his comrade, he was closely wrapped in a heavy oiled cloak, the hood drawn up over his face. She could see little in the darkness. There were no colors upon either his cloak or the horse's saddlecloth to indicate his origins. He had a sword strapped to his side—she could just see the tip of a pommel beneath his cloak—but this also told her nothing. Few men went abroad at night unarmed. She gave up. She did not have the energy even to feel afraid. She tried to comfort herself with thoughts of Taran as her captors bore her onward.

Despite her discomfort, she dozed until the horse slowed. They were on a snow-covered road rutted with hoof prints, and there were faint lights in the distance. Her eyes teared in the stinging wind, obscuring her vision. She heard the rasp of wood. The lights were closer than she had thought.

She was carried through a stout wooden gate and caught a glimpse of the guards who had opened it. They were muffled in cloaks, and not even the flare from the guardhouse brazier showed her more than dark outlines. They did not speak, merely pushed the heavy gates shut once more.

Her horse halted and the second one stopped alongside. Its rider jumped down and came across to her. "Give her to me." She was shoved down the shoulder of the sweating beast, to be caught by the man on the ground. "Can you walk?"

She tried, but her legs were too weak. Cursing, he picked her up and strode across a darkened courtyard. The bright, comforting brazier disappeared behind his bulk. She heard the second man following, and then he stepped in front to tap on a small door set into a stone wall. She caught a flash of the man's features as he turned apprehensive eyes on the one who held her. She did not recognize him.

The sound of bolts being drawn took her attention and she fixed her gaze on the door. It opened onto stygian darkness, and she could see no one behind it. Her captor walked through, leaving the other man outside. The door swung shut, trapping them in utter darkness.

"Through here."

The voice was low and harsh; she hardly heard the words. Her captor obeyed, carrying her through another door. She heard the swish of robes as someone moved in front of the man holding her. Her eyes, more used to darkness than light these past two days, had already become accustomed to the gloom, which wasn't as absolute as she had first thought. She could detect the ruby glow of a banked fire, its warmth a blessing to her cold, aching limbs.

She stiffened. Part of the ruby glow detached itself, becoming two points of light that moved in a disquieting manner. A strange smell emanated from the man who held her—the smell of fear. She almost sympathized when she realized he was shaking as hard as she was. She could feel every cord of his muscles, every heave of his frightened breath. This alarmed her more than anything else. If this strong swordsman was so terrified, how much more frightened should *she* be? She tore her thoughts from the man who held her and fixed her gaze on the twin points of sullen light that moved and behaved like eyes.

"So, my dear, we meet again. I cannot tell you how pleased I am to see you. Put her over there."

The order was given in a completely different tone to the silky voice that had addressed Jinny. She recognized the voice and gasped in shock, hand flying to her mouth. She had managed to convince herself she had imagined hearing him speak at the mansion the night of her abduction, but it seemed she was not deluded after all. Somehow—impossibly—her uncle had escaped his prison and returned to persecute her. Her heart hammered in her breast.

"Secure her hands."

The man dumped her on a hard surface and grasped her wrists. Brought to life by her shock she tried to struggle, but it was futile. Even had she been warm and fit, he was far stronger than she was. He tied her hands with a slim rope. Then he stood away, arms dangling, looking like a puppet whose strings had been cut.

Jinny stared into the gloom, peering for her uncle. He seemed to have melted into the darkness. She could neither see nor hear him. She shuddered. This whole experience had a surreal quality, as if it was not really happening, and she was unsure how to react. If it was really her uncle who had abducted her, what did he want? Where was this place? How had he managed to escape his isolated island prison when everyone thought he was dead? She fought back tears. How she wished she were lying safe and warm in Taran's arms, in their own comfortable bed. Perhaps she would wake soon, his beloved face next to hers, and she would tell him of her nightmare and he would laugh and comfort her with his body, as only he could do.

A flare of fire revealed a stooped figure before her, but his face was in shadow and she could not see his features. Her gasp betrayed her fear and he gave a malevolent chuckle in response.

"What's the matter, Jinny my dear? Are you not pleased to see your uncle? Are you not pleased I am free, and we are together again? For I have to tell you, *I* am. I am so very pleased to see you here. I have waited a long time for this moment."

She could find no words to reply.

"Come, Jinella. Have you nothing to say to me? No words of greeting? You had plenty to say the last time we stood face to face."

She heard the malice in his voice and suddenly, with a lurch of panic, she realized what this was about. She knew his nature, after all—knew how he held on to grudges, how he nursed them and fed them until they became the reason for his existence. She understood why he had returned.

She shoved herself upright, desperate to flee. She had forgotten the swordsman behind her and fetched up against his breast as she turned from her uncle. He gripped her by the shoulders as she sagged in defeat.

Her uncle chuckled again, a parody of indulgent amusement. "Sit down, you silly girl! Where do you think you can go? There is nowhere to run to, Jinella, no friends to aid you. I am master here; you are under my control. Nothing happens here without my order, so you might as well get used to it."

Jinny swallowed painfully. The silent swordsman pushed her back onto the hard seat, and she did not resist. She was too weak for that, and if what he said was true, there was no point anyway. She might as well learn why she was here.

"What do you want from me, Uncle?"

"Want from you? Want from you, girl? What could I possibly want from you? What could anyone want from someone who betrayed them as thoroughly as you betrayed me?"

She jumped as the menacing voice crept out of the shadows. He had moved while she was struggling, and she had to peer about to locate him. His voice had a disembodied quality, as if it came from somewhere else and not the figure before her.

The ruby points of light fascinated her. She had thought they were eyes, but now she was not so sure. They seemed to blink and move like eyes, but then they disappeared altogether, reappearing somewhere else when she was sure her uncle had not moved. She watched them, mesmerized, as his gloating went on.

"You are wondering why you are here, my dear and loyal

niece. Well, I think you already know the answer to that. What would someone in my position want? What would anyone want who has been as persecuted, as wronged, as ill-treated as I? Revenge, of course. That is what I crave. Revenge upon all those who stood against me. Revenge upon my enemies, the enemies of our realm. Revenge upon *her*! And you, my dear, will help me achieve it."

The malevolent, silky voice sounded by her ear, and Jinella startled. She had thought he was beside the fire, yet now she could feel his presence right by her side. She held her breath. A miasma of evil flowed from him, a stench of sickness and death. She gagged, retching.

He paused and straightened as if he had heard something. Jinella raised her head, the sweat on her face stinging in the warmth from the fire. He turned toward another door, one she had not noticed before, and then she heard it too—a soft tapping.

Her uncle gestured to the silent swordsman, and Jinella gasped. His hand had the aspect of a bony claw. She stared in horror. Yet it was nothing to what she saw when the door opened.

Her gaze snapped to the new arrival, taking in the sumptuous velvets and flowing silks of the elaborate court gown. She registered the bleached and unfriendly features even as the disgraced former Queen smiled at her in triumph. Yet that was not the worst. The extra light from the hallway outside, dim as it was, illuminated the stooped, twisted specter crouching before her, and once she saw it Jinny could not wrench her gaze from its hideously contorted features.

Glaring from the ruined, mottled flesh were two malicious ruby eyes. And in the wasted muscles, the burned and dried-out tendons, the stooped and desiccated parody of a human being, Jinella recognized her uncle.

Overcome by revulsion and horror, Jinny screamed until she fainted.

Chapter Six

When General Blaine emerged from the substrate tunnel into the castle parklands, he could immediately see Sullyan and Vassa's changes. Vassa stood by the courtyard entrance, surrounded by swordsmen. Double the usual amount guarded the park gates, and many more than normal patrolled the perimeter wall. Blaine nodded his approval; his two colonels had put every measure in place they could think of to ensure Elias's safety. He followed Elias as he rode toward the waiting Vassa.

Before they reached him, a hail sounded from the gates. Blaine turned, alarmed. His hand went to his sword—as did those of the swordsmen around him—before he relaxed, seeing the familiar colors of one of Elias's runners. The horse sped toward them, the youth riding it calling out as he came, his voice full of urgency.

"Major Tamsen! Urgent message for Major Tamsen."

Robin frowned and wheeled his horse to meet the messenger. Blaine, his attention divided between the Major and his King, saw Elias dismount in front of Vassa. He turned impatiently back to Robin as the young man addressed the messenger.

"Feilin? What is it, man?"

The youth panted as he reined his horse to a halt. "Your uncle sent me to tell you your mother is gravely ill. He told me to bid you come with all speed, sir, but I have been over a week on the road in this weather. It might already be too late."

General Blaine saw Robin reel in the saddle, his face turning deathly white. His mother had suffered poor health ever since the death of his father. She grew frailer by the month. His uncle, the village blacksmith, took her into his home and looked after her, for which Robin was grateful. He visited her as often as his duties allowed, taking Sullyan and Morgan when he could, and had expressed concern over her declining health after the last such visit. So this news, shocking as it was, was not totally unexpected. But Robin clearly had not imagined she could die so soon. His face pale and his voice trembling, Robin turned in appeal to the General.

"Sir?"

Blaine briefly closed his eyes. He knew Robin still felt guilty for not being there when his sister, Jessy, died eight years ago. He would be desperate to be there for his mother and Blaine could not, in all conscience, forbid him to go. It was damnably poor timing, but that could not be helped. Still, something pricked at the back of the General's neck ….

"Think a minute, Major. Do you know this lad? Does his news ring true?"

He saw Robin pause and frown, sensed the Major using his Artesan gifts on the youth. Then the frown cleared. "He's speaking the truth, General. This is Feilin, my cousin Darral's friend. He has been in Elias's runner service for over a year now. Do not worry, sir. I'll slip through Endormir and I'll be back as soon as I can."

Reassured, Blaine nodded. "Very well. You're free to go."

Robin set heels to Tobias's flanks, manipulating the substrate before Blaine finished speaking.

"Report to Sullyan as soon as you arrive!" yelled the General, and Robin raised his hand in acknowledgement before disappearing into the tunnel, followed by the runner.

Blaine sighed. The last thing he needed was to lose Robin's leadership and expertise, and if the Major arrived too late to say his farewells, the tragedy would affect his ability to carry out his duties. Blaine dismounted in the courtyard, leaving the escort in Dexter's capable charge, the Captain already making arrangements for his two sick men. Shaking off the feeling Fate had dealt them a rough hand of late, the General clapped Vassa on the shoulder and followed the King, who stumped off into the castle muttering curses.

Robin's tunnel opened onto the white, featureless steppe that was Endormir in winter. The temperature plummeted by a good twenty degrees, causing the two riders to gasp. Both wore their warmest winter clothing, yet the ferocious climate of the First Realm was more than capable of penetrating the thickest fleece and toughest leather. Even the horses snorted in discomfort.

"I'll get us out of this before the sweat freezes and locks our muscles solid," Robin yelled over the howling of the wind. Feilin nodded, his teeth chattering hard.

Robin glanced at him, concerned. The young runner looked disoriented, and even if he had never been through the substrate before, it should not affect him like this. The youth's eyes widened abruptly and he reached out, gripping Robin's arm. The Major sensed his urgency and his stomach lurched.

"Is my mother that bad?"

Feilin only nodded, his eyes strange and fearful.

Robin cursed. Why was this happening *again*? He had never forgiven himself for not being there when Jessy needed him. Must he suffer the same agonies over his mother? Gritting his teeth against the cold and the tears that threatened to freeze his eyes, he gathered the substrate and formed a way through.

The winter that met them in the far west of Albia was almost warm in comparison, but no less miserable. The sleet whipping their eyes was only partially frozen and quickly worked its way down their necks, chilling them to the marrow.

They emerged onto the only road leading to Lychdale, Robin's tiny home village. It was dark, the winter gloom shutting out the light. Robin nudged Tobias into a trot, then realized Feilin had not followed. He turned, frowning.

"What is it, lad? Come on, we have to hurry!"

Feilin looked like he was going to faint. He swayed in the saddle and gave a gasp. "Major, I—" He toppled out of the saddle, landing in a heap on the road.

"Oh, for pity's sake!" Robin slid down his horse's shoulder and ran to the stricken young man. He bent to shake him by the shoulder.

"Feilin! Come on, wake up. What is wrong with you? Feilin! Come on, lad, I can't leave you lying in the road."

The soft step behind him was followed swiftly by pain blossoming beneath his ear. Robin had no time to react. He collapsed atop Feilin, twin points of sullen red light fading before his sight.

✣ ✣ ✣ ✣ ✣

Sullyan halted outside the door to the King's chambers and squared her shoulders. She doubted the news she carried would do anything other than increase the King's fury, which, judging by the sounds within, was already past boiling point. She sighed, remembering the gruesome sight that had met her search party when they finally traced the source of the dreadful smell that permeated the east wing.

Three whole hours of fruitless searching had ended with a maggot-ridden corpse, a body too decayed to have been someone involved in the incidents at the castle. Who he was and how he got there she had no idea, but those were the questions she would face when Elias heard her tale.

She took a breath and opened the door.

All sound ceased. The King stopped shouting at his daughter, who stood before him in an attitude of defiance, watched by General Blaine and Colonel Vassa. Taran was there too, and he looked dreadful. She recalled her promise to link with him to search for signs of Jinny, and guessed why he appeared so sunken and drawn. Deprived of her skill and strength, he must have attempted the impossible on his own, with no success. Her heart went out to him.

She briefly wondered where Robin was, but then realized he would be in the garrison. Bulldog should have contacted him by now concerning the second extra company of men she had requested. He would be discussing their deployment with Valustin. And then there were the arrangements for the funeral pyres of Denny and his men. Robin's absence left her to endure the full measure of Elias's wrath alone and she stepped farther into the room, closing the door behind her.

"Well?"

Elias's voice was curt and full of anger. His blue eyes snapped and she could almost feel the waves of furious indignation rolling off him. His home had been invaded, violated, and she understood his emotion.

"We found the body of a man in the east wing, your Majesty."

She used formal address to remind him of the proprieties. His body stiffened. She had the attention of everyone in the room, especially the young Princess, whose smug face turned stark white.

"Unfortunately, it cannot be our murderer."

Elias glared. "Why not? Who is it, then? Where did you find it? How the Void did he get in there?"

She related the tale of her search. Her attention was on the King as she spoke, so she only vaguely registered his daughter's frightened look. Seline edged toward the door.

When Sullyan described the corpse's shocking appearance, Elias bombarded her with questions. She answered as best she could. The body was now in the mortuary. Elias could examine it at his leisure, although she recommended staying a goodly distance from it. Elias, having extracted this information, turned his attention on Vassa, demanding to know how anyone could have entered the east wing without their—and especially Vassa's—knowledge. This left General Blaine free to speak with Sullyan. He moved close and placed a hand on her shoulder.

"What was the Major's report on the health of his mother, Brynne?"

She stared, perplexed. "What?"

She sensed the General's annoyance. "His mother. She is gravely ill. A messenger arrived just as we did, telling him to go to her. I told him to report once he arrived. Don't tell me he hasn't been in touch?"

She stared at Blaine in horror, feeling the blood drain from her face. Her muscles felt weak and useless; she feared she might fall.

Softly as Blaine had spoken, the King heard him. The conversation died as all eyes turned to the two of them.

Sullyan's whisper was harsh. "What are you talking about, Mathias?"

Blaine quickly told her about the runner from the garrison near Robin's village. Sullyan's breathing faltered. She felt nauseous and her eyes lost focus as she quested for Robin's psyche in the substrate. The agony in her shadowed eyes told the tale of her failure.

Her voice broke as she snapped, "General, your assistance, please."

Blaine nodded curtly, meshing his psyche with hers, his Master-level powers vastly increasing the strength available to her. Taran reached out too, but her rejection was harsh. "No, Taran, not you."

He ducked his head, although she knew he understood. He was too drained to be of use. He watched as the two Master Artesans struggled to find some trace of Robin.

Eventually, faces white and beaded with sweat, breath laboring from the strain, they had to admit defeat. The General turned away from the agony and blame in Sullyan's eyes.

"How could you have let him go alone?" she cried, collapsing into one of the King's chairs. She dropped her face to her hands. Taran approached her, eyes wide with fear. He laid a hand on her shoulder, which shuddered with the force of her emotions. The General had to clear his throat before he could reply.

"I told him to check the lad's information. He did, said he knew the fellow and he was telling the truth. What more could we have done?"

Sullyan raised her head and stared at them, her eyes prickling and sore.

"He has been taken. It is the only possible answer. If he were at home, I would have sensed him." She hugged her chest, trying to contain her fear and pain. "There is no trace of him anywhere. Whoever has him knew exactly how to trap him. They sent someone who knew the smallest details of his life and family, probably gave the boy false information, lured Robin with the one fear guaranteed to compel him. He would never have gone so willingly otherwise."

She faltered, her throat threatening to close on her emotion.

"So what are we to do?" she continued. "We are under attack with no form of defense. We do not even know who our enemy is. How can we protect ourselves? How can we fight back?"

No one spoke, they just stared at her. Fury erupted in her breast. Why did they always expect her to lead them? Why was she always the one to make the decisions? Could they not see how hurt she was? Could they not see the despair? The pain in her heart swelled, overflowed, claiming her soul, and she shook off Taran's hand, surging to her feet.

"Do not look to me for answers! I am out of ideas. My heart is torn and my strength is gone. I do not know how to proceed."

She turned away, stalked to the window, and stared into the darkness, head bowed, breath coming harshly, arms wrapped tightly about her chest as if that were the only way she could contain the pain.

✢ ✢ ✢ ✢ ✢

Seline watched the tableau in silence. They all stood there just staring at Sullyan's back. Taran looked haggard and defeated, as if all hope was dead. Her father, General Blaine, and Colonel Vassa stared at each other in helpless rage. Fortuitously forgotten, Seline slipped out the door, collected her lady's maid and guards, and returned to the private chambers Sullyan had allotted her. A small smile creased her lips, replacing the anxious fear she had felt on hearing of Sullyan's discovery of what could only be the vagrant's body.

Her smile widened as she considered the implications of this latest event. Maybe now her mother could return. Maybe someday soon she would come back and take her rightful place. Once all these interfering Artesans had gone, they could all get on with their lives.

Careful to hide the elation she felt, Seline settled into a chair and allowed the servants to bring her refreshment, their deferential attitude a balm to her haughty pride.

✢ ✢ ✢ ✢ ✢

In the dark, pain-filled caverns of his mind, someone called his name. The syllables sounded strange in the hazy shroud that smothered him like the cerements of the dead. He heard desperation and urgency behind the voice that called him, and fear. He struggled to reach out, to respond, but could not. The voice faded and he could have cried for the loss. He was alone, terribly alone. More alone than he ever recalled feeling before. The clamor of pain and the pounding of his blood were the only sounds in his mind, and for some reason he could not clearly grasp, that was the most frightening thing of all.

He tried to stay calm, struggling in vain to halt the sickening sway of his thoughts. If he could only dampen the insistent, dull thud of pain, he might make some headway. He tried to reach within, to access his powerful psyche and the life forces flowing through it. The null barrier repulsing his every attempt drove a needle of agony into his overburdened mind. With a sickening rush of terror, he realized what it meant.

Spellsilver.

His power was blocked off, smothered and surrounded by a terrible blank wall that denied his efforts to breach it. With this realization came despair. He was trapped, helpless. He had never succeeded in finding a way to combat the effects of spellsilver, no matter how many times he tried. That knowledge forced a cry from his lips. It echoed in the empty chambers of his mind and beat around his heart. Whether it sounded outside his head, he could not tell. The wash of agony it produced fired its way into the depths of his being, plunging him once more into oblivion.

As he sank, he thought he heard soft, frightened weeping, and felt a trembling hand on his fevered brow.

✠ ✠ ✠ ✠ ✠

With a curt gesture, King Elias dismissed the other men. Taran hesitated, casting a glance at Sullyan's unresponsive figure. Elias gave him an undecipherable look as he tore himself away, following Blaine and Vassa toward the door. The King heard what Blaine said to them before he closed the door.

"Jerrim, come with me. The Major's company deserves to know what has happened, and we must see to the funerals for Denny and his men. Those brave souls died in the service of their King and must be honored. At least the darkness will cover the smoke from the pyres. We can do without upsetting the city any more than we need to.

"Taran, I recommend you stay here until the King either calls for you or dismisses you."

Once the door had closed, Elias stood in silence. Sullyan made no move, standing rigidly unapproachable and cold, her head bowed over arms tightly clenched around her chest. Elias took two steps toward her.

"Brynne—"

"Leave me be."

Her voice was unrecognizable, rough and low, quite unlike her usual tones. Elias heard the ache of her soul in the raw-edged words and his face tightened. There was no remedy for her pain; he already knew that. Yet he was damned if he was going to let her descend into bleak despair. He did know how to combat that. Had she not shown him many times before? Taking a breath to shore up his heart against her anger, he came closer.

"Elias!"

There was real warning in her tone, real anger, and had he not cared so deeply for her it would have made him recoil. Such fury had never been unleashed on him before, but he would not falter. He could not fail her now.

Swiftly, before his better judgment intervened, he stepped up behind her and wrapped his arms around her shuddering body. He felt her stiffen in shock, and then she struggled. Yet he was stronger physically, at least when she was unarmed, and he had taken care to hold her in such a way that she could not reach her weapons. He held on, ignoring the vicious curses she hurled at him.

He trusted she would not hurt him, not even in such distress, and she could not sustain her rage with agony eating at her heart. Elias's silent compassion and dogged embrace finally broke through her barriers, releasing the storm of emotion dammed inside. It was a measure of the depth of her love for Robin and her despair that she could not hold out longer. Gently, knowing she would not fight him, he turned her, allowing her to bury her face in his breast, holding her tightly until the storm ran its course.

She mastered herself eventually. Trembling still, unable to fully purge herself of her terror, she raised her face. Her golden eyes were red-rimmed and full of hopeless fear. But the specter of debilitating despair had receded; she was able to function again.

"I thank you, Elias. You took a risk there."

"I know."

The sympathy in his voice and the slight smile on his lips made her frown. Becoming aware of their close proximity, she pushed clear of him. He relaxed his hold reluctantly. He could see she was far from calm, but for that there was no remedy, not while her life mate was missing, possibly dead.

He knew it was inadequate, but he said it anyway. "I'm so sorry, Brynne. I don't know what else to say."

"Then say nothing."

"But what are we to do?"

Anger appeared in her eyes again, but it was born of frustration and wretchedness, not despair. "Endure, Elias! What else is there? Endure and pray our enemy makes a mistake. And whatever else you do, my Lord, do not delude yourself. He has not finished with us yet."

Elias stared at her in alarm. Gone was the despairing weakness of a few minutes ago. Gone was the draining hopelessness. Now fury shone from her eyes, a deep and abiding anger that someone had dared harm those she loved. Whoever was behind these events, whether the Baron or some hitherto unsuspected enemy, Elias pitied them. When Sullyan caught up with them, she would show no mercy.

He attempted to divert the disquieting rage lurking behind her eyes. "What makes you say that?"

She inhaled slowly, controlling her emotions with difficulty. Nevertheless, her underlying anger still surfaced in her tone.

"Think, Elias. Ponder the execution of these crimes. Think how difficult they would be to enact. Neremiah's murder was easiest, as no one expected it. Yet the murderer risked planting incriminating evidence in the mason's yard to divert us. Then he arranged for brigands to waylay some noble's coach in order to keep the King's Guard occupied while he abducted the Lady Jinella and set fire to her mansion. Not to mention the murder of some poor woman who had the misfortune to bear a passing resemblance to Jinny. And then, while the mob bayed at your gates, distressed by the slaughter of crack troops sent to apprehend the brigands, he took another huge risk and used the disturbance to slip inside the castle in order to poison two seemingly unconnected people. And last of all, he used his intimate knowledge of us— virtually threw it in our faces—to so distress Robin ...," here her voice faltered, but she dragged it back under control, "... that he ignored the usual strictures of security and went haring off alone to answer a spurious but cunningly contrived emergency. Think, Elias: Why would anyone go to such lengths and take such risks unless they had a definite goal?"

Elias blew out his lips. "I think you've made some enormous assumptions there, Brynne, not least in assuming all those events are connected." He held up a hand to forestall her reply. "The murder of Neremiah might have been carried out by someone he upset or insulted. You know what the man was like; he could be insufferably pompous. I'd imagine there were many who would have liked to see him removed."

She shrugged. "I will grant you that. But how many people he might have 'upset' would have drawn that dreadful knife across his throat? How many who wanted him 'removed' would have implicated an innocent man in murder? No, Elias, that murder was not carried out by an offended dignitary or ambitious Churchman.

"But I agree I am making assumptions. I do so because I have no other choice. I have the strongest feeling a pattern exists somewhere among this mess—a pattern I have so far failed to see. There is purpose at work here, and I need to find and work through the clues to understand it. I am disappointed, although hardly surprised, that you found no evidence of collusion in Bordenn. Lerric is weak, Sofira little better. I doubt Lerric would willingly harbor the Baron, if he is still alive. As for Sofira, I would not care to speculate how she would react to a plea of assistance from one who betrayed her, but she would be unable to act without the support or permission of her father. From what you experienced there, her chief concerns still seem to be the strictures you placed on her relationship with her children. Her angry reaction to your mention of the Baron and her correspondence with him is what I expected.

"My assumption that the poisoner entered the castle with the city delegation is based solely on the lack of any other information. Jerrim and I thoroughly questioned the servants and castle staff. We could not discover any other way in which someone could have tampered with the food. He must either have been incredibly clever in avoiding the kitchen staff, or else the servant carrying the trays was distracted long enough for him to do it on the way to their rooms. Not that the man remembered anything out of the ordinary."

Elias heard the frustration in her voice. "And what of this decomposed body in the east wing? How does that fit in?"

She sliced the air with her hand and spun away. "How should I know? Maybe nowhere. Maybe some poor wretch crept in there for shelter before Sofira left, although the state of the body refutes that. This is all pure conjecture, as you see. I am shooting in the dark and striking wide of the mark. If you can formulate better answers, let me know. My heart is torn and I have no strength left."

Her admission of defeat struck at Elias's heart. While she was speaking, she could hold the despair of Robin's disappearance in abeyance. Now, her barely endurable pain overflowed and she lapsed into disconsolate silence. Elias was lost for a way to comfort her.

This might have lasted longer but for the discreet tap at the door. Irritated but unable to refuse the summons, Elias barked, "Come."

A deferential guardsman stood in the doorway. He approached the King, one eye on the silent Sullyan, who did not move. Elias raised his brows. "Well, man? What is it?"

The guardsman straightened stiffly and the King felt brief remorse at his brusqueness. The entire garrison was on edge because of the slaughter of Denny and his band, and the news of Robin's disappearance had not helped. None of them was used to feeling so angry and helpless and Elias should have been more sensitive.

"Your Majesty, General Blaine sends his compliments and begs to inform you all is now ready for the funeral ceremony."

Elias's heart sank, hearing Sullyan's soft groan at the reminder of the night's sad duty. He dismissed the guard with a nod and the man left. Elias turned to Sullyan, seeing her closed, pale face.

"We can't shirk it, Brynne."

She swung on him and he thought she would snap, but the anger in her eyes died before reaching her lips. She sighed. "Nor do I wish to. Denny was a true companion and a fearless fighter. He deserves our respect and attendance, as does every one of that brave company. I intend to honor them all tonight."

Elias raised his brows, but forbore to comment. He offered her his arm and, after a brief hesitation, she took it. It was not strictly appropriate for neither of them wore court dress, but the close presence of a good friend was a comfort to both. They left together, collecting the silent Taran, who waited patiently outside.

The garrison courtyard was crowded. Every swordsman not on duty stood by the group of pyres, and many of the castle dignitaries were present. They came to attention and paid homage to their King, and Sullyan saw many pairs of eyes trained her way, not least those of Ghyllan Ardoch and the men of Robin's company. She would have to speak with them once this ceremony was over. Dexter and Wil, in particular, looked quite wild about the eyes.

She knew how they felt. Her own heart clamored at her, urging her to *do* something, to look for him, to search through the Veils, tear through every realm, to run, shouting his name—anything, *anything*, rather than do what she was doing. She was not sure how she contained her fear and urgency. All she knew was that to rush off unprepared and alone was the very worst thing she could do and, for all she knew, it was exactly what their enemy hoped she would do. If so, she would disappoint him. There were clues here somewhere, and she would fight down the rising tide of terror and despair and she would take the time to *think*. Maybe then she would have some idea of what she could do. But first, she must honor the fallen.

Colonel Vassa approached and saluted the King. "All is in readiness, your Majesty."

The dead wore their parade uniforms, adorned with battle honors and rank insignia. Their weapons lay on their breasts, and drapes bearing the King's symbol of a sun-circled crown covered the bodies, hiding the dreadful wounds. The swordsmen lay together on four solid pyres, but Owyn Denny lay alone, sword across his breast, hands clasped about the hilt. Blaine, grim-faced, held a burning brand, awaiting only his sovereign's signal to ignite the mound. Valustin stood by the second pyre and Master Ardoch by the third, both holding brands. Elias glanced down at Sullyan before replying to Vassa. "Brynne?"

"Begin the ceremony, my Lord. I am ready."

Elias nodded to Vassa, who offered a brand to Sullyan before moving to the fourth pyre. She shook her head and drew Taran with her as she approached the final mound of logs, and left him standing beside it. As Elias addressed the throng, telling out the names of the dead and honoring their achievements and loyalty, Sullyan moved along the line of pyres, reaching a hand, now and then, to touch one of the bodies, remembering them all, saying farewell in her own way. She lingered longest beside Denny's pyre, stroking a finger along his cold cheek, tears glistening in her eyes.

Elias reached the end of his speech and those beside the pyres lifted their brands. Sullyan reached out to Taran's psyche and meshed her powers with his. Allowing the Adept to call the Fire, she closed her eyes as the brands entered the logs and the pitch smeared on them crackled and spat as the flames ran inward.

Leaping red and gold reflected in the eyes of those assembled as they stood in respectful silence, heads bowed, honoring their fallen comrades. Smoke wreathed high into the air, as the night was still with no wind to stir it. The only sound was the snap and crackle of the hungry fire as sparks leaped high to spangle the smoke.

The flames grew hotter and the crowd edged back. The blaze intensified, tongues of blue and gold leaping high into the cold, higher and straighter and brighter than any flames had a right to be. Heads turned toward Sullyan who stood immobile, eyes closed, arms upraised. She had no need to open her eyes to see the spectacle for the flames were not wholly corporeal. They burned on two planes. Deep within the substrate, within the natural home of Fire, burned a duplicate funerary pyre, raging with all the anger of Sullyan's wounded heart.

People moved farther back from the unnatural flames, the intensity of their light so fierce it hurt the eyes.

Sullyan and Taran stood unmoving, closer to the flames than anyone else. The heat had no effect on them. Taran raised his arms and the power of the blaze flared white-hot. With a great roar of all-consuming hunger, the fire flashed to conflagration, destroying all within its maw, pounding at the ears, causing some to cry out in fear. Yet the awful noise and searing heat died quickly, and as Elias opened his eyes he saw the incredible sight of the entire flaming mass sucked into the blossoming mouth of a shimmering substrate tunnel. So exquisite was Sullyan's control that not a cinder, not a smut, not an ember remained. What the fire had been set to consume had disappeared utterly from the earth.

Silence and darkness returned, alleviated only by the courtyard torches. The fire was but a memory, an afterglow imprinted on the backs of the eyes. Unwilling to talk, the crowd dispersed. Soon, only a few remained, and even they found it hard to break the silence.

Ardoch, Valustin, Dexter, and the rest of Robin's company

gathered around Sullyan. The old Torlander had tears in his eyes as he laid a hand on her shoulder, and his face was sad and pale.

"He would have appreciated that show, lassie. They all would have."

Sullyan nodded, her throat too tight to speak. She managed a smile for Valustin as he silently thanked her for her homage, too upset to voice his feelings. He was led off by Ardoch, no doubt to be plied with tarn brandy until some of his pain dwindled.

That left her with Robin's company, who were obviously waiting for her to command them. She read the fear in their eyes, fear she would have expected given the love and respect they felt for Robin, but there was also something deeper, something more damaging, and she guessed what it was.

"You are not to blame." Her voice, rough and low, still carried conviction. "You could have done nothing. Our enemy knew how to compel him, and Robin went of his own choice. None of you are to blame."

"But we could have stopped him, Colonel!" The anguished voice was Dexter's. "We *should* have stopped him."

She captured his gaze, reading his torment. "Do not torture yourselves with what could have been. What is done is done. We must concern ourselves with our next move." Hope flared in their faces and her heart fell. "No, my friends, I have no plan as yet. But I will not go searching blindly, not until I have given the matter more thought. Believe me, I am as desperate as you are for action, but I will not waste our efforts or spend our strength until I have a definite aim. Remember your training. Know your enemy before you strike. Know his strengths and his weaknesses, and you will prevail. Go in blind and unprepared, and you will fail. I am here to tell you now: I do not intend to fail."

Murmured agreement met her words and she knew she had their wholehearted support. When the time was right they would be ready, honed, and nothing would stand in their way. Yet for now she had no target, and this ate at her soul.

She sent them back to the barracks, telling them she would see them later, not least to check on the two recuperating men. She knew Ardoch and Valustin would drag themselves out of their sorrow to see to them. Vassa would expect no less. She watched them walk dejectedly away and turned to Taran, standing lost in his own thoughts by her side.

"Memories, Taran?" She drew him with her back to the castle. Elias and General Blaine were already inside, out of the cold and away from the grief.

Taran glanced at her. "I was thinking about Denny. I am going to miss him so much. He was a staunch friend to me. And it wasn't just that he enjoyed relieving me of my gold."

She nodded, appreciating his attempt at levity. "Many purses will be heavier for his absence from the card table."

Taran continued distractedly, eyes unfocused. "When I decided to accept Elias's offer to work in the castle, I wasn't sure how Denny would react. I was apprehensive about approaching him after … what he did to you and Robin. I thought he might feel I would not want his friendship. It would not have surprised me if he had not wanted mine. I did rather force him and Jinny into confronting Robin during the Baron's trial, and I know what a traumatic experience that was. Denny did his part after that, giving evidence and all, but I did wonder whether he might have held it against me."

Sullyan stopped abruptly and Taran turned to her, alarmed by the strange expression on her face. "What, Brynne? What is it?"

She shook herself and the look, if anything, intensified. "Oh, you have it, my friend! The first piece of the puzzle, the one fact that links the whole. The pattern I could not see. You have found it!"

He frowned. "I have? How? What did I say?"

She smiled grimly, grasping his arm. "I was right all along, at least in part. It *is* the Baron behind these attacks. I do not have all the answers, but it is a starting point, and you, my friend, have found it! Come, we must bring this before Elias."

She tugged the limping Adept with her, Taran still trying to work out what "this" was.

Chapter Seven

It was late and Seth was tired. He stared disinterestedly at the half-empty tankard of ale on the table and abruptly pushed it away. He had tasted none of it, if he was honest, even though it was the best the tavern had to offer. He could have had wine or even brandy, and a few days ago he would have said that having enough coin to buy such luxuries was his ultimate goal. Yet now that he had it, being wealthy wasn't as fine as he had thought.

What was wrong with him? What had changed? He stared at the tavern's other patrons, none of whom sat alone, as he did. It was a quality establishment; not top quality, but good enough. Seth did not feel like parading his newfound solvency in the haunts of the nobility. Apart from feeling out of place, he did not want the attention his appearance was bound to engender. Not with the changes to the running of the city and the jumpiness of the King's Guard.

Instead, Seth found himself a reputable but unremarkable lodging house and took a modest sized room. Aware that anyone splashing coin around right now might find themselves suspected of stealing Neremiah's gold—and by association, of his murder— Seth refrained from wild purchases and avoided the gaming houses. It was sensible to follow this course, and yet the young man felt cheated. He had come by his coin legitimately, but he could not tell anyone that. He couldn't even tell them where it had come from; no one would believe him. With the mansion in ashes and the body of "Jinella" no more than charred bones, mention of his former employer was out of the question. Although he had more than enough to last him a good few years if he was careful, Seth was far from content.

In truth, he felt abandoned, used. Had he not helped his master achieve one of his greatest aims? Had he not faithfully followed orders and stayed loyal to his duty? Had he not gone well beyond what might reasonably be expected of a manservant? *As you have for years*, said a sly voice in his head. Yes, he had been rewarded, but what use was gold if you couldn't enjoy it? What use was enough gold to live on in comfort if there was no one to share that comfort with?

He had to face it, he was bored and lonely. He had felt excited by what his master had demanded of him. He would be the first to admit he had been scared, but that was mostly because the vagrant wouldn't tell him what he was planning. Had Seth known from the start, he would have been prepared. Yet he had still accomplished everything his master asked of him, had he not; even down to cold, bloody murder?

He shivered, remembering Alice's terrified face and the mess he had made of the job. Well, he wasn't a killer, was he? He had no weapons skills. He was only a manservant. For a complete novice, he had done rather well, despite the vagrant's lack of respect.

So why had he been abandoned? Why had his master not contacted him? Had the vagrant left the city? Was he even now about some other task? If so, it was likely Seth would never see him again. The city was shut down tighter than a whore's purse, and no one could get in or out without a valid reason.

Seth was jostled hard on his shoulder and he swore, half standing in protest.

"Your pardon," mumbled the black-haired man, pushing himself clumsily farther from Seth's seat. *Drunk, no doubt*, thought Seth, rubbing his stinging shoulder.

He sniffed, the wisp of a vile, familiar smell catching at his nostrils. It was fleeting and he didn't bother identifying it. He sat again, staring at his tankard in a pool of spilled ale. The tavern's patrons were beginning to filter out as closing time approached; he would soon be asked to do likewise. Seth made up his mind and stood. There was no reason to stay and he did not want to draw attention by being the last to leave. Not that he had cause to be so careful. There were no witnesses and nothing to tie him to either the death of the whore or Alice. *Same thing!* sniggered the voice in his head. Grinning, Seth walked out the tavern door.

The dark streets were quieting down, most honest citizens heading for home. It was bitterly cold and frost glittered on the cobbles. Smoke hung on the air tonight, although that was not rare in Loxton. Most houses were heated by fire and Loxton's chimneys belched smoke all winter long. Tonight, though, the smoke smelled different, reminding Seth of the fire at the mansion. He wondered what had become of Jinny's Artesan lover after he had told him the fabricated suicide story. Seth was proud of that achievement and wished he could tell his master what he had done. He was sure the Baron would approve. The thought warmed his heart as he walked toward his lonely lodgings.

A sound caught his ear and he stopped. Despite the increased presence of guards, footpads still operated, and Seth carried coin. Anyone in the tavern would have seen it. It wasn't all on his person, of course; he wasn't that stupid. He rented one of the civil depositories for the balance, keeping only enough for his living expenses. Even so, what he carried would feed a pauper's family for months.

But there was no sound now and he saw nothing. The street

lamps were lit, and he was not in one of the poorer quarters. He knew enough to keep away from them, especially after his last foray. He moved on, keen to reach his bed, even if his lonely evening ended in another lonely night. He had gone to the tavern looking for companionship, but none of the younger men there were alone. He sighed and plodded on, careful of the slippery footing.

He must have been watching his step too intently or he would have seen the man approach. People did not materialize out of thin air, and this fellow was too large to hide. Seth almost walked right into him as he put one foot in front of the other.

"Here, watch what you're doing. What's the matter, street not big enough for you?"

The black-haired man stared at Seth, not bothering to apologize. Seth opened his mouth for another barrage of abuse, then shut it again, cold sweat beading his skin. The knife in the fellow's brawny hand glittered in the lamplight.

Seth's teeth chattered as he reached into his pocket. "I don't have much, but you can take it all."

His assailant's hand shot out to grip his forearm. Seth yelped. The man's touch burned like fire, even through Seth's thick jacket. And the icy cold of the knife blade burned the palm of his hand.

The man stepped back, releasing Seth's arm, leaving the knife in the astonished manservant's hand. Seth frowned up at him. "What are you giving me this for? Who are you?"

"Ah, Seth, my loyal servant. Still slow on the uptake, I see."

The familiar stench of rotting meat floated on the air, stinging Seth's nostrils. The hint of a ruby glow shadowed the man's blue eyes, and Seth relaxed. "Master. What happened to the other one?"

"And still asking stupid questions!"

Seth cringed. That was one of the things the Baron always tasked him over. He resolved not to ask anything else. Still ….

He held up the knife. It was medium sized and unremarkable, only Seth could swear the blade was made of silver. "What do you want me to do with this?"

"Put it away, man, it's not a plaything. Don't show it to anyone and don't, whatever you do, try to use it."

Seth frowned. "Then what is it for?"

The black-haired man laughed low in his throat. Seth wondered whether all the Baron's special servants had the same twisted sense of humor, or whether the twisting came from the Baron himself. Although this new man differed in physical form, his attitude and manner were much like the vagrant's.

"A very special purpose." His voice was different now, and he waved a burly hand at Seth. "Come on, mate, why don't we go back to your lodgings? Master says you've been lonely and we can't have that, can we? While I tell you the purpose of the master's gift, we'll see what we can do to make you … feel better. What do you say to that?"

Seth swallowed, not sure he understood. Not sure he *wanted* to understand. Yet he had little choice. He led the way, the black-haired fellow walking just behind.

✠ ✠ ✠ ✠ ✠

"**H**ow did you manage this, my love?"

Sofira's voice was full of admiration tinged with a little fear. She tore her eyes from the sorry sight before her and fixed them on the stooped figure by her side. The firelight was reflected in the glitter of his eyes and the gleam of his yellow teeth. They both ignored the weeping of one of the cell's occupants.

They stood in the scarecrow's killing room, although Sofira was unaware of its purpose. Reen had kept her ignorant of the terrible events that took place here, although that might soon change. He glanced at her, turning his leer to the semblance of affection. Soon, but not quite yet.

"Have I not told you I am more powerful than they, my love? Did you not believe me?"

She heard the warning in his tone and paled. Reen did not need the benefit of keen eyesight to sense her sudden wariness. He felt her body stiffen through the control he held over her. His glee intensified as she hastened to placate him.

"Of course I did. I would never doubt you. You must now that by now. I only meant to ask how it was done."

"By cunning and skill, Madam. Cunning and skill."

The Baron moved farther into the room. The weeping faltered and stopped as Jinella drew a frightened breath. He ignored his trembling niece, who sat on the edge of the small, hard bed, and looked down on the man chained to it by steel manacles fastened about his wrists. He lay still, unconscious. Jinella had cleaned some of the blood from the wound beneath his ear, but was unable to wash it from his hair. His handsome face was drained and white, his naked torso slick with the sweat of fevered nightmares. The Baron looked down on this most valuable of captives and was pleased.

"But what of his powers, my love?" Sofira ventured the question softly, unsure of her betrothed's mood. She sensed a corner had been turned, a milestone reached, and his demeanor had changed. He was more assured, more distant. This latest venture, to capture this very man, was at the root of his previous uncertainty. Now that it had been accomplished, a transformation within the heart of her beloved had taken place. He knew she did not like it.

He turned his head to glare at her, sending an image to her mind: a dark-feathered carrion bird, ravager of the dead. She shivered.

The Baron gestured contemptuously at the half-naked young man. "Have no fear of him, Madam, I hold him securely. Do you think I would risk his arcane powers without the means to combat them? Look at his fetters, my dear. They might be steel on the outside, but the inner surfaces are coated with spellsilver, enough to silence an army of such deviants. He is fettered as securely in mind as in body."

Sofira gasped. She knew all about spellsilver. She had learned of it during their dealings with Rykan, the renegade Andaryon lord. The weapon he helped them build had been destroyed by Brynne Sullyan, as was all the other spellsilver the Baron had obtained. The Baron had been beside himself with fury at its destruction. So ....

"Where did it come from, Hezra? Where did you get it?"

The scarecrow straightened from examining his captive. He was disposed to be generous, the anticipation of the dark pleasures he intended to indulge in later making him more than usually accommodating. His plans were going well and nothing could hinder him now.

He moved around the bed, ignoring the accusing stare his frightened niece cast his way, and strode to the chamber wall. His third captive lay chained there—with ordinary steel, as the young runner had no witch's powers—and he too was unconscious. The scarecrow considered it best to keep him that way till he was needed, a small dose of brown powder sufficient for the task. A little nausea was no obstacle once his participation was desired. A smile creased the Baron's crooked lips as he contemplated slaking those desires.

He glanced at Sofira. "I did not leave my prison wholly bereft of possessions. And the journey to reach you was long. I had ample opportunity to make certain arrangements."

Sofira looked perplexed. "There was spellsilver on the clerics' island? I thought it didn't exist in Albia. Why would the clerics have a supply?"

Memories rose to his mind. He had gone through agonizing death throes during that tortuous time after the accident and should not have survived. Stripped of everything—flesh, identity, even humanity—he had nevertheless been granted riches beyond his dreams: the means to rid the earth of its abominations. His God had flayed him of impurities and replaced them with Holy Fire to sear away the arcane powers that stalked the earth. Fire he was now fully empowered to use.

He spat. "Clerics! What do they know? What use are they, shut away on that pustule of an island, chanting their pious rituals? How can they hope to bring people to the Path of the Wheel shut up in isolation, brooding over their sterile faith? Pah! Once we have the reins of power, my love, I intend to destroy their precious island. I will swamp it with the sea, burn out their nest of complacency, drown them in their own self-righteousness!"

He fell silent, realizing his passion had overtaken him. The small gasp that escaped his cowering niece dragged him back to reality and he soothed his temper. He cared little if Jinella saw his true form—she had glimpsed it before—but it was still too soon to reveal himself to Sofira. She had not moved from her position by the door and was farther from him than Jinella. The dim lighting had fortunately hidden the worst of his lapse. He left the youth and returned to Sofira's side.

She was anxious, and this pleased him. Keeping her on edge increased his hold over her, but he must not push her too far. Not before this night was over.

He spoke gently. "Forgive me, my Lady, I fear I will never recover from their cruelty. No, the clerics had no store of spellsilver. They do not know what it is. I found it by the merest chance. The guiding hand of God led me to it and showed me its potential. It will play a vital part in the conquest to come. But before that, we have a happy event to anticipate, do we not?"

He smiled and she melted, unable to see the feral ruby glow lurking in his ruined eyes. She returned the smile, clasping his withered hand. "Will it be tonight, my love?"

Her question, so trusting, irritated him. The sooner he was rid of her simpering ways, the better. It would not be long now.

"Yes, my love, it will be tonight. And although we must conceal ourselves from the people and conduct our ceremony in private, you shall have attendants, and you shall have witnesses."

He turned from Sofira to his shivering niece. "What do you think of that, Jinella? You are to witness the wedding of your uncle to the object of his love."

Jinny's eyes widened and she made a choked sound. She stared at Sofira in horror. "What? You're going to *marry* him?"

Her grating voice made Sofira narrow her eyes. The Princess strode closer and glared into Jinny's pinched face, bristling with anger.

"Yes, we will be wed, little traitress. Together, we will right the wrongs of this realm, starting with that sham of a trial. We will have vengeance upon those who spoke against us and we will reclaim everything that was taken from us. And you will help us. Yes, even you, you faithless trollop. Willing or no, you will play your part. You will see your unnatural lover destroyed, along with all of his kind, and you will see them beg Hezra for mercy before they die. *You* will beg for mercy too, but it will not come. You will rue the day you turned your back on your family and betrayed your uncle's trust!"

Much to Reen's amusement, Jinella cowered before Sofira's fury. The Princess had not shown such backbone in his presence since he arrived. He sensed Jinella's fear and grinned.

"My Lady speaks the truth, dear niece. We will be wed before the night is out, and you shall be a witness. You and this other. Guard!"

The swordsman came forward, his movements jerky.

Reen pointed to Robin. "I want this one awake. Give her what she needs to tend him." He turned his gaze upon Jinella, a sneer quirking his lips. "You have one hour in which to rouse him. I suggest you do not fail."

Turning to Sofira, he took her by the elbow. "Come, Madam."

As he left with his bride to be, he heard his niece give instructions to the guard in a frightened, quavering voice.

Chapter Eight

Sullyan faced Elias, General Blaine, and Colonel Vassa in the King's chambers, Taran in tacit support behind her. Vassa did not venture an opinion, but the King and the General picked over every facet of her reasoning, trying to find holes in her theory. They had little success.

Elias spread his hands in a gesture of futility. "It could still be a coincidence, Brynne."

She snorted. "Is that the best you can do? Well, I do not care for coincidence. An explanation that fits all the known facts is not coincidence, especially with such diverse facts as these. And if the connection of the trial between every victim is not enough for you, consider this. Who could have known Robin would be in the castle parklands at precisely that moment? If it is coincidence you want, there you have it. That young runner did not go to the Manor first—I checked with Bulldog. And it would be a convenient coincidence indeed that he happened to be a friend of Robin's cousin."

She shook her head, holding the King's gaze. "Unpleasant as it is, we have to face it. The Baron is behind these deaths. He has managed to find someone willing to support him and provide him with the means for revenge. Whether by person or by proxy, he is systematically removing everyone who spoke against him at the trial. What other explanation can there be for the attack on Levant and the deaths of Alice, Denny, Bessie, and Neremiah? What other connection do they have?"

Elias stared at her, no ready answer on his lips. She knew it wasn't that he found fault with her reasoning; he simply didn't want to admit, even to himself, that the traitor might still be alive, at large, and capable of such far-reaching revenge.

General Blaine stirred. "If we accept that you're right, there must still be a connection between Bordenn and the Baron. And more important than that, others are still at risk."

She nodded. "Yes, General. Lord Levant is still at risk, having survived one attack, as are Ardoch, Taran, and, of course, his Majesty."

Elias capitulated in the face of overwhelming odds. "Not to mention you!"

Sullyan sobered. "Indeed. And also Prince Aeyron. This time I must not shirk my responsibility, however much I might wish to. I cannot leave him ignorant of this situation."

"Pharikian knows," Elias said. "Could he not protect his son without Aeyron's knowledge?"

She eyed him archly. "Would you be happier, my Lord, if the General and I conspired to protect *you* behind your back? How would you react to us keeping such intelligence from you?"

He ducked his head. "All right, Brynne, don't belabor the point. I was only trying to find an alternative."

She smiled, but her eyes were hard. Their expression had not softened since the news of Robin's disappearance. The lateness of the hour and her inescapable duties warred with her desire to take positive action, to move toward his rescue. If he was actually still—she squashed that thought with ruthless savagery. Although she could find no trace of his psyche within the substrate, she would *not* presume his death. Too many factors could affect the psyche's imprint. Being deep underground, deliberate muffling by another Artesan, spellsilver—all these could baffle hasty attempts at detection. Besides, on a purely instinctive level, she was sure she would feel it if he died. They were too close, too deeply bonded for her to be unaware. What she really needed was time; time to calm her mind, to still the ache in her soul, to concentrate her will and bring her skills to bear. Yet there were still too many things she must do.

A gasp from the King brought her back and she focused on him. "What about my son?"

Her heart skipped. Eadan had played no part in the Baron's downfall except that which the Baron had forced on him. Yet the control of Elias's heir was a crucial part of the Baron's original plan, and there was no reason to suspect he had changed his desires. Sullyan had already taken measures to ensure Eadan's safety; he was surrounded by Artesans and the might of the King's forces, and would be safer at the Manor than here with his father. It was of a different little boy that she thought now. She had not yet told Morgan of his father's abduction. She was not sure she could.

She responded to the fear in Elias's eyes. "Do not concern yourself. I gave you my word Eadan would be safe and I intend to keep it, on my life if necessary. I have already told Bulldog what has happened. He is guarding your son and will arrange for his security. Eadan will never be left alone, of that you may be sure."

Elias was comforted by her words, but the General regarded her narrowly. "And what of Morgan?"

The King shot her a glance, shamed he had not even thought of the potential danger to her own son.

She answered quickly. "Bulldog will watch over him, too."

Blaine shook his head. "That's not what I meant and you know it."

She hardened her heart against a painful surge of fear and saw understanding in the General's eyes.

"You haven't told him."

She waved a hand. "It is late, he will be asleep. Why disturb his rest just to distress him? Time enough for sorrow in the morning."

To forestall Blaine's retort, she turned to Elias. "My Lord, with your leave I will withdraw. I wish to check on Lord Levant, and then I must attend to my men. I am still concerned over the wellbeing of the two who fell sick in Bordenn, and I wish to test out another theory. The General was right when he said there must be a connection between the Baron and Bordenn, even if it does not involve Lerric or Sofira. Reen was a courtier there for many years. He may still have supporters among Lerric's men, or friends in the court. After that is done, Taran and I will pool our strength and trawl the substrate once more. We may have missed a clue, something that might come to light now that we have a better idea of what is behind these terrible events."

Elias nodded curtly. "And you should get some sleep. You too, Taran. Don't wear yourselves out pushing your energies past their limits. That won't help anyone."

"If you can show us another way, we will gladly take it."

Sullyan smiled to take the sting from her words. Elias bowed his head and the two Artesans left his chambers.

✤ ✤ ✤ ✤ ✤

Once they were alone in the Baron's private chambers, Sofira turned to Reen. She regarded him with shining eyes.

"Did you mean it? Are we really to be married tonight?"

He tried to curb his irritation. "Why, Madam, will you not be ready? I understood you wished the ceremony to be performed as soon as possible."

"I do, my love. And yes, I can be ready. It's just that I thought … I mean, I know we have to be circumspect and I know we cannot have the formal celebrations that would normally accompany such a joyous occasion, but I had hoped—"

"You hoped to throw a ball, did you? Invite the nobility in the dead of winter when travel is impossible? You hoped to swear them to secrecy and sit in regal splendor while they fawned over the beautiful bride? Is that what you hoped? Despite all I have told you, is that what you wanted?"

She frowned and he realized he had gone too far. He had not unleashed the full weight of his displeasure, but still, scorn was evident in his tone. Yet she did not crumple as she had on other occasions. That little scene in the killing room had made her realize she still held power. The burst of temper had emboldened her, especially with Reen's presence to support her. He caught her grim look and smiled.

"Forgive me, Sofira, I should not have spoken so harshly. With what I have had to bear, I sometimes forget I am among friends, and that you are a Queen. You are right to remind me. Of course you long for the trappings of a royal wedding. They are your due, and I do not wish to deprive you. Although we must hold this night's ceremony in private, witnessed only by your father and our captives, I will pledge you this. When we come into our power and restore you as High Queen, your second coronation shall be a spectacle such as never before seen. We will proclaim the news of our union and you will host the most splendid of feasts. I will bow to your beauty and share you with all."

She softened, her frustration leaking away. "I wish Seline could be here."

Mention of her daughter reminded him why she had come to him in the first place, before being sidetracked by his desire to parade his captives.

"What did you want to say to me, my dear? Is your father unwell? I heard he took to his rooms before Elias left and did not bid the King farewell. Was the visit too much of a strain?"

Sofira's face fell and he read her reluctance. Something had happened. Lerric must have let something slip, and she feared what Reen would say. Controlling a desire to shake it out of her, he stood patiently while she related what Lerric had nearly done.

His reaction was as intense as she feared. Though he tried to control himself, his skin reddened with fury and his eyes burned with rage. Clawed hands curled into tight fists that trembled as he struggled to maintain his disguise. He had not expected this, had never thought Lerric so craven as to endanger his daughter's safety—or his own miserable skin, come to that. Reen would never have allowed Lerric to meet with the King had he suspected the older man might crumble. He had truly believed Lerric feared his daughter's suitor more than he did Elias.

The scarecrow knew how to deal with Lerric, but it would have to wait. The crisis was over. Elias was unlikely to return. Reen needed to consolidate his hold over Sofira before removing the threat of betrayal by Lerric. She naturally harbored filial feelings for the man and Reen must not let this incident distract him from his purpose.

Calming himself with thoughts of how he would deal with Lerric, the Baron found a smile for his betrothed.

"Do not fear, my love. I was angry, but I can see that the effort of dealing with Elias would exact a heavy toll of your father. I can only imagine how galling it must have been to exchange polite conversation with the man who cast off his daughter and deprived her of her children. I have noticed that Lerric has not enjoyed the best of health lately. Once our ceremony is over, you must convince him to visit with me. Perhaps I can recommend a remedy for what ails him."

Sofira smiled back. "You are too generous, my dear. I thank you for your understanding. I am sure my father did not intend to jeopardize our careful plans. It must be as you say. He was weakened by the strain of the occasion. I have to admit, even I found it hard to face Elias, and I am supported by your love and loyalty."

"You did well, as I expected of a queen of your caliber. Now, I ask you to leave me. You have preparations to make, and so do I. I need to rest before we celebrate our marriage. I want to ensure I can fulfill my promises to you about our wedding night. I have arranged for a cleric to attend us at the first hour after midnight. Will that give you the time you need?"

Sofira took his hand and gazed deep into his eyes. Her anticipation pleased him. She would experience so much more than she thought when the time came to consummate the union. He would need more strength to carry out what he had planned, and he now had a ready source of vitality close at hand. He permitted the malicious pleasure he felt to show on his face; it was a fair substitute for the desire Sofira hoped to see. The widening of her eyes told him his deception had succeeded.

✠ ✠ ✠ ✠ ✠

Sullyan and Taran approached the guard stationed outside Levant's apartment. "Is Healer Endor still within?" she asked.

The guard shook his head. "Healer Endor judged the First Minister's condition to be satisfactory. He left one of the junior healers on duty."

"Has he awoken yet?"

"Endor said he spoke briefly before slipping back into sleep. That's all I know."

Sullyan turned to Taran. "I will just take a moment to look in on him. I do not wish to waken him. He must be on the mend if Endor has left his side."

Taran grinned. "He would not want to incur your scorn again."

"Was I so very hard on him?"

Taran just shook his head.

She pushed open the door, and the young healer dozing in a chair beside the banked fire raised her head. The door to the sleeping room was open, revealing Levant slumbering peacefully, his breathing regular and deep. No evidence of his sickness remained and the rooms smelled fresh and clean. Sullyan nodded to the young healer and stepped into the sleeping room.

Levant was oblivious to Sullyan's regard, and she was pleased. He lay in comfort; no dark dreams disturbed his slumber. She gently stroked his brow, feeling no hint of fever. Relieved, she left him to rest and returned to Taran.

"You did a fine job, Taran. Your support of his psyche has ensured he will take no lasting harm. I am glad. We cannot afford to lose nobles such as Rendan Levant. His tolerance and acceptance have done much to improve the standing of Artesans within Elias's court."

Taran accepted her praise without demur. It was a measure of his growth, she thought, that he no longer tried to turn her praise and showed no embarrassment when it was given. Not so long ago he would have protested his involvement, saying it was she who had saved Levant. Now, he could acknowledge that the battle for Levant's survival had been a joint effort, and he was content to have played his part and be rewarded for it. It pleased her that this should be so. She told him as much as they emerged from the castle's portico and made their way toward the torch-lit barracks.

He nodded soberly. "Yes, I've come a long way since I first showed up in your office at the Manor, full of my own importance, terrified by what I'd done and thoroughly embarrassed because of it. Not to mention mistaking Bulldog for you."

She smiled, remembering. "You are not the first to have done that, my friend."

"Oh?"

She took a breath so swift it was almost a gulp. "Robin did the very same thing. Bulldog had gone out recruiting, and he discovered Robin in the garrison near his home. He called me out from the Manor before talking to Robin, who was told only that a Major Sullyan wished to speak with him. His commanding officer made the introductions, and Robin naturally assumed it was Bulldog who held the rank. When told of his mistake, his reaction was much the same as yours."

Taran had never heard this story before and she knew he wondered why she told it now. Tears glistened in her eyes and he put a hand on her shoulder.

"We'll get him back," he murmured, his voice low and fierce. "We'll find them both and get them back."

Too choked for words, Sullyan bowed her head.

They entered the barracks. Normally a bustling and cheerful place even during the night watches, tonight the entire garrison lay below a pall of sorrow, as if the smoke of the funeral pyres lingered in the air. The somber atmosphere settled on the two Artesans like a heavy cloak as they made their way to the hut where Dexter had settled the company. The muted mutter of conversation could be heard before they opened the door.

Heads turned and Dexter gestured to the man nearest the fire. He poured two mugs of fellan and brought them to Sullyan and Taran. Sullyan sat on the nearest unoccupied bunk. Taran took a seat at the long trestle table.

"How is everyone, Dex?"

The Captain perched on the edge of the table, one leg swinging. Sullyan's heart lurched—the posture was a favorite of Robin's. "We're all right, Colonel. We just want to get out there and look for him. It doesn't seem right to sit here doing nothing."

She raised her brows. "Where would you look, Captain? What trail would you follow?"

He stared at the ground and did not reply. She saw his

frustration and relented.

"I share your desire. You must know I would never leave him languishing in an enemy's hands if there was any constructive action I could take." She glanced around the room. "Which is why I am here."

The whole company took heed, gathering round, faces anxious and full of trust. Taran shook his head. The close bond that existed between the swordsmen of the Manor and their commanders never failed to move him, and nowhere was it clearer than with Sullyan's command. The entire band would follow either her or Robin into the blackest pit of destruction.

She fixed Dexter with a serious gaze. "Tell me exactly what occurred during your stay in Bordenn. *Exactly*, do you hear? I especially want to know the details of what happened to Col and Pengar. Their experience may provide us with vital clues. Where are they?"

The Captain sent a man to fetch the two she had named, both of whom lay wrapped in blankets on their bunks at the far end of the hut. Were they avoiding their fellows as much as resting from their ordeal? She thought so, seeing shame and misery etched on their faces.

"What is this? Do you blame yourselves for the enemy's malicious actions?"

One of them replied in a low voice, head hanging. "We failed the Major and the King, Colonel."

"And how was that? Did you have foreknowledge of the attack? Could you have avoided the incident? Did you willingly go aside with those men?"

Anger rose in the other man. "No, Colonel, of course not!" He faltered when he saw her smile.

"Well then, Col, it is as I thought. You were not to blame and you know it. The whole company knows it. It could have been any of you—it could have been Dexter! So have done with this despondency and assist us. The two of you met with agents of the enemy, and I tell you this: I consider it a gross mistake on their part to have left you alive. You might carry vital knowledge that could help us in our search."

Both men perked up; they had clearly not considered the advantages that might be gained from their dreadful experience. If they could only provide some useful facts, it would go far toward alleviating the nagging feeling they were responsible for aiding the enemy in the Major's capture.

The company found seats on the bunks close to Sullyan. Dexter related every detail he could remember of their visit to Bordenn, aided by comments from the men and Wil in particular. When he was done, Col and Pen relived their experience as best they could. It wasn't easy as their memories of the tavern were hazy, and the time between leaving the tavern and waking to terrible nightmares was a complete blank. Sullyan was especially interested in their symptoms once they returned to the barracks, and had Dexter describe what they had gone through in distasteful detail, including the smell and the color of their vomit. Once Dexter finished describing it, she turned to Taran.

"Does that sound familiar?"

He wrinkled his nose. "You think it was the same as the substance given to Bessie and Levant. If you're right, it's very strong evidence to support your theory."

She glanced back at Col and Pen. "And if I am right, the two of you are fortunate indeed. That poison was both virulent and violent."

Dexter looked worried. "Do you know what it was, Colonel? Is there a way of countering it?"

She knew he was thinking of Robin. "Poisons are not my forte. It may behoove us to ask Rienne. The Manor's pharmacy might have had experience of it. Good thinking."

Dexter grinned and Sullyan relaxed. The mood of the company had changed. The anger and distress over Robin's disappearance lingered, as did their desire for instant action, but this necessary exercise of intelligence gathering had concentrated their minds, alleviating the dangerous state of despondency that had threatened to undermine their efficiency. Instead of moping and feeding each other's grief, they were now united in what they did best—second-guessing the enemy. It was what they were trained for, it was bred into them. It gave them a sense of purpose, cementing the bond that held them together as a fighting team. And while this was an essential part of the planning process of any offensive, Sullyan knew it was just what they needed right now.

"Tell me more about the palace's lower floor, Dexter. What was the reason behind its abandonment?"

"We were told it had become unsafe, and that Lerric was unhappy about the cost of housing and feeding the stonemasons while they repaired it. The door was locked and all the windows bricked up."

She raised her brows. "Bricked up? With mortar? As by stonemasons?"

Dexter frowned. "Why didn't I notice that? Yes, every window was properly bricked up."

"Why go to the bother and expense of bricking up any of the windows if the place was to be repaired? Why not just board them? Much cheaper if thrift was the reason. None of you saw Lerric's men taking an interest?"

The men shook their heads.

"Well, that is interesting. An entire floor abandoned. And very few nobles, if any, at the palace."

Dexter nodded. "We saw only Lerric, his daughter, Lerric's swordsmen, and the palace servants, although we did hear the sounds of a hunting pack. The quality of Lerric's hounds is famous, so presumably there were huntsmen. We never saw them. The Major said Lerric told them the bad weather had kept his councilors at home. He didn't expect them back until the thaw."

"How convenient."

Dexter looked unconvinced. "Colonel, we kept our eyes peeled for any signs of treachery by Lerric or his household. The lads and I did all we could to get the guards to talk, and talk they did, coming out with all sorts of complaints about their pay, their food, their duties. We saw evidence of the poor conditions for ourselves. Their rations were basic, some of them had the winter fever, and I know the Major was concerned about lice. But not one of them ever dropped so much as a hint of knowing something they shouldn't. And neither the Major nor the General thought Lerric or Sofira were acting out of character. So where does that leave us? What good does the connection of the poison do us? For all we know, it may be an easily obtainable substance, coming from the same source as that rancid narcotic they smoked. Are we any further forward in finding the Major?"

"Not yet, Dex."

The captain's disappointment was reflected in the men, and she felt for them. "But there is another connection between what happened in Bordenn and the Major's disappearance."

That sharpened their attention and she could feel them willing her on.

"The young runner who appeared at the castle gates this evening came here *directly* from Robin's old garrison. Not only was he a friend of Robin's cousin and knew his family circumstances intimately, but he also knew *exactly* where to find the Major at that precise moment. Who, apart from the King's escort and those you met in Bordenn, knew the hour of your departure? That runner would have been carrying the monthly report from the Lychdale garrison. He should have been bound for the Manor. The General would have been there if not for these recent events."

Taran spoke up. "But how did they persuade the runner to trick Robin? I understand that someone in Bordenn must have known of his movements, but how did they know the runner, or that Robin's mother had been ill? How did they even know about Robin's connection to the Lychdale garrison? He left there years ago."

Sullyan glanced at Taran, wishing he had not voiced that particular question. "I do not have all the answers. I am struggling to understand myself. But the facts are inescapable and must be explained."

She rose. "This has been a trying time for us all and I have kept you from your rest. Before I leave you, a word of warning. If the basic theory is correct and Baron Reen has somehow escaped his island prison and is bent on revenge, certain precautions must be observed. If his intention is to target or destroy anyone who spoke against him at the trial, then Ardoch, Taran, Lord Levant, and the King are still in mortal danger. It is our duty to ensure they stay safe. We must all be on our guard at every moment. Question anything that seems odd, take nothing for granted. Colonel Vassa will address the garrison in the morning, to the same effect. I will speak with you again when I have more to tell you. Once I have even the slightest suspicion as to the Major's whereabouts, I will be counting on your support. Get what rest you can."

Chapter Nine

Taran fell in with Sullyan as they made their way back toward the castle. He waited until they were in the courtyard before speaking.

"Did I say something wrong back there? I saw the way you looked at me. Should I not have asked that question?"

He noted the slight sag to her shoulders. She had not eaten much all day and had not rested since waking him that morning. "You really do need some sleep," he told her. "Even you can't go through what's happened today without feeling the effects."

She smiled. "There speaks a man who goes lame on one leg! Fear not, I do intend to rest, and I know I shall sleep. You and I have a final task tonight, and it will likely take all the strength we have. I certainly hope so. I could not sleep without the benefit of exhaustion, not while Robin is missing. As to your question, yes, you are right. I would rather you had not said what you did, although your point was valid. Despite what I told Col and Pengar, I fear they were the medium through which our enemy learned enough to trap Robin. Why else were they given an incapacitating drug that left them with no recollection of the evening? Why else lure them from their fellows? Every one of our company knows of Robin's origins. Who else could have supplied the knowledge that allowed the abduction to succeed?"

Taran halted. What she said made sense, but if it was true … He frowned. "But wouldn't that mean an Artesan was involved? There's no other way to have organized that trap without using the substrate. There simply wasn't time."

She nodded.

He stared in confusion. "How can you look so calm? How can you simply accept it?"

"Because you are right. And because I have feared it for some time. There is a precedent, after all."

Taran blew out his cheeks. "Surely he can't have found another like poor Huw?"

Sullyan shook her head. "Huw was unique. I doubt there is another like him in all the Five Realms. Nevertheless, if you think of recent events in the light of the logistics involved, you will come to the same conclusion as me. Our enemy has recourse to an Artesan's services."

He was appalled. "But who? And how?"

Sullyan closed her eyes, her face pale and strained. "If I knew that, would I be standing here while Robin endures God knows what torment? And if we are right about this, we are even further from finding our enemy than before, for with recourse to the substrate he could be hiding anywhere in the realm, directing these attacks without ever showing his face." She sighed. "I do not have the answers, Taran. All I have are theories which seem to fit the facts."

He heard the anguish in her voice and took her by the shoulders. "I'm so sorry. It's just all so strange. I, of all people, ought to understand how you feel. I'm as frantic for Jinny as you must be for Robin. And I fear for him too—he's one of my closest friends."

"I know. No need to apologize. None of us is at our best. Come, we will do that sweep of the substrate I promised you. I did not offer it lightly. I do believe we might find a lead, a trail to follow, if we only look hard enough. I intend to look so hard that I exhaust both of us into sleep. But first, I must let the General know our intentions."

✤ ✤ ✤ ✤ ✤

A deep, tortured groan issued from the man on the bed, and Jinny applied the cool, damp cloth to his brow. She could hardly see for tears and her breath hissed through her teeth as she tried to bite back sobs. One hour, the Baron had told her; one hour in which to rouse him. Jinny had no idea how much time was left, but she was beginning to think Robin would never come round.

He twisted against his chains, fresh blood seeping from the tight cuffs. She pressed her bound hands to his shoulder, trying to restrain him, murmuring his name constantly. She fought to keep the desperation from her voice, pleading with him, willing him to open his eyes.

She could see his pulse jumping in the pit of his throat. His fevered movements had reopened the wound beneath his ear, and the folded cloth under his head was red and wet. The herbs she had requested from the guard were supposed to alleviate fever and pain, but she wasn't certain she was using them correctly. She had steeped some of them in water; they scented the cloth she used on Robin's brow.

She cursed herself. Might the herbs work better if she could get him to drink them? Jumping to her feet, ignoring the guard's jerky movement as he took a threatening pace toward her, she dipped more water from the metal pot over the fire and poured it onto the herbs in their wooden bowl. Trying to avoid glancing at the other captive who lay slumped and unmoving by the wall, she stirred the brew with a finger and cupped the bowl in both hands. But now she had a problem. With her hands bound, she couldn't hold the bowl and raise Robin's head to give him the drink. She sighed in frustration and turned to the guard.

"Come and take this bowl."

The swordsman stared at her outstretched hands. She frowned.

"I can't do this with my hands tied! If you want me to help him, you'll either have to untie me or do some of the work yourself. If you don't want to take the bowl, lift his head for me. Quickly! How much of that hour do I have left? I don't suppose my uncle will be pleased with you either if I tell him it was your fault I couldn't do as I was told."

Jinny's tone, coupled with her angry desperation, did the trick. The swordsman stepped closer, avoiding Jinny's eyes, and roughly lifted Robin's head from the bloodstained bed. The young man gave another deep groan, frightening Jinny, who was aware that head injuries could be serious and permanent. She wanted to rage at the silent swordsman for his rough handling, but she bit her tongue. If Robin was that badly damaged, nothing she did would make any difference. Slowly and carefully, she dribbled the medicinal brew between the young man's lips.

She watched in desperate hope, not knowing how fast such herbs might work, cursing herself for not thinking of this sooner. If this didn't work, she had failed.

More heart-rending groans came from Robin's throat, the sinews taut with strain. She poured more of the infusion into his mouth, praying he could swallow. Suddenly he twisted, coughing violently. The guardsman let his head fall and some of the herbal brew ran down Robin's cheek. But enough had gone down to begin its work, and Jinny saw the merest hint of reflected firelight gleam below Robin's lowered lids.

"Robin! Come on, open your eyes! Oh, please, Robin, *please!*"

Jinny laid aside the bowl and took up the cloth, wiping Robin's face and mouth. The smell of the herbs on the cloth made him cough again and she saw him struggling to open his eyes. Then, a miracle.

"Brynne?" he managed, his voice a low croak.

Jinny gulped, half in relief and half in anguish. "No, Robin, it's me, Jinny," she said, keeping her voice as soft and soothing as she could while stroking his brow with her hands.

He forced his eyes to open, but she could tell his vision was blurred. He blinked and frowned in the poor light, confused and alarmed. Then he focused on her face and she heard his gasp of fear.

"No, this can't be," he moaned, twisting away, but the chains on his wrists held him fast. The pain of the movement made him groan.

"Don't move, Robin, just lie still. You'll only hurt yourself. Try to lift your head for me. I think you should drink more of this."

Robin tried to avoid her hands on his face, turning his cheek so his lips touched the bowl. He was clearly too weak and confused to work out what was wrong, but the warm steam from the bowl, refreshingly herbal, seemed to awake a raging thirst. He managed to hold his head up as she gave him the water. This time, more of the liquid went down his throat, warming and easing his pain.

"Who are you?" he croaked.

Her heart fell. His brain must be damaged after all.

"I told you, Robin," she said, trying not to cry. "It's Jinny."

"But you can't be. You're dead."

The whispered words cut through Jinny's heart with a cold shock. "What?"

"The fire. You died in the fire."

"What fire?" she demanded fearfully, setting aside the bowl and taking his face between her bound hands. "Robin. Look at me! What fire?"

Robin frowned, trying to remember. She could see he wasn't fully aware of what he was saying. But her cold fingers on his face and the urgent tone of her voice helped to restore some of his senses, and she saw his vision begin to clear. He stared up into her eyes.

"Jinny?"

She gave a gasp, a choked-off sob, and a single tear rolled forlornly down her cheek. "Oh, Robin!"

She fell forward onto his breast, her unbound hair hiding her face. The deep shiver of her body was due as much to relief as it was to the terror of her ordeal, and the low fire had done little to chase the bone-deep chill of hypothermia from her weakened muscles. Robin instinctively tried to move his arms, to embrace her, but the steel of the chains held him still. He moved his head slightly, turned his lips toward her ear.

"Jinny? Jinny. It's all right, I can think now. Jinny!"

The sound of his voice, stronger and more normal, gradually registered. Sniffling, she pushed herself upright and gazed down into his dark blue eyes, seeing sanity there, and recognition. He smiled at her and it nearly broke her heart. She fought against her tears. Collapsing in uncontrollable sobs was not going to help either of them. She would have to find some core of courage if she was to give him any support at all. She was terrified of what her uncle had in store for them, and there was still the other youth, the silent one, lying by the wall. She wiped her hand across her eyes and took a shaky breath.

"Are you all right, Robin? How are you feeling?"

He gave a choked laugh. The fact that he could react to her at all was a blessing, and she allowed herself a wan smile. He sobered immediately, however. This situation—the spellsilver and the chains upon him—was no laughing matter. "Where are we, Jinny? Can you tell me what's happened? I can't remember anything after arriving in Lychdale with Feilin."

"Feilin?" she repeated. "Is he a young lad, about sixteen, with short brown hair?"

Jinny's fearful voice and worried eyes made Robin's breath hitch. "Oh no," he murmured, "not him too."

Jinny nodded. "He's lying over there, chained to the wall. Robin, he's not moving and I've not been able to rouse him."

Robin tried to turn his head to see, but nausea rose in him. He groaned again and Jinny used her damp cloth to wipe the fresh sweat from his brow.

"Do you think you can sit?" she asked. "You might be more comfortable, and I think that chain is just about long enough …."

The cuffs that encircled both of Robin's wrists were linked by a short length of chain. But the length that secured him to the bed itself ran from the middle of the short chain and might just permit him to sit, leaning against the iron bed frame. He nodded and Jinny awkwardly used her bound hands to assist him as he struggled into a sitting position. Once there, he leaned heavily against the metal bedhead, waiting until his spinning head could clear. Jinny watched him anxiously, not liking the pasty gray aspect of his handsome face.

"Is there any more of that water?" he gasped. "It might help settle my stomach."

Jinny rose and dipped more water onto the herbs left in the bowl. She held it to Robin's lips. The chain wasn't long enough to let him bring his hands up that far. He sipped as much as he could, thanking her when he was done. As she reached to put the bowl on the small table by the bed, she winced. The tingle of restricted blood flow to her numb fingers almost caused her to drop the bowl.

Robin frowned at the rawness of her skin beneath the chafing ropes. "Maybe I could free those for you," he offered.

She shook her head, giving him a smile to let him see she appreciated the gesture. "My uncle would only replace them," she said listlessly. The shocked silence that followed her words tightened the atmosphere in the gloomy room.

"What did you say?"

The half-breathed words carried the taint of rage as well as fear. Jinny glanced at Robin's face, almost recoiling from the horror she saw in his wildly staring eyes.

"Jinny, are you telling me that Reen is behind all this? That Sullyan was right all along?"

His words drove like knives into Jinny's heart and she nodded miserably. "He and Sofira," she whispered. "They were here a while ago, gloating. He'll be back soon. He said I had one hour to get you to wake up. I don't know what he wants us for; I only know it won't be pleasant."

She faltered to a halt, that line of thought too horrible to contemplate. And she suddenly remembered something else, something she ought to tell Robin before the Baron came for them. The appalled disbelief she had felt when she first heard it uttered returned to haunt her, and she brought her sore hands up to her mouth.

"But I have to tell you … oh, Robin, he says he's going to *marry* her!"

✢ ✢ ✢ ✢ ✢

Robin's head buzzed with pain and he just couldn't seem to order his mind. The dreadful clamor of the head wound he had suffered and the sickening pall of the spellsilver lining his cuffs combined to interfere with his thought processes. He was reeling from Jinny's assertion that the Baron was behind their capture, and her revelation that Sofira was involved had dealt him a stunning blow. This news could only mean one thing: Lerric and the former Queen had succeeded in duping them all thoroughly. Not only the King, who might well be excused the slip given his history, but also two wary and powerful Artesans who had gone into her lair specifically to sniff out deception. They had all failed in spectacular fashion, and now he didn't know what to think. How long had he been here? Was Elias still safe? Was Sullyan?

He went icy-cold. Suppose the Baron wanted to use him to trap Sullyan, just as he had used Feilin to trap Robin? He felt sick and his skin turned clammy. Oh, gods, no! He couldn't bear that. And she would come, he knew she would. The Baron would only have to hint that he held Sullyan's beloved life mate, and she would come. He closed his eyes in despair. How could he turn this dreadful failure, how could he prevent himself being used to ensnare the most precious love of his life?

Jinny's last words finally registered with him, but in his confusion he couldn't grasp her meaning. "Marry her?" he repeated. "What do you mean? Who is he going to marry?"

Jinny's self-restraint suddenly snapped, frayed by terror and weakness. "The Queen! He's going to marry the Queen. Oh, Robin, I just don't understand what's going on! How can he be here? How can this be happening? Taran told me he was dead!"

Robin sagged. "Well, I thought *you* were dead until a few minutes ago." He shook his head wearily, unable to make much more sense of Jinny's words than the girl herself could. "They all think so. Sullyan told me Taran was convinced he had found your body in the ashes of your mansion, and although she later discovered it wasn't you, they still thought you were probably dead."

Jinny stared at Robin through shimmering tears, her hands to her mouth. "You said something about a fire before, but I don't know anything about a fire. What made Taran think he'd found my body?"

Robin tried to clear his thoughts. They weren't getting anywhere like this. They were only confusing each other. He took a deep, shaky breath, holding Jinny's tear-filled gaze, trying to show her a calm demeanor.

"Jinny, you said the Baron gave you an hour to wake me. I don't know how much of that time we have left, but I think we need to clear a few things up. Or at least *I* do. Will you tell me as much as you know of what happened to you, from the beginning? Try to be clear about the length of time involved, if you can. I need all the information I can get before the Baron comes back. Only the gods know whether we'll get the chance to talk again after that. Can you do that for me?"

Jinny nodded, gulping back tears, and haltingly told Robin all she could remember about her abduction. She was as sure of her timing as she could be, and the quantity of food that had been left for her in the hut convinced Robin she was right. It gave him some ease; at least he knew he hadn't lain unconscious for days.

He then told Jinny about the uncomfortable visit to Lerric, and the fact that he, Elias, and General Blaine had been here, in this very palace, not a few hours before. Robin had recognized Jinny's brief description of the darkened courtyard and knew without a doubt that they were being held in the supposedly disused ground floor of Lerric's home. This vital information gave him some heart. Sofira may have duped them, but he would stake his life on Lerric being an unwilling party to the deception. Or, if he had been willing at first, he was now very unhappy about it. Robin suspected he now knew what Lerric might have told them if Sofira had not prevented him. It gave him an edge, something he might be able to use. Whether it would do him any good or not, he didn't know. But it was one piece of information he knew their enemy would not wish him to have. And that brought him to something else of vital importance.

He turned his gaze on Jinny, seeing the anxiety in her eyes, and spoke soberly.

"Jinny, there's something I want to tell you. Something I want you to remember."

His serious tone arrested Jinny and she managed a small, frightened nod.

"I don't know any more than you what your uncle has planned," he continued, "but we both know it won't be good. So I want you to promise me something, and I want your sworn word you'll keep that promise. Will you do that?"

"What is it?" she asked.

He held her frightened gaze, trying to impress his meaning on her. "I want you to do whatever your uncle tells you. Whatever it might be, do you understand? Don't try to fight him or do anything that might get you hurt. Especially don't try to do anything to help me."

"But what if he hurts you?" she wailed, tears rolling down her cheeks.

Robin grimaced, trying not to show his fear. "We have to face the fact that he might very well want to hurt me. He's not gone to all this trouble just to invite me for tea, has he?"

The mere fact he could smile and even attempt a weak joke made Jinny gasp. "But—" she began.

"No 'buts,' Jinny," he cut in sharply. "I mean it. For myself, I can bear much if I have to, but if he starts threatening you or hurting you, I don't think I could stand it. And I can do nothing to protect you, not like this." He indicated the metal on his wrists. "So I want your sworn word that you'll do as I've asked. It's the only thing you can do to help. Believe me."

She stared into his eyes, reading the desperate plea behind his words. She had no fighting skills, and she wasn't trained in the bearing of pain. She would probably crumple at the first offer of violence; they both knew it. They also both knew her malicious uncle would not scruple to use her against Robin should he think it expedient.

"All right, I promise," she whispered.

He gave a soft sigh of relief. "Well done, my Lady," he said, warm approval coloring his formal tone. "We'll come out of this yet, you'll see. They'll have missed me at the castle by now and they'll be scouring the countryside. And I wouldn't want to be your uncle when my Sullyan catches up with him!"

Robin didn't mention how strongly Sullyan would react when she caught up with *him*, either. He knew he had made a bad mistake in allowing himself to be duped into following Feilin so blindly. Sullyan would be enraged he had not taken a guard with him. How many times had she berated him in the past for his hotheaded and often rash actions? They both thought he had grown out of those. Shamed and angry, he cast a glance over his shoulder at the unmoving young runner, wondering what his part was in all of this. Not just the entrapment, obviously, or he wouldn't still be here.

Robin sighed. He would find out eventually, no doubt. Well, he told himself, he deserved Sullyan's anger and he would endure her temper; he could only hope none of them would suffer the ultimate penalty as the price of his folly.

Robin stiffened. The silent guard, who hadn't reacted in any way to their discussions, had taken a step closer to the door. Straining his ears over the nauseating buzz of the spellsilver in his head, Robin caught the sound of a footfall.

"Be brave, my Lady," he hissed. "And remember your promise."

She nodded reluctantly and gasped in fright as the door to their prison slowly opened.

Chapter Ten

Sullyan approached the King's chambers down the silent and darkened hallway, pleased to see four of the King's Guard stationed at his door. Their faces bore somber expressions; the recent events at the castle would take some time to fade from memory, especially while the edict of military regnancy prevailed. As she approached the nearest guardsman, she found herself wondering whether any of the City Council had tried to gain audience with Elias to protest the edict, and what sort of reception they'd received if they had. It would be just like Elias to take some of his fear and temper out on the likes of Sir Regus. She smiled grimly. She almost hoped Regus *had* tried to disturb the King. A purging display of spleen would have done Elias a world of good.

"Is the General still within, Dugal?" she asked one of the swordsmen.

"He is, Colonel, but the King retired a while ago."

"I need to see the General," she told him, and he opened the door to the King's antechamber.

She slipped inside and found Mathias Blaine stretched at his ease beneath a blanket on one of Elias's couches, close to the banked fire. He glanced up as she came in, alarm on his features, but she reassured him.

"There is nothing new amiss, Mathias. Is the King asleep?"

"He went to his bed half an hour ago, after taking a look at

Rendan. Some of the City Councilors wanted to remonstrate with him, but I sent them packing. Their complaints will keep until morning. Did you want Elias?"

"No, leave him to sleep. In truth, I envy him."

Blaine pushed aside the blanket and heaved himself to his feet, coming toward her. He laid his hand on her shoulder and looked into her eyes. "And what about you? I don't suppose you'd let me help you sleep, just this once?"

She accepted his regard and his concern, but shook her head, astounding him with her reply. "I would gladly allow you to help me sleep, Mathias, but I believe that what Taran and I plan to do tonight will suffice. I just wanted to warn you that you can expect no metaphysical aid from me for the next few hours. Not that I think you might need it, but in the light of recent events I felt it prudent to inform you. We will be in Taran's rooms trawling the substrate. I fully intend to stretch us both well beyond our normal limits, and I hope that the resulting exhaustion will grant us at least a few hours of sleep. Who knows, we may even find something. That is what Taran thinks, at any rate."

The General snorted. "That's what you've let him believe, you mean. Ah, you witch! When are you going to think of yourself for a change?"

She tossed her head. "When I have the father of my child back where he belongs!"

She left him to his grumbling, trying to ignore the dull ache that the mention of Robin had touched off deep in her heart. She returned the guards' silent salutes and made her way back to Taran's rooms. The welcoming aroma of fellan wafted out to meet her as she opened his door.

He held a cup out to her. "I thought you might want this." She accepted it and sank wearily onto his couch. "What did the General say?"

"No more than I expected. Are you ready for this?"

Taran took a long drink of his fellan before replying. "I appreciate what you're trying to do, but I doubt I can be much use when both you and the General failed. He is a Master, after all. Wouldn't you stand a better chance with him than with me?"

She regarded him steadily. Where once he would have flushed and dropped his eyes, now he held her gaze. Discarding the glib answer she might have given, she replied to the need in his heart.

"Mathias Blaine might be a Master in rank, but in this particular instance you are more powerful than he."

Taran's eyes widened. "How do you work that one out?"

She sighed and swallowed the steaming fellan straight down before setting the cup aside. "My friend, the task we have set ourselves tonight is not reliant on skill alone. We have both suffered a loss—deep and personal. By incorporating the pain of that loss into our working, we empower ourselves a hundredfold. Remember what I have told you: emotion is a mighty tool when used the right way."

Taran pursed his lips. "But I still don't have the skills and reserves of strength a Master has. I don't see how my relationship with Jinny makes me stronger than the General. More motivated, maybe, but not stronger."

She regarded him frankly. "You are stronger than he is because you do not fear your inner Fire."

There was a small silence. Then: "Are you saying …?"

She dropped her gaze to her hands. "You are *never* to repeat what I am about to tell you, Taran Elijah, not to a living soul. And if you think you cannot swear to that, I will take steps to see that you *cannot* repeat it."

He stared hard at her before nodding his acceptance. She fixed her vision on the empty fellan cup, the amber gleam of the waning fire trembling across its glaze.

"The reason Mathias Blaine rarely uses his Artesan skills—and it is the same reason behind his failure to rise above the level of Master—is that he fears the use of his power."

Taran was struck dumb, unable to conceive of the confident General ever being afraid of anything, least of all his innate power. He struggled with the concept for a moment, finally shaking his head. "Of all the things I might have expected you to say, that was not among them. Do you know why?"

Sullyan answered the intended question rather than the obvious. Now was not the time for games.

"He fears to rely upon something possessed by only a few. If you think about it for a moment, you will understand. Who makes all the rules that we, who were trained at the Manor, have to obey? Why do you think we do not commonly summon one another through the substrate, or bespeak each other, when it is so easy and costs so little power? Why do we rely so heavily on the physical, instead of the metaphysical? Did you notice he lit Denny's pyre with a brand, despite his long Mastery over Fire?"

Taran frowned, thinking back. She was right. She could sense him recalling other instances where to use the skills he possessed would have made more sense, and cost Blaine less, than doing things the conventional way.

He opened his mouth, but she said softly, "He fears elitism. He always has. And he distrusts the intensity of his own emotions. He fears he will not be able to control them once he admits to their strength."

Taran closed his mouth, but his curiosity had been piqued. She knew he had never become close to the General. His knowledge that Blaine had refused to accept his father's reluctant plea for help in Taran's early training was always at the back of his mind. He would always wonder how different his life might have been had the General been more inclined toward sympathy all those years ago. Although he knew Blaine was well aware whose son he was, the two men had never discussed the incident, both shying from what the other might think. So he really knew next to nothing about the man. The one other person who might have enlightened him, the one who had served Blaine the longest—Hal Bullen—had never volunteered information. And she knew Taran would have felt awkward asking for it.

She hoped that her revelation, unsolicited and freely given, had allowed Taran a more sympathetic insight into the stern man's character. She knew it had when Taran saw a connection between them he would never have guessed at.

He sighed. "Well, if anyone should understand how that feels, it's me."

She nodded. "Indeed, although that was not precisely why I told you. And now you must forget it. We have work to do. Adept, are you ready? I will stay here the night, if you have no objection. The closer we are, the more energy we can expend in the search. Have you a spare blanket?"

He gestured. "Take the bed. I'll sleep on the couch."

"No need," she demurred, pushing off her boots and taking the blanket Taran lifted from the bedding chest. "The couch will serve me well enough. Make yourself comfortable. Once we are through with this, you will not have strength left to turn your head, let alone undress."

✢ ✢ ✢ ✢ ✢

Once they were settled and the room was dark and peaceful, Taran stretched flat under the bed sheets, slowed the beating of his heart, and wrapped his mind in the complex and beautiful structure that was his psyche. He allowed the potent flow of his life force to swirl around his consciousness, blotting out all other sensations. He reached for the power with his trained mind and metaforce flooded to his command, linked to him by Fire and by passion and by spirit. It pulsed with the rhythm of his life, beat with the love and vitality of his warm and generous heart. And when Sullyan's imprint joined with his, when he accepted the merging of their souls and allowed his forces to flow with hers, then his psyche sang with power, thrummed with the welling of his emotions, swelled with a potency he could scarcely bear. He was hard put to contain the might his soul could wield.

He felt rather than heard her lilting tones, sure like the skills of her training, deft like the touch of her mind. He acquiesced to her suggestion and allowed her to lead as they entered the gray-shot, shimmering aura of the substrate, one familiar pattern held fast before their minds.

We will look here first, as this is the most recent impression, he felt her say. They sampled the Veils around the castle parklands, easily picking up the imprint of Robin's tunnel to Endormir. They could see the echo of the shield he'd used to protect the ungifted Feilin, and had no trouble tracing the two young men as they left the terrible cold of the First Realm and emerged onto the road to Lychdale. But here the trail went cold, and Sullyan spent some considerable time sifting through the layers of the Veils, searching, prying, seeking. She eventually withdrew and Taran could sense she was troubled, but by what she did not say.

They followed their own tracks back to the castle and Taran felt her soft words echo once more in the open spaces of his mind.

I am yours to command now, Adept. I give you control. Use my powers and my skills as you will. Push them to the limits and beyond. Use the force of your love for Jinella and the fear that you feel in your heart. Do not stop until you feel you cannot endure any more. Hold her memory before your sight. Use the passion of your union together as a substitute for a psyche. Focus on your longing for her and hers for you as a beacon to guide your quest. She has reached you once, and what has gone before can be made to serve again. Use your Fire, Taran. Use your heart!

Her impassioned speech and the thrust of her spirit gave Taran's desperate terror for Jinny its freedom. Without further thought, he gathered up the tremendous energies generated by their twinned psyches and flung them out toward the Baron's estate. There was no resistance from Sullyan; she was as passive as if she were not there. Taran had never known her to give up her might so completely, so freely, and had he not been so caught up in the strength of his terror for Jinny, he might have questioned his ability to live up to her trust. But the heady thrill of controlling such puissant forces was lost within the immediacy of his mission, and he never gave it a thought. He spent their strength like water, pouring it out across the layers of milky substrate, searching and sifting, calling frantically for his love.

After some time, when his straining heart began to feel it could take no more, a peculiar shape impinged upon his psyche. He pounced toward it, feeling the faint echo of fear, sensing a scream, a moment of panic. He knew Sullyan had seen it too, but she kept her silence, holding to her word, submitting completely to Taran's control. The echo was too faint and insubstantial to read, too strange and twisted to be an imprint of Jinella, although something familiar about it nagged at the back of Taran's mind.

He was tiring, the Fire of his passion burning out. Even his spirit burned low as failure sapped his energy. With a shock, he realized that the reserves of their joint metaforce were all but gone, and he could hardly believe he had actually drained them both. He had exhausted the joint powers of an Adept-elite and a Senior Master, and yet he had failed.

He heard the soothing tone of Sullyan's voice. *Do not be so hard on yourself, Taran. You have done more than you know this night. And I do believe even I might sleep now. I thank you, my friend.*

Taran was scarcely able to stay awake long enough to separate their psyches. *It is I who should be thanking you,* he returned. *You didn't have to do that. I might have taken more than you wanted to give.*

I said I would stand for you, and I meant it. Do you think I would have scrupled to drain you *if I had scented Robin's pattern in the Veils? Now sleep, Adept. Tomorrow will be a weary day.*

Her aura faded almost immediately and he could just hear the faintest sigh of her breath from where she was curled on the couch. He lay in amazement for the one waking moment he had left, stunned at the generosity of her gift. Then he, too, slept.

✢ ✢ ✢ ✢ ✢

"Oh, how very touching."

The oily tones of the Baron's voice dripped with sarcasm as he regarded the two figures before him. As the door opened, Jinny retreated to the head of the bed and now stood with her arms clasped around Robin's shoulders; whether for protection or for comfort not even she could have said. Robin half-lay against her, his face pale from pain and from fear, feeling both helpless and enraged.

"What is it you want, Uncle? Why can't you leave us alone?"

Jinny's tearful plea was ignored. The scarecrow spared her one dismissive glance and spoke curtly to his servant.

"Take her out."

The swordsman moved woodenly and caught Jinny by the wrists, hauling her toward the door. She struggled, crying out, desperate not to be parted from Robin, fearing she might never see him alive again.

In truth, Robin feared the same, but he had to do his best for the frightened woman. "Jinny," he called through a haze of pain, "remember your promise."

She stiffened and then sagged in defeat, staring back at him out of brimming and pleading eyes. But he refused to look at her. He had other thoughts to occupy his mind.

The swordsman dragged Jinny from the room and shut the door behind him. The ensuing tense silence was broken only by the sounds of Jinny's reluctant steps as she was taken wherever it was the Baron had commanded.

Captor and captive stared at each other across the dimly lit room.

"So," the Baron drawled slowly, leaning upon a strange cane, "Major Robin Tamsen. We have never been formally introduced, have we?"

Robin had no energy for games. "I won't do it, you know. Your plan will never work."

The scarecrow raised an eyebrow, a sardonic twist to his crooked lips. "You won't do what, Major? What is it you think I have planned?"

"Sullyan," Robin rasped, short of breath from the sickness of the spellsilver. "I won't help you defeat her. I'll never betray her."

The scarecrow's ugly grin widened and he leaned slightly forward. "Oh, but my dear Major, you already have."

Robin's gut clenched and he thought he might vomit. He struggled to fight down the rising tide of panic and nausea, praying this was a cruel tactic, that the Baron didn't already have his love helpless within his power. He had to believe she was safe; he couldn't bear it if his unthinking stupidity had already sprung the trap.

The scarecrow moved closer to his captive, cane tapping lightly on the floor. Robin's muscles tensed involuntarily. Although he hadn't obviously moved, the Baron could tell he was combat-ready, watching for his opening, looking for that moment of weakness, of inattention, that would enable him to strike. Except, of course, that he couldn't strike. He was bound and helpless, totally unable to attack or defend.

The Baron smiled, enjoying the futile rage behind Robin's dark eyes, the demeaning knowledge of his own helplessness. He cocked his head. "Not pleasant, is it?"

"What?" grated Robin, torn between reluctance to give Reen the satisfaction of a reply and his need for information. He knew from Sullyan of the hedonistic pleasure the Baron took in gloating over his victims, and that she had been able to trick him into giving away more information than was wise. Any snippet Robin might wrest from his overly confident captor could prove useful.

The malevolent grin widened at Robin's tone. "Impotence. I doubt you've ever experienced that feeling before in connection with any of your vaunted skills, eh? Either with weaponry or with women."

Robin narrowed his eyes at the leering figure. "What makes you think I'm impotent?"

Oh, that's better, thought Robin. He had managed to crack the Baron's certitude. His swift and confident reply had inserted a worm of doubt, jolted that sneering air of dogmatism, even if only for a second.

"Ah, very clever, Major," approved the Baron, the oily sarcasm hissing through his words. "I can see why your witch-girl values you so highly. You are extraordinarily handsome, your body sleek and honed and superbly sculpted. Any woman—or man, for that matter—might find you desirable. And you know how to use your body in combat. Your reputation precedes you. And you are no weakling in intellect, either, it seems. Well, I'm going to enjoy breaking that proud and willful spirit. I'm going to enjoy it very much.

"But you're not so clever all the time, are you? It didn't take much to separate you from your friends. Just one little message, one little tug at your heartstrings—totally false, of course—and you scamper off into the unknown without so much as a thought. I took you as easily as I took that young boy over there, and here you are, chained and helpless and in my power. Tell me if that isn't impotence."

Robin didn't bother to reply. He was struggling to keep his mortification from weighing him down. The Baron's mention of young Feilin had reminded Robin that he wasn't alone. Jinny may have been removed—which Robin hoped indicated she was in no immediate danger—but the young runner remained. Robin was only too afraid he knew what purpose the Baron had in mind for his other helpless captive.

As it turned out, much to his horror, Robin was only partially right.

"You make no reply, Major? Well, no matter. I didn't come here to make idle conversation. I have a wedding to attend, and I have decided you shall be a witness. So you see, young man, you have no cause for that fear you hide behind your eyes. I intend you no harm this night."

Robin stared at the strange figure before him, repulsed and puzzled. His vision had cleared a little more, although it was still partially clouded by the numbing effects of the spellsilver. Yet even in his semi-confused state, he was aware something was terribly wrong.

Robin had only seen the Baron a few times before. Reen had visited the Manor on two occasions—once when Sullyan was promoted to colonel and Senior Master, and once when the King inaugurated the College. On the first occasion, Reen had congratulated Robin on his own promotion and made a point of shaking his hand. On the second, Robin barely noticed him. The only other time they met was at the trial, when Robin spoke as proxy for young Tad. And even on that occasion, Robin had had other things on his mind. Yet he was certain the Baron had never looked so shrunken, so drained.

Of course, three years on a barren island, deprived of freedom and constrained to a regime of worship and bodily denial, might deal harshly with any man, but Robin didn't think that what he was seeing now was due only to deprivation and hopelessness. There was an aura about this scarecrow of a man—an evil—that Robin couldn't define. It was out of his experience and, due to the spellsilver, he had only the instincts of an ordinary man to rely on. Still, those ordinary human instincts plucked at him with fingers of alarm.

"No, Major," the Baron said idly as he moved about the shadowy room, "I intend no harm to *you*. Not this night, at any rate. This is to be my wedding night, and you know what ladies expect on their wedding night. Sofira is no exception, and she has been a Queen; she deserves the very best. But you see, my dear Major, that gives me a problem. For I do not have the taste for women. Oh, I'll grant you, they have their uses, and on occasions I have … sampled, shall we say … the pleasures they provide. But my taste runs more toward my own gender, and I would hate to disappoint Sofira. What do you think I should do?"

Robin watched the pacing figure much as the rabbit watches the stoat. He knew his fascination might kill him, but he was mesmerized nonetheless. The tapping cane and the smooth, untrustworthy voice, so reasonable in its tone, held him in a stasis of dread, too confused and fearful to fathom the scarecrow's meaning. He held his tongue, not trusting himself to speak.

But the Baron didn't really expect a response. He advanced toward Robin, his aspect causing the young man's skin to creep, and it took an effort to refrain from cowering. The scarecrow's strange appearance seemed to be changing and shrinking, unless it was a trick of the flickering light. His flesh seemed to wither and slump. The hands that rested on the gnarled wood of the cane began to resemble claws, and there was a fiery glint to the myopic gray eyes.

Giving a low cry, Robin wrenched his gaze away. The feral glint he had thought was reflected firelight had grown in intensity to fill the orbs in the ruined face. A ruby glow suffused the gray, and the cracked and twisted lips parted in an evil leer.

"What's the matter, Major? Not *frightened*, are you?"

Shuddering with revulsion, Robin forced his gaze back to the dreadful apparition before him. The skin was mottled, livid, and hung slumped upon the grinning skull as if melted by some unimaginable heat. The body was stooped and sticklike, the tendons of the arms standing out stark and taut. But it wasn't this terrible transformation that so affected Robin's psyche. Even through the suffocating shroud of the spellsilver, the appalling emanations from the warped wood of the cane pierced Robin's soul with terror and dread. Unable to help himself, he cried out and shrank to the limits of the chain, terrified lest the loathsome thing come closer.

The Baron retreated a pace, grinning at the sweat standing out on Robin's torso and the sudden dampness of his breeches that betrayed the depth of his fear. The sudden flush of shame on Robin's pallid face made the grin widen. The sullen glow of his eyes faded, much to Robin's relief.

Reen nodded his repulsive head. "So now you understand how it feels to be brought so low as to lose control of your bodily functions, and to grovel in abject shame before the might of your enemy. So your witch of a wife served *me*, when I was chained and helpless before her."

Robin struggled for composure, or at least for understanding.

He had been badly shaken by what he had seen, and mortified by the treacherous reaction of his body. An enervating weakness surged through his spirit.

"Strength, Major, strength and power," Reen continued, watching as Robin's hopelessness spread. "That is what I lacked, and that is what I have now—as much as I could desire. And I shall have more, much more, once I wed Sofira, although it is not the power *she* expects. She thinks I intend to return her to the throne, but that is just her womanly folly. I will show her, before the night is done, just how deluded she is.

"And that brings me back to my problem, young man. In order to overcome my personal preferences, in order to give Sofira the satisfaction she thinks she desires, I need physical strength. And as you see, my natural strength has been stripped from me. So I must needs obtain it from somewhere else. Shall I show you how I satisfy those needs, Major Tamsen?"

He was repulsed and horrified, yet Robin couldn't tear his eyes away as the Baron approached the unmoving figure of the runner. He was sweating freely now; his heart limped painfully and quailed within his breast. The aura of evil was palpable within the gloomy room and terror beat about the walls. Robin wanted to scream, to plead, to beg for release, but his tongue was fixed in his mouth and his throat too dry for speech. His muscles were locked in a rictus of horror and he was forced to watch, appalled, as the Baron laid hands on the body of young Feilin.

The youth had been half-stripped, as Robin was, and chained by both hands to rings set low in the wall. He lay on the floor on his belly, unmoving and silent, his head turned to one side. Robin could see his eyes were closed. He watched, fighting his rising terror, as the Baron knelt beside the boy and produced a small knife from within the folds of his robe. But he did not use the knife on Feilin's flesh, as Robin feared. Instead, he used the blade to slice the breeches from the boy, leaving him naked and defenseless.

"Wake," he said curtly, and Robin's sweat-stung eyes widened in shock as Feilin stirred at the order. The Major gave a great involuntary gasp when he saw that the very same ruby glow glinted from the youth's eyes. His heart thumped in painful bewilderment; he had never experienced anything remotely like this. And then the Baron turned his head.

"I will show you why I am now mighty enough to defeat your Artesan witch, Major. I will show you why none of you can defeat me. For I have been granted powers far beyond your puny knowledge—powers birthed within me by the purging Fire of my God. And these holy powers enable me to renew my strength and to take vitality where I will. But the wisdom of my God did not end with that. He has empowered me to use even my enemies' skills against them. By sending me a sacrifice, he showed me how to fight Fire with Fire. As I take their life force, so I also take their powers."

As he spoke, the Baron repeatedly ran his claw-like hand over the youth's exposed flesh. The boy gave no reaction. Although his eyes had opened at the Baron's command, he seemed to be unaware of his surroundings. Robin, mesmerized and appalled by the almost tender motion of that twisted claw, was held transfixed by the terrible gleam of lust growing in the scarecrow's eyes. He could scarcely believe what he feared he would now be forced to witness. His throat grew tight with horror.

The Baron leered at Robin's revulsion. "You pagan demons are not the only ones who know how to wield arcane forces. But now you will see them turned against you, and you will be helpless against my might. And how fitting will it be that your own powers will be used to bring the witch Sullyan to her knees? Before I'm done with the pair of you, she will beg me to kill you, plead with me to release you both from the torment of holy retribution. I will see her grovel before me as she prays for me to end her life. But my vengeance will never end, and your days upon the Wheel of Perdition shall be as eons to the world!"

Spittle sprayed from his deformed lips, and he turned once more to the silent, helpless boy. He fumbled at his robes and Robin, shuddering and sickened to his soul, closed his tear-filled eyes. He might not be able to shut out the dreadful sounds as the Baron slaked his lust and sucked the vital life force from the passive youth, but he did not have to watch the terrible violation. Raging at his helplessness, he strained unconsciously to the very limits of the chain, the manacles biting into the flesh of his wrists and bringing a fresh flow of blood across his tightly clenched hands. But no matter how hard he tried to block out the sounds of the Baron's brutal pleasure, he could not prevent the creeping of his flesh and the dreadful, nauseating heave of his stomach as the Baron's harsh, climactic cry echoed around the killing room.

Robin lost the fight. He slumped forward, his whole body rebelling against the knowledge of what the scarecrow had just done. His throat achingly raw, he retched as he tried to rid himself of the horror. For he had felt, somehow, impossibly, even through the spellsilver, the boy's shrieking agony as his spirit was dragged from its roots and consumed. And Robin saw, with icy despair, the blank and dreadful face of his future.

Chapter Eleven

The sky was red with fire, the night air ringing with screams and the thud of galloping hooves, the cries of men urging him on. Breath panted harshly through lungs too cold to work and blood thumped painfully through overworked veins. His legs churned for speed. Faces passed before his eyes in a confused procession, blurred with fear and tense with fright. Voices rang in his mind. His heart strained over useless powers. He was too slow, too late. Buckets passed from hand to hand. Water hissed and fire sparked bright. Pain seared his body.

Then he was falling, flailing for balance, his eyes whipped by fire and snow. Men cried out behind him and his breath trembled. "It's over, Taran. You can do no more." Denny's face swam before his eyes, but the features blurred and faded, becoming cold and gray. Fire licked with golden tongues, eating through crumbling wood. A terrible smell arose; the miasma of rotting meat. Blackened timbers caught at his feet, smoke burned his nose. He heard a scream and turned to look, but no one was there. A silver gleam captured his eye and he stretched forth his hand. Fire sparked and crackled. His hand flamed red before him.

Sickness lurched in his mind and he struggled to hold life within the poisoned body. A melodious voice murmured, "This whole place reeks of evil." Purging waters smothered the fire, but smoke still curled from the ashes. The scream sounded again and he tried to run, but his muscles throbbed with agony and he couldn't move. Jinella stood before him, arms held out in supplication. He strained to reach her, but she drifted away, her heartbroken sobs tearing through his soul. "How could you *do* that, Taran? I thought you *loved* me."

He fought to cry out, but his voice made no sound. Someone handed him a deck of cards, and he pushed a pile of gold across the table to the sounds of raucous laughter. He turned his hand and lost the bet, crying out in rage and frustration. A man's whispered voice by his shoulder sneered, "I'm a bit surprised you're so upset, sir," and then Jinella was there before him again, an accusing glare in her pale green eyes. "Where's your damned *honor*, Taran?"

Denny dragged him off for another hand and he never saw her leave.

Taran's body shifted restlessly under the goad of the nightmare and whimpered protests escaped his lips. Clammy sweat stood out on his body, a frown creasing the lines of his brow. But he didn't wake and soon the images faded, receding from the forefront of his mind. His panting breaths returned to normal and the racing heartbeat calmed. The blanket-wrapped figure lying peacefully on the couch never stirred, her deep and even breathing undisturbed by evil dreams.

✤ ✤ ✤ ✤ ✤

Robin startled in fear as the swordsmen entered the darkened room, but the absence of the Baron soon calmed his pounding heart. It was likely they had come to take him to the wedding ceremony, and he cursed himself for his lack of spine. Since the Baron's dreadful act of violation, Robin had been left to brood upon his fate. The discarded body of Feilin—whether dead or yet alive, Robin didn't know—was silent testament to the veracity of the Baron's claims to power. It had not been necessary to reinforce those claims. Robin had seen with his own eyes how the Baron's body had swelled with stolen life. He had seen vitality return to those sere and withered limbs, and reinvigorated blood pulse through muscles firm with new life.

The Baron had spared not one glance for the used and ruined body that had fed his vengeful heart. He had reached for the livid wood of his cane, though he no longer needed a prop for his steps; he had walked with ease toward his other captive. Robin had raised his head and watched him come, revulsion in his eyes and terror in his heart. The Baron had said not a word, simply held Robin's gaze with his own. He had then passed behind the bed, trailing one hand slowly and deliberately across Robin's naked shoulders. His touch burned like fire and Robin flinched, crying out. He was trembling and panting when the Baron left the room.

Now, drained and defeated, no thought in his beleaguered mind for how this evil might be fought, Robin offered little resistance as the four swordsmen manhandled him to his feet. They unfastened the chain from the iron bedhead and refastened it about Robin's narrow hips. His manacled hands held secure at his waist, they jostled him roughly out of the room, two of them gripping him painfully by the arms while the other two prodded him in the back with their swords. The despairing young man felt his skin pricked more than once, thin rivulets of his blood soaking down into the leather of his fouled breeches.

He was in considerable discomfort. His muscles had cramped from his awkward position on the bed, and the manacles pained his wrists. His head swam from the effects of the blow to his skull, as well as the constant buzzing of the spellsilver. The urine-soaked leather of his breeches chafed his skin. Apart from the water Jinny had given him earlier to aid his return to consciousness, he had been offered no other opportunities to relieve the needs of his body.

Defeated and confused, the dreadful images of the Baron's

violent act still swaying before his eyes, Robin was hustled toward a lighted room where he imagined the ceremony would be held.

✣ ✣ ✣ ✣ ✣

Jinella tried hard to be brave. She realized her struggles and terror had added to Robin's concerns, and she tried to force the panic down. She had promised to do as she was bid and understood his reasoning. He thought it would appease her uncle and make it less likely that she would be harmed. Robin could more easily bear what would happen to him if he knew she was untouched. Yet she still had to endure the terror of not knowing what her uncle intended. She was so very afraid he meant to murder them both.

The swordsman who took her from the room guided her down a lightless hallway. A short way down he pushed her into another room, this one lit with lamps trimmed low and set with a table at one end, on which sat a silver chalice and a wooden bowl. On the wall behind the table hung a representation of the Wheel, its spokes picked out in gold, its rim painted with depictions of the stages of Enlightenment. This, she gathered, was where the wedding would take place.

He thrust her toward a chair and she sat, grateful for the rest. She was weak from lack of food and trembling from the effects of severe cold and extreme fright. She still wore only her flimsy nightshift, and it was stained and torn around the hem. The room where she and Robin had been held was warmer by far than the freezing hut, but not warm enough to calm her shivering. Terror and confusion had added to her tremor, so that she found it hard to stand and harder still to walk. She collapsed onto the plain wooden chair and tried not to think.

The swordsman stood silently beside her until a faint tapping alerted Jinny to the presence of someone outside. Her jailor opened the door and a young serving girl stepped in, a wrapped bundle in her arms. She gave the taciturn guard a nervous glance and swerved around him as she crossed to Jinny.

"My Lady, I've been sent to serve you. Will you let me help you dress?"

Jinny gasped and clutched at the girl's arms with her bound hands. "Oh, can you help me? Can you get me out of here? I need to escape—I'm in terrible danger! Please, please help me."

The girl's eyes stretched wide and she pulled away. The swordsman approached and the girl cringed, obviously fearing a blow. "Please, my Lady, don't ask me that. They'll beat me if I don't do as I'm told. I can't help you, Lady, I'm only a serving maid. Let me get you dressed and then I have to go."

Jinny's flare of hope died and she subsided in despair. Her outburst had been instinctive, born of terror. She had known, deep inside, that a serving girl could do nothing in the stronghold of her uncle. She bowed her head and nodded, no fight left inside.

The maid placed her bundle on the floor and glanced nervously at the hulking swordsman. "You'll have to untie her hands," she said timidly. The guard came closer and freed Jinny's hands, but he stayed beside her, watching warily. Jinny was grateful for the chance to rub some life back into her wrists and didn't move from her chair.

The maid laid open the bundle which contained a warm winter gown of dark-green wool, plain and serviceable, a selection of underthings, and a light cloak. The maid had also brought dampened cloths with which Jinny could refresh her face and body. A hairbrush completed the bundle's contents.

The maid shook out the gown and turned to Jinny. "Let me help you off with that shift, Lady."

Jinny stared in disbelief before indicating the silent guard. "I hope you don't expect me to disrobe in front of *him*?" Her voice held as much scorn as she could manage.

The maid's face fell. "Please, Lady. He's not allowed to leave. Can't you just … pretend he's not here? If you're quick, you'll hardly know you've done it. And you really need to get out of that thin shift. They'll be here soon. Please hurry! I'll be whipped if you're not ready."

Jinny's heart sank. She would be allowed no privacy and no complaint. She trembled to think what her uncle might do if she didn't comply with his orders. Fear and frustration making her sharp, she snatched the dampened cloth from the girl and scrubbed furiously at her arms, tears of anger and fright pricking her eyes.

She cleaned as much of her body as she could without removing her shift. She used it as a dressing gown, pulling her arms inside it and completing as much dressing as she could before removing it. The maid helped her pull it over her head and had a fresh cotton one and the green gown ready for Jinny to step into. The guard didn't even watch her. As long as she made no move toward the door or the table, he ignored her.

Jinny felt better for the wash and the clean clothes, especially so for being able to brush her matted hair. She was still weak and trembling, but she could feel warmth creeping into her arms from the good quality wool gown. She cast the cloak about her shoulders to increase her chances of staying warm, and thanked the maid quietly as the girl gathered her things and hurriedly left the room. She even meekly held out her wrists as the guard approached her with the rope, thinking he might not tie her so roughly if she cooperated. But the bonds still bit into her sore skin and she subsided dejectedly onto the chair, too drained to do more than sit and wait.

After only a few more minutes, she heard the tramp of footsteps in the passageway. Jinny gasped in shock as the door was pushed roughly open. Two guards dragged Robin inside, hauling on his arms. She gave a cry and surged to her feet, running over to him too swiftly for her guard to stop her.

"Robin, dear gods! What did he do to you? Are you all right? Oh, you look awful!"

Jinny's eyes brimmed with tears as she took in his gray face and saw the dreadful fear behind his eyes. She could tell something terrible had happened, but at least he was alive and unhurt. Or not hurt too badly. She gave another gasp.

"Robin, you're bleeding. What have you done to him, you bastards? Leave him alone! Can't you see he can barely stand?"

"Your concern is very touching, my dear, but quite misplaced."

The smooth tones behind her made Jinny wheel in fright, and she gave a small scream as a heavy hand descended on her shoulder. The Baron gave a curt nod and the swordsman turned Jinny roughly, forcing her back to her seat. She did not resist. Her uncle's changed appearance had thrown her off balance, evaporating the brief flash of courage she had felt at seeing Robin. Her uncle came before her and stood staring down at her, a small, nasty smile creasing the corners of his lips.

Jinny stared back in total confusion. Her uncle looked much the same as always, if a little thinner. Gone were the sticklike aspect, the skinny arms, and slumped flesh. He even walked with a stronger step and the cane no longer bore his weight. He had changed his clothes and stood in soft black velvet, unadorned and plain, yet shimmering faintly in the dim light. She frowned and opened her mouth, but what she would have said, she didn't really know. She cast a glance of mute appeal at Robin, catching the barest hint of a warning look, the merest shake of his head. She closed her mouth, mindful of her promise.

The Baron waved a hand in Robin's direction. "As you can see, my dear, your friend is quite unharmed. The blood is only superficial. It is nothing to one so highly trained for combat. I'll wager he has taken many wounds far worse than those."

He turned to Robin's guards. "Put him over there."

They hauled on Robin's arms, forcing him to a seat across from Jinny. She watched him in consternation, not at all reassured by the Baron's casual assessment of his injuries. She was frightened by the look in his eyes. Whatever had occurred after she had been taken from the room had left a deep and terrible impression on the young man. And if *he* was so afraid, what chance did she stand? She swallowed, trying to lubricate a throat dried up with terror, and caught the glance of Robin's haunted eyes. Dragging in a steadying breath, he gave her the ghost of a smile.

Jinny wasn't convinced, but allowed herself to be reassured. If he could manage a smile, he must be all right. But her thoughts were wrenched away from Robin's condition by the arrival of another man, this one in the shabby livery of a captain in King Lerric's personal guard. He entered the room with no ceremony and obviously intended to approach the Baron. However, when his eyes fell on the two seated captives, they bulged with astonishment, lingering longest on Robin.

"What is it, Bassan?" said the Baron. "Have you brought the cleric?"

Captain Bassan closed the mouth he had opened in shock, but Jinny saw the flicker of puzzled anger in his eyes. She wondered at it. It was clear the man hadn't expected to see her or Robin and was far from happy. But why? Did he perhaps know Robin, or was his anger for some other reason?

The Baron pointedly held Bassan's gaze until the captain dragged himself back to his appointed task. "Er, yes, my Lord. I came to tell you that Cleric Eskel awaits your pleasure and that the Princess is ready to attend the ceremony."

"Then let it begin."

The Baron stared hard after Bassan as the man turned and left the room, and Jinny could see his displeasure. She felt a small measure of hope. Not all the Baron's servants approved of his actions.

The Baron stood facing the door, his back to the table. Jinny heard slow footfalls approaching and then a cowled figure appeared in the doorway. He was dressed in the simple robes of an initiate into the Faith of the Wheel, his silver belt adorned with circular decorations depicting the eternal circle. He carried the Book of Joining, from which he would read the marriage ceremony, and he preceded the bride. He passed the Baron and came to stand in silence behind the table, resting his book between the chalice and the bowl. He gave no sign of surprise at seeing guarded captives in the room. He must have been forewarned.

Jinny knew they could expect no aid from the cleric. He was probably in Lerric's pay and would be mindful of his duty to his lord. Junior clerics often found themselves in penury unless they found a patron to retain them. This one would not jeopardize his living by questioning his master's actions.

Jinny and Robin watched the door. The rustling of silk heralded the arrival of the Baron's bride. Sofira paced serenely into the room, leaning on her father's arm. She was dressed in elaborate court robes of pale gold, the pallor of her skin fading further with the unflattering hue of the gown. She wore a fillet of gold in her hair and precious gems glittered at her throat and on her hands. She glanced neither left nor right as she entered the room; the captives did not rate her attention. Her eyes and her thoughts were on her intended groom.

Lerric, however, was another matter. He looked pale and ill and leaned as much upon Sofira as she upon him. He, too, refused to look at the captives, but the unhealthy flush that colored his skin as he passed them betrayed his discomfort. Jinny saw Robin fix his eyes on Lerric and could almost hear him willing the king to acknowledge their desperate plight. She could see his body trembling and would have given much to know what he was thinking. She wouldn't want to be in Lerric's shoes when the High King discovered what he had done.

With a visible effort, Lerric ignored Robin's glaring. As if she felt his discomfort, Sofira's hand tightened on his arm. Jinny caught the brief, intense glance she shot him, one that boded ill for her father if he dared spoil this day for her. Then she turned from him and smiled with radiant joy as she halted before her beloved.

Jinny and Robin sat through the mercifully short ceremony, taking little notice of the proceedings. They were not required to take an active part. It seemed that Sofira and her paramour desired only to parade their achievement before their enemies. They had eyes only for each other as they repeated the cleric's ritual phrases, exchanging the life gifts of wine and bread from chalice and bowl.

Robin kept his gaze on Lerric the entire time, trying to make the man feel as uncomfortable as possible. Lerric glanced his way only once, but Jinny could tell that he was fully aware of Robin's hostile scrutiny. Lerric could not keep still; he fidgeted with his robes, shuffled his feet, and cleared his throat. But he could not return Robin's baleful stare, and neither could he bear to look at Jinny.

For her part, Jinny kept her eyes on Robin. She was terrified of what might happen at the end of the ceremony. Images of pagan sacrifices churned around in her head. These macabre fancies sent fingers of dread down her spine and pricked hopeless tears in her eyes. She had never heard of her uncle following any of these barbaric practices, but he had changed so much in recent years that she no longer knew what to think. She was beginning to think she had never known him at all, and wondered what her father would have made of all this. He surely would not have recognized his younger brother.

The ceremony finally ended with no one making a move toward the captives. Lerric, having given his daughter's hand into the scarecrow's keeping with trembling reluctance and signed the official papers acknowledging Reen as a member of his House, fled the room as soon as he could. Reen watched him go with a malevolent glare. A swordsman escorted the cleric away, which left the two captives alone with their tormentors and their guards.

Sofira was resplendent with joy and triumph. Her bleached, cold features were as animated as Jinny had ever seen them, her hard gray eyes alight with desire. She approached Jinella purposefully and Robin stiffened in his chains, although the reaction was purely instinctive. He was helpless and he knew it.

But it seemed Sofira had no intention of sullying her wedding night with physical violence. She had other things on her mind and greater pleasures to anticipate. Still, she couldn't resist parading her triumph and regarded Jinny with haughty scorn.

"So, my dear," she sneered, "you and I are now related. But don't think you are safe because of it. You have committed an act of base betrayal and have forfeited your rights to family loyalty. When we ascend the throne as High Queen and Consort of the realm of Albia, there will be no place for you within the capital. Nor for any of those who dared speak against my husband. The cleansing has begun and will not end until everyone who worked his downfall is destroyed."

Jinny was incensed, her anger lending her sudden courage. "Except for you, your Highness!" Sofira's air of righteousness nauseated Jinella, as did her constant harping on the theme of betrayal. Jinny had been at that trial and was well aware it was Sofira's own treacherous words that sealed her uncle's fate, and very nearly condemned him to a tortuous death.

Sofira's face darkened and she struck out, her hand connecting sharply with Jinella's left cheek. Jinny cried out, her hands flying to her face. Robin leaped to his feet before he could think better of it, but was instantly felled by a blow to the head from one of the swordsmen. He crumpled, groaning, to the floor.

The Baron regarded his furious niece. "It seems the little hellcat has claws, my dear," he drawled. "You would do well to remember that."

Sofira's head snapped round at the tone of her new husband's voice. "I'm not going to be spoken to like that, and especially not by the likes of her!"

He replied smoothly. "Of course not. Don't worry, Sofira. Her claws will be drawn soon enough. The fight will go out of her when she realizes what my plans are. Until then, I intend to keep her unharmed. I may still have to make use of her. We're not in Port Loxton yet, you know. Be patient a while longer, and then we will have all the revenge we desire. But enough of that. I promised you a wedding night like no other, and I am eager to keep my word. You have shown your faith in me by joining with me this night. Now I wish to show you how we can both benefit from our new status. Is our bedchamber prepared?"

Jinny felt nauseated by her uncle's silky tone. She raised her head, pressing cold fingers to her stinging cheek. Sofira had allowed herself to be sidetracked from her fury by her groom's speech. She didn't seem to see the faint ruby glow deep within Reen's eyes—or if she did, she didn't care. She turned from Jinny with a smile.

"Yes, my love, all is as you ordered. Are you ready? Shall we go?"

Reen turned to the swordsmen standing over Jinny and Robin. The young major was stirring on the floor; the blow to his head had only stunned him. "Take them back to their room," the scarecrow commanded. "Give them water and food. I will come to them again on the morrow. Guard them well."

Without another glance, Reen took up his new bride's arm and led her from the room. His step was firm and level, the cane tapping lightly on the floor.

Jinny winced as the guards hauled on Robin's arms, dragging him to his feet. He moaned once but then was silent, biting his lips as they were escorted back to their gloomy prison.

Chapter Twelve

Once back inside their room, Robin was secured to the iron bed as before. He made no resistance. Whatever strength he might have had was gone now. His one consolation was that Jinny's brave but foolhardy show of defiance had not earned her more of a reprimand. She was his only hope of rescue, and it was a slim enough hope without her courting serious injury or worse.

He heard her furious voice over the suffocating hiss in his head and wondered what she was doing now. He strained to make sense of her words.

"And how do you expect him to manage with *that*?" she was shouting, fear making her reckless. "For the gods' sake, loosen that chain! What are you, barbarians?"

Robin saw that the guards had set a pitcher of water and a bowl of dried fruit on the table. That was well enough, and Robin's parched throat yearned for the water. But they had also provided a slop bucket, and this was what had enraged Jinella. It was all very well for her. Her bound wrists did not prevent her from coping with such facilities. But Robin's bonds did not allow him to use his hands at all, and he could not even rise from the bed. Jinny's furious protests on his behalf were not entirely altruistic.

The guards ignored her, shrugging their shoulders. "The Baron's orders, Lady," one of them muttered. They both withdrew, closing the door behind them. Jinny swore, a very unladylike word, and Robin raised his brows, amused despite their plight. He couldn't claim to know Jinella well, but he had never heard her utter profanities before. She had been spending too much time in Sullyan's company, he thought wryly, before the pain of that image burned his heart. He turned from it hastily.

"Jinny, don't. You'll wear yourself out. Come over here."

Jinny turned slowly toward him and his heart broke to see the tears on her cheeks and the hopelessness in her green eyes. Her left cheek still bore the mark of the Princess's slap, but the rest of her face was pale. She approached Robin and sat beside him on the bed.

"Robin, are you all right? I nearly died when I saw him hit you. I'm so sorry, it was all my fault. I was just so angry with that haughty bitch—carping on about loyalty when she's the worst traitor of the lot."

"You were very brave to stand up to her like that." Robin put as much warmth into his hoarse voice as he could. "Although it was a mite foolish. Just give me fair warning the next time you plan to defy them, will you? Then I'll know not to react and risk getting a sword in my back."

His smile and weak attempt at levity burst the remnants of Jinny's resilience. She collapsed against him, burying her head in his chest as a storm of weeping swept over her. Robin was too firmly chained to hold her, but he murmured into her hair and comforted her as best he could. She was warm and soft against his skin and the feel of her lent him strength. Strength would be an issue, he was sure, in their struggle to survive this hellish situation.

An insistent need nagged at him and he knew he would soon have to test Jinella's strength once again. But before he did, there was another issue badly needing attention.

"Jinny?" he said softly once her fit of weeping subsided. "Can you do something for me?"

She raised a tearful face to him and he saw the wariness in her red-rimmed eyes.

"Will you see if there's anything you can do for poor Feilin? I don't know if he's even alive. Would you look at him for me?"

He could tell Jinny hadn't even noticed the lad was still in the room. The fire was very low, the light it cast shadowy at best. She gasped in shock when she turned her head and saw his naked body on the floor. She rose and approached him slowly, her hands to her mouth. Robin doubted she had ever seen a dead body before, and he didn't know if she was looking at one now. She turned to him with an anguished look.

"What on earth did he do to him?"

Robin shook his head. He didn't feel up to telling that tale right now. He didn't think Jinny could stand it. "Later," he murmured, hoping she would forgive him. "Is he still alive?"

"I don't know. How would I tell?"

"Feel for his pulse in the pit of his throat. But if he's still warm, that's a good sign."

Privately, Robin almost hoped the poor lad was dead. That dreadful, silent scream had signified a terrible reaving of his spirit. Even if his body was still breathing, his mind must surely be gone. He watched Jinny anxiously as she bent to the boy's neck. Gingerly, she pressed a finger to the base of his throat.

"His skin is quite cold, but it's not very warm in here. I think I can just feel a pulse. Robin, why has he been stripped?"

Robin closed his eyes, trying to shut out the dreadful memories of what the Baron had done. He didn't know how to tell her; he didn't understand it himself. He could feel Jinny's eyes on him and her sudden intake of breath brought a flush of shame to his face. When he opened his eyes again, she had discovered the telltale signs of the Baron's brutal ravishment. She stared across at him, fresh tears of horror in her huge green eyes.

"No!" she breathed, her face turning gray, hands to her mouth. "No, I can't believe it! I can't believe he did *that*! How could he? What kind of monster *is* he?" She broke off, her gaze traveling Robin's body. "Oh, dear gods! He didn't ... oh, Robin, please tell me he didn't!"

Robin guessed what she was thinking and hastened to reassure her. Not that he *felt* reassured—he feared Feilin's fate might very well be his own—but he wouldn't torture Jinny with that private terror.

"Hush, Jinny, I'm all right, he didn't touch me." *Not quite true*, he thought, recalling that mocking hand of fire trailed deliberately across his shoulders. Trying not to shudder, he said, "Is there anything you can do to make him more comfortable?"

Jinny set about cleaning the lad's body. Robin was both amazed and proud that she didn't shrink from what she was doing. She had endured much torment and terror these past two days, yet she could still concern herself over a stranger. She did what she could for the unresponsive lad, and when she was done she covered him with her cloak.

When she approached Robin again, he could see she had come to some sort of decision. She squared her shoulders and looked him in the eye.

"Is there anything I can do to make you more ... comfortable?" She tried for friendly detachment, but fell just short.

Robin smiled in genuine warmth, her offer briefly eclipsing the dread in his heart. "Taran would be so proud of you," he murmured.

Jinny flushed and gulped down tears. Blinking away the moisture, she cocked her head at him.

"Well?"

He grinned. "You surpass me, Lady." He did not belabor the point when he saw her about to crumble. "I cannot deny that I do have certain needs at this moment. But I don't want you to do anything you can't cope with. I could probably manage somehow."

"Oh yes?" She eyed him deliberately, giving him a wan smile. "I'd like to see you try."

She sounded so much like Sullyan that Robin nearly broke down. He had to turn his face away, and when he finally mastered himself enough to look back, she already had the bucket in her hands.

Afterward, they sat together on the narrow bed, eating the dried fruit they had been given. Jinny had questioned the wisdom of eating it all, but it was Robin's opinion that rationing was futile. Food on the table was no good to weakened bodies. Besides, if the Baron intended them to starve, he would have withheld the food altogether. So she took the bowl on her lap and fed him pieces of fruit between taking bites for herself.

The food and water went far toward restoring their resilience. The matter of the slop bucket and the contortions necessary in order for Robin to use it had served to lessen the menace of their plight; the absurdity of the situation had actually lightened their mood. Robin was grateful, and not just for the relief it gave his body. Mutual embarrassment had resolved into wry amusement, even if it had stopped short of outright laughter. Taran really would have been proud of her, thought Robin. He had never expected to find such steel beneath her outward softness.

Once the food was consumed, the atmosphere tautened once more. They could not forget their desperate situation and Robin needed to tell Jinny what he knew and suspected. It wasn't fair of him to keep her totally ignorant, but he quailed at the thought of her pain when she heard the truth. Steel or not, she wasn't as strong as Sullyan. Nevertheless, it had to be done. They had only themselves to rely on. If he began by treating her with less than total honesty, how could he expect her to trust him?

She must have felt him shift behind her, because she turned to regard him. She had been leaning back against his chest, their shared warmth and touch helping her shut out the fear and heartache, if only for a while. But she sensed his need before he spoke and showed her steel once more.

"Robin, I want you to tell me exactly what happened here tonight. I may not understand it all, and I'm certain I won't like it, but perhaps I can help you make sense of it. Even if I say the wrong things, it might help you decide what's right."

He took a quick breath. "Oh, Jinny, you're a marvel, do you know that? You put me to shame. Taran Elijah is a very lucky man."

Jinny's pale face flushed, but the pleasure of Robin's praise did not last for long. "I wish I could believe I will see him again," she said, her voice choked and small. "Our last meeting was so full of anger and I said some terrible things. Do you think he could ever forgive me?"

"I'm sure he already has," murmured Robin. Unfortunately, Jinny was not so easily soothed.

"But you said he thinks I'm dead," she whispered, tears filling her eyes once more. "I can't bear him thinking I died without forgiving him. I wrote him a letter, you know, but I never sent it. Oh, I wish I had! I was going to tell him the next time we met. How stupid is that? And I can't believe I let such a silly little thing come between us in the first place. He was only trying to protect me, and I got so angry with him. You would think I would know him better by now, wouldn't you? After three years, I ought to. Robin, what will I do if I never get to see him again?"

Robin had no answer. He could not even offer the comfort of his arms. But she had led him rather neatly into an area he wished to explore, and had put herself in the right frame of mind to be receptive to his idea. This should save him the bother of trying to convince her.

"Jinny, did you and Taran ever talk much about his skills?"

She frowned. "Do you mean as an Artesan?" He nodded. "Yes, we spoke about it often. I wanted to try to understand as much as I could. I was so disappointed when I found out I had no talent whatsoever. I had hoped there might be a tiny little bit buried in my mind somewhere, and that if I understood it more, it might just surface. But apparently not."

This was not what Robin wanted her to say. If she believed there was no hope, his idea was doomed from the start.

"That may not be entirely true, you know," he said, catching her immediate attention.

"What do you mean?"

"Well, Taran and Cal lived with Rienne for a couple of years before they found out she was an empath. And people can develop Artesan talents well into their adult years. Even if they don't, there are other links, other bonds, between two people who love each other."

She stared intently into his eyes. "What exactly are you saying?"

"Just this. I'm completely helpless, bound in spellsilver like this. I couldn't reach Sullyan even if I were dying in torment. I doubt she could sense me even if she were standing in the courtyard out there. There's absolutely no chance of me being able to alert anyone to our whereabouts unless this silver comes off, and I can't see the Baron taking a chance like that. But there's no silver on you, and you and Taran have shared a very close bond. Is it true you'd be willing to wed him?"

Jinny watched him with wide, puzzled eyes. "Well, yes. But you can't expect *me* to contact Taran! I wouldn't even know how to begin."

"You don't need to know how." Robin saw the increasing confusion in her gaze and smiled encouragingly. "What was it you told me earlier about what you felt when you were taken from your house?"

She hesitated before realizing what he wanted. She had described her sensation of incredible pain when she was abducted, a feeling that had made her imagine she was being physically torn out of her body. Robin had told her she must have been taken through the Veils. It was the only explanation that accounted for such a dislocating sensation. "The strange pain I felt? Is that what you mean?"

"In part, yes, but that wasn't the only strange thing you felt, was it? What else did you tell me?"

Her eyes went wide. "That I imagined I cried out to Taran, begging him to rescue me."

"Yes! And you felt a response, didn't you?"

"Well ... I thought I did, but I was hurting so much and I was so confused when I woke in that hut that I could have imagined it. I so wanted it to be true ...."

"Jinny," he said, voice low and earnest, "you have to believe that's exactly what you *did* feel. You and Taran have been very close. You have shared passion, and that binds two people together with ties we don't really understand. And even if only one of those people happens to be an Artesan, well, strange things can still occur. Have you ever heard of a pair bond?"

"I'm sure Taran mentioned it once or twice," she said.

He nodded. "That's because he hoped you would form one. You have to try to call to him again. It may be our only hope. Something terribly alien has happened to your uncle, and it has changed him beyond belief. What I saw him do earlier tonight"— Robin had to fight to keep his voice from breaking—"was indescribably evil, warped, and perverted. It went way beyond mere sexual gratification. Somehow, he has learned how to steal another person's powers, even their life force, and he can use it to strengthen himself. I have never seen or heard of anything like it. I don't believe Sullyan has either. And the thought of her, or any one of our friends, coming here unawares and facing *that* is just too much to bear.

"I can't begin to imagine how we can fight him, Jinny, but I know he must be killed. I'm sorry to say this, as he's your uncle, but I think he might be the greatest evil the Five Realms have ever known, and unless he's stopped, none of us is safe. He can suck the life force from anyone he chooses—gifted or ungifted, willing or no. But that's not the worst of it." He took a breath. "Whatever his victim knows, the Baron knows too, once he's taken what he wants."

Robin fell silent and Jinny stared at him, incredulous and horrified. She could tell he wasn't quite done and his obvious revulsion and fear made her quail.

"What is it, Robin?" she whispered.

Robin closed his eyes, his voice harsh with horror. "I fear he's going to do to me what he did to Feilin. He's going to use me, use my powers, to destroy Sullyan, and every other Artesan and enemy he's ever made. And there won't be a single damned thing I can do to prevent him."

❖ ❖ ❖ ❖ ❖

Sofira led her new husband up the darkened stairway to the palace's upper floor and along the carpeted hall. It was a cloudy, moonless night, yet heavy drapes obscured every window and the fires were banked low. The scarecrow didn't intend to waste a drop of his stolen strength in protecting his body from light.

They approached the Princess's bedchamber and the two guards on duty outside her door. She pointed to them, saying, "I have done as you bid me, my love, but is this really necessary? No one will disturb us tonight of all nights. We are quite safe here."

"Humor me, my dear," he said. "Nothing shall come between us this night. I want to concentrate fully on you. You deserve nothing less, and I intend to see that you receive it."

"Oh, Hezra," she murmured, passing through the door as one of the silent guards held it open. The Baron followed her in, taking the key quietly out of the lock and passing it back to the swordsman. The door closed behind the newlyweds and Sofira heard the key turn. She raised her brows, but the scarecrow only smiled seductively. She returned the look and moved toward the bed.

Sofira's bedchamber was large and well appointed. The magnificent bed took up the center of the room, its gauzy hangings flowing to the floor. The two huge windows were tightly closed, hidden behind wine-red velvet drapes. Her dressing table and mirror stood between them, and a large hearth opposite contained a banked fire. Two trimmed lamps in niches burned on either side of the great bed, their faint golden glow lending an air of shadow and mystery to the room. Sofira's feet made no sound on the expensive woolen carpet as she reached the bed and turned to sit on the edge. She slipped off her shoes and lifted her arms to loosen her hair.

Reen had not moved from the door. He watched as she shook free the flowing river of her hair. Unbound, it reached almost to her waist and rippled like pale yellow silk over her bare shoulders. The tumble of it instantly softened the angular planes of her face and turned the hard gray of her eyes to pearl. It was a great pity, the Baron thought, that he was not the man to appreciate it. How much easier his task would be if nature had not made him indifferent to the beauty of women. But it mattered not. He now had strength enough and more to overcome his preferences, and erotic images aplenty to whet his lust. And after tonight, it would no longer be an issue.

She saw him looking at her and smiled coquettishly,

attributing his avid expression to his contemplation of her figure. She raised her hands to her breasts, fingering the fastenings of her gown, and arched her brows at him.

"Do you want to help me with these?"

He approached her slowly, not taking his eyes from hers. His precautions this night and his instructions to the guards ensured they would not be disturbed, no matter what sounds came from this room. Not even her father would get past the Baron's minions, not that Reen expected him to try. Lerric had become a liability and Reen would waste no more time on him. Once this night was over he would deal with Lerric permanently, for he now had the daughter completely within his power and no longer needed her father. Lerric had served his purpose in bringing succor to the Baron, and Reen was grateful for the haven he had provided. He intended to show Lerric just how grateful he really was.

Reen moved behind his bride and brought his hands sliding across her naked shoulders, down to the bodice of her gown. He unlaced the ties and loosened the fabric, sliding it farther down her arms. He ran his hands up the smoothness of her skin to caress the base of her neck.

"Sofira," he said, permitting a husky note to creep into his voice, "I think the time has come to reveal my plans to you."

"Can't it wait, my love?" she said, her own voice hoarse and low. He could feel desire swelling within her, linked to her as he was. He fed a little on it, feeling his own desires stir. "We have all the time we need now," she continued, trailing her fingers over the backs of his hands. "And I have other things on my mind right now."

"Ah, but that is where we differ, you and I," he murmured, hands tightening slightly on her neck. "My plans are everything to me. I thought you shared my ambitions?"

She tried to twist round to look up at him, but his grip on her throat prevented her. She was not apprehensive, not yet; she was too caught up in the anticipation of her fulfillment.

"You know I do," she protested, relaxing once more as he caressed the side of her neck. "But this is our wedding night and you promised me delights. Surely we can indulge ourselves this once and forget schemes and plans until we have consummated our marriage?"

"Delights, Sofira? Is that what I promised you? Is that what you want from me?"

He leaned forward until his lips brushed her ear. Her body gave a shudder of pleasure. His hands traveled down her arms, pushing the fabric of her gown farther down, exposing the swell of her breasts. He caressed them and she tilted her head back, moaning in pleasure and closing her eyes. Had she looked up at that moment, she might have seen a sudden flare of ruby light, but she did not.

Sofira submitted to her swelling desire. He used his hands confidently on her flesh and she lost herself in pleasure. He was before her now, pushing her gently but firmly back onto the bed, and she allowed him to do so. He straddled her body, still caressing her, leaning down to kiss her flesh, to nip with eager teeth. She writhed beneath him, hands and arms still pinioned by the bodice of her gown. She tried to free them, but he held her firm. She gasped in pleasure, giving herself to his touch, a touch that burned with passionate heat on her skin.

Soon that heat intensified, and she realized something was wrong, something about the feel of his hands and the burning heat within them. Concerned, she opened her eyes.

The scream that rang through the chamber probably reached even Lerric, cowering fearfully in his room. Reen knew he would do nothing, would make no move toward his daughter's defense. He was beaten and drained, no threat to the scarecrow.

Sofira stared wildly up into a face out of nightmare. Linked to her senses, Reen saw what she saw. Sullen red orbs that bored into her eyes with malice beyond her imagining. Livid flesh that lay limp on a grinning skull as if plastered by some inept child playing with clay. Clawed hands that gripped her throat, dried and hard and tipped with talons so strong they would have served an eagle. And the stooped, sticklike body shuddering with hatred, ropy tendons straining as they squeezed those dreadful claws ever tighter around her throat. She tried to scream again, but the sound died unborn. Those red eyes flared and her voice was not her own.

"So, my passionate bride, not so full of lust now, are you? What's the matter, proud Queen, don't you find me desirable? That's a great pity, because this is what you married. It's too late to revoke your vows now!"

Sofira's eyes were wide with shock as the monster's terrible voice dripped into her ears. Her body trembled as she saw his decaying smile.

"Oh, you do right to fear me, Sofira. I am your worst nightmare come true. And you have bound yourself to me willingly—you have made my task so much easier. Did you not know that, my love? Did you not know that you cannot take something back once it has been willingly given? That Artesan witch Sullyan knows it. That's how she defeated Rykan. If he had not given in to his lust and raped her, made her a gift of his innermost essence, she would never have been able to take his life force from him. He made a bad mistake there. But I do not intend to make the same mistakes, or any others. She will not be able to defeat *me* that way. Oh no. I would never sully myself with the touch of *her* flesh. No, I will take something much more precious to her, something she values far more highly than even her own life. And I will see her beg for mercy—beg for *all* of them—before I'm through with her. And then she will die in despair and hopelessness, as I nearly did deep in the fires of that cursed island!"

Sofira was transfixed by his malevolent glare. She didn't feel the spittle that sprayed her face. She had no thought for the palsied clench of his hands round her throat, even though they were choking her. For she was seeing her future, her precious vision of the future, and it receded by the minute, fading from her grasp, eaten by the vengeful hatred of the terrible thing crouching like a cancer over her body.

"I will have my revenge," the dreadful voice continued, its raw and husky tones a cruel parody of the desire she had felt just moments before. "On her and on you. I have waited long for this. I have sat in the darkness and nursed my despair. I have cried out my torment in silence and solitude. And I was heard, Sofira, *I was heard*! I thought I had been abandoned, thrown to my enemies, discarded as a worthless, broken tool. But I was wrong. I was wrong to despair and I was wrong to give up. You might have betrayed me, you faithless, treacherous slut, but I should have known my God never would. He placed me there for a reason and he tested me—tested me as steel is tested—in Fire and in Water.

"And I passed the test. I have been tempered in God's Holy Fire, and I have been empowered to fight, to bring down my enemies, and to take my revenge! And who better to pay the price of betrayal? Who better than you, who begged death for me? Who better to feel the strength of my power than the one who first cast me down?"

Sofira wept, but the carrion creature took no notice. He was lost in his own malicious mind, savoring the emanations of terror flowing from her heart, drinking her fear and feeding on her quailing spirit. But that was not the worst and he felt her realize, with a growing sense of horror and hopelessness, that her ordeal had not even begun. For she felt his flesh stir and his hand creep down to her skirts. Then the full terror of what he meant to do flooded through her.

She struggled and screamed, but it was no use. The strength he had taken from the young runner stood him in good stead as he effortlessly mastered her unwilling body. He held her down, pinning her arms within the folds of her gown, forcing her body to open to him as it would have done so willingly just a few moments before.

The Fire of his touch seared through Sofira, starting in her belly and traveling through her being, flaring with every thrust he made. His panting breaths filled her ears and his body shuddered. She heard his gloating cry even through her own screams of pain. Then he collapsed atop her, spent and trembling, and she lay unmoving, unable to utter the gibbering whimpers crowding her throat, terrifyingly aware that her mind and body were no longer wholly her own.

Chapter Thirteen

R obin had fallen asleep. Jinny envied his soldier's ability to sleep whatever the circumstances. She could feel the regular rhythm of his breathing from where she lay close against his smooth, warm back. They had made themselves as comfortable as possible on the narrow bed, although their bound wrists were a problem. Robin had attempted to loosen Jinny's ropes before they lay down, but his fingers were weakened by poor circulation, and the restriction of the cuffs. The knots were just too tight.

So they lay back to back for comfort and warmth, and Jinny listened to Robin's murmured instructions on how to go about contacting Taran.

"Don't think about *how* you might do it," he had said, "just believe that you can. Close your eyes and let your mind drift. It's your heart you need for this—your heart and your emotions. There's nothing logical about being an Artesan, but everything emotional. Imagine a dream. Imagine yourself in Taran's arms, his hands on your body. Think about how he makes you feel—how he speaks to you, what he says to you, the sound of his voice. All those little words you use between you. Imagine the two of you making love, imagine the passion. Use your fear and your yearning to reach out to him. Think about what you would say if he were here with you now. Feel the love flowing between you. Take hold of it and reach out with the passion of your heart. Feel him next to you, feel his skin beneath your hands. Breathe in the scents, hear his voice. You are with him, Jinny, you can feel him ....”

And she could. As Robin's low tones faded in her mind, she moved her hands and felt the smoothness of Taran's naked skin. She could hear him breathing, lying warm and sensual next to her. “Taran!” she whispered, longing for the deep, masculine sound of his voice, the touch of his hands. She saw in her mind's eye all the delicious evenings they had spent together, the passionate nights in her chamber, the laughter, the companionship, the love. Tears rolled from her eyes, but they were tears of joy. He was so considerate, her lover, so attentive to her needs, so unselfish in his passion. He never took, he gave, his pleasures gained from the fulfillment of hers.

She murmured his name again, yearning toward the sound of his voice, desperate for a touch, for the scent of his skin. She turned over on the bed, felt him next to her, and she smiled. She whispered his name a third time, frowning when there was no reply. But there couldn't be, could there? She had sent him away, rejected the love he had offered, thrown it back in his face, all for the sake of an error, a mistake, a slip of judgment. And now she was alone, fearful and cold, abandoned and in terror.

“Taran!” she cried, her own voice jolting her awake. But he was still beside her, he had not abandoned her, and she was safe. “Oh, Taran,” she murmured, running her hands over the smooth muscles of his back.

Robin murmured in his sleep and shifted slightly. Jinny snatched back her hands with a gasp, grateful they were still bound. She had been so convinced it was Taran beside her; who knows what she might have done had her hands been free? She felt her face flush with shame. She and Robin might have reached an understanding about issues like the slop bucket and essential human bodily functions, but he would probably draw the line if she tried to seduce him.

Tears rolled down her cheeks. Her attempts to reach Taran had failed. She had felt nothing in return. It was no use, she had no talents, and she would just have to face it. She had done her best and she had failed. No one knew where they were and no one would rescue them. What Robin so feared would come to pass and she would be responsible. They would die in this place—or worse, be used as poor Feilin had been used, and then they would wish they had died.

Cold in heart and sick in spirit, Jinny huddled closer to Robin and tried to will herself back sleep.

✢ ✢ ✢ ✢ ✢

"Jinny!"

Taran's cry rang sharply in the room as he struggled upright. He stared wildly in confusion, for he could still feel her arms around him and smell the perfume of her hair. His body had even responded to the dream, but his arms held nothing and the bed was empty. He was quite alone. It was only a dream.

He glanced at the couch near the window. It was dawn, and Sullyan had left him already, the blanket neatly folded and laid upon the chest. It was like her not to have woken him. He hoped he hadn't disturbed her with his troubled sleep.

Shaking his head to dispel the disquiet his dreams had left him, he rose. He was pleased to note that his leg was less painful this morning. He had hardly spared it a thought last night. Their combined metaforce could probably have healed it completely had he remembered. But still, he was grateful it seemed to be mending on its own. It was one less thing to worry over.

He moved about the room, dressing with no hurry. It was very early yet and not many were about. In breeches and shirt, he sat on the couch Sullyan had slept on and stared into the dying fire. He flicked it a thought, fresh flame leaping up at his command. He didn't feel the thrill of control such skills usually brought him; his thoughts were concentrated elsewhere.

The strange nature of his dreams nagged at his mind. He remembered them clearly, which was unusual in itself. The first few were full of bitter self-reproach. He had tormented himself over and over with his failure to talk to Jinny, both about his concerns over their relationship and after their argument, when he had told her what steps he had taken to ensure they didn't make a child between them. How he could have let himself be sidetracked by Denny's card school that night he didn't know, and he would berate himself to the end of his days. Yet once his sleeping mind had dragged him through several variations on the theme of blame and castigation, it was almost as if he—or someone else—had forgiven him. After that he had dreamed of the times they had spent together, of companionable evenings and loving glances. He had imagined himself holding her, kissing her. He had felt her lying warm and passionate next to him, and had woken still thinking she was there. Even his body had been convinced she was there. And this puzzled him, for he had never experienced such vivid dreams before.

He thought about what he and Sullyan had seen before they slept, when they had pooled their resources and searched the Veils for signs or clues. He knew she had seen or suspected something about the area where Robin's imprint had disappeared, but she had not told him what it was. What he really wanted to examine was the strange echo he had found in the Veils close to Jinny's mansion. He dug the memory of it out of his mind and went over it again.

The trouble with the substrate was that from a distance you could never quite pin it down. You could tell the general vicinity of an imprint, but you could never fix it to a physical place. He knew the Veils existed in a state of constant flux. This was what made fixing the egress of a trans-Veil tunnel so difficult. It needed a Master's strength to control the Veils sufficiently to anchor a portway, and this was also the reason why access through the Veils was never attempted too close to human habitations. So although Taran had found this peculiar echo in the substrate, and although he knew it originated somewhere in the vicinity of Jinny's mansion, he didn't know its exact location. It could be as far as a mile away from the burned-out house, and he stood no chance of determining that from the castle. But he could probably pin it down from the estate.

He would go to the house and do a more detailed search. It would satisfy his urgent need to do something useful, and he might get a more specific image of the echo. He might even get an impression of who had made it—if it was a person, and not some natural phenomenon. He could then give Sullyan a clearer view of what it was, and that would save her the effort of doing the sweep herself. Vassa was addressing the garrison this morning, and Elias would be hearing complaints from his nobles and councilors about the edict of military regnancy. Sullyan would have her hands full too. She still had to tell little Morgan that his father was missing and in grave danger of his life, and would more than likely return to the Manor sometime today, if she hadn't already gone. Anything Taran could do to further the search had to be worth it. The King had the General with him if he needed to contact the Manor. Besides, the residue from his dreams still nagged at him. A good ride in the cold might blow the sad cobwebs from his aching heart.

His mind made up, he completed his dressing, adding his warm jacket and fur-lined cloak for protection from the wind. He made his way down the silent hall and staircase to the lower floor. He was headed for the garrison, as he would not risk going alone to the estate. That would be pure folly, and Sullyan would have his hide if he attempted it. He would take a guard, and he knew that someone from Dexter's command would be happy to go with him.

He passed through the great castle doors, nodding to the guards huddled over the warmth from the braziers and drinking their morning fellan. They nodded back; no smiles, just grim expressions all round. Last night's funeral pyres and the news of Robin's abduction had hit them all hard.

Taran entered the garrison compound. There was more movement here. Guards were being changed and horses exercised, and grooms were completing their morning stable duties. The air of purpose that always surrounded the garrison soothed Taran's troubled spirit. The normality of the routine was something solid to hold on to when all else was uncertain, even if the usual cheerful banter was currently absent.

He found the long hut where Dexter had settled Robin's company and tapped lightly on the door. He entered without acknowledgment and was hailed immediately by some of the men. Dexter came over as Taran accepted a mug of the ubiquitous fellan. He often wondered how the King's forces would cope had someone not discovered the fellan plant growing in the rainforests of Beraxia. He thanked the man who had poured for him and smiled at Dexter.

The captain managed a smile back, but it lacked its usual cheer. Dexter was normally irrepressible, but recent events had cast a shadow over his cheerfulness and dampened his habitual high spirits. "Morning, Taran," he said. "What brings you here so early? I thought you city types slept in long after dawn."

Taran appreciated Dexter's attempt at levity. "I just came to make sure you lazy lot hadn't overslept."

Normally, this would have elicited a barrage of jeering from the lads, but today Dexter only grinned. Taran sighed.

166

"Dex, I want to go over to Jinny's mansion this morning. Sullyan and I found something odd while we were searching yesterday, and I need to sniff it out. I don't think it would be wise to go alone, so can you spare someone to ride over there with me?"

Before Dexter could reply, a voice sounded from across the room. "I'll go, Captain."

Both men turned at the quiet voice and Dexter raised his brows. "Are you sure you're up to it, Col? Neither of you were fit yesterday."

Col turned anxious eyes on his senior officer, obviously keen to prove something, either to himself or to his captain. "I'm fine, sir, really I am. I don't think I could cope with a full tour of duty, but I can do this. Save you from detailing one of the fitter lads."

Dexter shot Taran a glance. "That all right with you?"

Taran nodded and grinned at Col, recognizing the young man's need to do something useful. Both he and Pengar were still feeling inadequate after what they perceived as their failure in Bordenn. An easy spot of guard duty might help one of them forget. "I'm not fit myself, yet," he said, indicating his injured leg, "so we'll do just fine together. I'll meet you out in the compound. I have to see if my poor horse is fit to be ridden. Thanks, Dex," he murmured to the captain.

Dexter waved his gratitude away. "Just help us find them," he said gruffly. Taran left, pretending he hadn't seen the fear in Dexter's eyes.

He went to the stables and spent a few moments talking to Bucyrus and rubbing his small ears. The scrapes on the horse's sides had healed well and the hair was already beginning to grow back. Sullyan had done a good job on him, Taran thought with relief. When completely healed, there would be no telltale white hairs in Bucyrus's hide to prick his conscience. Satisfied, he went to collect the horse's gear.

Col was awaiting him on a dusty black when Taran nudged the stallion into the compound. He fell in beside the swordsman and the two of them rode companionably out into the town, heading for the northern road.

✤ ✤ ✤ ✤ ✤

Sullyan had risen just before dawn and decided not to wake Taran. She had heard some of his soft cries in the night and guessed he was dreaming of Jinny. She stayed away from his mind, although she could have soothed his sleep. In truth, her own slumber had been far from refreshing and she still felt drained. Her eyes felt gritty and sore and her heart was heavy. Today she could no longer put off the task of telling Morgan about his father, although what she would say to her son, she did not yet know. Everything she thought of sounded false. Morgan would see through her in an instant. Besides, he might already have tried to bespeak his father and failed. She could only imagine how that would feel to a small child who had no concept of evil. For the first time since she had birthed him, she dreaded looking into the eyes of her precious little boy.

Telling Morgan was not the only unpleasant task she must undertake today. It was high time Aeyron knew of the probable re-emergence of their greatest enemy, and his hurt when he discovered she had kept the news from him for nearly a week would only add to her pain.

And then there was the Manor. Bulldog knew as much as she knew. He had offered to tell the rest of her company and she had accepted his offer, berating herself for a base coward. Bulldog—dear, loyal, faithful Bulldog—had known how she would dread telling young Tad that one of his heroes was in desperate danger. And Cal, one of Robin's closest friends, would share their anger and fear, not to mention Rienne. Yet she had to go there today.

Once she had told Morgan, she had to make other arrangements for the safety of Elias's son, Eadan. Her conviction that the Baron once again had recourse to an Artesan's powers made nonsense of their complacent view that Eadan would be safe at the Manor. She knew there was only one way to guarantee Eadan's security, and she intended to see it done. While she was at it, she would include Morgan, Elisse, and Taric as well. Rienne might not like it, but her friend would see the sense of it once Sullyan explained. She also needed Rienne's medical expertise if they were to discover anything at all about the virulent poison that had been used to kill Bessie and seriously incommode Rendan Levant.

She knew she ought to check on the First Minister, but the day would be short enough with all she had to do. She would have to leave his health to the healers and his protection to the castle's vastly increased security measures. General Blaine would stay with the King for the time being. Elias would value his stern, impressive support when he had to face the nobles and councilors who were up in arms over the closure of the city.

Let them rant! she thought irritably. If they wanted their king protected from whatever stalked him, they would have to obey his protectors. It would do them no harm to acknowledge those who truly held the reins of power.

After a swift visit to the main dining hall, where she made quick work of a quantity of fellan and some fruit, she made her way to the King's chambers, unsurprised to find the outer door already open. The presence of the two lady's maids waiting a discreet distance down the hallway and the angry voices coming from the King's chambers only made her heart fall further. She had hoped to avoid this, but she should have known better. Nodding to the two guards at the door, she squared her shoulders and entered the room.

As soon as she appeared, the furious clamor ceased. Three heads turned toward her, two pairs of eyes showing sympathy behind their anger and one pair holding only hostility. Princess Seline's hard gray eyes bored into Sullyan like gimlets until she turned her back deliberately to face her father once more.

"Well?" she demanded, hands planted firmly on her hips.

Sullyan knew what this was about. Seline had come to her father to complain about the slap Sullyan had given her for her uncaring dismissal of Bessie's death. She should not have done it, deserved though it was. Seline was Elias's daughter and a Princess. Sullyan had sworn an oath to protect the royal family and that did not allow her the liberty of striking one of them. Never mind that her status was equal to Seline's; the young girl cared nothing for the honor conferred on Sullyan by Andaryans. An Albian Princess of the ruling House had been grossly dishonored and she was here to claim her due.

Elias cast his colonel a helpless look, but he opened his mouth once again to try to reason with his daughter. Sullyan knew it was futile. Seline would not back down until she had what she wanted. And Elias's day would be full enough of acrimonious anger; he could do without the petulant demands of his spiteful daughter. So Sullyan made a slight gesture with her hand and Elias fell silent.

"Your Highness."

Sullyan spoke softly from behind Seline. The Princess was forced to face Sullyan and acknowledge her presence. The King and the General watched as she slowly turned.

"Colonel." The girl's voice dripped venom, her stance that of someone expecting a fight. Sullyan disappointed her.

"Your Highness, I apologize unreservedly for striking you yesterday. It was unforgivable. The terrible circumstances of your maid's death and Lord Levant's condition must have left me bereft of my manners. I was concerned for your safety, that you weren't taking matters seriously enough, and acted out of fear. I hope you can understand that I had my duty to protect you uppermost in my mind."

The girl's eyes narrowed. "What was uppermost in your mind, Colonel, was plain dislike! Don't think your soft words can fool me. I know how much you hated my mother. I know how much you hate me."

"Seline!" thundered Elias, his furious tone and expression making even his rebellious daughter jump. This time she had gone too far. What she had uttered was tantamount to an accusation of treason.

Sullyan, realizing things could get ugly, knew she had to act. She dropped to one knee before Seline. The girl's eyes grew wide; color rose in her cheeks and her mouth hardened.

"Your Highness," said Sullyan, keeping her voice low, "I have apologized for my dishonorable actions. My strength and my sword are at your command. I hold to my Oath. I swear and declare before witnesses that I do not desire any harm to you, or to your lady mother."

Seline was trapped and she knew it. Sullyan's unforced apology and witnessed avowal of her Oath could not be refused. Seline was honor-bound to accept her apology and pledge, no matter how much she might wish to refute both. Yet still she hesitated.

Elias was dumbstruck and Blaine wore an expression of distaste. He understood what this gesture had cost his colonel; she could see his hands twitching as if he itched to slap the Princess himself.

Sullyan remained where she was, concealing her irritation, her face expressionless under Seline's hard gaze. This was necessary if they were to progress. They had no time to deal with the tantrums of a spoiled child.

Eventually, with no room to maneuver and no insult left to claim, Seline was forced to capitulate. She had pushed this as far as she could. It was over, for now.

"Your apology is accepted, Colonel," she spat, turning on her heel and stalking from the room. Sullyan stood, her eyes following the Princess's stiff back.

Elias sighed heavily and sank into a chair. "Ah, Brynne. I would have done anything to save you that shame. I don't know what's got into her lately. She's worse than her mother."

Sullyan was too weary for this. "Pay it no mind, my Lord. It cost me little enough."

The General came forward and laid a hand on her shoulder. "Even a little is too much at present. Are you all right, Brynne? In truth."

Sullyan abandoned her usual, evasive replies. "Of course not, Mathias. But what can I do?" She saw the answering sympathy in his eyes, but she had no time for that either. Cutting straight to her purpose, she briefly outlined what she intended to do that day. He gave his permission, though he would clearly have preferred her to stay at the castle.

"I have to explore every avenue, seek out every clue, try to get one step ahead. If it really is the Baron behind all this, he will have laid his plans carefully. He will not risk some half-thought-out scheme. He has had three months at least to build up his power base and form his defenses, so I will not go running blindly into a trap, no matter how perfectly baited."

"Just be careful, Brynne. I don't want to lose you, too."

She gave him a pale smile. "I will. I have no intention of meeting the Baron until I know more about his plans. Just pray that Robin has the strength to endure. And if that bastard harms one hair of Robin's head, he will pay for it a thousandfold. I will make him wish he had suffered Execution by the Wheel before I am done with him."

The General's nod let her know he understood.

Chapter Fourteen

When Sullyan rode through the Manor gates, Bull was already on the training ground drilling the cadets. It was only an hour after dawn, but they had obviously been there some time judging by the churned snow underfoot and the red faces of the sweating cadets. Bull saw her immediately and yelled to one of the weapons master's assistants to take over the exercise, and for one of the cadets to take Drum to the stables. He came over to her, pain and anxiety in his honest brown eyes.

"Oh, gods, Sully!" he said when he reached her, bereft of anything else to say which would adequately express his fear and heartache. She thought he might hug her, yet he refrained. He would know such a display of affection and sympathy might undermine the show of calm strength she had carefully built around her.

"I know, Bull," she murmured, unable to hold his gaze. "Where is Morgan? Has he said anything?"

"He spent the night with Rienne. I don't know if he knows anything yet. I've not heard from Rienne, so I suspect not. But he'll be awake soon, if he isn't already. You know how he likes to be up early. Would he try to contact his father?"

She shrugged. "Probably. He has not called me yet, though. I have to tell him. I cannot allow him to find out for himself. But I have no idea what to say. How do you tell a little boy that his beloved father may never come back?"

Sullyan's voice broke and tears sprang into her eyes. Bull didn't make the mistake of reaching for her; that would only open floodgates she was already struggling to hold shut.

"Don't write him off just yet," he told her, his voice low and intense. "He's strong, he's resourceful, and he has the knowledge of your love behind him. He won't crack or give up until he has no other choices. And we'll find him before that happens."

She gave him an anguished look. "Will we, Hal? How? And where will we look? We do not even know for sure if Reen is behind all this. If he is, then he once more has access to an Artesan's powers, and I do not even want to contemplate what that might mean. You know what he tried to do last time."

Bull stared at her in horror. "You think he'd try it again? But where would he get the spellsilver?"

She did not reply, merely held his gaze. Bull's jaw dropped open.

"Oh, dear gods … he wouldn't … would he?"

"Who else does he know with connections to Andaryon?" she hissed. "He knows I would do anything to regain Robin. And I would, Bull, believe me! If I thought for one moment he would exchange Robin—alive and unhurt—for spellsilver, then I would rob Timar's mines myself! I would give him all the silver he could possibly want in order to get Robin back."

Bull's florid face was aghast at the vehemence of her tone. She was deadly serious. "But what would be the point? If he destroys the Veils like he planned to last time, there'll be no world left for you to live in!"

"But at least we would die together," she whispered, turning her face away from the big man. She sighed heavily into the ensuing silence. "Oh, do not fear me, Hal. I have no intention of providing the Baron with the means to destroy the world. But I have to face the fact that refusing to do so may mean sacrificing Robin."

Bull stared helplessly at her. "We'll think of something. There's been no ransom demand yet, has there? And if that's what he intends, then he has to keep Robin unharmed. That may buy us time."

"I certainly hope so. For I have the damnedest feeling time is fast running out."

Bull left his cadets in the capable hands of the weapons master's assistant and accompanied Sullyan to Rienne's quarters. As they went, she told him some of what she intended to do, both for the security of Prince Eadan and the other children and in regards to her visit to Andaryon. They were still discussing it in the hallway leading to Cal and Rienne's rooms when a door ahead of them burst open and a small figure hurtled desperately toward them. Sullyan's eyes filled with tears as she knelt down to embrace her frantic son, who had obviously just tried to bespeak his father.

Cal appeared in the hallway, his daughter, Elisse, and Prince Eadan hot on his heels. Both children were crying, upset by Morgan's terror. From within the room, the sound of baby Taric's shrill cries could be heard over the soothing murmur of Rienne's voice as she tried to calm him.

Some of the strain in Cal's dark face relaxed when he saw Sullyan. Rienne approached their door, her sobbing son held tight in her arms. Her face was pale, her eyes soft with unshed tears. She took one look at Sullyan's anguished expression and turned abruptly away, Taric cradled to her breast. The children were upset enough without seeing her break down. Cal gathered Elisse and Eadan to him and tried to comfort them.

Sullyan did the same for Morgan, but her communion was silent. She had to let her son into her mind. If she tried to hide from him, she would frighten him all the more. So she let him see her grief and fear, but she tempered it as best she could. Her anger and deep desire for vengeance were shut away; they were the last things he needed to see. But she could not conceal the danger from him, not with so many worried Artesans broadcasting fear and anxiety.

He eventually calmed. Her familiar presence enveloped him with the assurance of her love, lending his fragile spirit strength. She carried him into Rienne's apartment and sat with him on the couch, turning his pale, tear-streaked face to hers.

"Morgan, my son, I am going to ask a very hard thing of you," she told him seriously. He hiccoughed once and wiped his eyes, looking back at her anxiously. "Your Papa is in danger, as you know." Morgan nodded, another tear sliding down his cheek. She tenderly brushed it away. "But we have told you before that danger is part of our lives, do you remember? We are members of the King's forces. Sometimes that means one of us has to endure danger so that the King may be kept safe. Do you understand?"

Morgan nodded again, although he only accepted her words rather than appreciating the reasoning behind them. His gold-flecked blue eyes, still moist from crying, were intent on Sullyan's.

"But this does not mean he will not come back. He is a very strong man, your Papa, and much of his strength comes from our love for him. It is all right to feel fear, Morgan, but we must never give in to that fear, and we must never let it become stronger than our love. Papa will feel that love and he will not give in to his fear because he knows we will be doing all we can to help him. And that is the best way you can help him right now—by being brave.

"Now, I have to go away again. I have to do everything I can to find your Papa, and that means I cannot be with you. But you always know how to reach me, and I will never leave you alone. Do you hear me? And just because you cannot speak to Papa at the moment does not mean he has left you either. Remember your lessons. There are many reasons why we might not be able to feel each other at certain times. This is one of those times, but it will not last. Do you understand me, Morgan?"

The little boy nodded silently, his eyes brimming with more tears, his arms creeping up to encircle her neck. She caught him up in a sudden, fierce hug. His arms came around her with desperate strength and she felt his young heart striving for courage. It tore her to pieces. Her spirit filled with hate for her enemies, who could do this to such a little child, and her natural instincts yearned to strike out at the source of so much grief. Holding him tightly to her, she strove for calm.

Eventually, both Eadan and Elisse came forward to share in the hug. Sullyan caught them all up together while Cal, Rienne, and Bull exchanged worried glances. When the children had been pacified as much as they could be, Sullyan turned to the healer. "Rienne, I have a request for you, if you will."

Rienne handed Taric to Cal and drew in a steadying breath. "What is it, Brynne? What can I do to help?"

Sullyan explained about the poison used on Bessie and Levant, and also on the two swordsmen of the King's escort. When her description of the symptoms drew no recognition from Rienne, she asked, "Can you search the pharmacy records and see if you can identify it? If you can discover a remedy to counter it, I think it might behoove us to lay up stocks. It is both virulent and violent. I would not wish to see anyone else suffer the agonies poor Bessie went through. Rendan only survived because he had two Artesans supporting his life force. A younger man might have lived through the purging unsupported, but an older man certainly would not."

Rienne nodded. "I'll do what I can. I'll ask Hanan to help me. Toxins are a specialty of hers."

Sullyan nodded her thanks. "There is one other thing. Cal, this affects you, too."

She lowered her voice so as not to disturb the three older children, all of whom huddled together for comfort. Bulldog was crouched down beside them, murmuring encouragement.

"It is my belief that the Baron, or whoever is behind these attacks, once more has recourse to the skills of an Artesan," she said. Cal burst out with an expletive, reddening at the sour look thrown him by Rienne for swearing in front of the children. "Until now," continued Sullyan, ignoring Cal's slip, "I have considered Eadan to be safe here within the confines of the Manor. Yet if I am right about this, all is changed."

She turned her head to include Bulldog, who looked up expectantly. "Bull, from now on the children are never to be left without two guards, one of whom must be an Artesan. If Cal cannot be with them, either you or Tad must take over. I am including Taric, Morgan, and Elisse in this order. We can guard them better if they stay together. But there is one other thing. It may be that whoever is providing Reen with metaphysical force is either untutored or less … scrupulous, shall we say? … over the uses of power than the rest of us. I will take no chances he might try to take Eadan from right under our noses. During the day we can guard them, but at night it could prove difficult. Therefore, I want all the children and their guards to sleep in the College's healer suite. The spellsilver in the walls will prevent any unauthorized entry."

Rienne gasped in alarm. "Do you really think that's necessary? Surely he won't try anything here?"

"He sent for Robin in the castle parklands, in full view of an entire company and right under Blaine's nose!" countered Sullyan harshly. "He is devious and amoral, Rienne. He cares nothing for human life and even less for an Artesan's. He might try anything. How would you feel if we ignored the possibility and lost one of the children? The King's Heir apart, once he sees I will not be tempted into his noose for Robin's sake, he might well try for my son. And there, as I doubt I have to tell you, he would succeed!"

Rienne was frightened, but she nodded her acceptance. The children would be guarded well, of that Sullyan was sure. It took one small worry off her mind. Save locking them up, there was not much else she could do.

She clasped Rienne's arm in thanks, and then turned to Bull. "Hal, I must leave for Andaryon at once. The General will stay in Port Loxton for the time being, but he may send Vassa back here. Elias has decided to leave the edict of military regnancy in place until this business has concluded, but the nobles and the city councilors are not happy. The General may ask you to send more men if the level of unrest rises. I suggest you ask for volunteers, select a company, and have them standing by."

Bull nodded. "Who will you take to stand for you?"

"I will ask Jay'el. I do not want to take any of you away from guarding the children at present. Jay will be quite happy to visit his future brother-in-law."

Bull managed a wan smile. "You'll have to dig him out of his bunk first."

Sullyan took an emotional farewell of her son, Eadan, and Elisse. She charged them with looking out for each other and with obeying their guards' and parents' commands. All the children solemnly agreed. Morgan's fear for his father was too raw and they all felt it equally. Sullyan was loath to leave them—at times like this she seriously questioned whether her way of life was fair on her young son—yet she pushed that thought to the back of her mind. Time enough to ponder it when she had Robin safely back.

Leaving Cal and Bull to arrange for guarding the children, she and Rienne made their way through the Manor, parting at the final turn in the hallway. Rienne headed for the pharmacy to begin her search for the toxin, while Sullyan made for the College. The wind was still bitterly cold when she emerged from the confines of the Manor, and she hugged her fleece-lined jacket about her body. She crossed to the College doors and hurried inside.

The College was by no means full, though it housed the greatest number of students since its inauguration. She felt intense pride that this had happened in her lifetime, and enjoyed her hours teaching here. Every Artesan at the Manor shared teaching duties, even Mathias Blaine. His willingness to impart his knowledge had surprised Sullyan, knowing what she did of his attitude toward his own powers. If not for Elias's enthusiasm and unflagging support, the College would never have existed, and she was damned if she would let bigots like the Baron destroy all their hard work.

She made her way through the College toward the refectory. She could hear voices and smell the aromas of the morning meal. The Manor cook, Goran, managed to split his forces admirably between the College and the commons, but she knew that if the College continued to grow as it had these past two years, they would need an increase in kitchen staff.

She pushed open the refectory door and walked in among the students. The atmosphere of the College was more informal than the barracks; there were no salutes to her military rank here. But every student was aware of her metaphysical status and she was held in awe by all of them.

Casually acknowledging the many greetings she received, Sullyan spied the person she had come to find. Contrary to Bulldog's prediction, Jay'el showed every sign of having been awake for some time. She thought he had probably even been out on the practice ground. He wore his sword at his belt and his face was flushed from exercise. She approached him and caught his eye.

"Highness!" he exclaimed, his already flushed face reddening further when he saw her disapproving look. She never paraded her Andaryan status among her colleagues at the Manor, and even her friends were forbidden to use her title. "Sullyan," he amended hastily, "good morning. What can I do for you? Is there news?"

She ignored his second question. "I intend to visit Timar this morning, Jay. Bulldog, Cal, and Tad cannot be spared from their duties and I need someone to stand for me. Would you be willing to accompany me?"

"Of course," he said, eagerly. "Do you mean now?"

"Yes, now. It is a matter of some importance."

Although Sullyan had taken up Bull's offer to tell the men about Robin's disappearance, she had asked him not to go into too much detail. So much of what she suspected was still supposition, and the last thing they needed was to encourage rumors. So Jay'el did not know what she intended to do and she did not enlighten him. He would hear of it soon enough. Once Aeyron knew, he would make his own arrangements for personal security, and might very well wish to include Jay'el among them. Until then, she would leave the Andaryan seaman in the dark.

Jay'el swallowed the last of his fellan and snatched up a piece of fruit. He offered some to Sullyan, but she shook her head. "Have you everything you need?" He nodded and followed her out of the College.

At the horse lines, Drum awaited her. He whickered softly as she appeared. A young stable lad hurriedly harnessed a mount for Jay'el, and they were soon turning their horses' heads down the lane, making for the first patch of open ground where they could construct a crossing in safety.

Normally, Sullyan would have made Jay'el provide the strength for the tunnel. He was still a raw Apprentice and needed the practice, but this was not the time for lessons. She handled the whole thing herself and soon they emerged onto the Citadel Plains, half a mile from the southern gate. She had alerted Anjer to her imminent arrival and they heard the horns and saw the gate opening long before they reached it. She and Jay'el rode swiftly up the Processional Way and into the Palace courtyard.

Grooms took their horses and Commander Barrin came forward to greet them. His manner toward Pharikian's human allies had thawed considerably since Elias's disastrous invasion, but Sullyan still missed his predecessor, Torman Vanyr. She acknowledged Barrin's greeting and thanked him as he directed her to where her adopted father awaited her. She and Jay strode through the corridors of Pharikian's Palace alone. No one would dare to suggest that a Princess of the royal House needed an escort. And she knew her way very well, having spent many happy hours here since her adoption, watching her young son playing with Marik's twins, Tyrian and Mallin. But today the corridors were quiet. Marik's two hellions were at their father's palace in Kymer, and the entire Citadel was catching its breath before their next onslaught.

Sullyan and Jay found the aging Supreme Ruler of Andaryon relaxing in his private rooms. His son and Heir, Prince Aeyron, was handling the morning's business and Pharikian was alone. He stood and beamed in pleasure when Sullyan entered the room, throwing his arms wide and pulling her close to him. She entered his embrace, feeling, as always, the intense rush of love that contact with her true father's closest friend always brought to her heart. She was more than deeply grateful to this powerful yet gentle man. His love for her father and care of her mother had enabled Sullyan to be born, and his wholehearted transference of that love and care to her had seen her through more trials than she cared to remember. She owed this man so much, and not least for his unstinting inclusion of her into the bosom of his family. It was all she could do not to break down in the comforting circle of his arms.

Insightful as ever, he quickly divined her troubled spirit and saw more deeply into her heart than she might have wished. He drew back a little and gazed deeply into her eyes. "You are much troubled, Brynne. I take it this is not a social call?"

Fighting back tears, she shook her head. "Unfortunately not, Father. I would that it were."

Pharikian's eyes narrowed at her choked tone and he drew her with him to the fire. "Sit, Brynne. You too, young man. There is fellan brewing and I have sent for some food. I'll warrant you've not eaten yet?"

Sullyan shook her head. The bit of fruit she had snatched at the castle that morning was already forgotten. Pharikian gestured for Jay'el to pour the fellan and he sat watching Sullyan as she accepted the steaming cup in hands that were suddenly unsteady. She knew he could feel the emanations of distress that escaped her tight rein, and his gentle and comforting presence was making this harder for her than ever. Keeping her feelings from her adopted father was something she found almost impossible to do. They were simply too close.

Before she broke down completely, there was a discreet tap at the door and a young page entered. Sullyan glanced up at him and smiled. The shock of fair hair and cheeky smile were the same, but where Norkis had blue eyes, Maxin's were pale gray. Apart from that, the twelve-year-old lad was the image of his older brother, who had held the post of Pharikian's page before him. Maxin grinned back as he carried his heavy tray across the room and deftly deposited it on the low table before the fire.

"Highness," he said quietly, making a respectful bow.

"Maxin, it is good to see you. Are you well and enjoying your work? How is your scamp of a brother?"

"I am very well, Highness, thank you, and I hope I am giving my lord good service. Norkis is progressing well, although the weapons master says he should practice more and talk less."

Sullyan smiled, grateful for the chance to forget her troubles, even if only for a few moments. "And his other skills?"

Maxin's mischievous grin widened. "He practices those *very* hard, Highness."

Sullyan was sure of it. Norkis's Artesan skills had been slow to develop, but once he had begun formal training, they had burgeoned. She was sure his friendship with Tad, and Tad's commitment to and enthusiasm for his military training, had had some influence on Norkis's own decision to join the Velletian Guard rather than continue as a steward in Pharikian's Palace.

"He doesn't want to be overtaken by young Tad," confirmed Pharikian wryly. "Their friendly rivalry keeps him on his toes."

Maxin bowed and left the room. Sullyan clearly remembered his brother at that age, and how strikingly he had resembled the slightly older Tad. Much had changed since that time. Memories of her first visit here returned to haunt her, and Pharikian gazed at her intently.

"What is it, Brynne? What troubles you so?"

She raised brimming eyes and he caught his breath. He saw the pain she fought to contain and offered her his mind, thinking to make the telling easier for her. She refused his offer, knowing that if she let him in, if she accepted the loving care and sympathy he yearned to offer, she would never be able to close the floodgates of her emotions. She needed a clear head right now, and dispassionate planning. She ruthlessly slowed her thudding heart and drew in a shaky breath.

"Father, it seems my suspicions over the apparent suicide of Baron Reen were correct. I am as certain now as I can be that he not only survived the leap into the sea, but that the whole episode was a carefully planned charade to convince us he had taken his own life. With the time this bought him, he built up a power base and gathered strength, and now I very much fear he is nearing the time when he will bring his plans to fruition."

Pharikian's lined face paled at the implications her words held for his son. "What has so convinced you of this?"

Sullyan ran through the events of the past two days, beginning with Taran's chance remark concerning the trial. Pharikian agreed that the connection between the victims was too clear to be coincidental, and when he heard about the poisonings in Bordenn and Loxton Castle, he was even more firmly convinced. Yet he could tell she had not told him everything, and when she fell silent, he sat and watched her, pouring waves of strength toward her, waiting for her to gather her courage. He knew the trouble had to concern either Elias, Robin, or her son. It was obviously of momentous proportions.

When she finally told him, he could sit still no longer. He reached for her shuddering body and enfolded her in a tight embrace, sharing the pain in her soul and flooding her with love. Jay'el sat awkward and forgotten at the side, trying to process all he had just heard.

Sullyan was lost. All of her careful barriers crumbled before the power of Pharikian's love. Her facade of strength and calm evaporated like so much mist in the sun. Her will was shattered and her pain overflowed. Her fear and her terror crashed over her soul and carried her composure away.

Pharikian just held her, unable to speak. His fear for her and for Robin mingled with worry for his own son, who would soon be finishing his audiences for the morning and would be making his way to this room. He knew Sullyan would not want to inflict such deep emotion on her brother, not until she was calm. And not even Pharikian could guess how Aeyron might react.

Some of Aeyron's scars ran so deep that he might never fully heal. He had his confidence back, thanks largely to Sullyan, but it was a fragile thing, easily broken. Pharikian closed his eyes against the anger he felt. Hadn't they all suffered enough?

It was Jay'el who rescued them, remembering that strong fellan was Sullyan's anodyne for most situations. She had not touched the food and he knew she would not unless forced to. So he added more grounds to the fellan pot and poured a stream of the rich, bitter liquid into her cup. Without a word, he took one of her hands and loosed it from its grip on Pharikian's shoulder, curling her fingers around the hot cup.

"I thank you, Jay," she said shakily. Pharikian released her and took his own refilled cup, held out to him by the young seaman. He nodded his appreciation to Jay, who indicated the food with a nod. Sullyan might accept fellan from him, but he held no power to force her to eat. Pharikian did, and he recognized Jay's wisdom. He took up a piece of fruit from the plate and handed it to her. She stared at it for a full second before she capitulated, although her mouth felt like dust and her stomach rebelled at the thought of food.

"How can we help you?" murmured Pharikian softly. "There must be something we can do."

She replied listlessly, her strength used up. "I came here mainly to warn Aeyron. I can keep this from him no longer, and he must take steps to protect himself. But there is something I would ask you, and it may be that I also have a task for Gaslek, if he is willing."

Pharikian waved a hand. "Speak on. Aeyron will be here soon, and we can always send for Gaslek. What is your question?"

"Father, I am as certain as I can be that Reen has, once again, some recourse to the powers of an Artesan." The Hierarch nodded grimly, having gleaned as much from her description of Robin's abduction. "What I do not yet know is how. I did not tell you this when I was last here, but while visiting the island where he spent his exile, I learned of the friendship Reen had formed with a young cleric named Serrin. By all accounts, the two of them became very close. How close, I can only speculate, but I was struck by how alike they sounded. Shortly before the Baron's apparent suicide, Serrin disappeared. I believe that boy was an untrained Artesan."

The Hierarch leaned forward. "And you think Reen somehow subverted this Serrin? Convinced or forced him to work for him?"

Sullyan frowned. "That would be the most logical explanation. But I found no evidence that Serrin had managed to leave the island, and there is also the matter of the large pool of blood found in the Baron's rooms. That blood could not have come from Reen's body. Having lost that amount, he could never have scaled the heights of the crag, nor survived the plunge into such a cold and stormy sea, no matter how close the boat he had waiting. I am convinced that the blood came from Serrin. I am sure the Baron killed him."

"Then he has somehow found another poor soul to dominate, as he did with Huw." Pharikian turned his head. They both heard the footsteps approaching from far down the hallway. Aeyron had finished his appointments for the day.

Sullyan glanced at the door and lowered her voice. "There is yet one other possibility, Father." Pharikian narrowed his eyes. "If you remember, the Baron had latent powers of his own. We discovered that at the trial. And this brings me to my question: have you any knowledge of a latent Artesan being able to activate his powers? It was my thought that perhaps the Baron somehow used Serrin to help him unlock his potential. It may have been the reason why the poor lad was killed. Perhaps the Baron grew frustrated and slew him in a jealous rage, or maybe his death was an experiment in control that went awry. Perhaps Reen always intended to slay him once he had what he wanted. I can only imagine his fury and sense of betrayal when he discovered that his one companion in his lonely exile possessed the very qualities Reen so loathed and which he had tried so hard to destroy. That knowledge may well have sent him over the edge of sanity. I was told he fell into a very strange state of ill health once the lad was gone. It is the only explanation I can think of at this time."

Pharikian frowned at the question. "I cannot bring to mind such an occurrence, Brynne, and I have to say I very much doubt the Baron's ability to bring to potency such long-buried talents, even with the help of an experienced Artesan such as you or me, let alone an untutored boy. I fear your hypothesis leaves much to be desired."

Sullyan closed her eyes. Her father's words were what she had feared to hear, and they sounded a death knell over part of her theory. The Hierarch saw her frustration and grieved at the fresh pain he had given her.

"Let us not discount the possibility entirely," he soothed. "Just because I have no experience of such a thing doesn't mean it's impossible. Our archives hold information gathered over hundreds, if not thousands, of years. I would not care to say what might be recorded."

He glanced at the young seaman. "Jay'el, would you be so good as to go to the door and ask Maxin to fetch Baron Gaslek. If anyone can find references to help us, he can."

Jay'el strode to the door, but it was opened before he reached it and Prince Aeyron, co-ruler of Andaryon, entered the room. Jay'el swept a low bow, but the Prince only had eyes for his sister. He crossed the room in two fluid strides and caught her to him in a fervent embrace. Jay'el continued to the door and relayed the Hierarch's request to the young page waiting outside. Maxin nodded and scampered away.

Aeyron eventually released Sullyan and stared down into her eyes. His immediate pleasure at seeing her again swiftly evaporated as he registered the dark crescents under her eyes and the pallor of her face. He shot a concerned glance at his father, seeing the same traces of emotion on the elderly ruler's face. "What is it?" he asked warily. "What's happened?"

The Hierarch spoke heavily. "Sit down, my son. Your sister has some unwelcome news for you."

Chapter Fifteen

Seth woke late that morning and groaned softly, stretching his aching limbs. The beds provided by the lodging house were comfortable, and normally he had no complaints. Yet last night he had not slept on the deep down mattress due to it being monopolized by the snoring man lying naked at full stretch on the counterpane.

From his roll of blankets on the hard floor, Seth stared at his companion, trying to decide whether he was pleased or irritated by the man's presence. Certainly, he had provided the companionship and other pleasures Seth had missed for so long, but he had also dominated the younger man and given no thought to his comfort.

Seth reflected wryly that he ought to be used to that. This hulking swordsman was his master's latest tool, and his master had always been the taker, with Seth the giver. He supposed he ought to be thankful. His master obviously still needed him and valued him enough to seek him out. Once the Baron was back where he belonged, Seth hoped he would once again enjoy the benefits of his employment.

His lower body aching from last night's excesses, Seth cast off the blankets and stood, stretching cramped muscles and reaching for his breeches. He wondered if he ought to wake his companion, then decided food was his priority, that and hot fellan. He moved toward the fire and the kettle of water.

The smell of fellan eventually roused the snoring swordsman

and he grunted, rolling over onto his hairy belly and leering at Seth from one bloodshot eye. Seth did not return the grin. He didn't feel like repeating last night's activities just yet, and besides, he wanted to know more about the purpose of the strange knife he had been given. The black-haired man had been sidetracked from his explanation as soon as they closed the door of Seth's rented room, and the manservant had been able to get little sense out of him. Once his seemingly inexhaustible lust was finally spent, the swordsman collapsed onto Seth's bed as if he owned it and was snoring in moments. This morning, Seth decided, he was owed an explanation.

He poured fellan for both of them and passed a mug to the other man, who took it with huge hands calloused from long practice with the sword. He grunted his thanks. Seth sat on the wide windowsill, cradling his own drink. "What's your name?" he asked suddenly.

He didn't really expect an answer. The vagrant had never vouchsafed his name, or any unnecessary information, come to that. Seth was taken aback when the fellow replied gruffly, "Varth."

Seth nodded. "So, Varth, are you going to tell me what last night was all about?"

The man grinned wickedly. "Thought you'd have worked that one out by now! Didn't realize you'd been without so long you'd forgotten what it was. Though that's not what it felt like to me."

Seth sighed and refrained from the frustrated retort he wanted to make. He ought to have seen that one coming. Clearly, the Baron chose his minions for their dreadful sense of humor. Seth determined to phrase his questions more carefully in future. "I meant the knife, as you well know," he pressed, keeping anger from his voice. He had experienced the man's physical strength during their liaison and didn't want to incur his wrath.

Varth swung his muscular legs off the bed and sat on the edge, slurping fellan and making no move toward his discarded clothes. His hirsute and powerful body was grimy, but it wasn't the dirt that caught Seth's attention. It was the infected patch of raw skin he could see on the swordsman's belly. He hadn't noticed it the night before. The room was in darkness when they had returned and they hadn't bothered to light the lamp.

"That looks nasty," Seth said, pointing to the weeping sore.

Varth glanced down at the patch as if he had never seen it before. Then he looked back up. "My business."

Seth raised his brows. "I was only—"

"Well, don't. Do you want to hear about that knife or not?"

Seth wisely backed off, not liking the redness lingering around Varth's bloodshot eyes. There had been times during the night when he was sure he had seen a ruby glint, just like in the eyes of the vagrant. He really didn't want to antagonize this man. So he shut his mouth and nodded, seeing the mocking grin return to the man's face.

"That's better." Varth leaned down and reached for Seth's discarded jacket. He felt through the pockets and brought out the knife Seth had stowed there the previous evening. He tossed it casually to the puzzled manservant, who caught it gingerly, angling the blade to the light from the window. Varth's eyes narrowed in disgust as he saw Seth's inept grip on the haft. "Gods, man, it won't bite you."

Seth glanced at him, confused. "It won't bite anyone. This knife's made of silver!"

Varth grinned widely, showing uneven, brown-stained teeth. He put down his empty mug and stretched out an arm, snagging his breeches from the bottom of the bed. He extracted a grubby leather pouch and a slender pipe from one pocket. A strange, pungent smell emanated from the pouch and Seth eyed it warily. "The master said you weren't the sharpest blade in the scabbard," the swordsman sneered, "but there's no fooling you, is there?"

Seth watched, fascinated, as the swordsman took out a few pinches of a crumbly, plum-colored leaf from his pouch and tamped them down into the bowl of the pipe. "Get me a light," he said, more command than request. Seth did as he was told, already in awe of this hulking fellow. He took a taper from a box on the mantel and lit it from the fire. He handed it to Varth, who touched it to the pipe. A gentle wisp of purple smoke wreathed up from the bowl. Varth took a pull and savored the aroma, leaning back against the headboard.

"You're right," he said flatly, "it is silver."

Seth pursed his lips. "What use is a knife made of silver? It'll never hold an edge."

"No, but you'll feel one right enough if you don't shut up. Just listen."

Seth cowered back against the window, trying not to breathe in the peculiar smoke streaming from Varth's nostrils. The man stared hard at him for a few seconds, but Seth held his peace.

"Better," Varth approved mockingly. "That knife there has a very special purpose. It's not for killing—leastways, not like a proper knife. It's for catching them damned witches the King likes so much. You know, *Artesans*."

Varth said the word as if he was describing something foul, and he spat on the floor after he said it. Seth frowned and opened his mouth, but then thought better of it. Varth grinned and eyed him slyly. "You know one of them, don't you?"

Seth replied warily. "Sort of. Taran, the mistress's lover. Is that who you're after?"

"Me?" The swordsman snorted and pulled on the pipe. "Who said I was after anyone? Master gave you the knife, didn't he?"

Seth yelped, aghast. "The master wants *me* to do it? How am I supposed to do that? The man doesn't even like me. How can I get close enough to catch him? And how is that little knife supposed to help, anyway?"

Blowing a cloud of drowsy smoke, Varth chuckled, a throaty and unpleasant sound. Seth had heard it before, many times during the night, usually right before being instructed to do something he wasn't at all keen on. The same seemed to apply now.

"Oh, don't look so pained, mate. You've no need to worry. I'll be right behind you. The master knows you're no use at this sort of thing. You're only the decoy."

Seth breathed a sigh of relief even as he felt slighted by his master's casual assessment. He had killed Alice, hadn't he? Clumsily, maybe, but he had still done it. Although, he reflected, Taran would be an altogether different proposition, because Artesans had powers he knew little of, and they could call others of their kind when they were in danger. His eyes strayed to the silver knife in his hand.

"So where does this come in?"

Varth blew a stream of smoke toward him and Seth gagged. It smelled odd and it made his head spin. He didn't like to think what it was doing to Varth's lungs.

"That little beauty is the secret to killing their powers," Varth said slowly. "It's made of special stuff—stuff that makes them helpless. They can't use their witchery when one of these is stuck in them, and it also weakens their muscles and makes them sick. All you need to do is get close enough to stick him with it, and then I'll come up behind him and clobber him. That way, he can't call out to any of his mates."

"And then what?"

"You can leave that bit to me. You'll just wait for your next job."

"When are we going to do this? And where?"

Varth's lazy smile was already getting on Seth's nerves. It was both patronizing and possessive, and it made Seth very uncomfortable. The Baron's other servant, the one he thought of as the vagrant, was every bit as infuriating and dismissive, but at least he never had that lustful gleam of domination in his eyes. Of course, reflected Seth, he hadn't entered into a physical relationship with the vagrant. That one's tastes had run along more conventional lines, although the memory of what he had suggested in the brothel still chilled Seth's spine. Varth seemed to consider Seth his personal property and the manservant was beginning to fear he might regret giving in to his lonely desires and allowing the liberties he had permitted the man last night.

It was too late to worry over that now. They had a task to complete and it was one Seth didn't find too distasteful. Risky, maybe, but certainly not distasteful. He might even welcome the opportunity to watch Taran's fear when he realized who had worked his downfall. And his removal would mean one less obstacle to hinder the return of his master.

But Varth still hadn't answered his question.

The swordsman had been watching the play of emotions across Seth's face from within his wreath of smoke. His smile widened. "You're getting a taste for this."

Seth bridled and replied archly. "I'll do anything to further the causes of my master. But I need to know what you have planned."

"Oh, I'm not doing any planning." Varth chuckled. "That's your job, mate. I'm just the muscle, you're the brains."

Seth was about to snap a retort when he heard what Varth had said. He knew enough from his brief association with the vagrant to realize these men had little of their own thought processes left. They only said what the Baron put into their minds. Varth wasn't being sarcastic for once; he meant it. That left Seth with a problem.

"He didn't give you any specific instructions, then?"

Varth shook his head, his greasy hair falling in his eyes. "Only to take him alive and mainly unhurt. As soon as possible."

Seth frowned. "That doesn't help me much. Taran is the King's court Artesan. He works in the castle during the day. He used to visit the mistress some evenings, but mostly he would stay at the castle. He's only free when Colonel Sullyan's on her tour of duty, which she isn't right now. Although with the city shut down and the King's Guard up in arms over the murder of Neremiah and the company in Loxton Forest, who knows what's happening up there? How on earth are we going to lure Taran out where no one can see us?"

"Your problem, mate," muttered Varth, stretching out atop the bed once more, still unashamedly naked. He drew strongly on his pipe and closed his eyes. Seth watched him in annoyance, his stomach churning from the reek of the thickening purple smoke. The swordsman's voice crawled out from the haze. "Doesn't he have anywhere else to go?"

"What do you mean?"

"Well, he doesn't live at the castle, does he? He must have his own place."

"No, he doesn't, not really," said Seth, "not since the mansion burned down." He was silent for a while, thinking. Then he brightened. "Matty!"

Varth opened bleary eyes. "What?"

The beginnings of a plan were forming in Seth's mind. "Matty," he repeated, "the young lad who looks after the mistress's horses. If I could get him to send a message to the castle, Taran might come and speak to him. He wouldn't come for me. I … upset him last time we met."

"And why would he want to speak to the young lad?" asked Varth.

Seth shrugged. "He likes Matty. The boy must be wondering about his job, and what's going to happen to the horses. He had to find temporary stabling for them. If I were to suggest he ought to ask Taran about them, he might just send him a message. Especially if I offer to take it to the castle."

Varth sat up, swirls of smoke curling about his head. Seth wondered why his eyes weren't watering in the acrid haze. "Where do we find this boy?"

"He'll probably either be at what's left of the mansion stables or at his father's house in the village."

Varth stood up and began pulling on his breeches. "What are you waiting for?" he growled.

✤ ✤ ✤ ✤ ✤

Bull stood silently in the entrance to the cellar holding the pharmacy records, watching as Rienne pored over an enormous book propped open on the table. Her back was to him and she was bent low over the pages, her curtain of lustrous hair flowing down her back. She was sitting on a tall stool, her chin cupped in one hand, the other holding the aging parchment flat. The book she had opened was a collection of single parchment sheets loosely bound with gut, and it was fragile.

Rienne reached the end of her parchment and gently turned over the sheet. The writings were old and often illegible; many of the inks used had been crudely made from plant extracts and were subject to fading. It was often a punishment detail for unruly cadets to be sent to this room to laboriously copy out, under the watchful eyes of their sergeants, the less well-preserved medical texts. Bull smiled in memory. He had dealt out some of those punishments himself.

Rienne reached for a quill and made a note on the fresh sheet she had at her elbow. There were few such notes on its surface.

She had not yet found what she was looking for. He frowned, remembering Sullyan's graphic description of the poison's symptoms. The nursemaid's death had been a deliberate and brutal act. No one deserved to die like that, and least of all someone whose only crime had been to see too much. Bull's heart filled with anger at the thought of Bessie's agonized death throes.

"What do you want, Bull?"

The big man pulled himself from his thoughts and stared at Rienne's back. She had not shifted her position nor turned her head, yet she had sensed him. He grinned with genuine pleasure despite the gnawing fear in the pit of his stomach.

"My, you are growing skillful," he marveled, stepping into the room. "I was shielded, too."

He came to her side and Rienne straightened her back, turning sober eyes to his face. The smile she gave only just moved her lips and was gone in a moment. "I can't claim any credit for it. It was your breathing that gave you away, not any innate skill."

Bull's heart fell at her weary tone. During the three years she had been at the Manor, he had grown close to Rienne, as close as a man and woman could get without actually being lovers. The big man had felt drawn to her from the first, eliciting a mildly jealous reaction from Cal until he realized Bull would never trespass on their relationship. A confirmed bachelor wedded to his profession, Bull had come to think of Rienne almost as a younger sister, and Rienne returned his love with the freedom that came from knowing she never had to watch her step.

Bull did sometimes visit the women in the nearest village, taking advantage of those who were more than happy to accommodate the King's men for gold, but he would never take advantage of her. She could talk to Bull on any subject and trust in his total discretion. In his turn, Bull confided in Rienne, and their bond was deep and unbreakable. Rienne had told him she didn't know and couldn't imagine what she would do without him were he to be killed in combat or succumb to his ailing heart. This loving dependency was the only reason she had given in to his recent confidential request.

Now, seeing her careworn face and weary aspect, Bull stepped closer and gathered her into his arms, hoping to ease the burden on her soul. She leaned into his embrace, but didn't allow her emotions free rein. She had work to do.

She pushed him away and gazed up into his eyes. "Have you run out again?" He nodded and she pursed her lips. "Then you're taking too much. I warned you about that. When are you going to tell her, Bull? You know I hate deceiving her like this."

Bull dropped his gaze and moved away from the table. He walked around the room, glancing at the shelves of records and parchments, unable to meet her serious expression. "I can't tell her right now, can I? Not with Robin … Maybe when all this is sorted out. When things are back to normal."

Rienne ran a hand over her face. "You really ought to ease up on the training. It's not helping. I've told you that before."

"Yes, dear heart, I know you have. And I've done my best, truly I have. But if I stop, it'll be noticed, won't it? Someone will tell her and then I'll really be in the shi—Oh, sorry. Look, I've slowed down, it's the best I can do. I supervise the cadets. That way I can step in and correct them, and then step away again. I don't have to do a full session. But if I gave up weapons training altogether, I'd have to tell her why, wouldn't I?"

Rienne sighed in exasperation. "As opposed to *me* explaining to her why you've collapsed because your heart stopped beating. Only you won't have to worry about that, will you, because you'll be dead!"

Bull ceased his pacing and stared at her teary eyes. "Oh, Rienne love, I'm so sorry. I do know how hard this is for you, believe me. I've lost loved ones, too. But look at it from my point of view. I've been doing this for more years than I care to remember, first as a young lad, a member of the Lord's household, and then under Blaine's command. If it hadn't been for Sully's appearance at the Manor and her willingness to keep me on, Blaine would have pensioned me off long ago. I tell you, Rienne—and I mean this—I wouldn't be alive now if he had. I'd be dead of boredom, if not alcohol poisoning. It's my life, dear heart. It's all I've ever known and all I've ever wanted. And if I did drop down dead in the middle of a practice session—or better still, in the middle of a bloody good fight—it would be the best way I could think of to go. Hard on those who love me, maybe, but the best way for me. Sullyan understands that. Can't you?"

"Of course I *understand*, you great ox!" Rienne fought her tears. "I just don't want to see it happen. There's too much sorrow about right now. I can't cope with the weight of it. I get everyone's fears, you know—I can't shut them out. And having to lie to Brynne about supplying you with drugs to strengthen your heart is not helping. I don't like it and I don't want to do it."

Bull stepped in close and took hold of Rienne's shoulders. Her huge eyes still brimmed with unshed tears and he could see she was fighting her fear as well as her sorrow. He had never before truly appreciated how hard it must be to be an empath. He looked intently into those shimmering pools and smiled for her, gently and with love.

"Oh, dear heart! You are the rock on which we all depend, do you know that? You keep us all sane and our feet firmly on the ground, and you get precious little back except gratitude. We sometimes forget how sensitive you are to all these emotions, but we never take you for granted. You know that, don't you? Anytime you feel you want to be shielded from us, you only have to say. Any one of us could give you a respite from the constant bombardment you must get from us. Hasn't Sully been able to teach you any shielding?"

"A little," she replied. "Mostly, I can cope with it. It's only at times like these that it overwhelms me. I'm sure that's part of why Brynne asked me to search these records out. She knows how peaceful it is down here."

"Have you had any luck?" Releasing her shoulders, he turned to peruse the parchment she was reading.

She shook her head, dark hair rippling. "Not really. I've found substances that can cause some of the symptoms, but not one that includes them all. It may have been a mixture of herbs. We'll probably never know. Has anyone spoken to Lord Levant yet? Maybe he could help with the puzzle."

"Not as far as I know. I expect he's still pretty weak. Next time I speak to Blaine, I'll ask him. Anything we can learn would be helpful, although I'm sure the poor sod would probably rather forget it. It sounded horrendous.

"Now, do you want me to give you a hand until Hanan's free? I suppose it won't hurt me to spend a little time on my backside, although I don't want you accusing me of getting fat and lazy."

His easy manner and solid presence broke the back of Rienne's dark mood and she smiled, her youthful face lightening, the lines under her eyes smoothing. "Thank you, Bull, I'd appreciate it." She laid her hand on his forearm. "When Hanan comes to relieve us, walk with me to my office. I've some more of that medication you can have, although I'm altering the dose."

Trying to conceal the rush of relief her words sent through him, Bull pulled over another stool and perched beside her, taking the pile of dusty parchments she indicated and scanning their contents.

Chapter Sixteen

Aeyron sat stunned once Sullyan fell silent. His yellow eyes were unfocused and blank, his face pale and pinched. Sullyan shared an anxious look with Pharikian, but neither of them spoke. Jay'el had tactfully removed himself to the other side of the room and sat unnoticed, a cold cup of fellan in his hands. The atmosphere was tense and strained.

"I cannot believe you didn't tell me."

Aeyron's voice was low and full of confusion, his usual pleasant baritone colored by pain. Sullyan closed her eyes against the rush of chagrin she felt.

"Didn't you think it important enough? Or was it that you didn't trust me to handle it?"

The hurt in his voice brought Sullyan to her knees beside the couch, her hands on his arms. "Oh, my brother, can you not understand? Why would I cause you pain for no good reason? We had no proof at first, only vague suspicions. We still have no proof, but now I am sure. All the clues point to him, and this latest attack on Robin ..."

She could not go on. Aeyron looked at his father and saw the censure in his eyes. The Prince colored. He should not berate her for doing what she thought was right, especially in the light of what had happened. He sighed.

"I'm sorry, Brynne, I'm reacting badly. I should have known you had your reasons. I ought to trust you by now."

She stared up into his pale face. "Maybe I should have told you before, but I had to tell you now. You could be in the gravest danger, Aeyron. You must look to your security. You must never go about without a guard, preferably one who is also an Artesan. The Baron is obviously intent on exacting revenge from all who spoke against him, and it was you and I who ultimately sealed his fate. I implore you, do not dismiss his threat merely because he is in Albia and you are here. That does not guarantee your safety. He has done things already for which we can find no immediate explanation, and it is my firm belief that he once again has access to metaphysical powers."

"We have sent for Gaslek," put in Pharikian. "Brynne thinks there's a possibility the Baron has learned to use his latent powers."

Aeyron frowned, taking Sullyan's hands to raise her. He drew her onto the couch beside him and refreshed her cup of fellan from the warming pot. His hands were trembling as much as hers. She guessed his earlier reaction was due as much to a resurgence of his old fear of the Baron as to anger.

Seeing she had noticed, he clasped his fingers tightly round his cup. "But is that likely? Whatever natural powers the Baron possessed would surely have atrophied after so long. He had spent his entire life trying to bury them. How would he ever accept them enough to allow them to surface? What are the chances of him suddenly learning to use them at all, let alone so effectively? It takes the best of us years of practice, and that's with the benefit of teaching."

"That's why we need Gaslek," said his father, before Sullyan could reply. "We need to know if there have been any other such cases, as they might give us an insight into what is possible. Brynne, was there anyone else on that island who might have had the relevant expertise?"

She shook her heard. "Not to my knowledge. If they had, they might have recognized Serrin's problem for what it was, and divined the root of the Baron's deep hatred."

Their heads turned at a light tap on the door and Maxin appeared, ushering in the plump, fussy Baron Gaslek. The little secretary bowed politely to Sullyan, his ringed hands clasping each other. As he straightened, he regarded the room's occupants quizzically through his spectacles.

"How may I help you, my Lords, my Lady?"

"Come and sit, Gaslek," Pharikian said. "Brynne has a question for you, one which might involve some research through the archives."

Sullyan could see Gaslek's interest engage even as he crossed the room to take a chair opposite her. Jay'el moved to serve the Baron with fellan, also refreshing Pharikian's cup. Gaslek nodded his thanks absently, his attention fixed on Sullyan's pale face.

"Ask your question, Highness."

Sullyan was disinclined to go over the entire story again, so she stuck to the matter at hand. "My Lord, have you any knowledge or memory of an instance when a person possessed of latent or repressed Artesan powers suddenly became able to access them? Effectively?"

Gaslek stared at her, but she could tell he did not see her face. His gaze was turned inward, his plump hands constantly twisting as he thought. His spectacles slid lower down his small nose and one hand came up automatically to push them back.

"You're talking about trauma, I take it?" he said eventually.

"Am I, my Lord? Then I was not aware of it. I do but shoot in the dark."

Gaslek spoke slowly. "I think I can recall one case, although I would want to confirm it from the records. I seem to remember reading about the son of a senior noble who never developed the talents he had been born with. His father tried everything he could think of to encourage his son's powers to emerge. He hired the greatest teachers, he offered him gifts, and even punished the lad. Yet nothing worked, and as he grew older they gave up, thinking his early show of power must have been a mistake and that the boy was ungifted after all. Later on, though, once he was grown, an extraordinary thing happened. I cannot recall the details, but he suffered some kind of life threatening trauma and the instinct for self-preservation caused his dormant powers to surface. He managed to save his own life."

Cold fingers trailed down Sullyan's spine, making her shiver. "And after that? Was he then able to function as an Artesan?"

Gaslek shrugged apologetically. "I will have to check the records if you want the full details. I can only recall what I have told you."

The Hierarch leaned forward. "I think that might be useful, Gaslek."

Sullyan guessed he had seen the look of anguish cross her face and knew she had hoped for another explanation. The vengeful Baron in possession of an Artesan's knowledge and power was not only a travesty; it was also a horrific prospect. What tortures might he inflict on the gifted if he had access to metaforce?

Pharikian dismissed Gaslek and the little secretary bowed as he left them. Sullyan didn't see him go. She was staring into Aeyron's fearful eyes, sharing his dreadful thoughts and memories. Why should their lives have been so blighted? Why could they not have been spared that terror? Yet had they not shared such desperate closeness while awaiting the world's end, they would never have bonded as tightly as they had. Such reflections did not help their current situation.

Pharikian stirred. "What will you do now, Brynne?"

She came out of her communion with Aeyron slowly, the

shadow of their shared memories etched across her face.

"I will await the Baron's confirmation," she said, looking for more fellan. Jay'el once again played the page and poured for them all. "If it is as he says, that trauma can unlock powers long buried, then I will need to make another visit to the island where Reen was held. Something happened to him there, something that drove Reen to murder his only friend. And if I am to counter his threat, I need to understand, as fully as possible, what now drives him and what he might be capable of."

She turned the full force of her gaze on her father, allowing him to see the depth of terror in her heart and read her innermost feelings. He understood that she feared she would be unable to prevail against the evil ranged against her. She had already challenged and triumphed against incredible odds over the powerful renegade Lord Rykan. She had thwarted the Baron's plans to destroy the Veils and with them the world. She had rescued Aeyron and saved his life. She had returned Prince Eadan to his father, thereby averting a full-scale realm war. She had even given birth to her son when she had thought herself barren. How much more could one Artesan woman accomplish? Surely the reserves of her luck had run dry. Surely this time she would have to concede defeat. If she did, she would lose the mate of her soul, one half of her heart. And it would kill her.

※ ※ ※ ※ ※

King Lerric roused reluctantly that morning. His chamberlain even had to enter his bedchamber in order to wake him. He permitted his servant to help him wash and dress, but had no appetite for the laden breakfast tray. He bade the man leave him and sat nursing a cup of hot fellan, staring out of the window at the flurries of snow swirling past. He had not slept much after hearing the awful noises coming from his daughter's chamber late last night. Evil dreams had dogged his sleep and now he felt old and fearful. It was cowardly, he realized that. He ought to go to his daughter and comfort her, but his heart quailed at the thought that *he* might be there. He didn't have the strength to face the scarecrow this morning, not now the dreadful creature had what he wanted.

By mid-morning, Lerric still had not heard movement within the castle. The king had already guessed the Baron had taken control of his small force of swordsmen. He had fully expected it, but he had no idea how totally enthralled they were. He imagined Sofira had ordered Bassan to obey the Baron. He had no idea that, in fact, Bassan was the only one *not* chained mind and soul to the terrible creature.

Eventually, gathering his courage like a tattered cloak, Lerric prepared to leave his rooms. He could not stay here forever, and he needed to know exactly what the situation was. There might just be a possibility of sending the letter he had written in desperation after Elias had left the palace. If what he feared should come to pass, Elias should at least know Lerric had not deceived him willingly—not once he knew for certain what Reen was planning, anyway.

Lerric sneered at himself. Who was he trying to fool? He had known from the start Reen had revenge on his mind. He had not fallen for the creature's speeches about justice for Sofira and her children. He had had plenty of opportunity back then, when the creature was still weak, to back away from him, to inform the King and put a stop to this madman's schemes. Yet he had let Sofira dissuade him, had been blinded by her love, her despair, and her trust in him.

Ah, you cowardly, craven, toothless old dog! he thought. *Why could you not have been stronger? Why could you not have ruled her? She betrayed her own husband and King, after all. She committed treason. No one forced her to do that. She made her own decisions and paid the price. You should have left it at that!*

But he hadn't. He had never been able to rule Sofira, not since her mother died when she was just eleven years old. Now they were all paying the price. A price he feared would cost them more than everything they had.

He left his rooms, emerging into a chilly hallway. He heard nothing from Sofira's rooms, but there were faint sounds coming from the floor below. He strained his ears. It sounded like hammering. Frowning, wondering what new mischief this was, he made his way to the stairwell and descended to the second floor.

There were no servants about and the fires had already been tended. Instead of flaring brightly to warm the cold stone walls, they were banked low, barely alight. Lerric shivered, and not just from the cold. He wrapped his velvet overrobe tighter about his body and moved closer to the sounds.

They came from his throne room. The hallway leading to it already had its windows boarded up, with heavy dark drapes pulled over the wooden slats. The palace was gloomy, cold, and unwelcoming. Lerric advanced reluctantly through the anteroom and toward the entrance to the throne room itself.

He pushed the door open slowly and peered into the shadowy depths, just able to make out four of his erstwhile guards as they nailed the final slats over the last window. The vast room was shrouded in darkness, relieved only by the light of a single lamp trimmed low. Lerric stepped into the room, looking about in consternation.

"What the Void do you think you're doing?"

The four men took no notice.

"What's the matter, Lerric? Don't you approve of my alterations?"

An icy shiver trailed down Lerric's spine. His breath clogged in his throat. He spun around, his eyes sufficiently accustomed to the gloom to pick out the scarecrow figure standing right behind him. The creature's closeness startled Lerric; he had not heard its approach. The dull ruby glow deep within its ruined eyes was blatant and baleful.

"What's the meaning of this?" blustered Lerric, surprising himself with the strength of his voice. Its lack of tremor pleased him. He waved a hand at the obscured windows, allowing his indignation to show.

The scarecrow grinned horribly, showing decaying teeth. "Do you wish to register a complaint?" it sneered in a wheezing voice. "Go right ahead. But I don't know who will listen to you."

"This is *my* palace, Reen! Who gave you the right to do this?"

The dreadful skull thrust close to Lerric's face, spittle striking his cheek as it hissed, "Oh, but I am master here now, *your Majesty*. Do you doubt it?"

Lerric stared in horror. The terrible screams from last night came back to haunt him, and his imagination ran wild, showing him all sorts of dreadful possibilities. His control snapped.

"What have you done to her, you dreadful creature? And what do you want with those two poor wretches you paraded last night? That girl was terrified! Let her go, Reen, I command it. And the other is one of Elias's senior officers! You know what will happen if you harm him. You'll bring the wrath of the High King and all his forces down upon our heads. Is that what you want? Are you insane?"

"You *command* it?" repeated the scarecrow, ruby eyes flaring. "You have no right of command anymore, you spineless coward. Do you think your pathetic band of peasants will protect you? Think again! They are mine, as is all that you once owned. You don't believe me? Call for help and see what you get. Go on, Lerric. Try it."

Lerric opened his mouth to do just that, but he knew it was futile. He was helpless within a prison of his own making. He stared hopelessly into the blazing red eyes of the scarecrow, the creature he had given his daughter to, the creature who had lain with her, taken possession of her, and who was now taking possession of everything else. Lerric had handed it to him on a plate. He buried his face in his hands.

Through his despair, he heard the sound of laughter. His head snapped up. It was not the scarecrow gloating over his abject surrender—it was Sofira.

She appeared at the shoulder of her travesty of a husband, laughing in the face of her father's dejection. Horrified to the depths of his soul by the menace in her laughter, he fixed her with a desperate pleading gaze—only to see the same ruby glow glinting deep within her eyes. He stumbled backward as if struck by a blow. Sofira fell silent.

"All is now mine," came the scarecrow's venomous hiss. "Mine to do with as I will. Mine to enjoy at my leisure. You ask me what I intend, you miserable excuse for a king? You warn me against the wrath of Elias? Well, I laugh in the face of your craven fears. Do you think I fear Elias when I hold the key to mastery over him and his most powerful allies? What do you *think* I want with my two captives? What did you *think* I wanted with your heartless, brittle daughter? Did you think I had fallen for her sharp-edged charms? Did you think me enamored of the hard angles of her body? Oh no, Lerric, her body holds no attraction for me. Do not mistake me, King of Bordenn. She is mine by marriage and by right. I have taken care to consummate our union, distasteful though it was. And in so doing, I have gained control over her mind, such as it is. Do you wish me to prove it?"

Lerric listened in growing despair to the creature, unable to tear his eyes from the red glow that flared from its ruined mess of a face. He was scarcely able to credit what he was hearing. How could the creature possibly control Sofira? But if he could not, how could she stand so still and fearless in the presence of such a monster? Why was she not running in terror from the leprous aspect of the creature she had wed?

Lerric soon got his answer. At a gesture from the creature's hand, Sofira stepped close to her father and wrapped her arms tightly about him. Lerric was taken by surprise and did not move as she pinned his arms to his sides. But the passionate kiss she forced upon his lips broke his stasis and flooded him with horror. This was not the chaste touch of a daughter's lips, but the lascivious kiss of a whore, and her hands were suddenly exploring his body, causing him to shudder in revulsion.

He let loose a cry of disgust and thrust her away. She stood where he had pushed her, her face devoid of expression, her arms hanging slack. Lerric, panting in horror, turned his head deliberately toward the grinning scarecrow.

"Come on, then, Lerric," taunted the creature, "show me you're not the coward I know you to be. Show me you're a man, not a feeble lackey of Elias. Here I am, unarmed and defenseless. Use your anger. Do what you know you should have done months ago. Take control and kill me."

Lerric roared in rage and flew at the scarecrow, grasping fingers extended to gouge at his face, claw for the vein in his neck. Reen watched him come and did not move, eyes flaring to blinding scarlet, mouth open in eager anticipation.

Lerric's hands closed about the creature's throat and he screamed in triumph. He tightened his fingers, digging deeply into the desiccated skin, feeling the heart pound and the tendons strain. He heard the creature's gasps even through the tumult of bloodlust in his overheated brain.

Yet they were not gasps of panic or breathlessness.

A white-hot needle of fire shot into Lerric's arms and he jerked back with a cry. He tried to loosen his hands, to release the scrawny throat, but could not. He shrieked as yet another stab of fire shot through his body, and struggled to flee. Although the creature had not touched him, he could not release his grip. He was held in a pincer of fire and it burned through his soul, charring his heart and blasting its way to his brain.

"Do you understand now, Lerric?" the scarecrow drawled. "Do you see why I have no fear? Your anger is a balm to my soul and your baser desires feed my body. I am your master now, as I am your daughter's, as I will be to all my enemies. I will suck them dry and become ever stronger. Those two confined below are only the start. They will provide me with the means to lure others, those I most wish to destroy. The girl may be useful for a while yet, but the Major, that very handsome young man with the body and the strength I desire, will be the final step toward achieving my goal. He possesses the knowledge that will gain me the prize.

"But you will not see my triumph, Lerric. You will not be here when my enemy is brought to her knees. You will not see her beg me for mercy, beg me for death, and you will not see me take my ultimate revenge as she gives me, freely and of her own will, those arcane powers that have so blighted my life. You will not be here when she realizes, at the last moment, that even her willing sacrifice will not save her—will not save *him*—and will not save her world.

"No, Lerric. You will not be here."

Lerric's hands suddenly came free of the dried, livid flesh and he fell heavily to the ground. All of his strength was gone, the fight sucked out of him by the leech who exulted in his stolen strength. Lerric lay crumpled at his feet, gazing in despair at the unmoving figure of his daughter, knowing his end was near. He mouthed an apology, tears trailing from the corners of his eyes, but there was no response. Her face was impassive, as if she didn't even know he was there.

The scarecrow lifted his cane, the cane he scarcely seemed to need. Lerric stared in disbelief as its tip glowed dull red. His eyes followed it as it hovered over his laboring heart. His breath turned to ice in his chest.

✢ ✢ ✢ ✢ ✢

Reen smiled as he brought the cane down. Lerric didn't even have the strength to scream, but his spirit writhed in agony in the grip of Reen's power, wailing its horror into the Void. The scarecrow watched the light of life fade from Lerric's eyes and felt new strength flood into his being. He laughed. If only his victims realized how much strength they actually possessed, he would stand very little chance of overwhelming them. If they only used their fear instead of giving in to it, they could throw him off easily. But they never realized. They never knew how vulnerable he was until it was too late. And he understood the power of terror only too well. Provided he tapped into their deepest fears before he attempted to enter them, he was safe.

He removed the cane from Lerric's blasted body and glanced over his shoulder at the four swordsmen who had not moved throughout the entire episode.

"Remove this," he said, nudging the body with his foot, "and then get on with the rest of it. I want it completed by nightfall. Come, Sofira."

He turned on his heel, the Princess by his side, the red glow fading from the depths of her eyes.

Chapter Seventeen

Taran and Col took their time over the ride to the mansion as Taran's leg was still sore and Bucyrus's flanks were not fully healed. Col didn't have much in the way of his usual energy, so the slow pace suited him too.

They gained an impression of the city's mood as they passed through the streets and heard the disgruntled mutterings and saw the nervous unrest of the populace.

"You would think that having the military on heightened alert and ready to deal with any situation would be comforting, wouldn't you?" Taran commented as they passed yet another group of ladies out with armed escorts. He was growing tired of the suspicious looks and behind-hand comments his Artesan's rank badge and Col's military insignia elicited.

"Not with the city shut down," the young swordsman said. "Reminds them too much of the civil war, I reckon. I've heard it said that Loxton nearly went under during that time. The port was closed due to worries about invasion by sea, and trade was at a standstill. The King was away with his forces, and without his authority, the city constables couldn't keep the peace. Looting was rife and the streets weren't safe. No one who traveled the forest went with less than ten armed guards. More, if they were bringing in supplies. People don't want to see that sort of thing happen again."

Taran could believe it. "But we're not in wartime. All of this is for their protection as well as the King's."

Col shrugged. "Makes them nervous, though. Can't say I blame them."

They passed through the north gate with no problem, recognized by the guards there. They completed the rest of the ride in silence. When they arrived at their destination and sat staring at the ruined house, Taran realized the wind was increasing. It smelled of snow. He and Col huddled into their fleece-lined jackets and turned up the hoods of their cloaks. The horses laid their ears back as the wind whipped their manes and tails. Taran glanced sourly at the sky, sensing a winter storm approaching. He would have preferred a still day for what he planned to do, but the weather would only be a slight inconvenience; it would not hinder his Artesan senses.

They sat their mounts with their backs to the wind and surveyed the devastation. Col whistled through his teeth. "Must have been terrifying," he murmured, taking in the broken and blackened timbers, the soot-stained stone walls.

The two corpses, what the fire had left of them, had been removed. Alice had no family anyone knew of; her remains were buried in the garden nearby. The bones of the other woman had been interred with no ceremony at an unmarked spot on the estate, as no one had any idea who she was. Enquiries in the city had turned up no missing women. The building itself had not been touched. The weather was too bad to attempt any clearing, and there was nothing left to salvage. No one wanted to waste time and energy in the freezing cold when there were more important things to do.

Taran and Col dismounted, and Col took the horses into the stables. Taran surmised that Matty had been back at some time. The stables had been cleaned out and all was left tidy. He appreciated the lad's diligence and realized he must be concerned for his livelihood, as must all the mansion servants. Taran knew he ought to make some arrangements for them soon, at least help them find other positions. That's what Jinny would have wanted. Yet he had a more pressing concern this morning, and it flooded his soul as he stood and stared at what was left of Jinny's home and his hopes for the future.

Col gave him space, recognizing the weight of sorrow and confusion burdening his heart. In truth, Taran hardly knew what to think. Mostly, he believed Jinny was dead and that the fire and the mysterious corpse were a callous and deliberate charade intended to divert attention from the killer—rather like the planting of the Minster's offertory chest in the master mason's workshop after the murder of Neremiah. Yet part of him desperately wanted to believe she was still alive, that she had been taken for some unknown purpose and that there was a chance he could get her back. The letter he had found in her silver box relieved him of one burden: the fear she had taken her own life and died hating him. Yet even if she had forgiven him, he could not yet forgive himself.

Steeling himself for the task at hand, Taran approached the ruins of the mansion and picked his way once again through the charred and tumbled timbers. He shut out all outside influences; the chill of the wind, the moan as it blew through the derelict house, the presence of Col standing watch by the stables. He reached within for his psyche, pleased to find his energy levels back to normal after his exhausting search the night before. That was one of the advantages of linking with another Artesan: recovery times were usually shorter. He wrapped himself in the complex layers of the incredibly beautiful pattern and sifted out his memories of Jinny.

In the absence of a recognizable imprint for her, he used his inner perceptions. The way she felt under his hands, the way she smelled, the way she tasted, the sound of her voice, and the many different ways in which she expressed her inner nature. All these things were personal and unique and combined to form an essence of the blonde woman. Taran fixed this in his mind in place of a psyche and then cast it about, searching for signs of her in the substrate.

He succeeded almost immediately. He was in the vicinity of her chamber, albeit a floor below. Much of the debris here had fallen from her rooms, and the sense of her presence was clear. The one thing that hit Taran strongest about the aura of his love was the fear she had felt. The stronger emotions—terror, love, passion, pain—left the deepest impressions, and it was no surprise he should find them here. The fact that he sensed her fear the strongest only fueled his efforts to find out more.

Yet try as he might he could pick up nothing else. He remembered Sullyan's strange comment—*this whole place reeks of evil*—but could find no evidence of why she had said it. He wished he had paid more attention at the time and sampled its texture for himself, but he had not. Now he didn't know what to look for, and all he could sense was Jinny's overriding terror. He cast about in wider and wider circles, but had no more luck.

His meanderings brought him to the kitchens, where he received a shock. The emanations of terror in this part of the house were overwhelming, forcing him to retreat. The sensations were jumbled and confused, and he was convinced they came from more than one person, but he was not skilled enough to be sure. This, of course, was where Alice had died, so he should not be too surprised to find residues of intense emotions lingering here.

Full of sorrow and aching in his soul, Taran let go of his working and returned to the normal world. He shook his head to clear it of the clinging echoes of screams and struggling, and looked about for Col. He saw the young swordsman standing just inside the stables, arms wrapped about his chest under the folds of his cloak, trying to keep out of the wind.

"I'm going to have to widen the search," Taran shouted to him. "I've had some success here, but I've still not found what I sensed last night. I'm going to walk the surrounding area and try to pick it up. It'll be a bit boring for you, I'm afraid. Do you want to wait here for me? Be a bit warmer."

"Better not," replied Col, trying not to shiver. "Captain said not to let you out of my sight and he'll have my hide if I do. A bit of exercise might warm me up. Come on, let's get on with it. I've given the horses a bit of hay. They'll be fine for a while."

Taran grinned gratefully and cast around, trying to decide which way to go first. He pictured the scene as it must have been when whoever had done this left the scene. The house had been set alight, but the servants' wing was still safe. If he had been the perpetrator and wanted to get away without being seen, which way would he go? It would have been dark, so that would have provided some cover, but he still wouldn't care to pass too close to the servants' wing. If he went to the right he would be heading for the village, where people might be stirring if they saw the flames. Left, then, out into the fields.

He started off, Col trailing, and once again wrapped himself in the complex swirls of his psyche, hunting for that strange impression in the milky shimmer of the Veils.

✢ ✢ ✢ ✢ ✢

Seth and Varth strode through the city, unremarked by the townsfolk. Seth was nervous about going out so openly, but as Varth had said, they were more likely to attract unwanted attention if they tried to sneak. What could be more natural than for Seth to have a bodyguard? He only had to act as if he had every right to be there, and no one would ask questions.

The hulking swordsman was right. The townsfolk kept to themselves and the two men went unnoticed and unchallenged. They made for the northern gate. Here, Seth suffered another pang of uncertainty. What would he tell the guards? How would they get past them? Varth stared at him as if he were an imbecile.

"Who's got more right to visit the estate than you?" he growled. "Used to work there, didn't you? Concerned for your fellow servants, aren't you? Come on, man, show some backbone! Don't you know the biggest giveaway is fear? You can get away with anything if you act confident. And you have my sword at your back. What better provider of confidence could there be?"

Varth's last statement was as two-edged as his sword and Seth wasn't sure how he meant it. But he was right nonetheless, and Seth stiffened his spine as he approached the gate guards.

"State your business," one of them said, moving forward to block the way.

Seth looked him in the eye. "We're going up to the mansion. You know, the one that burned down."

The guard cocked an eyebrow at him. "And what do you want up there, me lad? Not much left, by all accounts."

"That's what we want to see," said Seth, improvising. "We want to know what the chances are it'll be salvaged. A lot of us lost our jobs that night and we need to know what the future holds."

"Servants there, were you?"

Seth nodded glumly. "Don't suppose I'll get another job like it if it's gone for good. Most of the others stayed on the estate and we need to talk to them. Time we decided what we're going to do."

The guard stood aside and nodded to his fellow. "Good luck to you, mates." They heaved the gate open and Seth passed through, his bodyguard following. As the gate rumbled closed behind them, they heard the guard call, "You'll have company up there this morning. The place is popular today."

Seth turned to ask what the fellow meant, but Varth's expression forestalled him. "Just wave and walk on," he growled. "Don't push your luck."

Seth did as he was told and they held their peace until the guards were out of earshot. "What do you suppose he meant by that?" said Seth.

"That someone else has gone up there today," snapped Varth. "What do you think?"

"Yes, but who could it be?" returned Seth, ignoring his companion's sneer. "What would anyone else want up there?"

Varth shrugged. "Who knows? At least we've been warned. Don't forget you've got a perfectly good reason for coming here. Don't act guilty if we're seen. Just go looking for this Matty fellow and don't get sidetracked."

* * * * *

Baron Gaslek looked up as Sullyan appeared in the archives doorway. He had a bundle of old parchments laid on the table before him and when Sullyan offered her help sorting through them, he gladly accepted.

They kept a companionable silence as they perused the parchments, Gaslek occasionally reaching up to reposition his spectacles. His small nose was not an ideal platform for the heavy lenses. After half an hour had passed, Gaslek stiffened and plucked a parchment from his pile.

"Ah, Highness, here it is," he exclaimed, putting it flat on the table where they could both read it. And there it was indeed. The secretary's memory had not played him false; the events had happened just as he described them. A very young boy, born to a senior noble's family in the mountainous northern region of Morvaigne, had shown early promise of strong Artesan powers which failed to materialize. No matter what inducements or punishments were offered, he seemed incapable of accessing what they were sure he possessed. As time passed, his parents gave up trying and accepted their son would never realize the potential he had shown.

In his early adulthood, however, he suffered an accident. The young noble had become separated from his companions during a routine tour of his father's lands. A freak blizzard triggered an avalanche which swept down the mountainside, engulfing the company. Some were never found, but the young noble was one of the lucky ones. He was discovered some days later, wedged in a crevasse and badly injured. By the time the rescue party recovered him, they expected to find a corpse. Yet the youth had survived, and had even managed to stem the flow of blood from a partially severed arm and remain coherent due to the miraculous awakening of his innate powers. It was decided the life-threatening trauma had unlocked these buried powers, which then developed in a natural way. The young man went on to inherit his father's lands, despite the loss of his arm.

Gaslek glanced at Sullyan. "Was that what you were hoping to find, Highness?"

She laid a hand on his arm in thanks. Hope was not what she was feeling, but she could not lay her troubles on him. Once again he had helped her, and his willingness to put himself out for her touched her heart.

"I thank you for your time, my Lord," she said. "Your help has been invaluable, as always. If there is ever anything I may do to repay you, you only have to ask."

Gaslek ducked his head. "I am only too pleased to be of assistance, Highness."

She left him then, returning to the Hierarch's rooms where she found her father, brother, and Jay'el deep in discussion concerning

Aeyron's forthcoming visit to his betrothed, Lirina. Maxin had just deposited a tray of food on the table and Sullyan realized it must nearly be noon. She had to move quickly if she was to progress with her investigations this day. Every day she delayed in her rescue of Robin was another day of heartache for her and who knew what torments for him.

Pharikian saw the fire of determination in her eyes. "I take it Gaslek was right?"

She nodded. "I do not know whether to feel relieved or more fearful, and I must now pay another visit to Cleric Patrio Ruvar. I just pray there will be some answers now that I know which questions to ask. Jay'el, are you ready?"

She would not stay to eat and they didn't try to force her. Words were useless at this time, but their support and their love were offered freely and she took what she needed. The look on Aeyron's face nearly turned her resolve, reminding her of the days immediately after their liberation from the Baron, when he feared his maimed right hand would reave him of his birthright. That had not happened, but the terror was still there, ingrained and buried deep. She flooded his mind with her love, trying to erase the pain behind his eyes, and he smiled for her.

"Call us if you need us," he told her as she took her leave.

She and Jay'el fairly ran for the courtyard, finding their mounts ready and waiting. Drum caught the urgency in his rider and bugled in his impatience to be gone. They mounted up and rode swiftly through the lower town, heading for the gates. Once out on the Plains, Sullyan lost no time in forging them a passage back through the Veils and into her own realm once more.

✤ ✤ ✤ ✤ ✤

Bull retired to his rooms once Rienne had given him the packet of fresh herbs. The relief he felt in having them went deeper than he liked to admit. He dared not contemplate what might happen if she refused to give him more. He had come to depend on their calming effects and didn't think he could function now without them. She had altered the dose and told him to stick to it, and this time he intended to obey. Apart from anything else, she knew exactly how much she had given him, and if he went back to her too soon she would know he had ignored her warnings. Her threat to withhold the drug was enough to bring him to heel.

He took his kettle and poured warmed water over fellan grounds. The familiar aroma wafted through his apartment, and he smiled. The scent of it always brought back memories of Sullyan's reaction when she first tasted fellan at the age of ten, here in this very room. His astonishment when she had not only taken to the brew but preferred it the way he made it still made him chuckle. She had fascinated and surprised him from the moment he had met her, and even after all these years she could still do it.

He sprinkled the prescribed amount of herbs into the fellan and gulped it down before the drug could affect the taste. The relief from the nagging pain was instant and Bull sighed contentedly. Apart from the ache in his chest and the slight breathlessness he felt if he exercised too hard, he was in great shape. He was nearly sixty years of age and there might be more gray than brown in his hair, but he was still agile and muscular, still able to teach those cocky young cadets a trick or two. And still useful to the love of his life, which was his main reason for cajoling Rienne into doing something behind Sullyan's back. It was a measure of Rienne's deep regard for him that she had allowed him to persuade her, for it went against everything she believed in.

Artesans were often able to detect falsehood, and Rienne, being an empath, had more trouble concealing deception than most. Add to that her special bond with Sullyan, which enabled the two of them to sense what the other was feeling, and you got a very good set of reasons why Rienne was reluctant. Bull knew he ought to be ashamed of himself for taking advantage of Rienne's love for him and putting her in that position. He would have to tell Sullyan soon, if only for Rienne's sake. But not just yet.

He was about to return to the training ground when the door to his rooms opened. To his amazement, Sullyan stood there. She would never normally burst in on him like this. General Blaine might frown upon his Artesans using their powers for casual communication, but it was rare for Sullyan not to notify Bull when she wanted him. Apart from anything else, it helped avoid those embarrassing situations that could occur if one was otherwise occupied.

Not that he ever was lately, he reflected regretfully. His days of dalliance were generally over. He had long since discovered that the women available to him—at a price—were not capable of comforting him as he wished to be comforted. Only one woman could do that, and she was not—and had never been—attainable.

He smiled at her, and then sobered immediately as he caught the urgency and turmoil of her thoughts. "What is it, Sully? Has something happened? Is it—?"

"Bulldog, I need your help. I have to return to the island where Reen was held and speak to the Cleric Patrio. There is a piece of the puzzle missing and I believe that he, or someone on the island, can supply it. I need the benefit of your experience. Can you be spared from your duties?"

"Of course," he said, ignoring the questions crowding his head. "If I don't turn up for training, Ramsy will take over. They won't miss me for one session."

He grabbed up the pack and cloak that were always ready by the door, thankful he had already taken Rienne's remedy. It should last him for some hours and enable him to function at full efficiency without Sullyan sensing anything amiss. If she sensed he was feeling under par, she would take someone else, and she had been doing that far too frequently lately for his liking. Being permanently relegated to the position of cadet nursemaid was not a role Bull relished, even if it was preferable to enforced retirement.

"Are we taking the horses?" he asked as he followed her out, throwing his fleece-lined cloak over his broad shoulders and letting his door swing shut behind him.

"No. I know my way now, so we will use the Veils. It would take too long otherwise and I am fearful about the time Robin may have left."

He heard the deep fear in her voice and sensed it in the aura of her psyche. The fact she was unable to shield it from him told him how strident and powerful it was. As a Senior Master, she was three full levels above his skill and he should have been unable to read her. His mouth set in a grim line, he strode silently at her shoulder as they traversed the maze of corridors in the Manor and emerged into the freezing teeth of a strengthening wind.

Chapter Eighteen

Taran moved out into the fields, scanning the substrate. He was getting tantalizing glimpses of Jinny's aura from all angles and it was hard to separate them. The snatches of her presence indicated he was on the right track and he constantly probed for that strange flavor he had tasted last night.

Col trailed him disinterestedly, unable to see what Taran saw. To his eyes, the Adept was ambling aimlessly across the estate. Yet the Manor swordsman followed faithfully, wondering how much longer Taran would keep them out in this wind.

The cloud cover had increased and the first few flakes of new snow were falling. Although it was only just past midday, the light was failing, blocked out by the heavy clouds overhead. Col hunched deeper into the fleece-lined hood of his cloak and shivered. Taran continued searching doggedly, slogging across the fields, occasionally wading through knee-high snow. He approached a small copse of trees near the boundary hedge, wondering whether whoever had taken Jinny had hidden here while they did whatever it was that produced the strange impression. He stopped abruptly, causing Col to lift his head suspiciously. But it was only Taran's frightened imagination pricking him with hideous images of what he might discover when he finally found the site of that anomaly. He had begun to fear that it might be Jinny's body he would find hidden among the trees. He tried to dispel the awful image and concentrate on the trail.

✤ ✤ ✤ ✤ ✤

Seth and Varth approached the mansion from the south, walking down the long driveway leading to the house's ornate front porch. Very little remained of the impressive entrance other than two soot-stained marble pillars and the burnt planks of the heavy, iron-studded door. Varth raised his brows, only just realizing how complete the destruction was. "Not much left, is there?"

Seth didn't reply. He was more concerned by the hoof prints in the snow; two sets, leading around to the back of the house. What he could see of the rear courtyard was empty, but the trampled snow spoke of earlier visitors. Despite Varth's easy assurance that he had every right to be here, Seth was nervous.

"I think we ought to take a look round the back," he said. "If Matty's here, he'll be in the stables. Someone's certainly been here, and very recently too. I wonder where they are."

Varth followed Seth as he made his way through the frozen snow to the rear of the house. The devastation looked worse from here, the ruins of the kitchens and servants' wing adding to the overall sense of destruction. Seth shivered as he looked once more at the collapsed kitchens. He could still hear Alice's muffled screams and see the terror in her eyes.

Varth moved to the stables and disappeared inside. Seth began to follow, but the other man quickly re-emerged, a grin on his face. "The two horses we've been following are in here. Looks like your stable boy's been back too. There's fresh straw and hay in the stalls."

Seth put his head round the doorway and sucked in a breath. He instantly recognized the fine blood bay stallion munching its way through a manger of hay, although the other horse was not familiar.

"Taran!" he breathed, turning to Varth. "The mistress's lover, the one the master wants. That's his horse."

"And the other?" asked Varth, a dim red gleam showing briefly behind his eyes.

Seth ignored it. "I don't know. Someone from the castle, maybe."

"So, where are they?" muttered Varth, scanning the immediate area. There was no sign of the stable boy or their quarry, so the swordsman turned his attention to the trampled snow. "One of them went into the ruins of the house," he murmured, "while the other waited here, out of the cold. But then … move yourself!" he barked when the manservant didn't shift quickly enough. "No, not that way, you idiot, that's the way they went. You'll mess up the tracks."

Seth jumped out of his companion's path and stared balefully at his back, wishing the Baron would employ servants with better manners. He was getting very tired of their constant condescension.

Varth followed the tracks out of the courtyard and toward the fields, his eyes flicking constantly from the ground to his surroundings, searching for his quarry. The frigid wind blew straight into their eyes, throwing stinging bits of ice against their faces.

"What's out there?" he demanded, indicating the fields.

"Nothing," Seth said sulkily. "Fields and trees. Nothing."

The swordsman grinned mirthlessly. "Well, that's where they've gone. You better drop that sullen look, mate, and keep your eyes peeled. We're here to do a job, not get ourselves jumped. If you do something to get us discovered before we've got what we want, the master won't be pleased."

Seth knew it for the truth. He tried to forget his irritation and began searching the fields with his eyes, following Varth. He saw the swordsman loosen his sword in its sheath and felt for the little silver knife in his pocket. His heart thumped with the anticipation of striking another blow for his master. Taran was a peasant, no more nobly born than Seth himself. What right had he to come lording it over Jinny's household? What right had he to live in the castle and parade his arcane talents in the city? Seth's soul burned for the chance of retribution, and he barely noticed the evil grin his companion threw him. The sudden stinging ache in his shoulder went ignored as he concentrated on the chase.

Varth moved out into the fields, Seth dogging his heels. The tracks were plain and easy to read. They led in a meandering line toward a distant line of trees. Varth halted, cursing under his breath when Seth bumped into his back. "Keep out of my way!" he growled. Seth cringed away from the predatory gleam in Varth's eye.

"Looks like they're in that stand of trees," the swordsman whispered hoarsely. "If we go much farther out in the open like this, we'll be seen. Is there any cover around the other side?"

Seth shook his head. "Only more open fields."

Varth swore. "Looks like we'll just have to wait for them to come back. I'd rather pick my ground than be seen out in the open. It's too bloody cold to hang about here, anyway. This is what we'll do. I'm going back to the stables. You wait here. When you see them start back, come and warn me. It'll be your job to distract them so I can get behind them. Does this Taran know how to use a blade?"

"He's pretty good, so I've heard, but I don't really know. I'm no trained swordsman."

"That's the truth!" snorted Varth. "You're holding that tiny knife like a frightened girl. You going to be able to use it on him when you get the chance? Or will you run like a scared rabbit? I need to know if you're going to help or just get in the way."

"I can do it!" protested Seth. "I have killed someone, you

know. And not by accident, either. I slit her throat."

"Slit a woman's throat, eh? All by yourself?" Varth was clearly impressed by Seth's vehement assertion. "Just don't let me down, then. Now hide yourself as best you can and don't let your eyes wander. I want to know the minute they start back, and I want you to be ready with some sad tale or other to distract them. And don't be seen. Got it?"

Seth nodded, realizing he was in for a freezing wait in the open while Varth lounged in relative comfort in the stables, waiting for his call. He stared malevolently after the large man as he moved away, putting his feet down in the already trampled snow so as not to leave plain tracks. Seth wrapped his arms around his chest and tried not to shiver as he crouched behind a convenient bush, eyes fixed on the small copse of trees.

✣ ✣ ✣ ✣ ✣

The icy winds of Endormir swirled around Bull and Sullyan as they emerged from the substrate, pulling at the edges of their cloaks and wiping half-frozen tears from their eyes.

"Stand close to me, Bull, and do not move until you have your bearings. The place we are going has a very small landing stage, and it will be slippery with ice. You will not want to move too suddenly and miss your footing."

Bull held his breath and moved closer to Sullyan's back. He placed his hands on her slender shoulders, feeling her manipulating the substrate as she molded their passage back through. They took one small pace forward and the snow-covered steppes of Endormir vanished, replaced by a solid wall of rock and the booming crash of the sea.

The rock beneath their feet was slick. Brine-soaked air surged around them, sprinkling their cloaks with semi-frozen droplets. Bull cast a careful look over his shoulder, grateful for Sullyan's warning. If he had taken but half a careless pace backward, his foot would have slipped off the landing stage, toppling him into the waves pounding the black rock. He turned away from the disturbing sight to see she was already ascending the stairs cut into the sheer rock face. Treading carefully, he followed her, holding on to the frozen bight of rope secured to the solid rock.

Bull was panting and the big muscles of his thighs were protesting by the time they reached the gate. He was more thankful than ever he had taken Rienne's herbs before leaving. Without them his chest would have been tight with pain by now. As it was, Sullyan cast him an anxious glance as she reached for the muffled bell.

"Are you well, Hal?"

"Just puffed," he managed. "That's some climb."

She made no reply, but her eyes left his reluctantly as she released the bell's clapper and rang it. They had arrived at an odd hour and it was some time before they heard the sounds of hurrying feet coming toward them. Frar Varian appeared in the narrow passageway, his cowl thrown back from his face, alarm etched on his sunken features.

Sullyan didn't wait for him to identify them. "Frar Varian, I apologize for our abrupt and unannounced arrival, but we need to see Ruvar on a matter of utmost urgency."

Varian's eyes widened when he saw who it was. Bull could feel puzzlement emanating from him and saw his eyes flick between them as he unlocked the gate.

"But how did you come here, Colonel? None of the fishermen would let their boats put to sea in this wind."

"I came by my own methods, Frar. Would you be so good as to inform Ruvar of our presence? It really is most urgent."

Varian relocked the gate behind them. "*Cleric Patrio* Ruvar," he said, "is currently at prayers. You will have to wait until—"

"This cannot wait," she interrupted with none of her habitual courtesy. "Ruvar will forgive me when he hears what I have to say. And if he does not, then I must gamble upon God's mercy. If you do not fetch him, Varian, I will be forced to do so myself."

Varian's eyes widened further. "Come with me," he said, leading the way through the narrow rock passage toward the guest cottage. He did not turn aside at the cottage, as Sullyan expected. Instead, he led them directly to Ruvar's house and bade them enter. "I will inform the Cleric Patrio of your arrival," he said. Only once he had gone did Sullyan realize he had not insisted they remove their weapons.

She unhooked her sword and laid it on a table by the door, indicating Bull should do likewise. Their daggers and eating knives followed, making a gleaming steely array on the dark wood.

"What's this Ruvar like, Sully?" asked Bull as they entered the living area to wait.

Sullyan paced restlessly. "Surprising," was all she said, and Bull did not press her. Even this short delay had dragged at her nerves, and only her innate sense of propriety prevented her from ignoring the formalities and beginning her search unaided.

They didn't have long to wait. Varian must have conveyed their urgency, for Ruvar came at once. He entered his house, shaking snow from his robes, and came to stand before her. Bull's reaction to his youth and dark skin was much the same as Cal's and Tad's had been, his greater experience showing in his ability to keep his surprise to himself.

"Brynne," greeted Ruvar soberly. "I had not expected we would meet again so soon. What is so urgent that you force Varian to run for the first time in twenty years in order to drag me early from my prayers?"

"I apologize for our untimely arrival, and also for the inconvenience caused to both you and to Varian. But this is a matter, quite literally, of life and death and I hope you will forgive the intrusion."

Ruvar regarded her steadily before waving a hand toward chairs by the fire. "Won't you sit?" He transferred his gaze to Bull. "I don't know your name."

"I'm Hal Bullen, but my friends call me Bull," the big man replied, drawing a brief look of amusement from the senior cleric.

"I am pleased to meet you, Hal." He took the seat opposite Sullyan's and clasped his hands together. "What is this matter of urgency? Something to do with the Baron, no doubt. Were you successful in your search for young Serrin?"

"Serrin is dead," stated Sullyan, drawing a gasp from the cleric.

"I'm sorry to hear it. Did he make it home before he died?"

She shook her head. "He died here. He never left the island."

"What? Never left? What are you saying?"

She leaned forward, eyes intent on Ruvar. "The blood found in the Baron's rooms was Serrin's. Reen murdered him."

There was a brief silence and Ruvar's dark eyes narrowed dangerously. "What grounds do you have for that assertion?"

"None of the fishermen who serve you took Serrin off the island," she said, holding his gaze. "The blood in Reen's room was too much to have come from the Baron, and he did not slit his wrists. He would have been completely unable to make the trek to the crag if he had. The whole charade was a feint to deceive us. He colluded through written correspondence with someone who was willing to succor him, and he arranged with them to have a boat standing by. His scream as he jumped was their signal to rescue him, and the mighty leap he made was to avoid being dashed on the rocks of the reef. He has since murdered Arch Patrio Neremiah, orchestrated the slaughter of a company of twenty trained swordsmen, and abducted and quite possibly killed his niece, murdering two other women into the bargain. He has poisoned and killed the nursemaid of the King's daughter and very nearly his First Minister, and he has brought Port Loxton to the verge of civil revolt with his actions.

"Serrin was only the first, Ruvar. Reen has not scrupled to kill in the past and he will not balk at it again. He is removing, one by one, everyone who stood against him at his trial. He has now abducted my life mate, Robin, and no doubt intends to use him to lure me into confronting him. Then he will kill us both."

Ruvar sat in stunned silence, unable to take it all in. The news of Neremiah's death had shocked him; after that the rest just piled on top, causing him to shake his head in bewilderment.

"But why would he murder Serrin?" he said at last, dealing with the problem nearest to his personal experience. "What harm could that poor boy possibly have done him? He had befriended Reen. He made his life here bearable. Reen was beside himself once Serrin … left. Why be so distraught if he had killed him? It doesn't make sense."

Sullyan never relinquished his gaze, and Bull could feel her willing him to believe her, boring into the barriers of his reluctance with her compelling gaze. "I do not have answers to all of your questions. This is why we have come. Something happened to Reen on this island, something overwhelming. Something that caused him to change. Were you aware Reen possessed latent Artesan powers?"

The senior cleric's dark face paled and his head snapped up. "No! There was no mention of that in the papers I was given on Reen's arrival. Why wasn't I told?"

Sullyan shrugged. "It should have made no difference. He could not independently access his latent powers—they were buried too deeply and had never been developed. His gift was sterile."

"Then why mention it now?" Ruvar was growing impatient, unable to see the point of this.

"Put yourself in the Baron's place for a moment. You have seen all your righteous plans come to naught, your fervent service to your God denied. You have been publicly humiliated and have narrowly escaped a hideous and tortuous death. You have been betrayed by your only ally and forced to grovel in abject shame at the feet of your enemies. You have been cast aside, abandoned, exiled—left to live out your days in solitude and spiritual desolation. You have been rejected by your God.

"But then you find solace. In the midst of your despair comes comfort, and it gives you new life. A kindred spirit, a tortured soul, also needing solace and comfort. You become close. How close, we shall never know, but I can guess. And you dare to look beyond the prison of your soul, stop berating your God, and begin to pray once more. You even thank him for the gift.

"And then you discover how cruelly you have been deceived. You discover that this giver of comfort, this kindred spirit, is more like you than you thought, and you are appalled. You discover your ultimate nightmare—that you have been duped into intimacy with one who possesses those very powers which brought you down. You discover that you have been, quite literally, sleeping with the enemy."

Ruvar recoiled, his face tight with revulsion. "Are you saying Serrin was also … gifted? And that this is why he was killed? What grounds do you have for saying that? How can you possibly know? This is all pure conjecture, Colonel."

"It is not conjecture. When I discovered that none of the fishermen who serve you had ferried Serrin that day, I asked for the name of his village. I traveled there on my way home. The innkeeper told me most emphatically that they would not have welcomed the boy if he had tried to return, for he was known for his strange powers and disturbing ways. I have heard those same sentiments expressed far too often not to know what they mean. Serrin was an untrained Artesan, and for this he was murdered."

Sullyan's forceful voice, full of power and outrage, silenced Ruvar's protestations. It was a measure of her distress, thought Bull, that she made no apology for her vehemence. Her fear over Robin's plight and her failure to find him so far were eating into her control, fueling her fears. The vast energies she commanded could easily blow this island apart, sending its denizens to the bottom of the sea. Loss of control was always her greatest fear, and he could sense her struggling to calm herself. Unthinking, he reached out, offered his strength as he had done so often in the past. He caught the flash of her eyes with which she acknowledged his gift, and he suddenly remembered why he no longer did it. He could only hope she had not caught the flavor of the drugs in his system.

She had other things on her mind at the moment and spared no thought for Bull. She watched the confusion, pity, anger, and, finally, acceptance chase each other across Ruvar's face. He raised his deep brown eyes, resigned at last.

"What do you want from me?"

Sullyan sighed and Bull felt relief wash over her. "Two questions. How would Reen have disposed of Serrin's body? And what could have happened to him, here on this island, to cause such deep trauma that it forced the life-preserving powers he had buried and rejected to surface and become active?"

Ruvar spread helpless hands. "How can I answer you? I have already told you all I know of the Baron's time here. And you know Serrin was the only one to whom he would speak. The discussions I had with the Baron, few though they were, concerned our faith and our lives here, nothing else. He never confided in me. And apart from his obvious distress once Serrin had vanished, I saw no evidence of life-threatening trauma. Nor did any of our community here."

Sullyan was silent and Bull, who knew only what she had told him, held his peace. He knew she was sifting through what she had learned, trying to piece together a credible set of circumstances that accounted for everything she had been told. She raised her eyes to Ruvar once more.

"You said that Reen became reclusive and frail once Serrin had gone." Ruvar inclined his head. "But was there a time *before* the boy left when Reen kept to himself? Do I not recall you saying he had been unwell, and that Serrin nursed him?"

Ruvar nodded, his eyes unfocused, looking inward. She watched him intently, urgent for him to speak but unwilling to press him lest he lose his train of thought.

"Yes, yes he had been ill," said Ruvar hesitantly. "I do not remember exactly when it started, but Reen had been growing frailer for some time before Serrin's departure. He had taken to leaning upon that cane, but he didn't use it constantly. When he stopped attending our services regularly I sent Frar Durren to his rooms to enquire after him, and Serrin told him the Baron was unwell. We offered the services of our healer, but Serrin declined, saying he would tend to the Baron himself."

Ruvar's gaze sharpened and he stared hard at Sullyan. "That was only a week or so before Serrin left. The two of them kept to the Baron's rooms and I believe Durren may well have been the last person to speak with the boy. When the Baron finally emerged, the same day Serrin left his letter, he was emaciated, reticent, and unapproachable. We put it down to his illness and the loss of his close companion. But from that moment he grew increasingly strange. He suffered fits of ranting, shouting and raging in his rooms. He never went without his cane and he leaned increasingly on it. He rarely went abroad at all after that, and it was not long after his emergence from this illness that he leaped from the rock into the sea."

Sullyan's gaze intensified during Ruvar's speech and Bull could see she was thinking hard. "Would anyone have entered the Baron's rooms besides Reen himself? To tend the fire, to bring food, to clean?"

Ruvar shook his head. "There are no servants here. We are all in the service of our faith, not each other. Apart from the healer, who has been trained in the tending of the body, we all look after ourselves. Even the healer is helped by members of our community. No one would have trespassed on the Baron's privacy."

Sullyan turned to Bull, thinking out loud. "So Serrin could still have been in the Baron's rooms once Reen recovered from whatever had afflicted him. He must have restrained the boy until he committed his final act." She turned back to Ruvar. "And my first question? Accepting that the Baron could not have thrown Serrin's body to the waves, how else could he have disposed of it? What is your ceremony for honoring the dead?"

"They are given to the Holy Fire."

The shock that surged through the room touched even the Cleric Patrio, whose eyes widened. Bull felt an electric thrill run along his nerves; a disturbing sensation. He rubbed at his arms, where the hairs stood on end. "Sully!" he growled, drawing a startled look from Ruvar.

Sullyan had leaped to her feet and her eyes glittered with amber sparks. Her hands were clenched into fists at her sides and she was clearly unaware of the effect her unconscious show of power was having on the room's atmosphere. She outwardly ignored Bull's reprimand, but she did dampen her flare of power.

"Tell me!" she demanded, her compelling gaze boring into Ruvar's eyes. He stared at her, mesmerized.

"Those who die in the service of our faith are given to the Holy Fire," he managed, his throat sounding dry. "It is a sacred spot and dangerous, deep in the bowels of the volcano, and none are permitted to look upon it except at the Rites of Passing. I doubt Reen even knew of it, if that's what you're intimating. We held no such service while he was here."

"Reen may not have known of this site, but as a novitiate of your order, Serrin would, would he not? And as an Artesan, he would have felt the presence of Fire, untrained or not. I sensed the power of this place as soon as I set foot upon the rock, although I did not at first know from whence it came. Tell me, Ruvar, where is the passage that leads to the Holy Fire?"

Ruvar stared at her, his face turning pale. His voice was rough as he slowly said, "It runs from the passage leading past the Baron's rooms."

Chapter Nineteen

Taran cast his senses about as he stood beneath the trees. The impression of Jinny's presence was strong here, as was the imprint of another aura—a strange aura. He was relieved to find no woman's body concealed by the fall of snow, nor was there any sense of anyone having died there. He had discovered the site of the substrate anomaly within the copse, as he suspected he would, but finding it brought him no understanding. It tasted of death, but there was life here, too. Whoever made this strange imprint had been alive, and Jinny had also been alive when she was here. Her aura vanished abruptly, however, telling Taran she had been taken out of Albia via the Veils by whoever possessed that strange and disturbing impression.

He glanced at Col, standing watch under the trees. The young swordsman faced away from the burned-out mansion, looking out across the fields toward the distant swell of the cliffs. He stamped his feet and chafed his arms to keep his blood moving as the wind howled through the bare branches above him and fine sleet drove at his back.

On a clear day, Col would have been able to see the grass-covered backs of the impressive cliffs that sheltered the northern sweep of Loxton Bay, but today all was white. The weather was closing in and Taran didn't like the look of it. His instincts told him not to linger and he decided they had been here long enough. They still had the ride back to the castle to endure.

He made his way over to the swordsman, who was now blowing on his gloved hands through blue lips. Taran grinned. "You should have waited in the stables like I told you."

Col snorted. "And be flayed by Dexter for dereliction of duty? Not bloody likely. The captain learned his threats from Colonel Sullyan. Would *you* want to face that?"

Taran shivered, and not just from the cold. "Come on, then, the sooner we get to the horses, the sooner we can start back. I've found what I was looking for, though what good it has done I don't know. I'll have to speak to Sullyan later tonight, see what she thinks. Gods, Col, but this wind's evil!"

They put down their heads and forged into the full force of the wind, hugging their cloaks about them, holding their hoods over their faces. The stinging snowflakes blurred the features of the landscape into indistinct shapes.

✤ ✤ ✤ ✤ ✤

Seth blessed the sleet and the men's lowered hoods as he raced back to Varth. "They're on their way," he reported breathlessly, finding his companion inside the stables, hands buried in a horse's mane, sharing the animal's warmth. "What shall I do?"

Varth stepped away from the horse. "Distract them, like I told you. I could take them both on if blades was all we had to worry about. But your witch friend has other weapons we can't fight, and that silver knife is the only thing that'll stop him using them. I'll take care of the other man, but it'll be your job to grab the witch and stick him with that knife. You've still got it safe, haven't you?"

"Of course I have," retorted Seth. "I'm not as stupid as you seem to think. But how am I going to get close enough to use the thing? Taran's been trained in fighting and he's stronger than me."

Varth huffed. "Not once that knife's in his skin, he won't be.

It'll cut off his physical strength as well as his witch's powers. Just do what you came here to do. Pretend to be worried over your job. Ask him what he's going to do about you and the other servants. Get him off his guard, and then grab him. Once you've stuck him with that knife, you'll be able to overpower him easy. I'll deal with the other one, and then it'll be over."

Seth opened his mouth to protest again, then took one look at Varth's sullen red eyes and fled. He emerged into the lee of the stable block just as Col and Taran appeared out of the swirling snow around the side of the building, heads down against the wind. Seth's hands were shaking and he thrust them deep into the pockets of his jacket, feeling the cold smoothness of the silver knife and using it to lend him courage. He pictured himself overpowering the taller man, and seeing respect and fear for his superior strength in the helpless court Artesan's eyes. His imagined victory enabled him to reply almost calmly when Taran exclaimed in surprise.

"Seth! What are you doing here?"

Col reached for his sword at Seth's appearance, but Taran's recognition relaxed him. Seth ignored him, concentrating on Taran.

He could see the play of mixed emotions across Taran's face. Their last encounter had not been pleasant, and Seth imagined his unkind words about Jinny had not been forgotten. He faced Taran squarely, his excited shivering passing for cold in this bitter weather. He gave up trying to hide it.

"I'm out of a job, remember, sir?" he said, allowing dislike to color his tone. "Thought I'd come up here and talk to some of the others, see what we're going to do. I thought I might find Matty here."

Taran seemed to accept Seth's explanation; it was feasible, after all. "It looks as though Matty's been here recently," he said, "but he wasn't here when Col and I arrived. I expect he's at his father's house. How are you managing, Seth?"

The manservant flicked a glance at Col and edged sideways as casually as possible, trying to lure Taran past the stable door. "How do you think I'm managing … sir?" He kept his tone barely polite. His right hand tightly clasped the hilt of the silver knife concealed in his pocket. He had seen no sign of Varth as he glanced at the stable door. He really hoped the man would do his part. "I've got a small amount of coin saved, but it won't last long. I need to find work."

Taran's eyes held sympathy, much to Seth's relief. His story was working. Now all he needed was to get Taran's back to the stable door. Easier said than done.

Taran gave him a smile. "Seth, I'm in a position to help you, if you'll let me. If you will answer me a few questions as honestly as you can, I will be willing to see you're not too inconvenienced, at least until you can find another position. And I'll help you with that, too, if you like. What do you say?"

Anger boiled inside Seth at the man's temerity. Who did he think he was, to offer Seth his charity? What gave Taran the right to patronize him this way? His fury at Taran's well-meaning words suffused Seth's muscles with heat and stiffened his resolve. He bit back the spiteful refusal he wanted to give and swallowed, hard.

"What do you want to know?"

Taran took two steps toward him, passing the stable door and presenting his back to it. Col stayed where he was, and Seth cursed inwardly. Would Varth engage the swordsman if he refused to move? Seth wasn't sure how long he could keep his intentions hidden. He knew the rumors concerning Artesans, how they could see through falsehood and read people's minds. And he was already quivering with suppressed tension. He struggled for a way to entice Col into moving forward, but the young swordsman suddenly took it out of his hands.

Seeing Taran about to start what might be a lengthy conversation, Col said, "Why don't you two talk this over in the stable? I'm already frozen solid. If I stay out here much longer, I'll never move again."

Seth nearly cried out, biting his tongue just in time. Col took a step toward the doorway and Taran half-turned to speak to him. Seth whipped the knife out of his pocket and leaped desperately at Taran, bearing the startled man backward with the force of his assault. "Varth!" he screamed, praying the hulking swordsman would keep his word and not leave Seth to struggle on his own.

Col reacted instantly, turning toward the two men and sweeping his sword clear of its sheath faster than Seth thought possible. But Seth's cry had confused Col, and his split-second hesitation over whether he should defend Taran or look for a second assailant was his undoing. Varth surged silently out of the stable, his own sword naked in his hand, and caught Col high on the upper arm with a powerful sweeping slash. The young man cried out but rallied well, parrying Varth's return stroke and making a thrust of his own. Varth sidestepped the move and grinned.

Col was too caught up in the immediacy of the fight to wonder at his opponent's apparent mirth. The larger man's reach was greater than Col's and the Manor swordsman was already wounded. Col would need all his wits about him in order to compensate. The two men engaged in a bitter struggle.

Seth followed his wild leap by hooking his left arm around Taran's neck to avoid being thrust away, bringing his right hand up under Taran's chin. The Adept recovered from his initial shock, but he was unaware of his true danger and made the mistake of reaching for his sword. Seth was already too close and used his body to shove Taran off balance while he thrust upward with the silver knife. He tangled his left foot with Taran's right, and threw his weight against him, causing him to trip and fall. They went down in the snow in a grunting heap, Taran losing his grip on his sword hilt as he fought to break his fall. The attack was so swift Taran had no time to even think about calling for help. He needed all his concentration to fend off Seth's desperate onslaught. But he was too late and Seth had the advantage.

Unplanned and unskilled though his attack was, Seth knew what he was aiming for—the exposed skin of Taran's neck, just visible inside his hood. Plunging his right hand forward with all the strength of his hatred and fear, Seth thrust the silver knife hard against the side of Taran's windpipe. The tip of the blunt silver blade pierced Taran's flesh.

The Adept's instant collapse surprised Seth. His face went gray and he slumped beneath Seth. He looked as if he might vomit, odd noises coming from his throat. His hands twitched, straining to move, but he seemed as weak as a kitten. He stared at Seth in horror.

The panting manservant straddled his opponent's body, his trembling hand ensuring the knife stayed embedded in Taran's throat, his knees pinning Taran's arms. A triumphant leer twisted his flushed face. With Taran secured and helpless, Seth's attention turned to his companion.

�֍ ✤ ✤ ✤ ✤

Col and Varth swayed back and forth, trading blows, ducking and sidestepping. The deep slash to Col's upper left arm had weakened him, and blood flowed freely; it dripped to the snow from the fingers of his mainly useless left hand. Unbalanced, he didn't have his usual agility, and his opponent knew it. The man's eyes gleamed strangely red as he fought, pressing Col ever backward, wrong-footing him at every turn. He was maneuvering Col closer to the burnt-out mansion, probably looking for opportunities to trip him.

Col knew he was fighting for his life and Taran's. He could not spare a glance to see how the Adept was faring; if he took his eyes from his opponent he was done for. He didn't even know where Taran was. He could hear no sounds but the whistle of steel through the air, the clash of metal, and harsh grunts. He only just turned aside a vicious swing that nearly sheared his chest and leaped sideways, trying for some space in which to reverse the fight's advantage.

His assailant pressed on, keeping Col on the defensive, constantly attacking his left and forcing him to use his injured arm. The red drops in the snow were fast becoming splashes, and Col knew he couldn't last much longer. He had only touched the man twice; two small cuts that probably didn't even sting.

The man suddenly lunged inside Col's defense, managing to inflict another slash to his already wounded left arm. Col stumbled, but didn't fall.

He thought he caught a glimmer of respect in the man's eyes. He refused to give up, even though his wound was draining him. He kept parrying his opponent's blows, but now Col made no attempt at offensive strokes.

The man grinned again. "What's the matter, young 'un, can't you cope without your mates behind you?"

Col frowned, twisting aside to avoid a vicious sideways swipe. His blade rang on his assailant's as he managed to parry the return stroke. A mist obscured his vision, but a niggling thought in the back of his mind told him there was something familiar about this black-haired man.

The swordsman feinted left, drawing the tip of Col's sword as he moved to block. "You and your friend enjoyed our company that night at the tavern in Daret, didn't you?" he grunted, switching his grip and thrusting forward to attack Col's left side yet again. "Couldn't hold your ale, though, either of you."

Col gasped as he barely avoided yet another cut to his left arm. It was so painful and weak he could hardly move it, and the blood loss was telling on both his strength and his skill. Burning frustration inflamed his heart.

"It was you, you bastard!" he hissed, letting his anger provide the power for a backhand sweep. "What did you do that for? You nearly killed us both!"

The man danced out of reach, catching Col's sword on his own and twisting his wrist to deflect the younger man's blade. He moved quickly to his right, trying to catch Col before he regained his balance, aiming yet another powerful blow at Col's left arm.

"Didn't take much to do it," he taunted. "And it wouldn't have mattered if we had killed you. You'd already given us what we wanted. Most helpful, you was. Couldn't stop you talking once you started. Gave us all the information we could have wished for. Made it so easy for the master, you did. He took your pretty young major like he was stealing a baby."

"*What*?" The terrible, debilitating fear that washed over Col nearly caused him to stumble. His heart faltered and his skin went cold, icy shivers sliding down his spine that had nothing to do with the winter storm. The tip of the other man's sword sliced yet again into the useless muscle of Col's left arm, severing nerves and tendons. He barely swayed away from the lunge that reached for his heart.

"Oh, yes," said the man, his eyes glowing red. "He'd never have taken him so easily without your help. Did us a great service, you and your mate. Ought to be proud of yourselves."

Col gave a despairing cry. He and Pen had known there was more to their sickness than met the eye, but neither had dared to guess it was anything as damaging as this. It never even occurred to him to disbelieve the man. He could hear the ring of truth in the mocking words and knew it for fact. He and Pen were responsible for Robin's plight, and the knowledge drained him of what little strength he had left. He was done for.

A savage rage reddened his vision. He had failed in his duty twice over, both in Bordenn and now here, and the knowledge drove sharp stabs of anguish into his spirit. Furious for the brutal betrayal, for the cruel twisting of his and Pen's loyalty, he summoned the energy for one final thrust. Roaring in defiance, he came at his assailant like a demon.

The older man recognized a desperate move when he saw one, and Col was incapable of changing direction once committed. He sidestepped neatly and swung his blade with casual negligence. Col collapsed without a cry, his chest opened, his remaining lifeblood pulsing weakly onto the gory snow.

✢ ✢ ✢ ✢ ✢

Seth frowned as Varth gazed down at Col's drained and lifeless face and made a small, half-mocking salute. He cleaned his blade on Col's cloak and strode across to where Seth still straddled Taran's body. Seth watched him come, eyes shining with pride. Varth stared down at him, his expression suddenly furious. He reached down and wrenched at Seth's shoulder, throwing him bodily from Taran.

"You stupid, bloody fool! What do you think you're doing? If you've killed him, there'll be the Void to pay. Why did you go for the throat, you imbecile? Don't you know *anything*?"

He knelt in the trampled snow beside the senseless Adept, careful not to touch the knife still embedded in his flesh. Seth lay on his back where he had landed, staring malevolently at Varth, his fright and anger returning at this dismissal of his achievement.

"I overcame him like you told me to," he hissed, struggling to right himself. "What's wrong with you? We've got him, haven't we?"

"Fat lot of good that'll do us if you've killed him," Varth yelled, spitting his anger into Seth's face. "You've bloody near sliced his jugular, you lackwit! No wonder the master told me not to trust you."

Seth turned pale. He hadn't really thought about where he was going to strike as he leaped at Taran. The man's face and neck were the only exposed skin available under the heavy leather cloak. There had been no time to consider his target; he had seen skin and lunged for it. But Varth's words sank in as he knelt on all fours, staring at the unmoving body, a chill hand of dread curling about his heart.

"Is he … is he dead?"

Varth turned his head deliberately to stare at Seth, the red glow just visible in his bloodshot eyes. The grin that spread his lips was not his own, and neither was the voice that crawled sinuously from his mouth.

"No, my faithful servant. Fortunately for you, he is not. You have done well, Seth, and you will be rewarded. You can name your price after what you have done this day, but you may have to wait a while to claim it. I am not yet ready to show myself. But you have brought us closer to victory today, and I will not forget it.

"My servant here will bring me this prize, and also the body of the other man, and it would be best if you removed yourself. It will be up to you to conceal the evidence of what has happened here as best you can, and I suggest that once you have done that, you continue with what you told the gate guards you came here for. Go and speak to your fellow servants, so that if they are questioned later they will corroborate your story. Once you have done so, return to your lodgings and keep out of sight. Don't volunteer information unless you have no other choice, but if you are caught and questioned, stick to the truth. That way, they cannot hear the lie in your voice.

"Now, go into the stable and do not come out until Varth returns to you."

Seth did as he was told, warm excitement flowing through his veins as he brushed the snow from his clothes. He was aware he had very nearly slipped up. It was sheer luck the knife blade had not nicked Taran's jugular vein. He had not intended to shove it in so hard, but his nervous fear and untrained hand had taken over. Thankfully, it had turned out well and his master was pleased with him. Yet another obstacle to his return had been removed, and the Baron had another victim to use in furthering his aims. Seth stood by the horses, watching them eat their hay, ignoring the strange sounds from outside.

After a few minutes, Varth strode into the stable, shaking snow from his cloak and grinning evilly. "You really are one lucky bastard," he said, clapping Seth hard on the back. "Now get out there and cover up that blood. There'll be more snow soon to hide it, but better to be safe. Then we'll go talk to these other peasants of yours before we go back to your lodgings. I've worked up a powerful thirst here today, and a good sword fight always brings on other ... needs. I know just the man to take care of *them*, don't I?"

Seth's heart sank. He had hoped he would be left alone once this task was over, but Varth obviously had other ideas. Seth knew only too well what they involved, and he was none too keen to repeat the experience. Yet he really had no choice, and he needed Varth with him to get him back inside the city walls with no questions asked. Sighing in vexation, he wrapped his arms around his chest and went back out into the bitter, howling wind.

Chapter Twenty

Sullyan's gaze was hard as she faced Ruvar, who stared at her in consternation. "I need to see this place," she said, trying to keep the urgency from her voice. She feared Ruvar would refuse her access to the holy site and she knew, with a certainty too firm to be mere hope, that she was nearing the root of the puzzle. Something harrowing and dreadful had happened to the Baron here on this island, and this was the first indication she had that seemed to offer an answer. She held Ruvar's gaze.

"It's a very dangerous place," he replied reluctantly. "We approach it with care, and we do not go there willingly. The way is uneven and narrow, and the fires are unpredictable. There is a deceptive edge and no hope of survival if you fall. The heat can be unbearable at the best of times, and there are hidden pools of magma along the way, as well as tunnels and cracks in the rock through which flame or steam can spurt unexpectedly. If one catches you, you die, and even if you escape them, they can sometimes burn for days, trapping the unwary on the wrong side. Anyone so caught would perish. I can't see how the Baron could have made the trip, if that's what you think he did, and if a flare caught him, he would have died instantly, no matter what powers he possessed. The Fire is holy and should not be disturbed. Don't ask me to take you."

She moved closer to him. "I will not ask that of you. We need no guide, and my senses will warn me far in advance of any random flare of fire. I am a Senior Master, which means I have held mastery over Fire for many years. I could turn or dampen any magma flare and even protect myself long enough to pass through molten rock if the need arose. Bull and I will be quite safe, I assure you. All I ask is your permission."

Ruvar's eyes betrayed his skepticism, but Sullyan didn't have time to convince him. Her voice fell to a whisper. "Please do not force me to go against your wishes."

The Cleric Patrio acknowledged her need and lifted one hand in surrender. "I don't know why you're asking, since you're obviously determined to go. I can't see how I could stop you."

"I ask because I respect you and your order, Ruvar. I would rather go with your blessing than against your command."

Ruvar could hear her sincerity. Something passed between them in that moment, something deep, and Bull hid a smile. Not many men could resist Sullyan in that mood, and the Cleric Patrio was no exception. He inclined his head. "Go, then, with my blessing."

She smiled in gratitude and turned to Bull. "We will begin the search in the Baron's rooms, see if we can pick up any impressions of him in the substrate. Then we will follow any trail toward the fire until we reach the site of the trauma. I may need your strength then. Are you fit to stand for me?"

Once again, Bull blessed Rienne for her gift of strengthening herbs, for without them he would have had to refuse. And this was what he lived for; using what skills he possessed—physical or metaphysical—in Sullyan's service. If he were ever forced to give this up, his life would hold no meaning.

"Of course, Sully. I'll let you know if I get too tired."

Sullyan nodded and cast a glance at Ruvar. "We should not be long, and we will not disturb the holy site. We will report our findings to you before we leave."

Bull noted the man's resigned smile as they left his house.

Sullyan led him out into the fading afternoon light and the bitter cold. She made for the order's habitations and Bull expected her to turn aside at one of the neat wooden doors. Instead, she turned toward the sheer rock on their left and entered a narrow passageway he had not noticed. Steps wound unevenly down through the rock, ending in a wooden door cut into the rock face. Once they passed it, they would be inside the volcano itself. He could feel the emanations of Fire all around him, and sense the deep roar of its molten fury many miles beneath his feet. It was both a heady and a menacing feeling.

Sullyan opened the door and they passed through, leaving the biting cold behind them. She did not close the door in case they should need the flow of air, but the intrinsic warmth of the place soon seeped into their bodies, making their cloaks redundant. She paced swiftly past the many doors studding the long corridor until she reached the one she wanted. Bull felt her using her metasenses to check the room was unoccupied before she entered.

He took in the room's spartan aspect with interest. Sullyan turned to face him, her pupils dilated as she invited him to share what she could sense. Abandoning his inspection and opening his mind, he merged his psyche with hers, gasping as he always did at the vastness of her power.

Standing immobile in the center of the room, Bull felt her peeling back layers of the substrate, looking for traces of activity. She had no knowledge of Serrin's psyche pattern, nor of the embryo imprint the Baron must possess. Although she had discovered his latent talent during the trial, she had had no contact with him, so the traces of an Artesan's working were all she could hope to find. As Serrin was untrained, any traces would be vague and elusive indeed.

Each layer she examined represented a layer of time. Whatever had happened to the Baron or his unfortunate catamite occurred six months ago or more; it would take some searching out. It was some time before she found anything at all. Eventually, just when Bull was beginning to think she was looking in the wrong place, an imprint impinged on her senses. She pounced on it like a hawk on its prey and he narrowed his concentration so he could examine it, too.

It was terror. Sheer, pleading, uncomprehending terror. It beat about the room like a frightened bird, desperate for freedom. The childlike tones of its echo wrenched at Bull's heart, bringing tears to his eyes. Whoever had left such a poignant imprint was bereft of all hope, had poured all their draining energy into a final plea for succor. A plea that went ignored, unanswered, until the piteous cries abruptly cut off, leaving only the bitter flavor of malice.

Sullyan broke their link and Bull staggered, panting. "What the hell was that?" he gasped, wiping his eyes with the back of his hand. "That poor wretch, whoever he was! I could hardly stand it."

Sullyan was pale too, her eyes dark pools of anger. "Unless I miss my guess, old friend, we have just witnessed the death of Serrin. That poor boy gave his all to save his companion. Could you feel the love he expended, the effort he made? I would say he labored for many days alone in this room, just keeping the Baron alive. And that was how Reen repaid him. The boy exerted the very roots of his fledgling powers, brought forth skills he hardly knew he possessed, and death was his reward. A death he could not understand—a betrayal so fundamental, his spirit will spend eternity searching for the reason. I can only pray he finds solace."

She fell silent, brooding, while Bull watched in concern. What implications this discovery had for Robin, he did not care to speculate. He simply offered his solid presence, and soon she came out of her reverie. "Come, my friend. Now that I have a better idea what to look for, we must seek out the site of the trauma. Until I know what he suffered, I cannot know what threat we face."

They left the Baron's chambers and continued down the steeply sloping corridor. After leaving the residential area, the rock of the ancient lava tunnel was bare and unadorned. Several side passages led off the central tunnel, but their senses told them these were dead ends; old magma chambers long since cooled and disused. The volcano's interior exuded a slumbering sense of power, a brooding sense of majestic and terrifying violence, but the venting of the earth's inner forces was a natural phenomenon, only to be feared by the unprepared or the unwary.

The deeper they went, the stronger the smell of sulfur became. A soft red reflection was the tunnel's only illumination. They needed no light to guide them. The emanations of the earth and the signature of Fire were all the guidance they needed. The heat was increasing and the oxygen levels dropping the farther they went. Sullyan spared a portion of her power to call a whisper of Air down from the entrance high above them. It was just enough to keep them from passing out.

They approached another branch of the tunnel and Sullyan laid her hand on Bull's arm. He obeyed her unspoken command and waited by her side. A low hissing reached his ears, growing rapidly in strength and intensity until a superheated vent of steam shot from a fissure near the tunnel floor, not ten feet in front of them. Sullyan was ready to turn its might, but it came nowhere near them, spending its force swiftly before dying away to nothing. She shot Bull a glance.

"There are many such fissures in the rock, any one of which might vent at any moment. I would not care to be caught by one of those. It may be what happened to the Baron, although if such a vent caught him full on, he would have died in an instant. Perhaps he was scorched by steam, or suffered burns to his lungs. The dreadful pain might well have forced out such life preserving powers as he possessed."

"Do you want to search again here?" Bull asked.

She shook her head. "I would go a little farther, Hal, if you can stand it. I feel there is something else here—something more significant. It calls to me."

He waved her on, and she turned down the left-hand branch, drawn by the smooth floor, tamped by the passage of many feet over time. She had to draw more and more on her skills the farther they went to keep enough oxygen in the air. Bull knew she would not go much farther or she would have no strength left for the search. Besides, the Baron would not have survived if he had gone much deeper, and they both knew they must be close to the site of the Holy Fire, if not the place of the Baron's injury. She cast her senses about, searching for whatever pricked at her mind.

The tunnel curved sharply right in front of them and the constant roaring that had settled into their bones increased in intensity. The light had also changed, a pale golden glow replacing the sullen red. The smell of sulfur had receded, leaving the air more breathable, relieving Sullyan of the necessity to call Air. She released her hold and concentrated on her surroundings.

She felt it immediately and gave a small cry of shock. Bull gasped too; he had picked up the sensation on his own. It fluctuated and wavered, strong one minute, the next so faint it was barely there. Yet the two Artesans could feel it clearly, sliding over their skin with sinuous fingers, shrouding them unpleasantly with its peculiar signature.

Sullyan stared at Bull in amazement. Of all the possibilities she had considered, finding this here was not among them. It explained why the two men had come here, and Serrin especially would have been drawn to its call. For it sang in the blood and it plucked at the senses, promising greater control, mightier powers, increased potency, and was so strong that even a latent talent like the Baron's would have been unable to resist.

"Go forward carefully, Bull," she warned. "And stay shielded!"

Bull tore his mind from the seductive call and wove a strong shield. It was so hard not to incorporate the external power into his structure, but he knew he was lost if he did. He blanked it out, although it hurt him to do so. His heart gave a painful lurch and he started, suddenly fearful that Rienne's herbs would give out on him before their work was done. But he waved away Sullyan's concern, signifying his readiness, and she moved slowly forward around the bend in the tunnel.

It hit their shields like a battering ram, bombarding their senses with power. Stopping on the hidden brink, just one careless step from immolation, they stared in fascinated thrall at the seething molten pool that bubbled and frothed at their feet. Pale wreaths of hot steam and gold flame, beautiful in the still, thick air, writhed slowly above the pool, reflected from the shining surface, beckoning seductively. The tunnel roof was domed above the lethal pool, and the collected steam condensed on its slightly cooler surface, forming long, swaying ribbons of shining element that draped down from the roof to curl and waft above the roiling surface. They looked like ethereal dancers. Bull stared, mesmerized, feeling he had never seen anything more powerful, more deadly, or more beautiful.

Spellsilver!

He moved one foot.

A wrenching pain in his shoulder caused him to cry out. His whole body spun around, forced backward, away from the pool and toward the bend in the tunnel. An irresistible force bore down on him, shoving him out of harm's way. His back connected jarringly with the rock wall, its solidity cutting off the siren song of the pool. He blinked, looking stupidly down at two furious black eyes, the fright behind the fury boring into his soul. He shook his head, bemused.

"What happened?"

"You bloody great fool!" raged Sullyan, shaking him by the arms. "I thought I told you to shield!"

"I thought I *was* shielding," he said, wondering at her anger. "What did I do?"

"Oh, nothing much! Only nearly cast yourself into that bloody lake of death in there!" Tears appeared in her eyes. "I do *not* want to lose you like that, Bulldog! I would rather run you through myself."

Her vehemence and cursing let Bull know how near he had come to disaster. He stared at her helplessly. "I'm sorry," was all he could say. Now that the effects of the silver pool no longer overwhelmed his senses, he remembered what had happened. His skin turned clammy despite the heat. His heart painfully skipped a beat.

Sullyan's anger evaporated like snow in fire. She threw her arms around his huge body and hugged him. He returned the desperate embrace, the emotion of their close bond steadying his fear. His heartbeat slowed and returned to normal. "I take it that's what happened to the Baron?" he said, hooking a thumb in the pool's direction.

Sullyan dried her eyes, the irises golden once more as she dampened her power. By tacit agreement, they spoke no more of his near slip. He knew she would hold herself entirely responsible for his ineffective shield.

"I would think so. Neither of them could have resisted its pull, but Serrin may have held on longer. And if Reen fell into that maelstrom, his shrieks of pain would have snapped the youth from his thrall, enabling him to pull the Baron out. I will trawl the substrate once more, to be sure."

Bull was alarmed. "Is that wise? Won't you be exposing

yourself to danger if you use metaforce anywhere near that stuff? I can't imagine even you being immune to that."

"Not immune, no. I admit I also felt its call. But my shield is strong and I can resist. After all, I am familiar with the effects of this particular element."

Bull watched as she prepared to face the pool once more, not entirely convinced of her safety. Yet he did as she bade him and stayed where he was, where the solid wall of rock would protect him from the call of the elemental pool. He willed his strength to her as she vanished around the corner.

✛ ✛ ✛ ✛ ✛

Sullyan approached the blazing pool with caution. Shielding strongly, refusing to look at the seductive smoothness of the gently rolling surface, she sat cross-legged on the floor and tuned her metaforce to the substrate.

She was both amazed and fearful. She had never thought to find spellsilver in Albia, still less reverse-polarity spellsilver. And yet here it was: a vast molten pool of the deadliest substance known to Artesans. The clarion call of its lethal promise sang to her, ringing through her skull, offering her power beyond imagining if only she gave herself over to the flame of its touch.

She guessed that the unimaginable forces miles below her feet had twisted and changed the nature of the liquid metal, altering the flow of its magnetism as the lava heaved and pulsed. This pool must have formed the last time the volcano erupted, which was hundreds of years in the past. The tremendous energies of the venting magma must have ripped through a vein of spellsilver, lying dormant deep in Albia's mother rock, and forced it upward, vaporizing, changing, until it partially solidified into this incredible pool, the beauty of which moved her soul just as surely as it had moved Bull's.

Yet she was stronger than Bull, and she had greater experience with the effects of spellsilver. She had overcome it more than once and knew how to protect herself from the worst of its dangers. She blocked out the insistent pull of the molten metal and concentrated on sifting through the layers of milky substrate, looking for the fateful event that had activated the Baron's long-suppressed powers.

She found it easily, for the spellsilver enhanced the imprint, held it and deepened it, and she could read it clearly. She saw how the two men had come here, the younger leading the elder, naïvely eager to show his companion what he had found. She saw how mesmerized they both became, even Reen falling thrall to its beauty, creeping closer and closer until his foot slipped, pitching him to his knees as he partially fell, screaming, into the boiling liquid, clutching his cane and shrieking in anguish. She saw the frantic Serrin drag the thrashing, melting thing out of the pool, his own powers instinctively protecting his hand, and she saw him plunge the panicked strength of his untrained metaforce into Reen's mind, desperate to bring succor and ease from the pain.

Reen's terrible agonies unleashed forces of his own, and the amplifying nature of the burning pool thrust them into potency. He seized on Serrin's strength, the boy's ineptitude making it impossible for him to pull away, and took him over. Dragged unwittingly into Reen's agony, Serrin took the brunt of the pain, enabling Reen's mind to retain most of the sanity that the terrible anguish would otherwise have destroyed.

She saw how Reen mastered the boy, instinctively channeling Serrin's augmented powers to seal the worst of his hurts, holding himself back from the brink of death without even knowing what he did. And then he passed out. Released from the immediacy of the Baron's control, yet now joined irrevocably to the damaged creature's soul, Serrin carried the flayed and tortured body back to his rooms.

Shuddering in revulsion, Sullyan opened her eyes. The dreadful effects of the pool's great heat ought to have stripped the flesh from the Baron's body and melted his bones. In truth, it *had* done those things, but the bond between the two men saved the Baron, the spellsilver's puissance aiding in the unnatural preservation of his life. His awakened metaforce kept its hold on Serrin's soul, compelling him to serve the life he had saved, even beyond his normal limits. Serrin would have been sucked dry in saving the Baron's ravaged body, and Sullyan was only too afraid that she knew what had become of Serrin's soul.

She unfolded herself stiffly and stood, casting a glance back over the viscous silver surface and the tantalizing golden flames. The power still sang in the air, still moved through her blood with metallic beauty, but now she was repelled, not drawn. She had seen the Baron, swollen with stolen strength, ugly with the marks of his hatred, cast the limp and lifeless husk of his savior into the sucking silver depths. The innocent but corrupted young boy, drained of his lifeblood, his body violated by the lust of his companion, his trust and loyalty betrayed by the bigot's unreasoning hatred, died in bewilderment and anguish, ignorant of the true nature of the monster he had helped to create.

Tears pricked her eyes and she turned back toward the tunnel, suddenly desperate to leave this place. A dreadful fear gnawed at her heart.

Bull heard her coming and frowned at the expression on her face. "Sully! Are you all right?"

"I need to get out of here, Hal. I need untainted air."

Chapter Twenty-One

King Elias and General Blaine looked at each other as the door to the council chamber banged shut behind the last disgruntled councilor. Elias breathed a weary sigh of relief, and even the General ran his hand over his eyes.

"What the Void is wrong with these people?" the King demanded heavily. "To listen to them, you'd think it was my sole aim to ruin each and every one of them and divert their fortunes into my personal coffers. Don't they realize we're trying to protect them? Would they rather I ignored these terrible events? They ought to know by now that you and the King's Guard have no interest in taking over the city. Gods, if you had wanted a military-run state you could have had it years ago. You could have forced me into exile and taken control yourself. How can they not trust you? Have they forgotten who saved my reign? Do they really think they would be better off if we had lost the civil war?"

"Calm down, Elias," the General advised. "They're worried, that's all, and it's not so surprising. Neremiah's murder and the slaughter of Denny and his band have hit them hard. Not to mention what nearly happened to the First Minister right here in the castle. There have been no serious threats to the city for years now. The thought that someone can just walk in and cause so much confusion has frightened them. Our singular failure to discover who is behind these events has added to their distrust. They fear the military is looking for a scapegoat—someone to blame in order to save face. The fact that such deception is the last thing on our minds is neither here nor there if we can't convince them."

Elias slumped inelegantly against the padded back of his seat, snorting in frustration. "Regus put that idea in their heads. Haven't I compensated him enough for the theft of his coach and valuables? I don't believe for one minute he lost the amount he says he did. Oh, if only we had Levant here. He'd have put that irritating little weasel in his place. He knows exactly how to handle the likes of Regus. I hope it's not too long before he's back on his feet. I have a feeling we're going to need him."

The General agreed. The First Minister's natural air of veracity and competence had calmed many a heated discussion, and his unwavering support for his monarch had pushed through many an unwelcome proposal. He was universally respected among the councilors, and few would have continued to argue if he had thrown his weight behind Elias's decision to continue the state of military regnancy. A decision that the King, bereft of his First Minister's advice, now seriously doubted.

"Is there any word on Rendan's condition?" Blaine asked casually, hoping to divert Elias's attention.

The King shook his head. "Not since this morning. I left instructions to be informed immediately if there was any deterioration. Perhaps he's well enough to receive visitors. He must be wondering what the Void has happened."

The two men rose, glad to leave the chamber where they had spent such a frustrating day. It was now late in the afternoon, and Elias felt the need to stretch his aching back and forget the petty grumbles of venal merchantmen and grasping minor nobles. He eyed the General as they stepped into the hallway outside the council chamber, mercifully quiet now after the earlier barrage of raised voices.

"What do you intend to do tonight, Mathias? Are you staying here and sending Vassa back?"

The General returned his monarch's look. In truth, he had not decided. He wanted to wait until he heard from Sullyan whether she had uncovered anything new in her second visit to the island. As yet, he had insufficient information on which to base a military decision. He was unwilling to make any judgments on his monarch's or the city's safety without further intelligence. He hoped Sullyan would at least clear one possibility out of the way.

"I will let things stand for the moment. Vassa addressed the men this morning and instructed them all to be on their guard. I'm leaving him in charge of the increased security. We have restricted access to the castle and we can't reasonably do any more to protect the city without cutting off our trade completely. I have no sound reason to do that. We have men out scouring the streets as it is, looking for clues to Neremiah's murderer and Levant's assailant, but I doubt we'll find anything now. If it wasn't for the dreadful state of that body Sullyan found in the east wing, I'd have believed he was our man—that he tried for you and Seline after Neremiah, but got Rendan and the poor nursemaid instead. But he was too decomposed for that. He must have been there for weeks. How he got there, we may never know.

"Let's concentrate on the matter at hand. Wait until Sullyan reports, then we might know more. Although how she's keeping it together with Major Tamsen missing, I just don't know."

Elias pursed his lips at the mention of Robin's name. He felt so totally helpless, so completely unable to understand what was happening, and it was a sensation he didn't like. If he, his family, or his officers were being targeted, he wanted to know by whom, and why. The random nature of the attacks so far, and the inexplicable mystery of how they were carried out, left no room for reason or sane suggestion. Brynne Sullyan, he realized, was the only one who believed she knew the answer.

He went cold. What if she was right? Hadn't he always trusted her instincts? Why was he so reluctant to do so now? What if

Blaine was wrong to be so skeptical? How much damage had been done by their failure to act sooner? What had Sofira said to him when she stormed out of her father's dining hall? His face paled as he thought of the venom behind her words and he heard again her spiteful, lashing tones. *Look to your safety, Elias of Albia, and look to your throne!*

Had they been wrong to discount her words as the meaningless bile of a bitter woman? Were they more sinisterly significant than he had thought?

They arrived at the guarded door to Levant's chambers just as his physician emerged. The man jumped when he nearly walked into the King and he took a moment to compose himself. Elias realized that the events of the past few days had affected everyone's nerves.

"Ah, your Majesty." The healer bowed his head to Elias. "Lord Levant has awoken and is asking to see you. He is weak yet, but recovering well. I believe it would be beneficial if you were to speak with him. He is concerned for your welfare."

Elias gave an exasperated smile. "He's concerned for *my* welfare? I'm not the one who nearly died."

The healer declined to comment as he held the door open for his monarch. Upon seeing the aging minister propped on his pillows through the open bedchamber door, Elias gave the patient a broad grin and approached the bed.

"What's this, Rendan? Having a lie in? Trying to get out of your duties again? I'm not fooled, you know. I'll only save them up for you."

"I'm counting on it."

Levant's voice was rough. His throat had been damaged by the violent purging of the poison and would take some days to heal. A soothing drink, suffused with honey, sat in a goblet by his bedside. He reached out a shaky hand for it and took a sip.

Elias sat on the edge of the bed and examined the minister's pale, bearded face, seeing the undimmed blue eyes clear and free of confusion. He gave a silent sigh of relief. "How are you feeling, old friend?"

"I've been better," Levant admitted. "I really thought I was going to die, Elias. I've never known pain like it."

"Seems you're harder to kill than they thought. Although if it hadn't been for Brynne Sullyan and Taran Elijah, you would now be dead. They worked like devils to keep you alive."

"Then I want to thank them both," Levant croaked, his eyes sliding from the King's. "That was service beyond the call of duty. It can't have been pleasant."

Elias was sorry that his old friend could recall what had happened to him. The description of what the poison had done to him and to Bessie had turned the King's stomach. It would be better for Levant if he had been too far gone to realize what a state his body was in, but it seemed he hadn't been granted that mercy.

"I'll call Taran for you, if you like," the General offered. "He should be about somewhere, although I've not seen him since last night."

"I'd like that, Mathias, thank you," Levant replied, smiling weakly. Blaine strode toward the door to send a one of the guards in search of the court Artesan.

"How is the city, Elias?" Levant asked.

The King grimaced. "Unhappy. I've decided to continue the state of military regnancy until this crisis is past, and the people were not pleased to hear it. All the strange goings-on and the restrictions on movement in and out of the city have frightened them. Lord Blaine and I spent the entire day fending off outraged nobles and senior merchantmen, worried their profits will fall. They seem to think we're deliberately trying to ruin them. The gods know why. If the city does poorly, so does my Treasury."

Levant smiled, the unstrained expression bringing a semblance of his old self back into his eyes. "Let me guess. The dissenter with the loudest voice was a certain Sir Regus."

Elias snorted. "Well, that wasn't hard to work out. If you're trying to impress me with the sharpness of your wits, you've failed."

Levant tried to laugh, but his throat was too sore. The King frowned and reached for the goblet of warm liquid, which he pressed on Levant. The man took it, finally recovering breath enough to drink, and lay back against his pillows, his face pale once more.

"You're far from well yet," said Elias, standing up. "I don't want to tire you. I just wanted to let you know that Blaine and Vassa have put strict measures in place for the security of the castle. Not even a fly could get in here now without their permission. Once Taran has been to see you, you're to go back to sleep. I'll come and visit again in the morning to tell you what happened in Bordenn."

Levant's reply was interrupted by a commotion in the hallway. Elias's face darkened in displeasure. "Oh, gods, what now?"

Raised voices sounded by the entrance to Levant's chambers. Elias heard Blaine swear viciously—a serious departure from habit—and he left Levant's side with a low oath of his own. The First Minister struggled to raise himself from his bed, desperate to know what was wrong, but he fell back, too weak to support himself.

"What the Void is it?" demanded the King, striding up to the General. Blaine didn't answer. Elias took one look at his face and recognized the signs of an Artesan at work. He turned to the waiting guard fidgeting in the corridor. "What, man? What did you tell him?"

The guard looked worried. "Adept Elijah was not in his

rooms, your Majesty, so I sent a runner to the garrison. It seems he went out this morning with a guard and hasn't been seen since."

Elias turned pale. "This morning? Where did he go?"

"Captain Dexter said he went to the Baroness Jinella's estate. He wanted to check on something. I didn't really understand what."

Elias turned his attention back to the General. This was Artesan business. He wouldn't expect the guard to understand, but Blaine obviously did. He watched the General's face in an agony of suspense as the man's eyes regained focus. The anger, distress, and fear Elias read there caused his heart to clench. "Dear gods, no!" he breathed. "Not Taran, too."

"There's no sign of him," the General confirmed curtly, his voice hoarse, his angular face pale with fury. "I've searched as far as I can. I can sense his imprint in the substrate over to the north, but he's not there. He's gone, Elias. He's been taken."

⁜ ⁜ ⁜ ⁜ ⁜

Patrio Ruvar's house smelled pleasantly of brewing fellan and hot food. Bull hoped Sullyan wouldn't refuse sustenance. She had not eaten since morning and he knew how the experience by the pool had drained her. She would accept the fellan without question, but she also needed food.

He need not have worried. The knowledge she now possessed had impressed on her the seriousness of the situation. Depriving herself of food would be foolish. She took the chair offered by Ruvar and accepted the plate of meat handed her by Frar Varian. Bull remained standing and served himself, placing a large mug of fellan by her elbow.

Ruvar had not yet spoken, but once his guests were seated and served he turned to face Sullyan, his expression grave. "I can tell by your demeanor you found what you sought. Does it help you?"

Sullyan paused before replying, her face turned to the fire. "Help me?" she said, her voice distant and vague. "After what I have seen, I doubt if anything can help."

Ruvar glanced at Bull, who shrugged. He was unwilling to voice an opinion. Sullyan would have to assimilate and consider all she had learned, and it might take some time—time she feared Robin did not have.

"I take it there was more to the Baron's relationship with Serrin, and the manner of their leaving us, than we were given to know," Ruvar said, his voice taut with ire. The thought that the Baron had so deceived them all and had committed murder on their sacred island struck to the depths of his soul.

Sullyan raised her head to gaze on the cleric. There was a strange light behind her eyes, a gleam of fanaticism, or maybe instability, and it disturbed him. She saw Ruvar's uncertain frown, but made no effort to control herself.

"It is as I feared," she murmured, her voice carrying the taint of her horrified thoughts. "Serrin was foully murdered after giving his all and yet more in saving the Baron's life. The dreadful injuries Reen sustained caused his latent powers to surface, and the peculiar qualities of the holy pool augmented those powers, enabling him to draw on the succor Serrin offered so freely. Unfortunately, those same powers also alerted Reen to the fact that his companion, the one person to befriend him and warm his withered heart, actually possessed those same despised traits that had worked Reen's downfall. Despite Serrin's brave efforts, Reen's mind was affected by the agonies he suffered, and in his rage and confusion he ignored the gift of life Serrin had granted him, seeing only the imagined betrayal. In his unreasoning abhorrence, he destroyed his savior, devouring his soul as he did so.

"The dichotomy of his actions—taking revenge on a despised

enemy yet killing his innocent young lover—drove him to the ranting fits of despair that you and your clerics witnessed."

"But how did he hide his injuries?" wondered Ruvar. "If he was as damaged as you say, why did we not see evidence of it? Apart from the changes wrought by deprivation and madness, he was much as before."

Sullyan's eyes strayed back to the fire, her hands cradling the warm comfort of her cup, the remnants of her food forgotten. Her face was pale and Bull was sure he could see a tremor running through her body, whether from weariness or fear for Robin, he could not say. He needed to get her back to the Manor. To be with her son and recover some strength was what she needed most right now.

"Reen devoured Serrin's soul, Ruvar," she repeated, her voice crawling reluctantly into the tense atmosphere. "He took the boy's succor as it was offered, but at the last he took so much more. You were not permitted to see the extent of the Baron's injuries—that would have revealed far more than Reen could afford. It was necessary that you believed him to be frail and failing. That way, his apparent suicide would seem more credible, as indeed it did. He used the semblance of Serrin's youth to conceal the worst of his appearance. He stole the boy's strength when he took his life."

Ruvar's face betrayed shock and horror. "Is that what Artesans do?"

His tone was accusatory. Bull understood his reaction. Ruvar was the guardian of this holy community. Such things as Sullyan suggested should not happen here. He had failed in his God-given guardianship and had allowed a malignancy to enter their midst, to share their worship and live undetected. He had even given it one of their own, a troubled young soul entrusted to his care, whom he had allowed to be corrupted with unnatural practices, finally condemned to eternity on the Wheel of Perdition. He had allowed the Holy Fire to be desecrated. All this had been thrust upon him by Artesans, and by the King. His distress and his anger boiled over.

"Is that what your kind does?" he raged, leaping to his feet. "Corrupt those who come to you, defile their spirits, consume their souls? Is that what it is to be an Artesan? No wonder the world reviles you! No wonder people shun those with such evil powers!"

Sullyan's head snapped up, her eyes blazing with fury. The horror of what she had seen and the icy fear that clenched her heart had eaten into her already tenuous control and this unwarranted attack took her breath away. Ruvar's undeserved accusations flayed her like knives, resurrecting all her anger at the unreasoning prejudice of people who didn't understand, who didn't want to understand. She had not expected to find willing acceptance here on this secluded island, but neither had she thought to encounter the same bigoted hatred that squatted like a toad in the Baron's dead heart. She surged to her feet, power billowing from her, calling sparks from her tawny hair. Her eyes were black with fury and her face was the color of milk.

"Is that what you think of me, Ruvar?" she spat, her voice resounding with power. "That I am an eater of souls, a despoiler of spirits? How dare you judge me by the malice of one man! Do you truly think us all so corrupt? Why then did you speak with me? Why did you help us if we are such a threat to your lives?"

"Sully!" Bull warned sharply, fearing she might go too far. He could feel her teetering on the edge of control, anger boiling inside her, just waiting to be released. The floor of the house was buzzing, the earth and rock beneath their feet ready to explode at the least of her commands.

She heard the timely warning in his voice and recognized the danger. Ruvar was still seething, hovering threateningly before her, readying himself for another onslaught. But Bull could feel her drawing back, damping her unintentional show of power, and he breathed a silent sigh of relief. So did Varian, who removed his hand from something hidden beneath the folds of his robes. Bull caught the movement and raised his brows, recognizing it for what it was.

Sullyan faced Ruvar coldly, her emotions now fully under control. She still felt angry, but its heat had turned to ice, the urge to strike contained. She would waste no more time here among people so willing to judge, so quick to rescind their friendship, based only on the actions of one renegade and despite their knowledge of her character.

"I thank you for your hospitality, Cleric Patrio," she said stiffly. "We will take up no more of your time. Come, Bull, let us leave these narrow-minded bigots to their isolation." She turned to leave, only belatedly realizing Bull wasn't following. "Bulldog!"

He could not respond. His eyes were unfocused and his face had gone slack, a sure sign he was communing with someone. Sullyan watched him, frowning. She disliked his aspect.

Ruvar stood forgotten, his anger turning to shame. His faith reasserted itself, showing him how unjust and wounding his angry comments were. His face flushed with embarrassment.

"Brynne—"

With a curt gesture, she brushed aside what he was going to say, her attention focused on Bull. He had not included her in his communication, and she would never force herself on him, but the anguish in his slowly focusing eyes frightened her. She stepped close to Bull and took him roughly by the arm.

"Hal? What is it, what has happened? Tell me. *Hal*!"

Bull stared at her through eyes blurred with tears. He shook his head, clasping her arms.

"It's Taran," he whispered, appalled. "Blaine can't find him. He went to Jinny's estate this morning and hasn't been seen since. Sully, Blaine says he's been taken!"

Chapter Twenty-Two

The fire in the grate crackled sharply as Varian added more wood. Had Bull been less preoccupied, he might have wondered where it came from on this barren pinnacle of rock rearing out of the ocean. But his attention was centered fully on the woman sitting hunched on the seat by its warmth, her head in her hands, silently, desperately, expending her powers. He kneeled beside her and glanced up at Ruvar.

"Patrio, might I trouble you for more fellan? This is going to weaken her, and she's already drained."

Ruvar nodded to Varian, who set about brewing fresh fellan. The young cleric crouched down beside Bull, giving him an apologetic look.

"There's no need for such formality, Hal," he murmured. "I didn't mean what I said. I don't know what came over me. I suppose it was revulsion at such evil living here among us with none of us being the wiser. I suppose I feel responsible. Perhaps if I had paid Reen more attention, tried harder to reach him, none of this would have happened. Poor Serrin! He was such a troubled soul, and we failed him completely. It eats at me that he died so dreadfully. That he gave his soul to our faith, only to have it snatched from him by such unspeakable evil. I should have been able to prevent that—I should have protected him.

"I know none of you are like Reen—of course I do. Do you think she will forgive my harsh words?"

Bull sighed, not really concerned with the young cleric's feelings. He had deeper worries to occupy his heart. "I expect so. Sullyan never harbors grudges, except against those who injure her loved ones. Don't trouble her for absolution right now, though. She'll have other things on her mind if she fails to find Taran. And I very much fear she will."

He was right. Sullyan came out of her search abruptly, traces of her power still lingering in her dilated pupils. She made no apology for the vicious oath that ripped from her mouth.

Ruvar widened his eyes and Varian frowned in disapproval.

"He is gone, as Mathias said. Just like Robin. Damn him, the bloody fool—*damn him*! Why could he not have waited? Why did he have to go up there alone?"

"He took a guard, though, didn't he?" Bull pressed fresh fellan into her hands. "I thought the General said he had taken someone with him."

"Yes, Bull," she snarled, "though he could have chosen a better candidate. He took Col, one of the men poisoned in Daret. And look what good it did him!"

"Col's a good fighter," the big man protested feebly. "So where is he? What happened to him?"

"Gods only know!" she spat, thoroughly furious. "Mathias has sent a company up to the estate to find out. We are to return to the Manor to await his findings."

"And what about Taran?"

She stared at him, arrested in the act of swallowing the strong, bitter fellan. "What about him? There is no trace of him! Where shall I look? Where do I go? Perhaps he is with Robin, wherever *that* is. Can you tell me?"

Tears ran down her face, but the fury remained in her eyes. It wasn't for Taran's folly, Bull knew. Whatever had befallen him was obviously powerful enough to overcome two trained and experienced swordsmen. And the disappearance of Taran's psyche from the substrate meant only one thing. No, her anger was for her helplessness and the strength of her love—that and her fear for her friends. Bull wanted to enfold her in his arms, but he forbore. She was only just holding together as it was.

"Ruvar, we must leave you," she said curtly, then drew a deep breath to steady her trembling body. "I deeply regret our earlier harsh words and I sorrow that you hold such unwarranted opinions of us. Nevertheless, I thank you for your help. I now know more about the threat that we face, although it fills my heart with horror. I hope that one day we can meet again under pleasanter circumstances, and that you will come to think better of me and my kind than you currently do. Forgive our hasty departure, but I trust you will understand."

Her cold, courteous tone brought color to Ruvar's cheeks. He moved to block her way when she would have brushed past him, and Bull saw her hand move as if to reach for her sword. But she was unarmed and the hand fell back to her side. She glared at Ruvar.

"Brynne," he said quietly, his voice conveying regret, "I ask your pardon for my earlier outburst. My accusations were unfounded and born of shame. I have failed my people and endangered their lives. I ought not to have taken out my failings on you. I know you are not evil, and neither are the powers you control. I understand you must leave now, and I do not seek to detain you. But please do not go with your heart full of anger. I was wrong and I acknowledge it. Please forgive me."

She held his anxious gaze for a fraction of a second before nodding. Ruvar's eyes betrayed his relief. She did not stay; she was desperate to hold her son, to be among friends, to rest the ache of her heart, although without Robin the ache would not ease. She swept from the room, gathering her weapons and swinging her cloak about her shoulders.

Bull gripped Ruvar's arm as he left, giving the young cleric a glance of understanding. Then he was gone, leaving Ruvar alone with his uncomfortable thoughts of evil and of a friendship so nearly broken.

Sullyan wasted no time transferring them back to the Manor, not even troubling to descend the icy steps to the landing stage. There was no one abroad in the dark and the portway she constructed was barely big enough for two. They were soon hurrying through the darkness toward the Manor's welcoming lights.

Cal met them in the hallway outside his apartment, followed by Morgan, Eadan, and Elisse. Sullyan kneeled on the floor and swept the children into a fierce embrace, tears coursing down her face. Rienne appeared in the doorway with anxious eyes, pleading to be told the dreadful news from Port Loxton was not true. Her fear for Taran increased her fear for Robin, and Rienne was on the verge of collapse. When Bull shook his head, Cal had to support her in his arms.

"Come inside, love," he murmured. Taran was his closest friend. Cal owed him everything for finding him in that Roamerling camp, for befriending him and showing him what he was. If not for Taran, Cal might never have found Rienne, might have spent his days wandering with the nomads until he died of overexposure to alien lands. He owed Taran so much and now he felt so helpless.

Once inside, he assisted Rienne to the couch. Bull followed him, with Eadan cradled in one huge arm, Elisse snuggled into the other. Sullyan walked behind, still communing silently with her distressed son. Cal closed the door.

"What are we going to do, Bull?" said Rienne, taking Elisse onto her lap as Bull sat down. "What's happening to us? We can't just sit back and let ourselves be carried off one by one! There must be something we can do."

Bull stroked Eadan's blond hair as he regarded Rienne. "I don't know, dear heart. Sullyan made some discoveries on the island, something significant concerning the Baron. Once she's had the chance to work through it, she'll come up with a plan, you'll see. He's not going to get away with this."

"Then you have more faith in me than I do!"

Sullyan's harsh voice, devoid of its usual lilt, cut across Bull's deeper tones. They all turned to look at her. Sullyan held Morgan to her in a clutch so fierce the little boy could barely breathe, yet he lay against her neck, thankful only to be in her arms.

Rienne's face paled. "Is there nothing?" she whispered. "Have we lost them? Is there truly nothing we can do?"

Her plea was so piteous, her aspect so distressed, that Bull thought Sullyan might break down. She was drained to the point of exhaustion. Insufficient food, her search on the island, her fears over Robin, and now this latest disaster, all had sapped her strength. She needed to sleep with Morgan cradled safely in her arms and dreams of finding Robin comforting her painful heart. Rienne's need was just too much.

She stood, her son still clasping her tightly. "I am going to my rooms," she said wearily. "I need to sleep. Have no fear, I will be shielded. Bull, if you could bear it, I would welcome your presence on my couch. Is that too much of an imposition?"

He gave a wan smile. "Not at all. But wouldn't you be safer in the College? He may try for you next."

"He has no need. He knows I will come. I need my own bed tonight. I would get no rest in the College. Morgan and I will be safe. Wake me if you hear news from Mathias, but only if it is good news. Otherwise, let me sleep."

She left carrying Morgan, and they listened to her retreating footsteps. Rienne sat enfolded in her own misery, Cal's arm about her shoulders. Elisse and Eadan watched the adults with frightened eyes, not fully understanding the words but reading the intense emotions in the room. Cal cast Bull a determined look and spoke in a low, savage tone.

"When she leaves to find them, we're all going with her. Tad and me, Dexter, and the rest of the lads. We won't be left behind! If she orders it, we'll disobey. If she tries to deceive us, we'll follow her. Not even the King's direct command could keep us from this. Robin and Taran mean too much to us—*she* means too much to us. I just thought I'd let you know."

"I expected no less," Bull replied heavily. "You'd have had the rough edge of my tongue if you hadn't felt that way. I know she'll never let *me* go, so you're the next best thing. I'll need someone to keep me informed."

Rienne sniffed, blinking back tears. "At least someone is thinking straight. You have to stop her from throwing her life away, Cal. You do know she'll offer to trade herself for the two of them, don't you?"

Bull nodded. "I didn't know for sure, but it's no surprise. Isn't that what any of us would do, given the chance? Don't worry so, Rienne, it won't come to that. Cal and the rest of the lads will do all they can to keep her safe. Won't you, Cal?"

Cal nodded, but Rienne was not so easily reassured. This was more serious than anything they had faced so far, although Elias's invasion of Andaryon had come a close second. In that instance, however, the perceived enemy was reluctant to fight, and their real adversary had not possessed such resources. Now that he did, there was no telling how far his hatred might allow him to go.

Rienne caught Bull's eye. "You had better go. She's up there on her own with Vassa and Blaine away. I know she'll be shielded, but she's weak and exhausted. Watch over them, Bull. They need you."

Bull stood, handing Eadan back to Cal, the little Prince giving his thick neck a hug before disengaging his arms. Bull ruffled his hair. "Don't you worry, your Highness," he said. "You get to sleep in the College tonight, in the infirmary. That'll be an adventure for you. Just don't go trying any of your tricks, though, or you might get a surprise."

Eadan managed the ghost of a smile, his eyes wide and his face anxious. Bull exchanged glances with Cal and Rienne as he left, silently assuring them of his watchful vigilance.

�֍ ✖ ✖ ✖ ✖

Robin and Jinny spent a truly wretched day languishing in their gloomy prison, but at least they were left alone. Worn down by fear and exhaustion, troubled by the travesty of a wedding, and terrified for their lives and their loved ones, they spent most of their time in sleep. Robin was suffering the accumulating effects of the spellsilver; it drained his energies and confused his mind until he could hardly tell what was real and what was imagined. The wound beneath his ear still gave him pain, as did the manacles on his wrists, and his natural ability to heal was blocked by the spellsilver in his blood. The constant throb of his injuries and the infuriating buzz of the ore were slowly driving him mad.

Jinny woke in a mood of tearful hopelessness after her futile attempts to call out to Taran. Her strivings had worn her out, and she still wasn't recovered from the two days of incarceration in the freezing hut. All she had succeeded in doing was to reaffirm her deep love for Taran, and the memory of their bitter row and her harsh words at their last parting haunted her. Her vivid dreams only caused her heart and body to yearn for him all the more; the fact she was unable to tell him how she felt tore at her soul.

Robin tried his best to console her, to encourage her not to give up, and he planted in her mind the thought that the more desperate she became, the more likely she was to succeed. She accepted his words at first, but the energy to carry on sending her thoughts soon deserted her. All she could do was lie against Robin's warm body and allow her mind to wander.

Sometime during the morning—or what they assumed was morning, as there were no windows in their room and they had no concept of the passing hours—two of the silent guards appeared, bringing more food and water. They exchanged the slop bucket for an empty one, mended the fire, and removed the body of the young runner. Robin had tried to persuade Jinny to examine Feilin again once they had woken, but the lad's unresponsive features and the eerie staring of his unmoving eyes unnerved her. Robin let it go. He had no more strength than Jinny and didn't want to push her too far. She was already coping with more than she had ever endured before and he could not, in all conscience, fault her sensitivity. From what he had been able to see of the boy, he didn't think Feilin was truly alive anyway. He did his best to dismiss the lad, and the memory of the Baron's evil violation, from his thoughts. They had to concentrate on themselves.

They drank the water and ate what food there was. It was never enough to satisfy either of them. Robin almost blessed the pounding ache in his skull, for it took his mind off the unbearable emptiness in his belly. Once the food and water were gone and the needs of their bodies taken care of, exhaustion set in again. With nothing else to do but wait and fret over their fate and the safety of their friends, they huddled together on the uncomfortable bed, for warmth and for comfort, and either talked or slept.

Robin thought it was early evening when they were disturbed again. His trained senses, dulled though they were by spellsilver and sickness, still reacted to the sound of footfalls outside their room. The start he gave as the bolts were drawn roused Jinny from her torpor. She raised her head from his chest, eyes dull with fatigue, too drained and wretched even to show much fear. She would almost have welcomed her uncle, coming to deal them their fate, yet it was only two guards bringing another meager offering of food. Robin ignored them once he was certain Reen was not with them. They never spoke and he never troubled to demand answers of them. He knew they would not reply. He closed his eyes once more and bowed his head to Jinny's hair. She had also dismissed the men and lapsed back into her troubled reverie.

The sound of someone approaching the bed made Robin look up again, a frisson of fear shivering across his nerves. His muscles tensed instinctively, although he was helpless in the chains. He managed to focus his vision and a face swam into view. Robin frowned. He recognized those thin features.

The short man who stood before him turned briefly, waving a hand at the other guard. The swordsman withdrew after a moment's hesitation. The thin man watched him go before turning back to Robin.

"Major? Can you hear me? Do you know who I am?"

Robin's frown intensified. The man's voice was familiar, he just couldn't place it. It wasn't someone he knew well. A recent meeting, then, and here in Lerric's palace ....

"Captain Bassan," he murmured weakly, the low tones of his voice rousing Jinny once again. She reacted with a small gasp of fear at the man's proximity and he drew back, holding up both hands.

"I mean you no harm," he said, looking from Jinny to Robin. "You need not fear me."

"Can you help us then?" Jinny said quickly, her flare of hope bringing out more animation than Robin thought she possessed. "Can you free us?"

Bassan's face fell and he looked awkward. "I dare not," he said, unable to meet her eyes. "The Baron has the whole garrison under his control. I don't know how he's done it, but they're all loyal to him now. You'd never get past them, and even if you did, where would you go? The weather's foul and all roads are closed. You'd be tracked easily even if you did get out. You'd be cut down in minutes."

"That might be preferable to what the Baron has in mind." Robin spoke with an effort. He found coherent speech difficult, with his brain buzzing so nauseatingly. The energy needed to force his mind to work threatened to relieve him of what food he had eaten. "Captain, you must try to prevent Reen from carrying out his plans. He's thoroughly evil. He's developed powers that threaten the whole of Albia, and he plans to destroy us. Even if you can't help *us*, you can help stop the Baron. He hasn't taken you over. You can get close to him—he won't suspect you. A quick knife in the heart is all it would take. You could do that, Bassan. It's your duty to your king and the High King."

Robin knew he wasn't making much sense, but he didn't know how much time he had. Bassan obviously didn't feel comfortable with what was happening. That much had been plain at the wedding and was confirmed by his presence here. Robin didn't know why the man was taking such risks. All he knew was that Wil had spoken respectfully of the captain's treatment of him, and had recognized potential in him. That was good enough for Robin. If only the incessant clamor in his mind would leave off. Then he could order his thoughts and make the most of this unlooked-for ally.

"Bassan, you have to believe me," he urged, fighting the nausea swelling in his guts. "The best way you can serve us, and Lerric, and Elias, and the whole of Albia, would be to plunge a sharp knife into that monster's heart. Please, Bassan, you have to try! If you don't, you'll never forgive yourself. Your life will change forever, and not for the better. I'm not asking you to free us. Just do what you can about Reen."

Bassan looked uneasy. Robin wondered if the man even knew why he had come. He watched troubled thoughts chase each other across Bassan's eyes and knew it was hopeless. The man was alone. He was hardly going to risk his life over the confused ramblings of one captive. A fresh wave of sickness swept over Robin, causing him to retch. Jinny took a damp cloth and held it to his lips, tears on her face and wretchedness in her eyes.

"If you're not going to help us, get out!" she spat. "Leave us to die at the Baron's hands. Don't torture us with false hope. Don't you think we've got enough to cope with? How much more do you think we can take?"

"Jinny," Robin murmured when he could speak again. "Don't wear yourself out. He's not worth it."

Bassan reacted as if slapped. He moved away, stalking stiffly to the door.

"Bassan."

Robin's hoarse voice brought Bassan up and he stood immobile, his hand on the latch.

"Think about what I said," Robin pleaded wearily. "If you can't bring yourself to kill him, at least send a message to the King. Warn him of Reen's marriage to the Princess. Let him know the traitor is here. It's your duty, if nothing else. And you would have my undying gratitude."

Bassan stiffened at the word "duty," but Robin had no idea what it meant to him. Where did his loyalties lie? Surely not with the Baron, but he might be loyal to Lerric or Sofira. Would he consider a message to Elias a betrayal of that loyalty? Or did Bassan see the Baron's usurpation of Lerric's palace and all it contained as a blow against those he had sworn to protect? Robin could only pray for the latter.

Bassan turned his head slightly, casting a swift glance over his shoulder at the two captives. Jinny sat with her shoulder pressed to Robin's side. If her hands were not bound, they would be thrown around his neck. Robin lay half supported by the bedhead and half by Jinny, his face slick with sweat, eyes hopeless. Bassan frowned, as if affronted by the sight. He didn't speak, but he nodded his head just once, registering the flash of hope that leaped into those dark blue eyes.

Chapter Twenty-Three

Traveling the Veils while wounded was something Artesans learned very early to avoid. The substrate could do peculiar things to an unprotected bloodstream, and unless the affected person was shielded, the effects could be catastrophic. They could be likened to the effects of spellsilver, only magnified, and were exacerbated by the intense nature of the milky barriers. The experience had been known to kill, and to drive the unwary insane.

Spellsilver, however, blocked all metaphysical functions, and the effect of the Veils on a wound was mostly a metaphysical function. It was true that a non-gifted person would suffer pain and trauma if translated against their will, but a wounded Artesan under the influence of spellsilver suffered pain and confusion only, not permanent damage.

Taran was currently in a position to appreciate that. To think of spellsilver's nauseating effects as protection was not a connection he had ever made. It was not a completely alien concept. He knew that when the injured Prince Aeyron was abducted by the Baron, spellsilver had prevented him from dying in the transition. Yet Taran's screaming brain had no thought for the experiences of others. He was far more concerned with his own.

Rough, brawny hands hauled him up from the ground, adding to the pain of the wound in his throat. He registered words, but not their meaning. His entire world had turned gray and blurry. The contamination in his bloodstream dragged at the roots of his energy, leaching it away, and he had no strength left for struggle or concentration. His thoughts were focused on staying alive. Seth's shocking attack and Col's desperate struggle faded to insignificance beside the terrible effects of the knife in his throat.

Then came the agony. The soul-ripping, heart-jamming, lung-seizing anguish of an unprepared passage though the Veils. Taran's chest was locked in a vise of pain, his body unable to move. He was held in a rictus of agony and white fire blossomed with incredible pressure behind his eyes. His shriek, when it came, beat about his ears, spiraling desperately upward before being cut off by loss of consciousness.

Sense slowly returned to his world. Unfortunately, so did the pain. A low groan escaped his lips and he tried to move, to roll over so he wouldn't choke when the dizzying sickness roiling in his belly erupted. But the sharp pain that jabbed at his hands made him gasp, and he desisted. At least the pain had cut through the nausea, although he could feel it returning as the discomfort in his wrists eased.

A nasty chuckle nearby brought unwelcome memories flooding into his mind.

"What am I supposed to do with this?" a rough voice growled.

"Get rid of it, of course. I've got to get back. And keep your eye on that one—master wants him badly."

"I know, I know. You're not the only useful one round here. Now get out of my way."

Something heavy and cumbersome was dragged away and Taran tried to open his eyes. The pounding in his temples blinded him, but he finally managed to force his eyelids open a fraction. He instantly wished he had not.

The pearly shimmer of the substrate shone briefly in the air some ten feet away and then faded, as if someone had just passed through. It was too close, Taran was unable to shield, and another stab of agony shot through the base of his throat. He gave a small cry.

"Shut up, you, unless you want the toe of my boot."

The harsh voice came from somewhere to his right and instinct made him turn his head that way before he could think better of it. At least the movement saved him from choking on his own vomit, but the realization was small comfort in his misery. He coughed and retched until the spasm passed. When he recovered, his bleary eyes focused on the lifeless, bloody face of Col, lying on the ground nearby. The shock and grief that filled Taran's heart threatened to set him retching again. He controlled himself with difficulty and turned his eyes away.

The two men's comments now made sense. Col's corpse would be disposed of with no respect or ceremony, and as for Taran ....

He struggled to focus on what he knew, to make some sense of his surroundings. His throat still hurt, although the knife had been removed. Yet he could feel spellsilver coursing through his veins, hammering at the beat of his heart, causing his pulse to race uncontrollably. His wrists were bound, and in a sudden flash of clarity he knew what had happened. He bit back a groan; he didn't want to attract the attention of his rough captor. That would come all too soon, and he was in no position to resist or protect himself.

Despite his determination, tears came to his eyes. His precaution in taking Col as a guard had backfired badly and caused the young man to be killed. He could well imagine the anger and grief in Dexter's eyes when he learned the swordsman's fate. The worst of it was that Taran had gleaned nothing truly useful from his trawl of the substrate. He had only managed to place himself in a situation where his enemies could lay their hands on him. Poor

Col's brave sacrifice had been for nothing.

Taran marveled at Seth's betrayal. He had never even suspected him. The manservant had never been friendly, but he had served Jinny well in the three years since the trial. She may have been soft-hearted over the fate of her uncle's servants and concerned they should not suffer for his sins, and Taran had often teased her over her generous attitude, but she brooked no disobedience or lack of loyalty from any of them. He knew Seth had never given her cause for complaint. So why should the man turn on them?

But then, Seth's complicity in Taran's abduction didn't necessarily mean he had anything to do with Jinny's disappearance. Although given the man's taunting words after the fire, Taran thought it was likely. Sullyan had taught him to mistrust coincidence.

The thought of Sullyan pierced Taran's heart with fear. What if she tried to track him and sprang some sort of trap? If he should become the cause of her capture, or—oh, gods—her death, he would never, ever, forgive himself.

Tears spilled from his eyes. There was nothing he could do, whatever happened. He was helpless, bound in spellsilver, his hands chained. He would have to rely on the good sense of her friends and superior officer to dissuade her from anything rash. If she had not gone blindly after Robin, it was unlikely she would do anything foolish on his account. The thought calmed him, centered his courage. He would try to think as she would, he would do everything he could to get himself out of this mess, although right now he was too weak to even control the retching that constantly threatened to swamp him.

Under the guise of trying to alleviate discomfort, Taran turned his head to the side, away from the distressing sight of Col's lifeless body. Once the spinning vertigo had calmed, he took note of his surroundings. He lay on a deep fall of snow, and darkness had fallen. It had been dusk when he and Col were accosted, but he had no idea how long ago that was. He could not see very far from where he lay, but it seemed they were in open countryside. No lights studded the darkness.

About twenty feet away, he could just make out the shape of a horse tethered to a tree, but what he was searching for—signs of other men—he did not find. He turned his head the other way, ignoring the grunts of the man heaving Col's body into the deep depression he had made in the snow. They seemed to be alone. Once Col was buried in the snow, there were only the two of them.

The man approached Taran, eyeing him mockingly. "Don't think anyone'll find your mate until spring if this freeze holds up." He grinned. "Unless the wolves get him, of course. Fine bit of meat on him, for a wolf."

"You bastard."

Taran spoke as scornfully as he could. The immediate threat of death or injury had driven the burr of the spellsilver temporarily from his mind, and he was thinking clearly. If he could get the man angry enough to make a mistake, maybe he could do something to help himself.

"Oh, my, we are in a temper, aren't we?" the man said, refusing the bait. Taran would have to work harder to rile him. He had already ascertained that his legs were free. Praying the surge of nausea coiling in the pit of his stomach wouldn't suddenly erupt and spoil the move, he rolled and heaved himself to his feet. As soon as he was upright, he kicked snow into the man's face and then dove for his legs.

He was too slow. The deep snow under Taran's feet partially absorbed his desperate lunge. He would have fallen short of his target even if the man hadn't leaped aside. He landed on his face in the snow, his head pounding and his stomach lurching. He heard the evil chuckle again.

"You want to play rough, do you? Well, I'd be only too happy to oblige you, except the master wants you whole. Can't think why. Anyhow, I can't spare the time to teach you your manners— we've a bit of a ride to do yet. Best you sleep through that, I think."

Taran only half-registered the words. He was too busy throwing up. He didn't see the man line up the kick, but he did feel the boot that thudded into his temple. At least the agonizing shower of swirling light that burst within his head cut off the swamping nausea.

✤ ✤ ✤ ✤ ✤

Jinny wiped at her tears with her bound hands and looked guiltily up at Robin. "I'm so sorry," she said, her voice so small and piteous it brought tears to Robin's eyes. He longed to put his arms around her and comfort her, but all he could offer her was a smile.

"You've nothing to be sorry for," he said as warmly as he could. "I can hardly blame you for letting your feelings out when I feel like doing the same myself. I confess, I never expected you to show as much courage as you have, given the circumstances. I know I've said it before, but it's true; Taran would be extremely proud of you. *I'm* proud of you. I don't think anyone could have held up better than you have."

Jinny sniffed, flattered by his praise yet still trembling with terror. Robin had told her not to expect too much from Bassan. His assessment of the chances of Bassan getting a messenger out of the palace, let alone that message reaching the King in time for him to do anything to help them, quenched her hope like a dose of icy water and shattered the tiny bit of self-control she had left. But her storm of frustrated weeping had relieved some pressure. "I think Brynne Sullyan would hold up better."

Robin didn't reply and Jinny bit her lip in self-reproach. She wriggled closer to his chest and laid her head beneath his chin. "Oh, Robin, I'm so stupid. I shouldn't have said that. I should have thought. The last thing we need is more pain. We should be encouraging each other, not making silly comments. I was just trying to think of better things, but my brain's not working right. Can you forgive me?"

He tried to control the thudding of his heart and the shudder of his breath, struggling for composure. Forgiveness was not the issue. Calm was what he needed, what he had been striving for, and the need to take care of Jinny was the one thing keeping him from madness. It was a dreadful thing to feel, and incredibly selfish of him, but he was thankful for her presence. Without it, he would not have remained so clear-headed under the effects of the spellsilver.

She had, in truth, been a marvel. He knew Taran considered her so much more than the social butterfly she seemed, and Sullyan herself had reprimanded Robin for calling her that once. She had repeated the story of Jinny's efforts in rescuing Prince Eadan, and how she had duped Commander Izack, and pointedly reminded Robin that without Jinny's suspicions over the actions of her uncle, and her help in getting Taran and Ardoch into the mansion, they might never have rescued the boy. Reen might then have succeeded in his plans. Was that the behavior of a featherheaded socialite?

Robin had laughed and conceded the point, but he had never truly come to know Jinny. Now, during this time of enforced intimacy, he had come to know her better. Her capacity to cope with adversity stunned him. It wasn't just her resolve to see to his bodily comforts, although that was a blessing. He could not have coped without her help, and fouling either himself or the bed would have been a tremendous embarrassment. Not that the contortions they both had to endure in order for him to use the slop bucket were any less embarrassing, but Jinny had somehow managed to turn the whole thing into something approaching a comical farce, and they were able to laugh off their red faces. Repetition gradually reduced them to resigned acceptance; now they didn't even comment.

Yet she had shown her resourcefulness in other ways too, such as when she began asking him about spellsilver. She had heard of it from Taran, of course, but had never had direct contact with it. It didn't affect her, which they confirmed when she ran a finger around the edge of his manacles where the steel met the silver. He had half hoped for some reaction from her, some sign that she might, against all the odds, possess some faint hint of the gift, but there was nothing.

"It only works against the skin?" she had asked.

"It's only really effective against skin, yes," he replied, eyes closed, just resting. They had been woken by sounds of faint hammering somewhere far above them and Robin didn't want to speculate on what it could mean.

"So," she said slowly, "if we could slide some fabric or something under those manacles, do you think it would make a difference?"

Robin's eyes snapped open and he let slip a pithy oath. Jinny stared at him disapprovingly. She looked so much like one of the village Elders who had taught him as a child that he let out a snort of genuine laughter. "Oh, Jinny, you put me to shame! I'm not thinking straight—I should have seen it myself. Yes, it might help, but only if the fabric is thick enough."

They both looked at his bloodied, swollen wrists. Robin grimaced. "I don't think we can do it, though. This metal's been hammered on very tightly. And the skin is swollen. I don't think you could get the flimsiest gauze under there."

"We're still going to try," Jinny said fiercely, drawing a look of wonder from Robin. "If you think you can stand it, that is. I'd hate to hurt you."

He smiled in approval. "Go ahead, my Lady. I've heard your touch is most gentle."

His mischievous inference brought a blush to Jinny's cheeks and his smile widened. He knew she would not succeed, but he couldn't take this away from her. If they didn't try, she would always wonder if it might have worked, and it was a good idea. If only one of them had thought of it earlier, before his wrists swelled so badly. But that was his fault—he was trained for situations like this, she was not.

The experiment was, of course, a failure, and the memory of her tearful face brought Robin back to the present. How could he have let her innocent reference to Sullyan affect him so badly? If she needed to talk then he had to let her, and if her conversation threw up names he would prefer to avoid, well, that was his problem, not hers. He bent his head to her hair.

"Jinny, Jinny, there's nothing to forgive. And you're wrong, you know. Sullyan might well handle a situation like this differently, but she couldn't do it any better."

Jinny's beautiful green eyes brimmed, and Robin suddenly saw why Taran had fallen for her. For years now, Robin had had eyes for one woman only, and her delicate beauty was the benchmark against which he measured all other women. He loved Rienne as a friend, and her slim shape and dark hair always reminded him of Jessy, the beloved sister he lost to a terminal illness. But he had never felt the attraction that could have become true love from anyone other than Sullyan. Until now.

He shook his head to clear it. It was their terrible situation and the close bond they had been forced into that made him think like this. That and his intense need for Sullyan. Now he found he also understood the unbreakable tie that joined Sullyan to Aeyron. They had shared a similar experience in the stone circle while awaiting the destruction of the Veils. He had never been jealous of that, but it was good to finally understand how it had come into being.

He smiled for Jinny and drew a breath to assure her he meant what he had said. The words were never uttered. Footfalls approached their prison, a slithering noise accompanying them. Robin's head jerked toward the door, his face paling. Jinny gasped in fear, clutching at him with her bound hands. They both knew, somehow, that this was not just another delivery of meager food.

The door swung open and the Baron stood there, his slump-fleshed skull grinning, his mad eyes glowing red. Robin did his best for Jinny's sake, but he couldn't stop the panicked thundering of his heart or the fresh sheen of sweat that broke out on his naked chest. Jinny cringed back against him, staring in terror at the grotesque figure of her uncle. He took one step closer, his eerie eyes fixed on her face.

"Come here, my dear."

The smug voice crawled like a snake into the gloom and one withered claw beckoned to Jinny. She shrank back farther, but Robin's body was behind her and there was nowhere she could go.

"Leave her alone, you bastard!" hissed Robin, the strength of his fear making his head swim. "What has she ever done to you? What threat is she to you? Let her go. You've no need to harm her."

The Baron took two more steps closer, his face darkening, his whole body stiffening in anger. Yet the insane grin never left his dried-up lips and the sullen glow in his ruined eyes intensified.

"Harm her, Major? What makes you think I'm going to harm her? I have a use for her, that's all. Something better for her to do than sitting here conspiring with you.

"Jinella, come *here*."

The last words were said with force, and Jinny whimpered. Robin didn't believe the Baron for one moment, but he could do nothing about it if he did intend to harm her. What's more, Robin's futile protestations might incite the evil man to action even if he hadn't, at first, intended it. The only thing Robin could hope for was that Jinny would not be forced to witness what the Baron intended to inflict on Robin. He gazed down at the top of her head where she had pressed herself as close to him as she could.

"You'd better do as he says."

Jinny's gaze snapped up to his with a look of pure betrayal. Robin's heart clenched painfully.

"Remember what we said, my Lady?" he whispered urgently. "Remember what you promised? You have no choice, and I can't protect you. Do as he says and maybe it won't be so bad."

"How can you say that?" wailed Jinny, clutching at him. "I can't leave you. I might never see you again!"

One of the Baron's silent guards came into the room. He crossed swiftly to the bed and grasped Jinny's arm, wrenching her away from Robin. She cried out and struggled.

"Jinny!" Robin called weakly, desperately. "Remember what I told you. Remember your dreams."

He could only hope Jinny would understand that he was asking her to carry on her attempts to contact Taran. It was the only slight chance left to them, and he willed her to find the strength to continue. But he didn't know whether she had even heard him. She was still struggling against the swordsman, kicking and biting at him, screaming in his face. The Baron looked on in amusement, something in his eyes arresting Robin as he watched the ugly scene.

The scarecrow crossed to the struggling girl and raised his right arm, bringing his hand sharply down on Jinny's face. The slap resounded in the gloomy room, and Jinny's furious screams abruptly cut off as her head snapped back from the force of the blow. Robin reacted violently, unthinkingly, lunging against his chains, but he only succeeded in bringing a fresh flow of blood from his wrists. He fell back, groaning with pain and sickness. He saw Jinny hanging limply in the swordsman's arms, all the fight gone from her, her terrified eyes fixed on the grinning face of the creature that had once been her uncle.

"Will you behave now, my dear?" he asked smoothly. She summoned the energy to spit at his face, but missed. His grin widened. "Oh dear, Jinella, I fear you've been keeping very bad company lately. Your manners have deserted you, as has your good sense. Your feeble attempts at defiance are not doing your friends any good at all."

Jinny stiffened at the implied threat to Robin and her pale face drained still further. Robin's beleaguered mind latched on to the Baron's words even through the waves of sickness. He could have sworn the Baron had spoken in the plural. A cold hand of dread seized his heart and stopped it for a beat or two.

"What is it you want from us?" pleaded Jinny. "I don't understand you! Why are you doing this? Why are you being so evil?"

"Evil?" hissed the Baron, thrusting his dreadful face close to hers. "The evil here is not mine! You don't think I should be angry at my undeserved punishment? You think I should have been content to wither away on that barren, benighted island? Grateful that my life was spared, when all of you clamored for my death? That I should not want revenge against those who stripped me of everything I had?

"I'm disappointed in you, niece. You should know me better. You should know I would never give in to my enemies. And now that I have the means to destroy them all, that's exactly what I intend to do. You haven't guessed what I want with you? Well then, I'll tell you. Apart from wanting to teach you the price of your betrayal, I thought you might be useful. And I was right."

He grinned at Robin and the Major's blood turned to ice as he guessed what was coming. Hopelessness flooded his being. Jinny hung in the guard's grasp and watched her uncle's flaring red eyes in horrified fascination, unable to look away. Robin steeled himself not to react; he owed it to Jinny.

The Baron's voice went on, crawling across their skin, worming into their ears. "Yes, I was right, dear niece. You have performed your first task very well. And now I have another for you. My wife needs a maid, someone we can trust. I have decided that you will serve her, Jinella, and you will serve her well. You will see to her every need and you will be obedient and silent."

It was not what Robin had anticipated. Jinny had not seen it coming either. Incredulous fury suffused her face. "Like the Void I will!" she yelled. "I'd kill her first!"

"Now that wouldn't be a very sensible thing to do," the Baron chided smoothly. "Not when I hold someone you value in the palm of my hand."

His low, menacing voice and the clear threat in his eyes cut through Jinny's defiance. She cast a swift, apprehensive look over her shoulder at Robin. He closed his eyes, dreading what the next few minutes would bring. The Baron stretched his desiccated lips in a wider smile.

"And if you won't pledge me your good behavior on his account, then I have another inducement which might persuade you. Guard!"

Scuffling noises came from the passage outside, and then the slithering they had heard before. The swordsman holding Jinny pulled her roughly away from the door, and the Baron stepped back. A second man came into view, dragging a third who was barely conscious, his head hanging. Blood caked the left side of his face, coming from a nasty wound on the temple, and it trailed down the front of his shirt from a deep wound in the pit of his throat. He was groaning.

At the sight of him, Jinella thrashed in the guard's grip and cried out in anguish.

Robin sagged, partly with horror and partly, he was ashamed to admit, with relief. If it had been Sullyan in the swordsman's grip he might have died then and there, but he realized Taran's appearance didn't mean she was safe. He was desperate to speak to Taran, find out what the Adept knew. But Taran was in no fit state to speak right now.

Jinny cried out again, struggling with renewed strength born of desperation and terror, lunging for Taran. The guard held her tight and she turned furious eyes on her uncle. He forestalled her rage by stepping closer to her and producing a small knife from inside his robes, the same one he had used to strip Feilin. The sight of it froze Jinny's muscles and she stared at him in shock.

"That's better, my dear, now you're learning. You will become Sofira's maid, and you will do everything required of you, silently and willingly. Do you understand? For if you do not, it will go very hard for your friends here. Very hard indeed."

The Baron's eyes slid slyly to Robin's and the Major could not repress a shudder, feeling the echo of that claw trailing across his shoulders. The Baron grinned and turned back to Jinny.

"Your good behavior is surety for their safety, do you understand?"

"How do I know you won't simply kill them anyway?" spat Jinny, her eyes locked on Taran.

"You don't, dear niece. But this I guarantee you: if you step out of line, if you make one wrong move, then *you* will have killed them. Your actions will seal their fate. I promise you that."

She nodded and bowed her head, her shoulders trembling.

Reen brought the knife flashing up to cut the ropes that bound her hands. She gave a cry as the knife nicked her skin, and the sudden rush of blood to numb fingers was sharp and painful. She rubbed her wrists.

Reen gestured to the guard holding Taran and he dragged the Adept across the room, chaining him to the rings that had held Feilin, his back to the wall. He slumped there, unresponsive. Robin glared at the guard as he left the room. Reen beckoned to the last man, who gave Jinny a rough shove.

"Come, my dear. We'll leave your friends to ponder their fate while we introduce you to your new duties. Sofira will be relieved to have a trustworthy maid. Reliable staff are so hard to come by, don't you agree?"

With a final leer over his shoulder at Robin, the Baron followed his sobbing niece. The guard closed the door.

Chapter Twenty-Four

obin lay panting on the bed in the gloom. Harsh, labored breaths came from Taran's direction and he knew the Adept was far from conscious. So he lay as still as he could, trying to slow his pulse and control the dizzying sickness in his stomach. It refused to abate, and he knew why. It was generated by his fear: the fear that the Baron might also have Sullyan somewhere in this warren of a palace; the fear that he would kill Jinella, despite what he had said; and the fear of what he intended to do to Robin himself, and probably Taran as well. Sweat slicked his skin and chilled his flesh. Blood still dripped from his wrists onto the grubby mattress. The sight of it brought back the image of Taran's bloodied face, and Robin turned to stare at the Adept.

Taran's breathing changed, became less regular, and Robin knew he was struggling toward consciousness. The blood from the wound in his throat had dried, but that which caked the left side of his face gleamed wet in the glow of the fire. The injury to his temple looked nasty. Robin's professional assessment identified a boot as the weapon used. He only hoped Taran's skull wasn't fractured. That was a complication they could do without.

"Taran."

Robin tried to keep the tremor from his voice, tried to sound encouraging. Taran's breathing was ragged now. He was fighting the effects of his injuries as well as the numbing spellsilver. Robin called to him again, hoping a familiar voice might give him an anchor, a focal point, something to aim for.

"Come on, man, fight it. You know you can do it. Concentrate. Feel beyond it, look through it. Open your eyes, Taran, come on!"

He kept up a flow of instructions, not knowing whether Taran could hear him or not. The Adept's labored breaths were now interspersed with groans. The pain, at least, had registered with him. Uncomfortable though it might be, it was the first step toward him regaining his senses.

Taran tried to raise his head, the movement causing the stricken man to retch. Fortunately, he didn't seem to have anything to bring up. Robin didn't think he could stand to watch his friend choke to death. He called to him again, this time seeing a brief flash of white beneath Taran's lids. Robin panted in relief; he was coming out of it.

The Adept gave a deep groan and tried again to lift his head. Robin knew what he was feeling: The heavy limbs; the surging waves of sickness; the incessant buzz of the spellsilver; the pounding headache from his wound. He called his name yet again and was rewarded with a blind turning of the head.

"Robin?"

The weak voice was barely audible and his eyes remained closed, but Robin drew a huge sigh of relief.

"Taran, thank the gods. Open your eyes, if you can. It helps stop the spinning. Just don't make any sudden movements."

There was the ghost of a snort from Taran and Robin winced in sympathy. The Adept was hardly able to lift his head. Sudden movements were way beyond him. At least his wits were unaffected by the silver or the kick to his temple. Robin saw the bleary eyes slowly open.

"Oh, gods, Robin. I feel like shit."

"It's the spellsilver. Concentrate on the pain. It helps focus your mind away from it. You'll get used to it after a while."

"That's supposed to make me feel better?"

Robin fell silent as he watched Taran struggle with his nausea. There was nothing else he could do to help, and in truth he wondered whether the Adept might be better off if he succumbed to the spellsilver's effects. If what the Baron had in mind for Robin also applied to Taran, Robin would do him no favors by encouraging him to fight. It was only that he was desperate for news of Sullyan, of his son, and he willed Taran to wakefulness even as he reproached himself for his selfishness.

Taran blinked his eyes and Robin saw how he had to fight just to keep them focused. They were wandering and bloodshot and clearly not working too well. To give the suffering man something else to think about, Robin said, "Taran, was there … was anyone else with you when they caught you?"

Taran nodded carefully, as if his head were full of broken glass.

Robin's chest tightened and his lungs struggled to breathe. He wondered why his body was even trying. If Sullyan was already in the clutches of the monster, they were all lost.

"They killed him."

Robin closed his eyes. Tears spilled over his cheeks, splashing unheeded onto his chest. He didn't care. Why should he strive anymore? Jinny wasn't here to see him lose control, and Taran was scarcely conscious. Neither of them had the power to influence their future or their fate. Why not give up now and have done? Deprive the scarecrow of one of his victims, at least. Then Taran's words registered with him and his eyes snapped open.

"What did you say?"

Robin stared hard at Taran, dreadful images swarming in his

mind. Images of his son lying dead ....

Taran gazed at the floor, hovering on the verge of consciousness. His face bore no expression, his arms hung limply in the chains. He slowly raised his head as his ears finally delivered Robin's question to his brain.

"They killed him, Robin. They killed Col."

Once again, Robin felt a flood of inappropriate relief. This time he made no effort to suppress it. His body sagged with it, but his mind began to work once more. "Col? Who killed him? When was this? Taran!"

Taran glanced at Robin, his face pale with nausea. Once it receded, he said, "I'd gone to the estate with Col as guard. I thought we would be safe. I was going to search for a strange impression in the substrate Brynne and I found the night before, but when I did find it, it didn't tell me much. We were making our way back when we met Seth by the stables. I didn't expect to see him there and I didn't think he was a threat, anyway. But then he jumped me and yelled out to someone, and before I knew it he had thrown me to the ground and had a knife at my throat. The knife was spellsilver and when he cut me with it, I passed out. The next thing I knew, Col was dead and a stranger was burying him in the snow. I tried to tackle him, but I was too weak. He kicked me. Then I was here."

None of this meant much to Robin except that Taran made no mention of Sullyan being present at his capture. The Major drew a deep breath and spoke slowly and clearly.

"Taran, listen to me, this is very important. Was Brynne with you when you were taken? Is she here, too?"

Taran frowned as if Robin's question made no sense. "With me? Of course not. She was already gone when I woke up. She's at the Manor. Or in Andaryon. Or maybe on the island. I don't know."

Robin bowed his head, trying not to cry with relief. He did not know how far he could trust what Taran said. The Adept's wits were clearly still addled, but he was sure Taran would have remembered if Sullyan had been captured with him. If she had not, there was still hope.

Then Taran dashed that small comfort.

"She's coming, though."

Robin's head snapped up. "What do you mean?"

"She worked it out. She's convinced the Baron is behind this, and she believes he somehow has access to metaphysical powers. She was going to Andaryon to try to find evidence in their archives that someone like the Baron could learn to use his powers. It won't be long now before she acts."

Robin went white. "She must not! Oh, gods, she must not. It's so much worse than she knows, much worse than any of us could have guessed. Pharikian won't be able to help her this time. Gods, Taran, we have to find a way of warning her. Oh, if only I had been able to learn how to break through this damned spellsilver! She did it once, why can't I?"

Robin's violent desperation made Taran stare.

"Tell me, Robin," he pleaded, his voice low and strained. "What do you know?"

Robin lay back against the bedhead, his whole body trembling. He could see he had frightened Taran, yet he could not prevent the icy-cold dread surging through his veins from showing in his eyes or flooding his voice.

"He can consume souls, Taran."

"He can ... *what*?"

Robin knew how he felt. Taran's guts would be roiling, constantly threatening to heave into his throat. Robin's words would make no sense.

"What are you talking about? Consume ...? How?"

Robin was only too afraid Taran would get a graphic demonstration before much longer, and he had other information Taran should know before that happened. He did not know how much time they had left before the Baron returned. It would not take him long to introduce Jinny to her new duties. Then he would be back, and his intentions had been clear. Robin owed it to Taran to tell him as much as he knew. That way, the two of them might just stand a chance of contacting someone before it was too late. The thought of the Baron doing to Sullyan what he had done to Feilin was just too terrible to contemplate. But where could he start?

"Taran, did you hear what the Baron said before the guard dragged you in?"

Taran frowned, Robin's unexpected tack catching him off balance. "What? No, I don't think so."

"So you didn't … you didn't hear Jinny's voice?"

Taran started. His face, already pale, turned gray. "Jinny? Please don't tell me Jinny's here?"

Robin nodded.

"Oh, gods, no! Is she all right? Has he harmed her?" Without waiting for a reply, Taran rushed on. "It was because of Jinny that I went to the estate. I had such dreams—such vivid dreams. I felt she was calling to me, searching for me. I thought she was dead. I heard her, you know, the night of the fire. I felt her screaming in my head, but I didn't know what it was until it was too late. Brynne said Jinny had reached me through her love for me, that we had achieved a pair bond and that's how Jinny managed to overcome her lack of talent. I thought I had lost her, that she had killed herself in the fire, but then I found a letter she had written, telling me she had forgiven me. And then I had these vivid dreams, and I went to the estate to look for clues, to see if I could find her trail in the substrate. I took Col with me as a guard, but Seth jumped me and Col was killed. Somehow, I was brought here. Was it all a trap, Robin? Did that bastard Reen use Jinny to lure me out to the estate?"

All through Taran's rambling, a slow and dreadful realization had crept into Robin's heart. Taran's final words sealed the cruel irony of it and he did not know how to tell the man. Taran fell silent and watched him intently, his hazel eyes clear of confusion.

"Oh, gods, Taran," Robin breathed weakly. "It wasn't the Baron who lured you—it wasn't Reen. It was me. It's my fault."

Taran frowned. "What is? What's your fault?"

"That you're here. Reen didn't use Jinny to lure you. I did."

Taran stared at him, uncomprehending. Suspicion and alarm chased across his features, slowly replaced by disbelief.

"How could you have? What are you saying?"

Robin hung his head, too wounded and weary to hold it up. "She needed comfort," he sighed. "She needed something to do. And I … I saw what he did to Feilin and I knew I would be next. I was desperate to send a warning, to contact someone, but I couldn't get past the spellsilver. I encouraged Jinny to reach out for you, thinking her fear and her love might allow her to succeed. I never dreamed … oh, gods, Taran, I swear I never thought it might lead to this."

Taran watched him, still confused and troubled. "Tell me all of it," he said, closing his eyes. "Just tell me what we're facing. I have to know."

Robin went through the events leading from his capture, his eyes and voice conveying his utter shame at the simple way he had been duped. He described what had happened to Feilin in as much detail as he could, given that he didn't fully understand how the Baron had done it. Taran was white and sweating when he finished, the prospect of facing the same fate causing nausea to swell once again.

"I won't be able to stop him, Taran. All I can do is hope to use the pain to breach the spellsilver and warn Sullyan. And if I fail— if I'm not strong enough—it'll be up to you."

Taran looked shocked. "If you can't do it, how will I? He'll probably do the same to me. Gods, Robin, what if he does it to Jinny, too?"

Robin could not answer, but the Adept's first question sparked an idea. "You might try for contact with Rienne if you can't reach Sullyan. As an empath, she might be able to hear you. You've known her a long time. You're close to her. She will know you've been taken by now. It might add to her receptiveness if she's desperate for contact with you. Concentrate on her. She knows by now to tell Sullyan of any odd thoughts or feelings. Try to send Rienne a warning. Don't be too specific—just warn them off coming here."

Taran's eyes were huge in his sweating face. "I'll try, but I don't know, Robin. I've never—"

"You have to!" urged Robin. Now was not the time for fear or failure. They *had* to succeed. His anger startled the older man, making his face flush with shame.

Taran knew he was right. The impossibility of what Robin was asking had to be discounted. The impossible had been overcome before, after all. More was at stake here than their own lives. The safety of their friends and the very structure of their realm were once again under threat. Taran saw the light of desperate fervor in Robin's eyes and nodded.

✦ ✦ ✦ ✦ ✦

Jinny allowed the swordsman to hustle her along the cold, darkened hallways. She could not think and she could not feel. It was all too much and there was nothing she could do. Nothing except obey, and hope to whatever gods she still believed in that her obedience would buy her friends' safety. Or, at the least, it would leave her blameless of their deaths.

Jinny had no doubt that harm would come to Robin, if not to Taran. The Major was convinced of it and Jinny saw no reason to disbelieve him. Now that Taran was also in her uncle's clutches, her last feeble spark of hope was extinguished. She understood Robin's desperate plea—that she remember her dreams—but what use was that now? Taran was here and helpless, caught in her uncle's web. There was no one else she could call to. What could she do where two such strong men had failed?

Her uncle walked behind her, tapping his cane. She could almost feel the evil flowing from him. It crawled across her skin, sending shivers down her spine. She felt defeated, ashamed, and useless; a pawn in this game of power. Yet as she moved through the gloomy hallways, past deserted rooms, her anger rose and pricked at her conscience. Why should she allow him to use her? What gave him the right to discount her so totally, to ignore her so casually? Did he truly think her so helpless? Did he imagine her so spineless and cowed as to be incapable of causing him harm?

As her guard prodded her silently up the stairway to the palace's second floor, she tried to order her thoughts, force her weary brain to work. She might be deprived of her friends' comfort and she might well be forced to bow to her enemies' demands, but that didn't mean she had to stop using her eyes and her mind. Hadn't Robin drawn a response from Bassan? Hadn't the man agreed to send a message? What if she could speak with him again? What if she could persuade him to help her out of the castle? So what if the weather outside was foul? Surely she could find someone to help them. There must be a way of alerting the High King, or the General, or Sullyan. Just because she was alone did not mean she was completely without resources.

The swordsman directed her up a second grand stairway,

leading to the upper level where Lerric and his daughter had their private rooms. The entire palace seemed to be deserted and in darkness. No candles burned, no lamps lit their way, and the few hallway fires were banked low. Jinny tried to memorize her surroundings, to fix the way in her mind in case it should prove useful later. She straightened her spine, relaxing her shoulders, but then thought better of it and slumped again, as if dejected. She heard her uncle chuckle, a low growl in his throat, and shivered at the menace of it. Better if her captors thought her defeated and submissive than alert and watchful.

She remembered Robin's praise for her courage, and a measure of warmth crept into her frightened heart. She could not let him down. She now had Taran to think about as well. Robin had said he would be proud of her, too. She would see what she could do to deserve that pride. Seeing her lover again when she had thought him lost only served to strengthen her love, empower her resolve, and fuel her anger. He and Robin were imprisoned and helpless; she was not. She was their only hope and she would do what she could to live up to it.

When she was bidden to stop outside a guarded door, she tried to hide the light of determination in her eyes. It wasn't too hard.

Reen stepped around her and laid his hand on the latch. His myopic gray eyes, free of the sullen red glare, peered irritably into hers. He thrust his dreadful face close.

"Just you remember what I said, girl. Behave yourself and they will live. Make one wrong move and they die. Slowly, before your eyes. I may even force you to do the killing. I can, you know—you don't want to know how. So attend your duties and stay silent."

Despite her resolve, his threat withered her heart. She knew he would carry it out with no compunction. She also had a fairly good idea of how he could force her to kill her friends, and she had no wish to dwell on that. She meekly held his eyes, allowing her fear to show, and then followed at his back as he opened the door without knocking.

Sofira's chambers were huge, sumptuous, and comfortable; by far the most extensive private rooms Jinella had ever seen. With the bathing and dressing rooms, the apartment must occupy nearly half of the upper floor. Jinny guessed the other half must belong to Lerric. She suddenly wondered where the aging king was, and what he truly thought of his daughter's monstrous husband.

Then she caught sight of Sofira. The Princess cowered on her bed, her hands clutching folds of bedding protectively to her breast as she stared in horror at the Baron. Pathetic, wordless whimpers sounded in her throat. She wore a crumpled gown, clumsily laced at the bodice as if done up in haste, and Jinny realized it was her marriage gown, although the outer robe had been removed. There was a stain on the front of the delicate fabric. It looked as if Sofira had not changed or washed since her travesty of a wedding, or maybe even slept. Her face was bleached and pinched even more than usual, her eyes red-rimmed and wild. Her hair was disheveled and her jewels disarranged. Her whole aspect was of a woman recently woken from a dreadful nightmare—only to find the nightmare was real.

Reen advanced into the room and Sofira cringed away, wild eyes fixed on her husband's grinning face.

"Sofira, my Queen," greeted the scarecrow, a mocking sneer in his tone, "I have brought you a companion, a maid to serve you. She will see to your every need. You will find her obedient and silent, and if you do not ... well, she knows the consequences."

Sofira's white face blanched further, her gaze swinging fearfully from the Baron to Jinny and back again. Jinny watched her in puzzlement, trying to equate this disheveled, cowering woman with the spiteful harridan of the evening before. All

Sofira's fire seemed to have left her. She was a shell of the woman Jinny knew. Her brittle gray eyes came to rest on Jinny, and she read a kind of desperation there, a reluctant, terrified hope. She wondered at it.

Reen turned to Jinella. "You are to take care of her personal requirements. I will know if you do not, and I will know if you try to leave. Believe me, Jinella, there are no friends for you here, no matter what you might think. Lerric's palace is mine—his men, his servants, even the rats now answer to me. *All* of them. Do you hear me?"

Jinny tried not tremble. Did he already know of Robin's appeal to Bassan?

"You are to stay on this floor," the Baron continued, "except to meet Sofira's needs. You are not, under any circumstances, to venture to the lower floor. If you try to see your friends, I will kill them. Your pagan lover will be first, and you will both scream for my mercy long before he breathes his last. I trust we understand each other.

"Now I must leave you. I have business to attend and plans to take care of. If I were you, Jinella, I would stay safe and silent within these rooms. It may be that there will be fighting within the palace over the next few days. I would hate for you to get caught up in it."

Reen turned with a grin and stalked to the door. Jinny stayed where she was, watching the strange emotions that played across Sofira's face. Reen paused with his hand on the latch.

"One more thing," he said casually, his back to the women, "there are guards upon these rooms with orders to let no one in or out besides the three of us. One of them will accompany you if you leave the room, and he will watch you at all times. They are absolutely obedient to me, so do not trouble to question them. They have been instructed to relay to me any speech you might have with the servants. I trust you will remember this."

Reen opened the door and passed through, the guard outside pulling it swiftly closed. The latch clicked into place. Jinny listened to the footfalls as they receded down the hallway, then she turned back to Sofira.

The Princess ceased her whimpering and rose from the bed. The crumpled bedclothes fell away and Jinny gasped at the bruises on Sofira's bloodless flesh. The terror in her gray eyes had vanished, along with the hint of hope Jinny was sure she had seen. The woman who stood before her now more closely resembled the hard, cold Princess Jinny knew. Her brow creased in puzzlement.

"I have to bathe."

The curt, haughty tone startled Jinny. Sofira stared at her, daring her to argue. She held herself awkwardly, as if her belly pained her. Jinny's eyes were drawn to a long, damp stain on the satin skirt. Sofira saw her looking and glanced down. A high flush appeared on her face.

"Don't just stand there gawping, girl. Get about your business. Order the servants to bring hot water, and I mean *hot*, do you hear me? I want some of that soft soap the herbwife makes, and the soothing creams. I want a bath and I want it now. Well? What are you waiting for?"

Sofira's voice rose in pitch and Jinny heard the note of hysteria and saw the flash of insanity deep in the brittle gray eyes. She dipped a hasty curtsey and made for the door. As she left the room, collecting a silent guard, she vowed that should she survive this terrible place along with Taran, she would take pains to see that their own wedding night was full of tender pleasure. Whatever Sofira had experienced on hers, she thought with a shudder, had neither pleasured nor pleased her.

Trembling with anxiety, Jinny hurried down to the kitchens, where she found the strangely subdued servants. Her own fear making her harsh, she stirred them to frantic action.

Chapter Twenty-Five

Captain Dexter rode through the deserted streets of the dark city, his men ranged behind him. His orders were clear: to find the manservant, Seth, and bring him to the castle for questioning. The order had come down after Taran and Col failed to return to the garrison and a subsequent search of the estate turned up nothing but their horses. The captain might have had no luck locating the missing men, but he had learned from the gate guards that the manservant had been there at the same time. Even if it was a coincidence and the man had no connection to Taran's disappearance, he might have seen something that could be of use. Dexter volunteered to lead the search for Seth with grim determination.

He sent men into various parts of the city to the cheaper lodging houses, but so far had drawn a blank. Then they headed for the better quality houses, those serving the wealthier merchants. Dexter couldn't imagine how a manservant could afford such accommodations and was considering the possibility Seth had gone to ground somewhere. Yet it also occurred to him that maybe the man had stolen some of Jinella's coin on the night of the fire, using the confusion and the smoke to hide his crime. How else could a mere manservant afford a bodyguard? If that proved to be the case, he would be made to answer for it. If Jinella was dead, as an appointed noble rather than a hereditary one, and lacking any immediate dependents, all her wealth and property reverted to the

Treasury for the King to use as he saw fit. Theft of such wealth counted as treason. More than enough reason to bring the man before the King even if he hadn't seen anything of Col or Taran.

* * * * *

The district surrounding Seth's lodgings was respectable and clean, and its patrons were mainly merchants and traders. The house was currently full, as the restrictions on movement in and out of the city made many reluctant to leave on their traditional rounds for fear they would be unable to return. While they still had stock to sell, they would remain in the city and leave the lesser towns until spring.

The atmosphere in the lodging house was convivial, counter to the populace's general unease. Merchants were among the few traders who would profit from the military's closure of the gates, along with the local taverns, although these were also concerned for their supplies of food and ale. The merchants, being circumspect and not wishing to spend their profits prematurely, generally retired early, so the house was quiet.

Seth and Varth returned from the mansion mid-evening and spent a couple of hours in the nearest ale house. Varth carried no coin, so Seth was forced to dip deep into his pockets to keep the fellow supplied with ale and food. He picked glumly at his own supper while Varth demolished a vast plate of beef stew and several tankards of good brown ale. Seth's only consolation was that the ale might dull the gleam of desire in Varth's eyes, and that kept him reaching into his coin pouch. Unfortunately, it seemed to have the opposite effect, and the huge swordsman eventually gripped Seth's arm and drew him from the ale house, walking too close for comfort as they returned to Seth's room above the street.

When the brawny fellow was finally sated, Seth once again found himself wrapped in a single blanket on the floor, left to nurse his aches and bruises while Varth snored on the bed, naked and exposed. Seth thought longingly of using Varth's own sword on him, but after the trouble he had killing Alice he did not trust himself to get the job done. Besides, how would he explain a dead body to the landlord?

So he covered himself as best he could and lay brooding in sullen silence until he, too, fell asleep.

Seth dreamed of milling horses, men's raised voices, and fists thudding on doors. He tossed and turned, too weary to wake. A hard slap on the tender, naked flesh of his buttocks made him start up with a sharp cry.

"Wake up," hissed Varth, "we've got company."

He looked amused at the fear that leaped into Seth's eyes when he registered the brawny man's closeness, and he grinned as Seth clutched the blanket around him. Varth grasped one corner and tore it away, leaving Seth naked and shivering.

"I'd get some clothes on, mate, unless you want to go before the King like that."

Seth gaped stupidly. "What are you talking about?"

Varth grimaced. "Didn't I tell you to expect a visit from Kingsmen? They'll have found out two of them's missing, and the gate guards will have told them we went to the estate, so now they've come looking for us. Don't worry. Just tell them the truth—you went to talk to your fellow servants. They'll know you did. Stick to that and you'll be all right. Try to lie about anything else, and they'll hear it."

"But I can't go before the King!" Seth squeaked. "Blaine will be there. He's a powerful man—he's an *Artesan*. He'll see through me in an instant. You've got to help me, Varth. Get me out of here. I can't do this."

Varth's reply was interrupted by the sound of hammering on the lodging house door. Varth stared at Seth in dislike. "You've got to," he spat. "Master's counting on you. You don't have a choice."

"But what if they see through me?" Seth wailed. "They'll kill me!"

"What do you want me to do?" retorted Varth, stepping closer. Seth fell silent, mesmerized by the sullen red glow throbbing deep inside the swordsman's eyes. It had been there before, earlier, at the height of the man's lust, and it sent shivers sliding through Seth's vitals.

"Help me," he whispered, defeated.

Varth regarded him while they listened to the landlord unbolt the street door and converse loudly with the Kingsmen. There was precious little time. "There is a way I could help you, Seth," said the man, his voice no longer the swordsman's coarse drawl.

"Master!" breathed Seth, his heart racing. "Please!"

"You have to do this," intoned the voice that crawled from Varth's lips, "but I have no wish to see you killed. There is a way we can avoid that, should Elias's men see through you. You will go with them to the castle, and you will answer their questions and sow the seeds of doubt. And if they suspect you, if they detain you, well—I have a way of dealing with that. But if you want me to save you, you will have to allow Varth here to lay hands on you once again. What do you say, my faithful servant? One more willing act to save your skin?"

Seth shivered miserably, staring at the grinning swordsman who was already reaching for the fastenings of his bulging breeches. Seth went pale. How much more could he endure? But then he heard the sound of his name spoken in the street below, and someone calling for the captain. They were coming for him.

Nodding his head in resignation, Seth turned his back, gritted his teeth, and braced his hands on the bed.

✠ ✠ ✠ ✠ ✠

Dexter shouldered past the disheveled landlord, ignoring the curious stares fixed on him from behind half-opened doors. The whole house had been roused by the hammering on the street door and the guests were wary and anxious. He strode past the lower rooms, Pengar at his shoulder, and made for the dark stairwell. Taking the flight two steps at a time, the two men gained the upper floor. The room they wanted was at the end of the hallway, at the front of the house.

Dexter tried the latch, but the internal bolt had been used. It was not surprising in the current atmosphere of unrest, but it irritated him nonetheless. All the other guests showed more curiosity than fear at the appearance of the King's Guard. How significant was it that the man Dexter wanted was the only one to be shy?

He heard a sound from within the room, a muffled gasp of pain followed by a drawn-out, shuddering groan. Dexter cast a glance over his shoulder at Pengar before thumping loudly with his fist on the door. He called Seth's name. There was a moment of silence before he heard movement, and then the bolt was slowly drawn. Dexter shoved the door open, his sword in his hand, Pen at his back. They regarded the man before them in silence.

He stood there in breeches, pale and sweating. Dexter frowned at his shivering. The lodging house was pleasantly warm. Was the man fevered? He certainly had an odd look in his eye and he was panting as if he had been running. Dexter could see the bed was rumpled. A nightmare, then, or maybe the beginnings of the winter fever. That would explain the strange sounds they had heard. He eyed the man warily.

"Are you Seth, former manservant to the traitor Reen? Lately employed by the Baroness Jinella?"

The man held his gaze, but only just. "I am." His voice quavered and his eyes were faintly red. Definitely the beginnings of winter fever. "What do you want with me?"

"You are wanted for questioning at the castle," Dexter said curtly. "Will you come?"

"Do I have a choice?" Seth asked archly. Dexter only raised his brows. "Give me a moment to dress."

He made to close the door, but Dexter put his foot against it. Pengar moved a step closer.

"We also require the attendance of the bodyguard who accompanied you to the estate today," Dexter snapped. "Where is he?"

A red flush touched the man's brow. "I have no idea." He turned from the door and reached for his clothes. "I saw him at the alehouse earlier this evening. No doubt he found lodgings of his own."

"And where would they be?"

The manservant stared at Dexter. "Try the nearest whorehouse. How should I know?"

Dexter considered him. It had already taken him longer than he had expected to track the man down and he was reluctant to waste any more time. If Seth was right and his man had patronized one of Loxton's many pleasure houses, Dexter could spend the rest of the night looking for him. He made a decision. They could always find the fellow in the morning. Getting Seth to the castle was his priority right now.

The man was now dressed and Dexter beckoned him out. His stiff gait drew a frown from Pengar, who shot his captain a look. Dexter shook his head. Whatever troubled the man, the General would find it out. Dexter only hoped it wasn't the winter fever. That would sweep through the castle and garrison like a scythe through grass. They hustled Seth down the stairs under the blatant curiosity of the other guests and out into the falling snow.

Chapter Twenty-Six

The palace servants filled the ornate bathtub in Sofira's rooms with near-scalding water. Jinny received nothing from them but blank stares and was sure her uncle had terrorized them into silence. One or two of the male servants seemed almost on the verge of catatonia, their eyes glazed and their movements slow, and she had seen red marks on some of them, weeping like sores. Those, she avoided. The last thing she needed was to catch a disease.

She collected the soap and creams from the herbwife and also begged some calming infusions. Jinny would need something to help her through this experience and she was sure she could conceal what she had taken from her new mistress. Once the woman was asleep, Jinny could take the herbs in some water. She doubted her own ability to sleep otherwise, despite her exhaustion.

Her guard stayed by her side as she made her way back to Sofira, and then took up his station outside the door. The Princess sat as Jinny first saw her—slouched on the bed, staring blankly at the wall in front of her, small sounds of fear coming from her throat. She did not react to Jinny's return, nor to the shambling servants. Yet once they all left and the two women were alone, some animation returned to her eyes and she levered herself carefully to her feet.

"Let me help you, my Lady," said Jinny as Sofira began to

remove her jewels. The older woman cried out and jumped, as if she had forgotten Jinny's presence. The look of unhinged fear came back to her eyes and it brought Jinny up short. "Are you all right, your Highness?"

Sofira didn't immediately reply and Jinny was sure she caught the glitter of tears. Yet when the Princess turned toward her, her eyes were as hard as ever, although her face was white as chalk.

"Come and remove these jewels," she said curtly, and Jinny moved to obey, trying not to touch the livid bruises about the pallid neck.

Once the priceless gems were back in their casket, Sofira moved toward her bathing room. Jinny followed. She was beginning to have serious doubts about the older woman's sanity. She moved like a marionette and only registered Jinny's presence when she spoke. Remembering her uncle's comments on silence, she decided to try an experiment and started on the lacings of Sofira's gown without asking permission. They were not correctly tied and Jinny guessed Sofira had done them herself, not watching what she was doing. The Princess stood still for her to do her work.

Released, the gold satin gown sank to the floor with a hiss, leaving Sofira in her soft silk shift. Jinny saw that it, too, was stained, but more extensively than the gown. There were smears of blood and it would take some cleaning, if the rest of the stain was what she thought it might be. But what caught her eye most and caused her to frown in concern was the extent of the angry marks on Sofira's arms and chest. The bruising around her throat was not the only injury she had suffered. Her upper arms were circled with red welts, as if her arms had been pinned to her sides, and her shoulders and the area above her breasts were covered with what looked like bite and claw marks. Jinny was sickened and she tried not to gasp.

Sofira remained immobile, as if awaiting instructions. Jinny took hold of the hem of the shift, lifting it over the lean woman's body. She could not bite back the gasp of horror when she saw Sofira's thighs. Her worst imaginings were obviously not depraved enough, and it was all Jinny could do not to sob. How could her uncle do such things? How had he been transformed into such a ravening monster? Her whole body shuddered. The man who could do such things to a woman who was supposed to be his ally and wife might commit any atrocity. And Jinny's heart's-love and a cherished friend lay helpless in his hands.

Choking back her tears and trying to blank such thoughts from her mind, Jinny gave Sofira a gentle push toward the tub. The naked woman stepped straight into the steaming water, despite its high temperature, and Jinny handed her the soft herbal soap. Sofira sank onto her haunches and immediately began to lather her skin. Jinny turned to gather towels beside the fire, ready for when Sofira was done, but a gasp from the tub and the sounds of frantic splashing brought her hurrying back. The sight that met her eyes made her heart race.

Sofira's eyes streamed tears. Her face was puffy and blotched, the skin mottled red from the hot water. She scrubbed at herself with frantic haste, and her whimpering breaths grew shallower. While Jinny watched, stunned, Sofira snatched a rough sponge from the rack by the tub and attacked the flesh between her thighs, rubbing so hard and so frenetically she actually drew blood. Jinny ran to the tub, falling to her knees with a cry. She caught Sofira's hand, trying to stop the mindless, harmful scrubbing, but Sofira wrenched away and continued to scour herself, her breath coming in sobs and spiraling rapidly toward hysteria. Blood ran between her thighs, staining the water red.

Appalled, Jinny did the only thing she could think of to stop it. She drew back her hand and slapped the former High Queen.

Sofira gave a small cry and all other sounds ceased. Her hands fell still in the water and her eyes stared into the distance. The soap slipped from the red-tinged sponge and fell to the bottom of the tub. Jinny sat back on her heels and waited for a reaction that did not come. The Princess had to breathe, however, and soon her lungs heaved in a sob. She turned her eyes on Jinny; they were damp and lost and fearful. Jinny could not refuse their silent plea.

"Oh, my Lady," she whispered. "What has he done to you?"

There was another involuntary sob, and that one broke the barrier. Sofira crumpled toward Jinella, who caught her in her arms, heedless of the soapy water, and held her to her breast. She rocked the angular body, crooning words of comfort, feeling the sobs racking the hard bones beneath her hands. Her own eyes pricked with tears.

When she felt a lessening of the storm, Jinny pulled back and made the Princess face her. Sofira's eyes were red and swollen, her face flushed and puckered from grief. Jinny's slap had left a large red welt on her cheek, exacerbated by the hot water. She looked truly dreadful, but more like a normal woman than Jinny had ever seen her. She decided to take a gamble. The Princess had allowed Jinny to comfort her; perhaps they could go one stage further.

"Do you feel better now, your Highness?" she asked gently. "Let me find that soap and I'll finish this for you."

She retrieved the soap and took the sponge from Sofira's unresisting hand, finding a soft cloth instead. Wringing it out in the soothing water, she soaped it and massaged Sofira's hunched shoulders, taking care not to rub on the bruises. Some of the tension eased from the knotted muscles and Jinny breathed a sigh of relief.

"Was it my uncle who did this to you?" she murmured, praying Sofira wouldn't react badly. After a moment of stillness, the older woman gave a nod. Jinny pursed her lips. "I don't understand," she continued, keeping her voice low and level.

Perhaps a show of emotion was not what Sofira needed right now. Perhaps they could deal with it detachedly, as if they were discussing someone else. "It was your wedding night. Was he somehow displeased?"

A shudder ran through the hard body under Jinny's hands and she tensed. Had she said the wrong thing?

"Displeased? Oh no." Sofira's whisper was almost inaudible and Jinny had to strain to hear her. "No, he was most definitely pleased. He was vengeful, evil, triumphant. And I never saw it."

Jinny couldn't believe what she was hearing. Was Sofira admitting she was wrong? Certainly, her recent experience had staggered her. Maybe, thought Jinny, her uncle had made a mistake. Maybe his treatment of Sofira would play into her hands.

"What did you not see?" Jinny asked softly, still massaging the livid skin, using soothing strokes, calming and comforting. The herbs she had cast into the bathwater had a relaxing effect and she suddenly wished she had prepared some of the infusion she had begged from the herbwife. But she had hidden it and she did not want to leave Sofira to get it. Not while she was receptive to questions.

"His need for revenge," Sofira murmured brokenly. "His intentions. His plans."

The stricken woman stared up at Jinny, and she was arrested by the pleading terror in the Princess's eyes. She ceased her stroking and gave Sofira her full attention. "Tell me, my Lady. I want to help you."

"Help me?" The Princess's voice was harsh and Jinny's heart fell, thinking she had made a blunder. Yet the flash of temper evaporated. Sofira was too hurt, too beaten, to sustain it. Jinny was offering friendship—or companionship, at least—and Sofira needed that very badly right now. Her recent unspeakable experiences and the dreadful realization Reen had forced on her had crushed her spirit and left her floundering, no longer able to function. She slumped into the water, leaning against the tub, tears coursing freely down her cheeks.

"No one can help me," she moaned. "It's too late. He tricked me, he lied to me. He wrote me wonderful letters, speaking his heart, telling me he had forgiven my betrayal and asking me for help. He sounded so lost and forlorn in that terrible island prison, and he told me I was the only one who could help him, the only one who could save his life. He said he would cut his wrists if I couldn't save him, and I believed him. I have never known anyone so despairing, so broken.

"He vowed he would stay in hiding if I could persuade my father to rescue him. All he wanted was to end his days by my side, serving me and advising me like he used to before I went to Port Loxton to wed Elias. He said he had seen the error of his ways and that he repented of his actions against the King. A final few years of freedom was all he wanted before he died. And I believed him. I wrote back to him and I forgave him.

"After that, the tone of his letters changed. He was sounding me out, I see that now. He asked me about my children and he sympathized, telling me how cruel Elias was to keep them from me, how dreadful he was to keep me locked up like a hound in a kennel. He told me they would forget me and that it wasn't right. He played on my love for them and my desperation to see them. The last letter he sent me, once he knew my father would help him, said that he knew how I could get them back."

Sofira fell silent, her chest heaving, hands covering her eyes. Jinny applied the cloth again, murmuring soothing words, her own eyes wide with surprise. She had never expected this, that the Princess would confide in her, trust her, and so quickly. Yet she had to be careful. Sofira was a proud and dangerous woman, even if she was currently in need of a friend. If she suspected Jinny was manipulating her, or thinking only of her own situation, she would probably order her removal, or worse, betray her to her uncle. Jinny must proceed with care and do all she could to convince Sofira she could be trusted. If Sofira was thinking like this, perhaps Lerric was, too. Jinny had noticed Lerric's unhappiness at his daughter's parody of a wedding. Surely Reen couldn't own every single man in the palace? Surely either Sofira or Lerric could contrive to send a message? Her heart burning with sudden hope, Jinny resumed her questions.

"What happened then, your Highness? How did he trick you?"

Sofira raised her head, her eyes hard. Jinny thought she was going to flare at her, but the Princess's thoughts were elsewhere. Her voice was vicious when she spoke again.

"With love. He tricked me with love. He knew I was lonely, knew I missed my children. And we were always close. We shared a special bond, even when I was young. Although now I doubt that was real. He must have been grooming me even then. He persuaded me to take him to Loxton, you know, almost begged me—told me I could not manage without him, that I would be all alone there, and friendless. He offered to help me, guide me so I made no mistakes in my new status. He said he would help me become a truly great High Queen, with all the acclaim of the people behind me. And all the time he was planning his own rise, securing his own future. And I made it happen!"

Jinny had finished her washing and the slight flow of blood from between the Princess's legs had ceased. She rose and fetched one of the warm towels, holding it out for Sofira to step into. The woman rose stiffly from the water and stepped onto the floor, allowing Jinny to wrap her in warm folds and rub her dry.

"And so, after your father's men rescued him and brought him here, you agreed to wed him," Jinny said softly, not meeting Sofira's eyes, just concentrating on drying her sore body. She felt a shudder of horror travel through the Princess and decided to shun that subject for the moment. She led Sofira into the bedchamber and seated her by the fire. She picked up a brush to untangle her damp hair as the Princess continued her story in a mechanical voice devoid of emotion.

"He flattered me, played with me. I wanted to nurse him when he arrived, but he refused, saying he was too damaged, too ashamed to be seen. My father ..." Her voice faltered and broke, and she swallowed. "My father tried to warn me. He said Hezra had changed, that he was not the same man, but I didn't believe him. When I was finally allowed to see him, I thought my father was jealous. Can you believe that? He was frightened for me, and I thought he was jealous! I saw only what I wanted to see—my faithful, trusted retainer come back to me, professing to love me. I even sensed my father's fear, but discounted it as a foolish whim of the old. I thought he feared to lose me and I argued with him."

Jinny could see the tears in Sofira's eyes reflected in the large silver mirror as she stood behind the Princess, brushing her hair. She frowned, fearing Sofira and her father were estranged, and wondered how she could repair that breach.

"He nearly betrayed us, you know," the Princess continued. "When Elias was here with his escort, my father nearly told him. I was furious and I screamed at him, accused him of not wanting to help me, of not wanting to see me regain my children and my throne. That's what Hezra promised me, you see. He told me he would give me back my pride, restore me to the throne—that he would give me back my children. And I was so unhappy, so dreadfully unhappy, that I believed him. But now, I wish with all my heart my father had done what he so nearly did. I thought he was craven and I accused him of cowardice. Oh, Father! You had so much more courage than I."

Sofira bent her head to her hands, once more racked by sobs.

Jinny laid down the brush and took up the crystal phial the herbwife had given her. It was an emollient, soothing for the skin, and Jinny hoped it would also help leach the pain from the bruises. It was warm from the fire and Jinny poured a small amount into the palms of her hands, rubbing them together before she gently applied the sweet-smelling cream to the blotched skin of the Princess's shoulders.

Sofira looked up at her from puffy eyes. "Why are you doing this?" she asked coldly. "I haven't exactly been gracious to you in the past."

Jinny smiled sadly. "I am a prisoner here, my Lady, at the whim of my uncle. I was brought here to serve you and threatened if I did not. I was afraid, expecting to find you as you were last night, still vindictive and more powerful now you are wed to him. But that's not the case, is it? I think you are as much a prisoner as I, and you have suffered at his hands. It seems to me we would do well to comfort each other, do what we can to help each other survive."

Sofira held Jinny's gaze as if she had not expected the Baroness to possess such strength. Her face softened for an instant, the most natural expression Jinny had yet seen. It was fleeting, replaced immediately by a blank and hopeless fear. The older woman's head fell again to her hands.

"You are right, Jinella. We are both prisoners here. But you are freer than I. There is no help left for me."

Her despair cut at Jinny's heart and she came round in front of the Princess, kneeling by her side and catching up her hands.

"Don't say that, my Lady! There is always help, there's always hope. Reen hasn't won yet, and we still have friends outside these walls. Maybe even inside them. What about your father, Lady? You said he tried to warn you. I saw him last night, the way he looked. He was horrified. Wouldn't he help us?"

"My father is dead."

Jinny stuttered to a halt, staring at Sofira's pinched face. The color from her bath and Jinny's slap had faded, leaving her usual bleached pallor. But now her lips were gray and the strangely unhinged light was back in her colorless eyes.

"Dead?" Jinny repeated stupidly. "How?"

"Hezra killed him. Before my eyes. And he enjoyed it."

Jinny knelt there with her mouth hanging open. She found it hard to believe each new atrocity attributed to her uncle, but just as she managed to take them all in, just as she managed to convince herself of the depths of his evil, something new appeared to knock her back. Sofira saw this and shook her head.

"Don't ask me how, I don't want to say. I have told you too much already. Just believe me when I tell you there is no hope. No hope for you, no hope for me, and certainly none for your friend down there. If Hezra does to him what I think he will, he would be better off dead. *I* certainly would be. If I had the will to do it, I would cut my own throat. I wish I had never set eyes on your uncle. I should have left him to rot on that stinking island. *Damn* Brynne Sullyan for averting his sentence of death. He should have burned upon that Wheel, and if I had my way he'd be burning still!"

The note of hysteria had crept back into Sofira's voice and Jinny felt frightened. There was more to this than she knew, that much was obvious. But she had to give the Princess something. She couldn't leave her so broken and ruined. She stood, taking the shaking woman by the shoulders, and brought her face close.

"I won't give up, my Lady, no matter what you say. There are others with the power to fight my uncle and they may even now be on their way. We have to be strong, Sofira. We mustn't give up. We must be ready to do what we can when help arrives—"

A sharp hand clamped over Jinny's mouth, making her eyes

widen in fear. Sofira stared madly into her face, eyes wild and panicked, squeezing her hand painfully over Jinny's lips, crushing them into her teeth.

"Don't say any more, don't tell me anything!" she hissed, her voice terrible with rage. Her hands were shaking and she cast her gaze frantically about the room. "He knows what I know. He might be listening. We mustn't speak, we mustn't talk. Forget what I told you. Don't even think about it. He'll hear you, he'll know! He'll come for us if he thinks we know something, and he'll … do *that* again. To you and to me. I couldn't bear it. Kill me, girl, promise me! Promise me you'll kill me if he comes to do that again. Promise me. *Promise me!*"

Jinny stared at the Princess's strangely altered face, a worm of dreadful fear curling about her heart. What had Robin said about Feilin? Was it possible the Baron had done the same thing to Sofira? Had he done more than taunt her with his true intentions before forcing himself on her? Had he truly possessed her mind as well as her body?

Jinny shuddered, leaning away from the Princess. She thought she had found an ally, although in the strangest of places. She thought she was not alone, and from that belief she had drawn a measure of strength. But it seemed she was wrong. Sofira was untrustworthy, if only because of her fear, and Jinny might already have overplayed her hand.

"I promise," she said, failing to keep the tremor from her voice. "I promise."

The fanatical light died from Sofira's eyes and she collapsed back into her chair, the strength born of terror deserting her. She shivered and Jinny heard her teeth chattering. Appalled at what she had learned, terrified for both Robin and Taran—not to mention herself—Jinny still found room in her heart to feel deep sympathy for this misguided, abandoned woman. Foolish she might be and easily led, yet Sofira had never really been given the chance to develop herself. Groomed from early childhood to be given in marriage as a living treaty of alliance, she had succumbed to the cunning contrivance of a trusted advisor. Never having reason to doubt his sincerity, she had missed the hidden motives behind his wise counsel, his gentle guidance. Unused to subterfuge and unsuspecting, she was a willing pawn in the universal game of power. And now she had been tossed aside, her value gone, to wait on the sidelines until the game was played out. Her feelings and emotions counted for nothing; her use to the game master was all.

Jinny's heart hardened in anger as she considered the implications of her uncle's scheming. It was not only Sofira's life at stake, but also the lives of her children; two innocents who, due to their birth, could also be used as stakes. The thought made Jinny's blood boil, but there was nothing she could do. Her teeth ground in frustration and a dull ache began behind her eyes. The Princess was trembling freely now, mindless whimpers coming from her throat.

The least Jinella could do was look after the woman. It should keep her uncle pacified, if nothing else. And she refused to give up hope, despite what Sofira had said. Until there was no life left in her, she would not lose hope. This she swore while she encouraged the shuddering Princess toward her rumpled bed and coaxed her under the blankets. She made some of the herbal infusion and gave it to Sofira, ensuring there was enough for herself. Sleep would not come easily, and Jinny would do herself no good if she shunned it.

She watched over Sofira until the shaking subsided, the whimpers muted to soft, sobbing breaths. The blank, fearful eyes closed, heavy with sleep. Then Jinny swallowed the rest of the mixture, laid herself down beside Sofira without bothering to undress, and succumbed to the pull of the drug. Her final thoughts were pleas to the gods, and the name on her lips was her lover's.

Chapter Twenty-Seven

Seth came hesitantly into the General's presence. It was late in the night and his exertions of the evening had left him weary and aching. The fear of this meeting lent him some strength, and the knowledge of his master's power gave him more, but still he found it hard to meet the stern, angular countenance that faced him as he came to a halt before Mathias Blaine. Seth bowed his head, as a manservant should.

"We found him in the merchants' quarter, sir," Dexter reported crisply. "One of the better quality houses. His bodyguard was not with him and he professes ignorance of the man's whereabouts. I thought I should bring him to you before we search for the other. Shall I send the men back out or do we wait until morning?"

Blaine didn't immediately reply and Seth did his best to ignore the guards at his back; they were not his main concern. He kept his eyes downcast and tried to order his thoughts. Keep strictly to the truth, his master had said, and they can't catch you out. It's only falsehood they can detect; they can't read your mind. Don't let them cow you or fool you with threats. If they suspected any complicity in the fire at the mansion, they would have taken you before this. Hold their eyes, answer honestly, and all will be well.

"Why did you go to the estate today?" the General barked, making Seth jump.

He drew meekness around him like a cloak. "I went to see my

fellow servants, my Lord. I have no employment since the fire, and I wanted to talk with them."

"Did you go straight to the village or did you visit the mansion?"

This was trickier, but Seth was thinking now. "I did go past the mansion, my Lord. I was looking for Matty, the stable boy. I thought he might be there tending the horses."

"You told Adept Elijah you thought the fire had been started deliberately," the General said sharply. "Why did you do that?"

How did the man know that? Taran must have told him, damn him! Well, it was the truth, after all, and Seth couldn't hide it. "I did, my Lord, because I believed it."

The General's mouth twisted. "Did you think he really wanted to hear that just then? When he'd found a body he believed to be his lady's?"

Seth shrugged. He was beginning to enjoy this. "I was surprised he was so stricken, my Lord, given that they'd had such a serious argument."

"And what would you know about that? It was private business between the two of them."

Seth allowed himself the hint of a condescending smile. "I imagine all the servants knew about it, my Lord. It was a rather loud argument. And my lady made no pretense about how upset she was."

"And so you thought that was a good time to tell him."

Seth remained silent, holding the General's gaze like he had been told. It was harder than he expected.

"Why do you hate him so much?"

The question crawled insidiously into the room, causing Seth to catch his breath. What should he say? The truth, of course, although not all of it.

"I don't exactly … hate him, my Lord. I resent him, I suppose.

I had been some years in the service of the Baron and I found it hard to come to terms with another man taking his place."

"You were loyal to the Baron?"

Seth narrowed his eyes. Was the General trying to find a reason to accuse him? He felt himself flush and silently cursed. *Careful!* He didn't want to give anything away. "Of course, my Lord. I had no reason not to be. He treated me well and paid me well."

"And after he was convicted of treason?"

Seth hesitated. "I don't think I understand you, my Lord."

"Oh, come on, man!" The General's voice was harsh, his growing anger apparent. "Don't pretend to be naïve; you're too intelligent for that. The truth is that although Lady Jinella kept you on, you retained your loyalty to your former master. That's why you resented Adept Elijah. Not because he was seeing your lady, but because he was instrumental in your master's downfall. What other tasks have you performed for him, Seth? How is he sending you instructions?"

Sweat prickled Seth's flesh and he struggled for calm. This was harder than he had imagined. He had not thought the General might try that tack. Did they actually suspect the Baron's hand in these recent events, or was that a clever shot in the dark? Seth was fearful of saying the wrong thing, something that would give the General good cause for suspicion. He was fairly sure the man was fishing, but it would only take one slip, one trivial lie, and the powerful Artesan General would hear it. And so far, Seth had only heard one interesting fact that might be worth telling his master. How could he protect himself while drawing the General out? At least Seth had a slight advantage: he knew he was safe.

"I don't know how to answer you, my Lord. I'm not entirely sure what you are suggesting. My former master was disgraced and banished. I heard from my lady that he had died. Are you saying he is not dead?"

Blaine stared balefully at the younger man, clearly trying to sort through what he said. Abruptly, he came to the point.

"You say you went past the mansion today on your way to visit your fellow servants. Did you see anyone else there at the time? Anyone at all?"

This was tricky and Seth had to be careful, had to watch his phrasing. He knew what Blaine was getting at. He stilled his heart and calmed his breathing.

"There was no one but myself and my guard at the mansion when I arrived. I think Matty had been there earlier, but otherwise the place was deserted."

"Did you see any tracks, any prints in the snow?"

"There were some, my Lord, yes. Matty would have left his prints when he visited the stables."

"Were there horses in the stables?"

Seth shrugged. "There may have been. I hadn't gone there looking for horses."

Blaine watched him in silence for a long while and Seth managed to hold the stern gaze. What he had said was mainly true, he was safe in that, and, fortunately, the General seemed to accept it. He turned his eyes from Seth and the manservant sighed inaudibly. The General seemed about to address Dexter when he suddenly rounded on Seth once more.

"Where did your bodyguard come from? How can a mere manservant afford such luxury? Did you loot the mansion while it burned?"

The abrupt attack jolted Seth, as it was doubtless meant to do. He paled, but recovered as best he could. More truth, as far as it went, could save him.

"No, I did not! The man was a former servant of my master." Seth allowed a measure of fear to color his indignant tone. He didn't want to appear too confident, after all. "After the terrible events in the city, he approached me. I had some coin put by from what my master gave me—I told you, he paid me well. I had no need to loot the mansion. I swear to you, the only coin I have was what I was given."

That was true as far as it went. The vagrant had told Seth to gather what he needed, and the vagrant had been his master's tool. The truth could be stretched to cover his actions, but he could see the General was far from convinced.

Blaine frowned. "Very well, Seth. It's growing late. I'll accept what you say for now, but I require the presence of your bodyguard, and he will be asked to corroborate your story. If what he tells me matches what you have said, you will be free to go. Until we find him, you will stay here, under guard. My men will look for him in the morning and you had better hope we find him. If we do not, I will be forced to conclude there are things you have not told me. You may not have lied to me, but I hear evasion in your voice and I will get to the bottom of it before I am satisfied.

"Captain, remove him to a place of safety and post a guard. No one is to see him or speak to him until I am ready to interview him again. Dismissed."

The two Kingsmen hustled Seth out of the interview room and into a small side room. The Captain stared grimly at him as he withdrew and closed the door. Seth sat on the settle and blew out his lips in relief. He had held out well, he thought, despite the General's awkward questions. He had not given himself away, even if he had not fully convinced the man. And he wasn't really surprised at that. The General had not seemed like a man wanting to be convinced. He was looking for a murderer and an abductor, and Seth was the nearest thing he had to a culprit.

Yet Seth had gleaned a couple of interesting facts and he thought his master would be pleased. The only concern he had was that the Baron might not keep his word, that he might leave Seth at their mercy a little longer in the hope of finding out more. The last thing Seth wanted was to be here in the morning when the Captain's men failed in their search for Varth. For they wouldn't find him, that much Seth knew. The brawny swordsman had vanished before his eyes. The image of Varth stepping nonchalantly into a glowing nimbus even as he fastened his breeches would stay with Seth for some time.

That thought brought the young man back to himself and he remembered the dull ache of his bruised body. It was worse than before, but what it left behind was a lifeline for Seth, and so the pain was worth it. He could feel the connection to his master deep inside his mind, and to Seth it was no violation. He smiled slowly and closed his eyes, feeling along the pathway that had been opened within him until he sensed his master's response. Seth ignored the sullen heat that pulsed briefly behind his eyes.

✠ ✠ ✠ ✠ ✠

It could not be far off dawn; that was as much as Robin knew. He and Taran had finally fallen silent, talked into exhaustion. Taran had done his best to reach out to Rienne, but all he succeeded in doing was setting off the nausea, which scraped his throat raw with dry retching.

Taran soon succumbed to his enervation, though sleep eluded Robin. He heard the Adept's ragged breathing gradually slow and calm as oblivion claimed him, and he was glad one of them could rest. Taran was worn out by his injuries, his heroic efforts to contact Rienne, and his frantic terror for Jinny—not to mention for himself and for Robin. Sleep was a mercy, although it would bring little relief.

Both mercy and relief were strangers to Robin, for he knew worse was to come. He feared even to close his eyes lest his nightmare come to pass. He must meet the terrible fate the Baron had planned for him and he must do all he could to fight it. He would fail, he knew, but he owed it to his son and to the faith and love of his life mate to try.

He knew the full story behind her dreadful experiences at the hands of Rykan; he knew what she had lived through. She had told him it was only her love for him that enabled her to deny Rykan what he wanted, and Robin was determined to do the same. Moreover, he was a Master Artesan. He had gained the right and the power to give up his own life. It was what she had planned to do at the last, when she was finally bereft of all hope, and he was sure that what the Baron intended to inflict on him would sever his own final, instinctive grasp on life. Once the spellsilver was removed, he would cast himself into the Void, denying his tormentor the prize he desired. With any luck, and if he could summon the strength, he would be able to warn Sullyan before he was swept away by the maelstrom of oblivion. He would not—he *could* not—allow his powers to be used to defeat her.

He did not tell Taran his intentions, nor had he told him everything the Baron had taunted him with. The Adept had enough to contend with, and witnessing the Baron's violation would be terrible enough without the foreknowledge of what Robin meant to do. Taran's ignorance was Robin's security. He could not give the plan away, even unintentionally. The Baron was bound to gloat over them before he carried out his attack, and Taran would learn all too soon why they had been captured.

Robin hung his head and breathed as deeply as he could, focusing on his will and resolve. It was not easy to do through the spellsilver's sickening hum.

His head snapped up, his heart lurching painfully when he heard the tramp of feet. He began to tremble violently, sensing the hour had come. He glanced over at Taran, but the man was still asleep. Robin didn't call out to him. He could not; his voice was frozen in his throat. And anyway, what could he have said save goodbye? His blood turned to ice and his heart began to race. He felt his face drain of blood as the tremor of his body grew. He tried to curse himself into courage, but failed. He didn't have the strength. He stared at the door, desperately willing with all his might for it not to be the Baron.

His wish was denied.

The bolts shot back and the door swung open. Four silent guards moved ahead of the scarecrow, coming purposefully toward the young man. He watched them come with wild eyes, feeling his training desert him, his scant courage evaporate. Terror overwhelmed him and sweat slicked his skin. He panted and strained at the chains, futile though it was. The men closed in on him, two going round behind him and two approaching from the front. His muscles clenched, ready for the fight.

He felt his upper arms grasped painfully from behind. One of the men in front of him reached for the chain securing him to the bedhead and released it. Instantly, with no thought or finesse, Robin exploded into frenzied action, adrenaline and terror lending him strength. He wrenched his arms upward, free of the grasping hands, punching his fists into the face of the nearest guard and twisting violently to the side, trying to throw himself off the bed. The man he had hit grunted with pain and crumpled, but the other came straight for him, having expected such a move. A fist drove into Robin's belly, forcing his breath out in a rush, and as he doubled over the two men behind him grappled for his arms. Robin thrashed in their grip, kicking for the groin. The man who had punched him threw himself on Robin's legs, pinning them to the bed with his weight.

The noise of the struggle roused Taran. He shouted in alarm, yelling encouragement when he realized what was happening. Robin heard him and redoubled his efforts, the nausea of the spellsilver forgotten as waves of terror swamped him. He heaved mightily on the bed, dislodging the man on his legs and thrusting his manacles straight into the other's eyes. The guard cried out, clapping a hand to his face, blood pouring from a gash on his brow. The other two leaped onto the bed, taking his place, throwing their weight onto Robin's chest and squeezing the breath from his lungs.

The harsh panting of the guards, screamed orders from the Baron, and Taran's hoarse shouts rang about the room, making chaos of the scene. The man Robin first hit struggled to his feet, enraged, his nose bloodied and broken. He aimed a vicious kick at Taran, catching the Adept on the right side of his head, the site of his previous injury. Taran fell limp, his hoarse cries reduced to gasps.

Another guard sprinted into the room and it took all five of them to do it; four to hold Robin down and one to fasten the chains. Robin fought them with all the might of his terror, but he was weakened and sickened and, eventually, they subdued him. They fastened him to the bed on his belly, spread-eagle, his wrists and ankles secured to the four corners of the frame. They stood away then, their eyes hot with fury, all of them bloodied, chests heaving from their efforts.

Robin lay helpless, panting and sweating, his wild eyes fixed in mindless terror on the stooped scarecrow figure that moved spiderlike across the room. The cane tapped rhythmically on the floor. That slight sound, or maybe the cessation of the chaos, registered with Taran, and he managed to raise his head just in time to see the dreadful smile Reen turned on his sacrificial captive. The Adept groaned.

Reen shot a glance at the panting guards and curtly gestured with his head. They took the hint and left the room, closing the door behind them. Reen turned to his captive, eyes gleaming scarlet. He advanced slowly, reveling in the slick sheen of sweat, the clench of Robin's hands on the chains, the terror suffusing his flinching soul. It was a heady and intoxicating mix. He came close to Robin's head and looked down on him, staring deeply into his eyes, reading the fear and hatred.

"Yes," he murmured, "you do well to fear me."

He straightened and moved around the bed, trailing clawed fingers over Robin's straining muscles. Robin's flesh crept beneath the Baron's touch, and waves of panic flooded from him. To a creature like the Baron, it must have been the nectar of life. He sucked it up, feeding and swelling his malignant, shriveled soul.

The loathsome, purring voice came again, dripping with malice. "I have waited long for this moment, young man. I will take you, and take what I want from you, and use it as I will. I will leach your strength to feed my power, and leave you only with the knowledge that what you have given me will ultimately be used against *her*—used against all of them—as I fulfill my vow to rid the world of your evil kind."

The Baron reached into the folds of his robes and brought forth a knife, gleaming dully in the orange glow of the fire. The scarecrow moved to Robin's waist, where he rested his hand on the shuddering back, considering the muscular body and absorbing the fear it exuded. The slavering grin widened and the terrible eyes flared in anticipation.

Robin tensed as the knife flashed down, but it only clove through leather. The Baron ran it down the length of Robin's legs, first one and then the other, until his clothing could be pulled free and tossed aside, leaving him naked.

Robin panted hard, his eyes closed tight. His hands clenched the links of the chain so fiercely he thought they would surely break. His body shook uncontrollably and he made no effort to stop it. He was way past that. He did his best to detach himself from what was happening and center his will, what there was left of it, ready for when the silver was removed. If the Baron intended to devour his soul as he had done with Feilin, he would first have to remove the barrier from Robin's mind. And no matter how swiftly he did it, no matter how much pain and terror he inflicted, Robin would be ready. Reen would be unable to prevent Robin's escape, and the warning he would send.

He heard a rustle of movement, and the hard bed creaked. The young man felt the weight of the Baron's body straddling him and tensed again. He saw the creature out of the corner of his eye; saw it rise and settle like a vulture over his hips. The distorted skull grinned, saliva hanging from cracked and twisted lips. He heard a whimper from Taran as the terrible creature leaned over him, one hand grasping the bedhead. The livid face came close, fetid breath stifling Robin's lungs.

"I know what you're waiting for," the wheezing voice hissed into Robin's ear, the syllables dripping venom, the tone gleeful. "But I'm afraid I'm going to disappoint you. The silver that holds you captive is a part of me. There is no need for me to remove it, for it is no barrier. So you can forget your little plan, Major. Not even your great powers can save you now. But do not fear, I shall not leave your witch unwarned. She shall know what has happened to her pagan lover. I desire her to know. Why do you think I wanted my niece's paramour? He shall carry my message, and he shall play his part. So relax, my dear Major, and let go your fear. There will be less pain if you do. This is the end for you. Your great strength, your knowledge, your skills—all shall be mine, and my vengeance is ever the nearer!"

The creature reared back, hips thrusting forward. Robin's eyes flew wide. His mouth opened in a hideous shriek and his whole body sprang rigid, the muscles like hawsers. The chains squealed under pressure but did not give, and the Baron's grunts filled the room.

Robin's agony was indescribable, but it was not the pain of penetration. That was purely physical and could have been borne. He had endured worse in many swordfights. No. It was the anguish of his soul that tore at the roots of his sanity, a white-hot fire that rampaged through his spirit. It pulsed into him with every thrust his tormentor made, suffusing him with anguish, splitting him in two. Screaming, he felt the fire reach for the seat of his power, eating through his mind, leaching his secrets from him. Tendrils of fire like spiteful fingers stabbed at his heart, sending needles of agony to pierce him, and his life force weakened with every surge.

He struggled desperately against the violation, fighting with every nerve of his body and spark of his mind. Yet he could not force it out. His body writhed in fiery torture; the pain was overwhelming. He spun helplessly, falling and dying, and nothing could stop it. His power was denied him. The barrier of spellsilver, visible in the recesses of his convulsing mind as a vivid, shimmering parody of the Veils, wrapped him in shrouds of clinging mist, confounding his senses and blocking his will. He pounded in panic against it, but it refused to give. His mental cry of anguish rang loud within the scarecrow's mind, a mind now locked tight around Robin's.

He felt the creature's every sensation. Reen moved toward fulfillment, excitement swelling him, tension forcing his body close to bursting. His victory was complete, his target achieved; this was now purely physical gratification. He could have ended it then, but he chose to draw it out, to deny himself release until he tasted the full measure of Robin's bitter despair, the depths of his failure. His final, anguished scream, echoing soundlessly in the sterile depths of his captive soul, was the cue Reen had been waiting for. He let himself go and threw back his head in a triumphant howl, body shuddering in pleasure.

Robin's consciousness flooded backward in a mighty,

unstoppable surge. Dragged against his will, flailing and helpless against the ebbing tide, he felt the sucking of the monster's rapacious soul. Screaming, begging, and pleading, he was absorbed, snuffed out, one name on his lips, one thought in his mind. The maelstrom of madness took his soul and whirled it away, his final despairing cry fading to silence.

Chapter Twenty-Eight

he Manor was dark and peaceful. All was quiet in the main building. The servants had done their rounds, tending the fires and trimming the lamps. Outside, only those on night duty stirred, patrolling the grounds, ever watchful, ever alert. Nothing chanced to rouse them and no danger threatened as the watch stretched toward dawn.

All was still in the College as well. The students slept in their dormitories, contented and safe. In the infirmary, Rienne and Cal slept together, arms entwined, their fear for their missing friends shared and made bearable by their deep love for each other. Cal's sword lay in easy reach beside the bed.

In a small side room, three children slept and dreamed. Taric snuffled in his cot, fingers twitching as his infant mind replayed some earlier game. Elisse slept unmoving in the bed next to the cot, her gentle breathing even. Eadan snuggled up to her, two puppies curled together, gaining comfort from her warmth.

In the main body of the infirmary, Tad dozed in a chair, his blond head nodding, his sword naked across his knees. Strictly speaking, he shouldn't be there. Ralf, another of their company, had drawn the night watch and was stationed just outside the door. It had been agreed between Tad, Cal, and Bull that Cal's abilities were sufficient to guard the children at night, with one other swordsman to back him up. Either Tad, Bull, or Jay'el would relieve him at dawn, and they would share the day watches. Yet something had nagged at Tad's senses, telling him he needed to be here, even if he didn't have to stay awake all night. He knew he would not sleep unless he gave in to his instinct, and so he had settled himself by the door.

On the Manor's upper floor, Bull snored on Sullyan's couch. It was roomy and deep, and this was by no means the first time he had used it. Rolled in a blanket and close to the fire, he was as relaxed and comfortable as if he were in his own bed. Head pillowed on one arm, he slept as deeply as a trained soldier ever did, the wariness of his calling far too deeply ingrained after so many years to be thrown off now.

When he had entered the room earlier that evening, Emos, Sullyan's valet, had already trimmed the lamps and mended the fire. The living area was deserted; no sound came from the sleeping room. He padded softly to the half-open door and looked inside before coming fully into the darkened room to check on its occupants. Sullyan and Morgan were already deeply asleep, curled tightly together. Morgan's dark head was tucked under his mother's chin, Sullyan's gentle breaths just ruffling his curling hair. Bull looked down on the pair of them, his heart aching, his vision blurred. He left them to their slumber, praying for a swift and satisfactory outcome to what was fast becoming a trial of the worst kind.

Wrapping himself in his blanket on the couch, he opened Rienne's packet of herbs and dropped a pinch into a cup of water. It tasted foul taken this way, but he didn't want to rouse Sullyan with the smell of fellan. Gulping the water down and grimacing at the taste, he settled to sleep.

Some time later, he was standing on the edge of a fiery silver lake, trying to dive in. Something held him back. He struggled to free himself so he could obey the pool's call, but the clinging hands only grasped him tighter. He thrashed, trying to throw them off, and took a step nearer the pool ....

"No! NO! *NOOOO!*"

The shriek cut through the mist of his dream and he shot bolt upright on the couch, throwing off the blanket. He leaped to his feet, grabbing for his sword, eyes searching wildly for danger.

A strange light played in the room, although it was still pitch dark outside. Confused by the dreadful wail resounding in his brain, he searched for the cause of the light, looking first toward the fire. It was low and not flickering at all. He spun, and with an icy shiver of dread saw that the light emanated from the sleeping room. He crossed swiftly to the door.

As he flung it wide, the inchoate wail beat against his ears, deafening and terrifying. Yet what staggered him more was the roar and leap of the flames that ringed the bed and its two occupants. Bull gaped in horror.

The incredible heat forced him back and he shielded his face with his hand, frantic for Sullyan and Morgan. He could just make them out, huddled together in the center of the bed, arms clasped tightly around each other, heads buried in each other's shoulders. The terrible wailing continued, rising and falling, pulsing like the leap of the flames. Bull stood rooted in terror, helpless against the blaze.

He had never gained mastery over Fire. He could influence it and call it, but there was a core of fear deep within that he could never quite overcome: the fear of burning. His darkest and most terrifying nightmare was of being burned alive, and he could never banish it. It colored all his dealings with Fire and prevented him from learning its innermost secrets, and this held him back from its mastery. Never had he regretted it more.

The wailing increased, searing through his brain, forcing him to clap his hands to his head in pain. The heat scorched his face.

He cried out and staggered back, bolting from the room and racing for the stairs. The door to the chambers slammed shut behind him.

✢ ✢ ✢ ✢ ✢

An urgent hand on his arm woke Cal and he lurched up in the bed, seeing Rienne's fearful face inches from his own. She was shivering, he could feel it, and a stab of dread shot through his heart. "What is it, love?"

The room was quiet, nothing threatened. There was no sound from the children, nor from Tad or Ralf.

"I have to go!"

Rienne slipped from the bed and reached for a robe, flinging it about her shoulders. Her movements were hurried, her face lined with fear. Cal tumbled from the bed and caught her, preventing her from dashing to the door.

"What is it, Rienne? You must tell me."

She shook her head, frantic to be gone. "It's Brynne and Morgan. I can't tell you any more than that. Let me go. You and Tad stay here, keep the children safe. Ralf will come with me. Let me *go!*"

She spoke so quickly he could hardly make out the words, but her imperative tone brooked no delay. She wrenched her arm free and ran for the door. Tad leaped upright as she pelted toward him, eyes swinging from her to Cal. Cal heard her order Tad to stay with the children as she flung open the outer door, and then she was gone, calling to Ralf as she went. The swordsman glanced to his captain before he obeyed her, and Cal jerked his head in permission. Ralf turned immediately and ran after Rienne, drawing his sword.

"What's going on, Captain?" demanded Tad, coming closer. The Captain stepped back into his room, going swiftly to the children's door to check on his charges. Taric slept on oblivious, but Eadan and Elisse had roused. They needed his attention. Tad followed him in to help, his young face creased in concern.

✢ ✢ ✢ ✢ ✢

Rienne and Ralf ran for the Manor, the primal shriek that had pierced Rienne's sleep prodding her to haste, stabbing at her brain. She had no idea whether Cal had heard it, or whether Ralf heard it now. She didn't know if it was real or in her head. All she knew was it was urgent, and that it signified something truly dreadful. She passed the puzzled guard on the Manor's outer door without pausing or speaking, and pelted for the first flight of stairs.

They met Bull racing down the second flight, yelling for help as he went, and he jerked to a halt when he saw them. He was panting and sweating, his face white, his lips tinged with blue. Rienne grabbed him by the arm.

"What is it, Bull? What's happened? Where are they?"

Bull's thumb jabbed upward. "Fire!" he gasped.

Rienne's eyes widened. She turned to Ralf. "Get help!" she said and pushed him away. "Come on!" she cried to Bull, and hurried on up the stairs. Ralf was already back down, sprinting for the lower floor. Fire was their worst enemy and greatest nightmare. Getting sufficient water up to the top floor would be a struggle. He would rouse the whole place to help.

Rienne ran ahead of Bull, her youth and panic lending her speed. The frantic wailing was still urging her on. She drew breaths in great gulps and pushed her legs to their limits. Flying past the door to Vassa's deserted chambers, she slammed into the next door, thumping it open, and skidded round the jamb. She jolted to a halt, gasping in shock.

Bull puffed up beside her, doubling over with effort. The fire threw heat in his face and the siren shriek of the wailing hurt his ears. He put out a hand as Rienne took a step closer.

"Don't!" he gasped. "You can't help them, the heat's too fierce."

Rienne glanced at him, her gray eyes searching. "No," she said, her voice sounding strange, and Bull stared at her.

Rienne turned back to the fire. She took a step toward it and Bull let his hand fall. He watched, amazed, as Rienne glided closer to the fire, her eyes fixed on the sleeping room, her dark hair swirled and lifted by the wind of the flames. She stepped nearer the doorway and Bull gasped again.

"No, Rienne, don't! You'll kill yourself. The fire's too strong. Wait for water. What the Void are you doing? Come back! *RIENNE!*"

The healer merely turned to look at him. She shook her head. "It's not real. It's metaforce, not fire. She's hurt and she's frightened and she's protecting them both. But she won't hurt us. Come with me, Bull. She needs us!"

Rienne stepped forward, into the flames. With a cry, Bull went after her, terror in his eyes. But she was right; the fire did not burn her. She moved through it, her hair spreading out in the breeze of its force, uncharred, unburnt. She turned her head and beckoned to him urgently, but still he could not. It *was* Fire. He could feel the heat. It would burn him and he was afraid ... but she was inside and it did not touch her. The wailing intensified, as if recognizing her presence. It held all the panic, all the pain, and all the terror of every hurt Sullyan had ever endured, and he cringed at the thought of what had engendered such extremity. He could not let her down in this state. He could not fail her now when she needed him. If Rienne was right and this was metaforce, it would not harm him. Sullyan would never harm him. Taking a huge gulp of air and screwing up every ounce of his courage, Bull plunged into the flames.

And found them quite cool. They buffeted him with their force, but they did not burn. They were like a curtain of light, and he passed through and out again. Inside the ring, the fire-like roar was diminished, but the wailing grew. A strong hand grasped his arm and he allowed Rienne to pull him out of his amazement and into reality. What he saw made him pause.

"What are they doing? Are they both generating this?" he asked, indicating the fire wall behind him.

Rienne nodded, stepping cautiously closer; examining without touching the pair clasped in a desperate embrace on the bed.

"What's caused it?" he asked.

Rienne pursed her lips, unwilling to reply. "Let's just try to wake them before the entire Manor mobilizes in this room. Contact Cal and Tad, will you? Ask them to stop Ralf organizing buckets for the fire. I'll just see what I can learn …."

She sat carefully on the edge of the bed, trying to cope with the constant keening that shattered her nerves and tore into her brain. She already knew what had caused it—only one thing could possibly push Sullyan's trained and powerful mind to such extremes. Yet she shut away the knowledge and the pain it brought her, and concentrated on reaching through the fiery barrier.

She could touch the edges of their minds, but she was unwilling to go further without Bull there to help her. Sullyan would never hurt her friends once she realized they were there. But Morgan was another matter; his potential was yet unknown, his depths unplumbed. Not even his mother could tell how powerful he might become, and he was a child with none of the skills necessary to rein his emotions. He could do untold damage to well-meaning minds. Rienne needed Sullyan aware and in control before she tried to rouse them.

As soon as Bull finished communing with Cal she tapped him lightly on the arm. "I'm going to try to speak to Brynne. I want you to be ready to catch and shield Morgan if she forgets herself enough to give him free rein. I don't think she will, but I don't want to take the chance. They're both drowning in grief, and I fear they won't be rational. Are you ready?"

Bull flinched at the mention of grief, but he said nothing as he fished for his psyche, attuning himself to both Morgan and Sullyan. He wrapped his own signature in their patterns and flung it over them all like a cloak. He nodded once, unable to spare the attention to do more. Satisfied, Rienne turned away and sent her soothing empathic presence into Sullyan's mind.

The depth of agony took her breath away. She risked her own safety by exposing herself to this. Rienne was no Artesan and was unable to shield as they could. She relied on her natural defenses—defenses she had no control over. Normally she had no need of such shields. She rarely had cause to enter another's mind, but she and Brynne Sullyan shared a very special bond of intimate friendship; she knew her way into the private depths of Sullyan's psyche almost as well as she knew her own.

She called Sullyan's name as she went deeper, announcing her presence, waiting for the mighty forces to see her, to recognize. The controlling power, so torn in its grief, snatched at her presence and gripped her in panic. With a warning to Bull she could only pray he felt, Rienne allowed herself to be swept into Sullyan's consciousness, where she could immediately sense the gaping rent in her soul, the terrible pain her loss had inflicted. Steeling herself against the agony she knew she would feel, Rienne accepted the burden and took on some of the pain, sharing the grief, soothing the hurt. Hoping Bull could cope with Morgan, Rienne turned Sullyan's panic inward, directing it away from her outward show of grief, and began the slow process of sealing the rent.

Rienne eventually succeeded in walling away the worst of Sullyan's pain. The grief still remained, but the agony was less. It would have to be dealt with at some point, but for now it lay dormant, a shuddering mass of torment, contained by her skill and Sullyan's power. Still wailing in the depths of her heart, still bleeding from a terrible wound that would never heal, Sullyan was helped into a sleep of oblivion. Rienne felt it the moment the fire died. Sighing in relief, perspiring with her efforts, Rienne withdrew from her friend's tortured mind and turned to see how Bull was getting on with Morgan.

Bull sat on the bed, cradling the boy and murmuring to him. The big man's face was gray, his lips tinged with blue and his breathing ragged. He was nearly exhausted by Morgan's uncomprehending grief. The little boy would not listen to him, and Bull had been forced to encase his mind, attempting to compel it into calm. But Morgan was fighting him with infantile tenacity, and he could not hold on much longer. She cursed herself. She should have checked on him sooner, but she had counted on him to warn her should he not be able to cope. Now she realized his concentration was so stretched that he had none left over to call her with.

She took Morgan from his arms. As she wrapped her empathy about him, Morgan burst into great racking sobs that tore at Rienne's heart. She let the boy cry, hoping he would wear himself out. She could not put him to sleep as she had done with Sullyan.

"Are you all right, Bull?" she asked over Morgan's head. Bull nodded, some color coming back to his face. "Do you have those herbs I gave you handy?"

He gave a weak grin. "I took some before I went to sleep. I can't take any more without permission—my healer will scold me."

Rienne appreciated his attempt at humor, but her soul was too sore to join in. "Just get them and take a half-dose. You'll need it."

As Bull left the room, Cal entered. Rienne guessed he had been waiting for someone to emerge rather than disturb them. His dark eyes were full of fear.

"What is it? What happened?"

Rienne patted the bed and Cal sat down. Bull returned, having taken his herbs. His face already looked less strained, and for the first time Rienne blessed her decision to prescribe them. He still sounded infinitely weary when he dared to ask the question none of them wanted to voice.

"It's Robin, isn't it?"

Rienne nodded. Tears stood in her eyes as she hugged Morgan, as much for her comfort as for the child's. She tried to speak, but words wouldn't come. Cal laid an arm across her shoulders.

"She felt him go." Rienne's voice sounded strange even to her. "There was nothing she could do, it was too fast. He's been killed, and I don't know how she will bear it."

One thing Rienne did know. When Sullyan decided to act, when she knew where to go, the killer would find no hiding place. Until then, she would endure. Until she had slaughtered him, taken her revenge on him, she would find the resources to live. After that … well, that was what frightened Rienne the most.

Chapter Twenty-Nine

Swordsman Yadrin stood smartly to attention as Captain Benett walked toward him bearing a small tray of food. It was just about dawn and Yadrin was due a relief. He had stood guard on the manservant since being sent there by Blaine, and he was ready to stretch his legs and go for his own breakfast. He grinned at his captain as Benett approached.

"All quiet, I trust?" Benett asked.

"Not a sound, sir." Yadrin turned to open the door for his senior officer. Benett stepped inside the darkened room and went to the windows to pull back the drapes. His vicious curse brought Yadrin rushing in behind him.

"Stay where you are!" the captain snapped, and Yadrin froze, staring in bewilderment around the empty room. Benett dropped the tray on the table, looking about, searching for places a man could hide. He stooped to search below the settle, even though he could see no one was there, then turned and flung the drapes about, checking no one was behind them. There was nowhere else in the room to hide. He turned to the doorway and stood stock still, fixing an accusing gaze on Yadrin.

"He's gone! The bloody prisoner's gone! Asleep on duty, were you?"

"No, Captain," Yadrin stated, frowning. "No, sir, I swear it. I've been alert all night. No one went in or out of this room. On my life, Captain—no one."

"It may well be on your life, Yadrin. Tell it to the General." Benett strode furiously past, leaving Yadrin staring stupidly at the empty room, facing the ruin of his military career.

Benett questioned other guards of the night watch, none of whom had seen the manservant leave the castle, and gave the order for a search of the palace and grounds. Then he marched straight to the King's chambers to report to Blaine. He dreaded telling the General his prisoner had escaped, but he dreaded even more telling him one of his trusted swordsmen was guilty of neglecting his duty. Only the day before they had listened to Colonel Vassa's exhortations to vigilance and efficiency, and Benett would have sworn for any of his men, including Yadrin. Benett would never have believed him capable of such gross negligence. Nevertheless, the fact remained that the room only had one exit and Yadrin had been guarding it. It was his lapse that had let the man escape and his head would roll for it. Benett could only hope Yadrin's failure would not reflect too badly on *him.*

Reaching the door to the King's chambers, he squared his shoulders, nodded curtly at the guards on duty, and rapped on the wood.

He was answered from inside and entered to find Elias, Blaine, and Vassa within, all turning enquiring eyes on him. The General looked as if he already anticipated bad news. Benett swallowed.

"Sir, I regret to report that the manservant, Seth, whom you ordered imprisoned last night, is not to be found within his room. He has escaped, sir."

The initial reaction was everything Benett feared, but the end result was not. Blaine stormed out of the King's chambers, Vassa in tow, and rained his fury down on Yadrin, who staunchly maintained his story even in the face of Blaine's anger. The Artesan General heard the truth in Yadrin's voice and calmed down. He entered the prisoner's room and stood in silence while Vassa, Benett, and the anxious Yadrin remained outside. The foul curse that burst suddenly from the General's lips made Benett's face burn. He was not used to such language from his General.

Blaine made no apology for his slip. Without a word, he left them, stalking back to the King. A few minutes later, the order went out to abandon the search for both the manservant and the bodyguard, and Yadrin was exonerated. Hugely relieved but no less puzzled, Benett and his swordsman returned to the barracks to tell their strange tale.

⁜ ⁜ ⁜ ⁜ ⁜

"What exactly are you telling us, Mathias?" the King demanded, pacing before the windows, his hands clasped behind his back. "How did the man escape if the guard didn't relax his vigilance?"

"He was removed," Blaine replied curtly. "By metaphysical means. Sullyan was right after all. Our enemy does have recourse to the services of an Artesan."

Elias stopped his pacing and glanced at the General. "Have you heard any more from her?"

Blaine shook his head. "She was exhausted from her searching last night. I told her I would contact her today once we had spoken with the manservant, and she could give us her full report then. She found something on that island, Elias, something of significance, and it frightened her. It doesn't bode well for either Major Tamsen or Adept Elijah, and it's more than likely the Baron is once more at the heart of these events."

"She was right all along," muttered the King, staring at the rug beneath his feet. Vassa watched silently from his chair by the fire and Blaine stood immobile across the room. "Mathias, this is our fault for not listening to her sooner. Why did we not give more credence to her convictions? Why were we so reluctant to believe her when she told us Reen was once again in a position to do us harm? And if she was right about that, what about the rest? What about Sofira and Lerric?"

The General snorted. "If they are both involved, they did a damned good job of fooling the three of us. Major Tamsen and I went there specifically to look for evidence of falsehood or evasion, and you know we found nothing to convince us they were involved."

"But did we ask the right questions?" The King moved closer. "You know as well as I that Lerric badly wanted to tell us something just before we left. Sofira was terrified when she caught him—terrified and furious. From what you have told me, Artesans can only hear truth or lie. But lies are only one form of deceit. Careful half-truths would do as well, and if you remember, Sofira led us—led *me*—very easily away from topics that might have proved difficult. She has always been able to get under my skin, and she used my guilt and my love for our children as weapons. I did not suspect her motives because I expected it of her. It's what she always does. But what if she was goading me, playing on my anger, trying to shame me into leaving? She damn near succeeded, too. It was only Sullyan's insistence that made me stay as long as I did."

The General did not immediately respond and the King was about to speak again when he noticed the distant look in Blaine's eyes that meant the General was in communion with an Artesan. Elias cast a glance at Vassa and waited. When the General finally raised his eyes, Elias felt his face go pale. Even Vassa caught the tense atmosphere pervading the room.

"What is it, Mathias?"

Blaine looked away and swallowed. He was caught in the grip of strong emotions. He took a moment to compose himself before he raised his head and faced Elias. "I have just had word from Hal

Bullen at the Manor. I have to inform you that Major Tamsen has been killed."

Vassa gave a gasp and Elias stood stunned. Then he slammed his fist down on the table.

"By all the gods, Mathias! Where's this going to end? How are we going to stop this vicious vendetta? There must be a way to find where the bastard's hiding!" He stared in furious appeal at the General, who could offer no answer. Seeing the man's expression, Elias asked, "How's Brynne taking it?"

Blaine shared his monarch's fury, but he would not let it rule him. They were still in the middle of a crisis and he could afford no more mistakes. With the means of Seth's escape confirmed, he understood how many of the crimes within the city had been committed, and why no culprits were found. Nowhere was safe, not even the castle.

They were alert to Artesan activity now, but the General knew it was too late. If the Baron had a link to Seth enabling him to snatch the man to safety, then he could also have killed him in Blaine's custody, leaving the General still in doubt. The fact that Reen had chosen to reveal his access to metaforce meant that not only did Seth possess information the Baron did not want Blaine to know, but also that Reen cared little if his enemies knew of his resources. Blaine thought he knew why the Baron had chosen this moment to reveal himself, and it had much to do with Robin's fate. He cursed himself for not questioning Seth more closely last night.

Elias's question finally registered and Blaine started for the door. "Badly, of course. How would you expect her to take it? Hal Bullen says she is planning revenge. He's very worried and asks that we speak with her. I intend to leave for the Manor immediately and I want you to come with me. This is not a request, Elias. You're not safe here with the Baron in possession of an Artesan's powers. The Princess ought to come too. I cannot take the chance Reen will try for her."

He turned to his colonel. "Jerrim, send to the garrison and tell Dexter to ready his company. They will be returning with us. You will remain here and post guards throughout the castle. Levant, especially, is never to be left alone, likewise anyone else you can think of who might be a target. It is Sullyan's belief that all who spoke against Reen at the trial are at risk, and they failed once with Levant. They may well try again. Ardoch, too, must be guarded, and if he protests, you have my permission to confine him to quarters. Just do not leave him alone! Until we know more, I will rely on Sullyan's advice. There is no knowing what the Baron might do with the powers he now has at his disposal. I will send you more men as I can, and we will return once we know more. You will be out of contact until then, I'm afraid, but there's no help for that with Taran gone. Can you cope?"

"I'll do my best, General." Vassa came to his feet and headed for the door. "Shall I inform the Princess his Majesty wishes her to accompany him?"

"No, Colonel," Elias said. "Thank you, but I will speak with Seline myself. You concern yourself with the security of the castle. Remember the edict: you are the highest authority in the city while I am away and you have my full endorsement to take whatever measures you see fit in discharging your duties. Just ... Jerrim, do your best for Rendan, will you? I could not bear it if something happened to him now, not after what he suffered."

Vassa bowed and left the room, exchanging a significant look with Blaine as he went. He understood the seriousness of their situation. The General and the King went about their preparations and then made their way to the rooms Sullyan had allocated the Princess, the King walking like a man with a bruised and heavy heart.

✠ ✠ ✠ ✠ ✠

Taran woke to utter physical misery. Terrible nausea still twisted his guts and the throbbing of his aching head was almost unbearable. There were flashing lights behind his eyes and he feared his skull was cracked. His cramped shoulder muscles were afire, and he could not feel his hands or fingers. He wrinkled his nose when it became obvious his bladder had failed him too, but there was nothing he could do about it. He closed his eyes and groaned. It was some time before he summoned up the courage to turn his head and look about him.

When the room stopped spinning, he glanced at the bed, desperately hoping to see Robin. What he was not prepared for was the sight of the bed unoccupied, the chains dangling free. He bit back a gasp and had to breathe heavily for a few moments to calm the raging nausea. His heart clenched painfully with grief. What he had seen was true and not some terrible nightmare. The Baron had indeed done what he had threatened and Robin was gone. Taran slumped in bitter defeat and a sob escaped him.

The feel of a tear striking bare skin roused him, and he stared down at himself in horror. Although still chained to the rings in the wall, still bound by spellsilver, he was now stripped of his jacket and shirt. The implications sent trails of ice down Taran's spine. Such a fate was too awful to contemplate, and Taran didn't know how he would bear the knowledge. To give his quavering heart something to hold on to, he used his terror to try once more to contact Rienne. Perhaps the desperate strength of his memories would give him the power to break through the spellsilver barrier. Although if Robin could not, even in the grips of such extremity, Taran had no hope. Still, he tried.

He was still trying when the scarecrow came for him.

✣ ✣ ✣ ✣ ✣

Jinny roused after some hours, the herbal sedative having long since worn off. She lay unmoving, feeling Sofira's level breathing beside her, unwilling to wake the older woman. Jinny was more than a little nervous as to how the Princess would react when she did wake. Would she be rational or demented? Friendly or hateful? Would she regret confiding in Jinny the night before, or be grateful for her help? Jinny did not know and was in no hurry to find out. Her frightened thoughts centered on Taran and Robin, and whatever the Baron might have done to them. She was desperate to discover their fate.

She had no idea of the hour. The entire palace was wreathed in darkness; not a chink of light crept through the boards and heavy drapes, not even in Sofira's chambers. Jinny lay still and forlorn. Sofira never stirred. Eventually, insistent discomfort drove Jinny to slip from the bed, moving carefully so as not to wake the Princess. She padded into the bathing room and used the night pot, then poured water from the warming kettle into the porcelain washbowl, suddenly desperate to wash her skin. She had not troubled to remove her gown the night before, and it was crumpled and uncomfortable. She took it off and laid it aside. Twisting her hair away from her face, she took some of the Princess's soft soap and a cloth, and used them to wash her face before turning her attention to her arms and legs.

These simple everyday actions calmed her, their very familiarity making her feel less wretched. She allowed her mind to wander away from the terror of her plight and was patting herself dry with a towel when she heard the frightened cry. Her heart thumped in alarm and her situation rushed back on her with a sickening lurch. She dropped the towel, thinking Sofira must have roused and was frightened to be alone. Jinny came into the bedchamber, reassurance on her lips, but she froze when she saw Sofira.

The Princess sat upright, cowering behind the sheets and quilts that she had clasped up around her, her eyes wild and panicked. She whimpered, staring at the door to the hallway. Jinny spun around, stifling a cry of her own. The door was open and two guards stood there, just within the chamber. Behind them, Jinny saw the slumped flesh of her uncle's ruined face. Her hand flew to her mouth and she crossed to the Princess's side, gathering the trembling woman into her arms. Sofira didn't acknowledge her. She sat rigid in the circle of Jinny's arms, her muscles locked in terror.

"Leave her alone!" Jinny hissed. "Can't you see what you have done to her? Haven't you hurt her enough? Just leave her alone!"

The Baron stepped around his men and took three paces into the room, his strange, livid cane tapping gently on the floor. Jinny stared at him. There was something different about him, something almost *healthy*, where before there had been only evil and decay. She frowned, taking in his malicious grin, his glaring red eyes, and the way he held himself. He radiated dark pleasure. He seemed stronger, more powerful, but it was obscene and terribly wrong. His strength sat on him like an ill-fitting cloak, like something he had pulled over the twisted bones and ruined flesh. Jinny was only too afraid she knew where it came from.

"Leave her alone?" he echoed. Jinny stared even harder. Even his voice sounded different, firmer, and she studied him, fascinated despite herself.

His frame had filled out, less a twisted skeleton and more like a normal man. The hand resting lightly on the cane was not the desiccated claw she remembered, but a veined and living hand. She saw him watching her, assessing her, and realized he knew what she could see. The shared knowledge merely stretched his grin and she felt sick. What could she possibly do against a monster such as this?

Sofira trembled in her arms and Jinny felt a wash of lassitude suffuse her. She did not understand this; she did not know what she faced. She suddenly heard Taran's voice in her mind, telling her some tale of his training at the Manor and how all young cadets were taught that in order to fight effectively you must first know your enemy. Now she understood what he meant. Reen was her uncle, the brother of her father, and she had lived with him once. Yet she had never truly known him, never troubled to examine the mind behind the man. His treachery and the depth of his betrayal had come as a shock to her, as had his behavior at his trial. Sullyan's exposure of his Artesan heritage went some way toward explaining his deep-rooted hatred of their kind, but as he was then banished, Jinny gave the matter no further thought. Now, suddenly and far too late, she regretted it.

"Leave her alone, dear niece?" he repeated, his voice low and sinister. "What makes you think I want anything more to do with her? What makes you think I came here for *her*?"

Jinny gasped and the Baron nodded. "Bring her."

The two guards advanced into the room. Sofira shrank back under the bedclothes, gibbering in mindless panic. Jinny stared at the guards blankly, powerless to move, fright turning her muscles to water. Yet as they grasped her arms and hauled her from Sofira's side, she struggled.

"What do you want with me? Where are we going?" she pleaded. "You're not going to hurt her, are you? Please, Uncle, tell me what you want, I don't understand! At least let me get dressed. Uncle, *please*!"

Reen ignored her and stood aside as the guards hustled her past. He spared one despising look for the whimpering woman huddled in the bed and left the room, closing the door on her terror. Jinny heard him following as she stumbled along in the grip of the guards, the tap of his cane echoing softly in the dark hallways.

She soon realized they were heading for the lower floor and the room of the captives. She began to tremble. As much as she yearned to see them again, to know what he had done to them, now she wanted the opposite. Was he bringing her here to gloat over their deaths? Was he going to force her to witness their murder? All manner of terrible possibilities crowded her mind and she felt her feet drag, unwilling to carry her closer to what she might see. The two silent guards just tightened their grip and propelled her toward their goal.

They reached the stout door leading to the prison and the scarecrow came around before her. A single lamp on the wall cast a feeble light, but the sullen red glow in his eyes was all Jinny could see. The changed aspect of his body appalled her, repelled her, and she had no wish to look on him. Yet the demonic flare in those evil eyes held her, and she was powerless to look away.

"You will stay here in silence," he said, his voice menacing in the darkness, "until I have need of you. If you cry out, if you struggle, it will go worse for him. Do you understand me, Jinella? Do not make the mistake of believing either of you are important to me. I will not hesitate to dispense with you should you cause me trouble. It suits me to use you at present, and it will not inconvenience me to lose you. Do you hear me?"

Jinella nodded miserably. What else could she do? She was alone and beset. She had promised Robin to do as she was told, but was he still living to hold her to that? She knew she was about to find out and it terrified her. What the implications were for Taran, she could hardly bear to think. She closed her eyes as the bolts were drawn and the door to the prison pushed open.

Chapter Thirty

Sullyan rose after a few hours of heartbroken sleep, unable to partake of the comfort offered by her friends. Their eyes were too full of pain and their arms too reminiscent of another's for her to endure. She rose stiffly, barely holding herself together, and only nodded curtly when Bull told her he had informed General Blaine of Robin's fate. She gave Morgan over to the big man to be taken to the College to join Eadan and Elisse. The pale-faced little boy, every bit as overcome as his mother, made no protest except with his eyes.

Bull carried Morgan to the College and checked in with the children's guards. Cal was there, in charge of their care. While trying to console Tad, who had heard the dreadful news from Cal, Bull received Blaine's message regarding his imminent arrival and went to meet the King and his escort on the steps of the Manor.

Almost as soon as Elias brought his mount to a halt, he lifted a tight-faced Seline from his saddlebow and set her on her feet. The Princess kept up a constant stream of bitter complaints. Her maids had been left behind at the castle and she was furious at being forced to live like a prisoner among those she considered responsible for the disgrace and departure of her mother. Bull could see Elias was fast reaching the limits of his patience.

Chief Healer Hanan came to take charge of the girl and Elias had to speak quite sternly before Seline consented, albeit sullenly, to go with her to the College. Bull didn't envy the woman. She was used to dealing with awkward patients, but Hanan would have her work cut out pacifying the spiteful Princess. The strain on Elias's face was not only due to grief.

The King and the General entered the Manor, followed by Dexter. Blaine quizzed Bull as they made their way to Blaine's office and he gave what information he could, telling of Sullyan's dreadful discoveries on the island. Elias and Blaine were appalled and stunned by what they heard. When they entered Blaine's office, Sullyan was already there, accompanied by Rienne sitting in an attitude of hopeless despair in a large chair near the window, her hands clasped together. She glanced up as the four men arrived, shrugging helplessly and shaking her head at their anxious, enquiring looks.

Brynne Sullyan neither glanced up nor acknowledged their presence, not even that of her King. She had washed and changed since waking. Her hair was unbound, hiding her face from the men. She sat in a chair opposite Rienne, her father's sword naked across her knees. The rhythmic scrape of a whetstone rasped in the silence as she mindlessly honed the blade, her measured movements needing no direction after many long years of habit.

Every man in the room could sense the waves of fury emanating from her, controlled for now, but avid for the work she had planned. Elias recoiled from her aura, never having felt it so powerfully before. He appeared tongue-tied before the immeasurable depth of her loss, wanting to help yet knowing no one could. He hovered on the brink of speech, awkward and heart-sore.

Blaine clearly felt the same, aching for her grief yet powerless to aid her. What could he say, he who had failed her? He had let Robin go to his death, and although she had not blamed him, he had lost the right to comfort her. What words he might have said were useless, as were his sorrow and regret. He, like his monarch, stood silent.

It was left to Dexter to come to her aid. He gave her the only thing she needed, and he was the only one to gain a response.

Into the awkward silence, he spoke over the rasp of the whetstone, his low tone conveying respect.

"Colonel. The men of your company await your command."

Her head snapped up, haloed by the tawny fire of her hair, and Rienne stifled a gasp. Sullyan's eyes were pools of black ringed by gold, and the intensity of the hatred mirrored within shocked everyone, including Captain Dexter. Yet he could see it was not for him. He could see the anguish beneath, and also her deep, heartfelt gratitude. It was what she had wanted, needed, that show of support, and her lips framed a smile that did not alter the promise of death in her eyes. Strangely, her lilting voice carried no taint of grief.

"I thank you, Captain. I will speak with you shortly."

Dexter did not wait for the General's gesture of dismissal. He turned and left the room, going back to his men, preparations in his mind.

This promise of action galvanized the King, cutting through the mist of futility encasing him. Suddenly, he knew what to do, how to help her, and he did it unthinkingly, knowing it was right.

He met the black blaze in her eyes, answering it with fury of his own.

"I'm coming with you."

✤ ✤ ✤ ✤ ✤

The sound of bolts being drawn startled Taran from his desperate striving for contact with Rienne. He had tried so hard to reach her that his head was spinning and his vision blurred. Though his eyes were unfocused, he knew who had entered his prison. The tapping of a cane on stone was clue enough if he needed one. His heart pounded in fear and nausea roiled in his guts.

The tapping halted inches from him and Taran had the urge to lash out with his legs, to sweep the man to the floor. He was too weary to try it. It was just as well; he would only succeed in bringing himself worse agony, although what could be worse than the fate suffered by Robin he could not bear to imagine. He blinked and tried to concentrate on the leering face above him.

"Get him some water."

The words meant little to Taran in his confused state, but he drank automatically when the stale water was held to his lips, hellishly thirsty. It was not enough to satisfy him, but it was better than nothing. It helped to clear his mind and ease the dreadful churn of his stomach. He managed to raise his head, bringing a low grunt of approval from the scarecrow.

"That's better. I need you awake and alert. I have a task for you, my friend, and I would advise you to cooperate. I have ways of forcing you if you don't."

"Go screw yourself."

The scarecrow's grin widened and he crouched down next to Taran, a position of vulnerability had the Adept been in a state to notice. He stared the Artesan straight in the eyes. "You don't know what it is yet."

"I don't care what it is," Taran mumbled, his throat tight with grief. "You can still go to Perdition."

"Oh, I don't think so, my friend. It is you and your kind who will fall from grace, not I. I am doing my God's will. Let me tell you what I want and then I will show you why you will do it. I need you to send a message for me. That is what you do at Elias's court, isn't it, Adept Elijah? I ask no more than that. It should not be too hard for you."

Taran frowned, confused. "What sort of a message? Who to?"

Reen grinned, his eyes glowing red. His right hand clenched and unclenched on his cane, eagerness flowing from him like water. "I want you to call *her*, my friend," he hissed, his voice crawling sinuously into the gloom. "Tell her where you are. You want to do it, don't you? You want her to come and save you? Well, I am giving you the opportunity. Call her, Adept Elijah. Call the Sullyan witch."

Taran stared, stunned. His brain and body might be wracked with pain, his soul crying out for her help, but nothing he could think of would induce him to lure her into this spider's web. Nothing would make him betray her. He swore at the Baron, told him in the foulest terms he could think of just what he could do with his proposal. Unfortunately for him, the Baron knew him too well and had come prepared.

Reen shrugged and stood. "Yes, I thought you might say something of the kind." He turned to the open door and jerked his head. Taran heard movement but could see nothing past the Baron. The sounds that reached him woke fresh fear in his trembling heart and turned his blood to ice. *Jinny.* He groaned deep in his throat, turning his head away. How could he bear this?

"Would you like to reconsider?" the Baron asked. Jinny had made no sound except for fearful panting. Taran remembered Robin telling him how brave she had been. He hoped she would understand why he resisted. He shut his mouth and refused to answer.

Reen nodded to the two guards, who each slipped a foot behind Jinella's legs, sweeping them out from under her. She went down with a cry, a swordsman on each arm, and they held her to the floor where she struggled in panic. The scarecrow stood over her, knife in hand, and the blade caught the gleam of his eyes as he slit the length of her shift and tore it from her body, leaving her naked. She cried out again and tried to twist free, but the men held her easily in place, both looking to their master, waiting for his command. Furious tears pricked at Taran's eyes and he lunged against the chains.

"You bastard! You *bastard*! She's your *niece*, for pity's sake! Leave her be, let her go!"

"Give me a reason and I might do as you ask," the scarecrow drawled, watching Jinny's struggles with detached amusement.

Taran was trapped. The man was a monster. He would not scruple to have his niece raped if he believed it would further his purpose. Taran could see he was perfectly prepared to unleash his men on Jinny. They were only too ready and eager to do his bidding. Jinny caught his glance and her pleading, frightened face tore into his heart. There was only one thing he could do.

"All right, all right," he panted, fury warring with despair. "I'll do what you want. Just release her."

The Baron did not reply, nor did he turn from Jinny. He stood in dark contemplation and Taran felt his skin turn cold. What new torture was this?

"What's the matter with you, Reen?" he cried harshly. "Didn't you hear me? I said I'll do it, I'll send your damned message! But only if you let her go. For the gods' sake, man, call off your men. Let her go!"

The scarecrow turned slowly to face him, eyes burning bright red. Taran shuddered with loathing before that strange expression. "Are you begging me?" the Baron hissed.

Taran closed his eyes, unable to hold the evil gaze. "Yes, yes," he groaned, willing to say anything to spare his love. "I'll beg you, you bastard. Just let her go. Please, *please*, let her go!"

"You want me to spare her, Adept Elijah? You want me to release her from her fear? Is that what you're asking?"

The tone of his voice changed, became eager, and Taran opened his eyes. The scarecrow came closer, watching his captive.

Taran's hands clenched into fists, yearning to strike the man, to squeeze the life from him, to silence that dreadful, wheezing voice. Reen was obviously intent on wringing the last drop of submission from him. Taran prepared to abase himself, to say whatever the Baron wanted to hear.

"Release her, yes, release her," he shouted, flinging his anger into that leering face. "I'm begging you, man!"

"Then do as I ask and I will."

Taran bowed his head, exhausted, defeated. There was nothing more he could do. Sullyan would understand; she would feel his terror, she would know he had been forced into this. That would be enough to warn her. All he could do was hope.

"I've said I will," he mumbled wearily. "But I can't reach through the spellsilver."

The Baron straightened and snapped his fingers. Another guard came into the room and approached the Adept. He loosened the manacles about Taran's wrists and his arms dropped painfully to his sides, useless and numb. A knife was held to his throat and he saw with a shiver that it was made of spellsilver. One false move and it would bite his flesh as it had done before. Jinny still writhed on the floor, sobbing in fear, and he could not jeopardize her. He closed his eyes and reached deep within, trying to ignore the pain of his body as he accessed his powers.

Burning red orbs watched him avidly.

✢ ✢ ✢ ✢ ✢

The General exploded in fury at his monarch's preposterous statement, feeling his authority sliding away, feeling the pull of Fate too strong to resist. Nevertheless, he tried.

"The Void you are!" he retorted, hands on hips.

Bull and Rienne watched with widened eyes as the two powerful men confronted each other. Sullyan reacted neither to

Elias's statement nor the sudden tension in the room. Her head bowed over the whetstone as it once again mechanically stroked her blade. The sound was menacing and savage in the charged atmosphere of the office.

"You can't stop me, Mathias!" thundered the King. He turned squarely to face Blaine, his arms folded over his chest. "The bastard's gone too far this time. Do you think I will sit idly by and let others dispense my justice?"

"It is what you pay us for!" the General snapped. "It is what we are here for, to stop you doing foolish things like this—stop you getting yourself killed."

The King's face turned purple. "What I pay you for, my Lord Blaine, is to serve me. Or have you forgotten that? Have you forgotten who rules this land? You may command these forces here, but *I* command *you*. Or will you be forsworn? Is that it? Do you think you know better than I how to govern my lands? Do you think me incapable of dealing with traitors?"

The General's face turned white. Elias was being unreasonable. It was unthinkable that he should risk himself in combat against such vermin as Reen. His pride had been wounded by his enemy's actions and he was hot for revenge; that much Blaine understood. But to offer himself to Sullyan in such a way, with the full intention of joining her and her men, of leading them against the Baron, was the height of stupidity. Blaine would endure what insults he must in order to bring the King to his senses. Besides, Sullyan would never take him. To spare her the King's thwarted anger on top of her bereavement was what he strove for now. He only wondered why she had not responded herself to refuse her sovereign. Gathering breath to refute Elias's hurtful accusations, he cast her a glance.

The words died in his throat.

She sat rigid, her hands stilled on her blade, fingers gripping painfully tight. Her eyes stared straight ahead, unseeing. Her breath came raggedly, the fire opal at her throat pulsing with the frantic beat of her heart. Blaine's gasp drew everyone's eyes, and Rienne's hands flew to her mouth.

The tableau was broken by Sullyan's sudden, anguished cry.

"No! Ah, Taran, no! Hold on, man! *Hold on!*"

Bull and Blaine felt their minds taken over as Sullyan reached for their strength. Her controlling will smothered theirs. She drained their powers, reaching and stretching, grasping for her goal, desperate not to lose it. Bull faintly recognized the pattern of Taran's exhausted psyche and gave willingly to her, fighting with her to grip the man's mind. After the briefest of pauses, Blaine did the same.

The strain of the effort showed on Sullyan's face. Rienne and the King watched helplessly as the veins stood out on her body and her hands gripped her sword. Blood dripped from her fingers where her unconscious grip pressed them to the sharp of the blade, but she took no notice, did not even feel the cut. Sweat stood out on her face and she went white with effort. Bull and Blaine both swayed on their feet. Rienne moved to Bull to support him and hissed at Elias to do the same. The King reached hastily for his General, placing a steadying hand on his arm.

And then Sullyan's furious, despairing scream rang out, shocking them all again.

✢ ✢ ✢ ✢ ✢

Taran cried out as the knife bit his flesh, the spellsilver cutting him off from his powers and wrenching him back to his body. The agony piercing his mind was unbelievable. He had never been forced from his psyche before and the effect was like being stripped of his skin. The encasing power of Sullyan's might was ripped from his soul and he knew she would have felt the agony too. He sobbed for the loss and the pain, and also for his enforced betrayal. He had not conveyed what he wanted, had not been granted the time. He could only pray she had sensed his warning, and that her death would not burden his soul.

Dragging in painful breaths, he stared up into the baleful red eyes of his captor. The guard swiftly replaced the manacles, effortlessly securing Taran's useless arms, and the knife was removed from his chest, the shallow cut dribbling blood down his skin.

"Very good, Adept Elijah," Reen purred. "Very good indeed. How could she refuse such a plea, such a call? You have done your work well and you shall have your reward. Give him more water."

Taran stared at the Baron as he turned to Jinny, still pinned on the floor by the leering guards. She was crying in earnest, pleading and sobbing, but the scarecrow didn't seem to hear her.

"Baron!" Taran rasped, his strength almost gone. "Jinella …."

"Ah, yes," the scarecrow murmured, "my niece. What was it you wanted?"

Taran's head fell back against the wall. He was too exhausted to hold it up. "Please," he murmured brokenly, "release her. Please."

The Baron moved to stand over Jinny, both hands on his cane, sullen red eyes staring down at her. "This is what you want?" he asked softly.

"Yes," groaned Taran, closing his eyes, "oh, gods, you bastard, yes …."

"Very well," said the Baron.

The dreadful shriek that filled the room burst into Taran's brain. His eyes flew wide and his head snapped forward, a scream escaping his lips. Jinny's body bucked on the floor, nearly throwing off the guards, and a charnel stench flooded Taran's nostrils. Her shriek spiraled down, weakening, dying, until it faded to nothing. Taran plunged in his chains, wrenching his arms. He swore and he yelled and the Baron turned to him, a terrible smile on his lips.

"I did what you wanted," he purred, removing his cane from Jinny's ravaged chest. "I did as you asked me."

The imprecation that left Taran's lips only served to widen the smile. The Adept's mind snapped with horror, too broken to take any more, and he gibbered in meaningless rage and terror as the dreadful cane with its pulsing red tip approached his breast.

✣ ✣ ✣ ✣ ✣

"Taran! Oh Gods, *NO*!"

Sullyan's cry snapped the tension in the room like an overstretched bowstring. Blaine and Bull both staggered. Rienne only just held on to the big man as she helped him to a chair. The General irritably pushed the King away, holding his head in his hands. Sullyan slumped over her sword, her bloody hands wrapped tight around her, retching and swearing and shaking her head. Rienne ran to her once Bull was safe, going down on her knees.

Elias stood white-faced, understanding only so much. He gathered some calamity had befallen Taran, which only strengthened his resolve. Now nothing would stop him from hunting Reen down, no matter where he was hiding. He glanced from Sullyan to the General, meeting the bluff man's drained and angry countenance.

"What do you say now, Mathias? Still going to refuse me?"

The General returned his glare. "It is sheer folly, Elias. Your pride will get you killed or captured like Taran, and then where will we be? It is what he wants, you fool. Can't you see that? Come to your senses!"

Elias swelled with fury, his eyes bulging. He laid a hand on his sword and advanced on the General, who drew himself up, prepared to defend his position. Yet what the King would have said was forgotten as Sullyan rose from her chair, her face bone white, her eyes dead black, her bloody sword in her hand.

"*Enough!*"

The power of the word arrested them and they stared at her. She glowered in fury.

"Enough of this!" she spat, her voice flat and hard, her eyes promising death. She stunned the General and rocked even Bull as she continued harshly, "Elias, I will take you. In truth, I would welcome your sword."

The General spluttered in protest, but she ignored him, stepping deliberately closer to the King and holding his gaze with her own. The tip of her sword pointed menacingly at his breast and did not waver. "But I will have your oath before I do. I take you under one condition. You will be under *my* command, as a swordsman of my company, not as my King. You will obey my orders and those of my captains. You will put off your authority as sovereign of Albia and bow to my will. If you accept these terms, I will take you."

Blaine, Rienne, and Bull watched in amazement as the King drew his sword. Without hesitation, he went down on one knee and offered her the hilt, holding her gaze as he swore the oath. No emotion showed on her face as she briefly touched the hilt of his weapon, accepting his words and his submission. She turned from him and strode for the door.

"But where will you go?" the General demanded, furious still and stunned at the turn of events. "Sullyan, this is madness. Take some time to think. You need to plan, to confer. You don't even know where to look!"

"Bordenn," she snapped, half-turning her head. "The bastard is laired in Bordenn. I told you he would be, but you did not heed me. He was there all along, lurking and plotting beneath your feet, and now he has made his challenge. You had your chance to find him, General, and you failed. Now Taran and Robin have paid the price and I must answer his summons.

"But you are right. I need to plan, for I will not go blindly into his trap. I will speak with my captains and plan my attack. If you have need of me, you know where to find me. I will be with the men of my company."

She swept from the room, Elias and Bull following at her heels.

Blaine stood defeated, arms slack by his sides. He understood her rage and her need, but this was plain folly. Yet she had set her course and he was powerless to change it. Sullyan was all that now stood between Albia and utter ruination.

The End

Glossary

Albian Characters

Alice. Former nursemaid at Port Loxton, now Jinny's housekeeper.

Ardoch, Ghyllan, Master. Elias's legendary swordmaster.

Bassan, Captain. King Lerric's guard captain at Daret, Bordenn.

Benett. A captain at Port Loxton.

Bessie. One of Prince Eaden's nurses.

Brynne Sullyan. A Colonel at the Manor under General Blaine.

Bull, aka Bulldog, aka Hal Bullen. Colonel Sullyan's friend and aide.

Cal Tyler. Taran's friend, and life mate of Rienne Arlen.

Col. A Manor swordsman in Robin's company.

Darral. Young cousin of Robin.

Denny, Owyn. A Major at Port Loxton.

Dexter. A Captain at the Manor under Captain Tamsen.

Drum. Sullyan's black warhorse.

Dugal. Swordsman at Port Loxton.

Durren, Frar. A member of the Order of the Wheel on Serna Island.

Eaden, Prince. Son of King Elias and Queen Sofira.

Elias Rovannon. Albia's High King.

Elisse Arlen. Daughter of Rienne and Cal.

Emos. Sullyan's valet.

Endor. Master healer at Loxton Castle.

Eskel. A cleric in Bordenn who marries Reen to Sofira.

Falkerk. Weapons master at the Manor.

Fergus. A Kingsman at Port Loxton.